THE THIRD WARRIOR

A NICKY MATTHEWS MYSTERY

CAROL POTENZA

Tiny
MAMMOTH

PRESS

Copyright © 2021 by Carol Potenza

Published by Tiny Mammoth Press, LLC

website: www.carolpotenza.com

LCCN 2021913389

Names: Potenza, Carol, author.

Title: The third warrior / Carol Potenza.

Description: [Las Cruces, New Mexico] : Tiny Mammoth Press, [2021] | Series: A Nicky Matthews mystery

Identifiers: ISBN 9781736326213 (hardcover) | ISBN 9781736326206 (ebook) | ISBN 9781736326237 (paperback)

Subjects: LCSH: Policewomen--New Mexico--Fiction. | Pueblo Indians--New Mexico--Fiction. | Cowboys--New Mexico--Fiction. | Murder--Investigation--Fiction. | Spirits--Fiction.

Classification: LCC PS3616.O8435 T45 2021 (print) | LCC PS3616.O8435 (ebook) | DDC 813/.6--dc23

EDITOR: COLLEEN WAGNER

PROOFREAD BY GILLY WRIGHT

SENSITIVITY READER: SCS

COVER: BRANDI DOANE MCCANN

DEDICATION

Hey, Paula. I really miss you.

THE THIRD WARRIOR

CHAPTER ONE

Hummingbird Mesa
  Tsiba'ashi D'yini Pueblo
  New Mexico, USA

FIRE-SKY POLICE SERGEANT Nicky Matthews maneuvered her unit to a stop a few yards from a second police vehicle already on-site. She leaned her arms on the steering wheel and scrutinized the scene.

A tongued section of Hummingbird Mesa jutted into the surrounding desert, the vertical layers of rock face rising about thirty feet high. Directly in front of her unit, tucked into a concave hollow of the cliff, stood a heavy, kaftan-covered woman, her thick braid swinging with her movements. Gray tendrils of smoke puffed up from a greenish-gray bundle—probably a smudge stick—tied up like a fat cigar and cupped in her palm. The bundle rested on something gently cupped and white—probably a shell. In her other hand, the woman clutched a fan of large feathers to scoop the smoke. With repetitive motions, she waved the feathers in the direction of her body, washing the hazy air over her sweaty face and breathing deeply, her expansive bosom swelling. Then she dipped the feathers away from her, sending smoke up the cliff, the wattle under her arms quivering. She appeared to ignore the presence of both Nicky and the second officer, but periodically, the round purple-shaded lenses of her glasses flashed in their direction.

Nicky released an exasperated sigh. Why did she always have to do this at the hottest part of the day?

She grabbed the comm mic. "Two-one-three, Dispatch. Ten eighty-two at Hummingbird Mesa. Over."

"Copy that, Sergeant."

Leaving her SUV and air conditioner on, she opened the door. A wall of heat hit her, painful against the exposed skin of her neck and face. Nicky slipped on a FIRE-SKY POLICE–logo baseball hat and tugged her ponytail through the clasp. She adjusted her duty belt around her hips, her fingers gliding over the handcuffs clipped at the small of her back. Deliberately, she rested the heel of her hand on her holstered Glock and breathed deeply. Squaring her shoulders, Nicky walked toward the young police officer first on scene.

Officer Jinni Kalestewa Sundry stood hatless, her dark brown hair in a tight bun nestled on her nape, wraparound sunglasses over her eyes. In the harsh sunlight, the blue of her uniform looked almost black. Nicky stopped next to her and stared impassively at the woman by the cliff face.

"Hey, Sarge. I didn't expect you," Jinni said.

"I picked up another weekend shift."

"Me, too. I can use the extra money." Jinni shifted and shrugged. Her silver-and-gold badge winked in the sunlight. "Anyway, thanks for coming out. I, uh, appreciate the help."

"I have no problem backing you up, Officer, but normally"— Nicky nodded at the woman against the mesa—"she's a one-person operation. What's going on?" The young officer had been patrolling alone since January, but her recent lack of confidence worried Nicky.

They didn't have the manpower out here in Indian Country to double up like this.

"When I talked to her, she right away turned mean. Didn't want to cooperate. I wasn't sure...." She shrugged again, shoulders tense.

"Did you call her Jean instead of Gianetta? She hates that."

Jinni peered over her sunglasses at Nicky. "I guess so. But I don't get why that makes her so mad."

"She told me once. Said Jean was so plain and ordinary, and she didn't want to be that person."

Rhythmic chanting rose in the blistering air, interrupting their conversation. Jean Green, aka Gianetta Green, continued to wave smoke over her body and up the cliffside.

"She's smudging herself. Doesn't she know you have to use a cacique or medicine man on Fire-Sky?" Jinni asked.

"Probably. Where's her car?"

Jinni tipped her chin to the right. "Behind those rocks, but how she got a Volkswagen Beetle out here is beyond me."

"Where there's a will. She parked okay?"

"No dried grass underneath the chassis. No grass anywhere. I wish it would rain." Jinni wiped a hand over her brow and frowned. "So, what do we do? She's not breaking the law."

"Yes, she is. Tribal sovereignty law, Officer. Trespassing on tribal property, illegally parked on sovereign land. Disturbing the wildlife." Lips quirked, Nicky motioned to a pair of brown, white-faced cows lying in the scraggly shade of a cluster of cedars.

"How about an open, unsecured flame in an area under an extreme fire threat?"

"I like that," Nicky said, impressed. Officer Sundry wasn't known for divergent thinking.

"A couple firefighters live in my neighborhood. I heard it from one of them." Jinni dropped her gaze, a small smile curving her lips.

"With the number of fires they've been called to this summer, I imagine they're even sick of the tribe's name."

"Fire-Sky." Jinni's smile widened. "That's pretty good, Sarge."

The chanting increased in volume and speed. Gianetta lifted her face to the sky and spread her arms wide. An aging, clichéd flower child straight out of Santa Fe, her purple-flowered muumuu and beet-red face clashed vividly with the tans, yellows, and browns of the surrounding desert.

"So, we arrest her?" Jinni asked.

"Not if we can chase her off." Nicky tugged the collar of her blouse to unstick it from her skin. Underneath, she wore light body armor, and under that, a dri-fit T-shirt. Necessary, but too many layers for this heat. "Let's get this done before I melt and Gianetta gets heatstroke."

Both women straightened and shifted to police mode as they strode toward Gianetta.

Nicky angled her head toward Jinni. "Do you know what she's singing? Because it isn't Keres."

"It's not Zuni, either. As far as I can tell, it's *heh-ya, ho-ya, ha-ya-ha*. Sounds like Hollywood Indian. All she needs are tom-toms." Jinni gestured with her chin. "She's got the smoke signals."

Nicky's mouth curled. "When her car is closer, she usually has Andean panpipe music playing. Very lyrical."

Jinni snorted.

"I'll approach first, Officer. Flank me and look stern." Nicky wiped all emotion from her expression. Her boots crunched through a stunted, shriveled bush, and Gianetta, who'd turned her back to them, stiffened in midwave of feathers.

"Gianetta. How many times have I told you Tsiba'ashi D'yini doesn't smudge?" Nicky lied smoothly, keeping her tone pleasant. The pungent odor of sage and cedar mixed with an odd bitter scent wafted over the air.

"Of course they do." Gianetta scooped at the smoke, but her movements jerked faster now. "I bought the smudge package from J WhiteHawk's shop right here on the pueblo."

"Speaking of Hollywood Indians," Jinni said under her breath.

"Gianetta, stop right now or I'll cite you for trespassing."

"I have a few inches of my smudge stick left, and J was very explicit about the completion of this ceremony. So—*oink, oink*—be good little *pigs* and step back."

Nicky's shoulders dropped, and her exasperation with the woman tripled. "Aw, Gianetta. Insults? Really? It's too hot, and I don't want any trouble. Give me the shell and feathers, get in your car, and leave the reservation."

Gianetta swiveled on her heel, fleshy jowls set. Sweat dripped off the end of her nose, and her lower lip pressed out belligerently. "No. I'm exercising my First Amendment right to freedom of religion." She brought the hand cradling the burning smudge stick to her face and inhaled deeply, sucking two streams of smoke into her nostrils. Her eyes unfocused and her body listed, face slick and red. She took a step, stumbled backward, and bounced against the cliff. The chant began again, her voice thin and wobbling.

Nicky narrowed her eyes. "Officer Sundry? I think Ms. Green is burning a little more than pine needles."

Jinni stepped closer and sniffed the smoky air. She flinched and paled. "Salvia and who knows what else."

Nicky shot her a look.

"Seer's sage. It makes you see things that aren't really there," Jinni said. She pressed a hand over her stomach and took a step back. "She'll fight, I bet."

"I don't want to hurt her. Let me try one more time," Nicky said. "Gianetta? You need to stop. Otherwise, we'll arrest you for trespassing."

Gianetta's chanting only got louder.

Nicky lowered her voice. "We need to get her out of this heat before she passes out." She pulled her cuffs. "Together. Ready?"

A black shadow flashed overhead, blocking the sun for the blink of an eye.

"Now." Nicky lunged and clamped her hand tightly around a fleshy forearm, trying to hold the smudge bowl steady. She quickly cuffed Gianetta's wrist. The woman shrieked and clocked the side of

Nicky's head with a fist full of feathers. Her sunglasses went flying, and her hat tumbled off. Eyes watering, she lurched and clutched hard at Gianetta to keep from falling. The woman's free arm continued to swing.

Free arm? Nicky found Jinni's form frozen in place, staring at the sky.

"Officer Sundry!"

Jinni's stricken gaze snapped to Nicky's. She dove forward, wrenched Gianetta's arm back, and cuffed it.

"No!" Gianetta's voice wailed off the wall of rock. "He's still here! I have to complete the ceremony or more will die. I have to—" She yanked her wrist away. The burning smudge stick arced into the air, a thin line of gray following it like a contrail, and tumbled into a scraggly four-wing saltbush.

No, no, no—

Nicky's eyes widened as red-and-orange flames *whooshed* up the dry branches, igniting paper-thin seeds and licking above her shoulders. Intense heat and a powerful reek saturated the air.

"Get away!" She shoved Gianetta into Jinni's arms.

Choking smoke filled Nicky's lungs. She frantically kicked and scooped dirt onto the fire. At some point, Jinni pressed a folding shovel into her hand, and she heaped sand onto the blackened shrub until the final sparks were doused. Dizzy, heart racing, Nicky bent and coughed. A bottle of water appeared. She twisted off the cap, drank, and spat to rinse her ash-coated mouth. After a long swallow, she poured water into a cupped hand and splashed it across her face. Jinni handed her a rag, and Nicky wiped it over her skin. Soot stained the cloth.

She straightened and stared hard at Officer Sundry, jaw clenched. "What happened, Officer?"

"Muhukwi—Night Grandfather—his shadow. It ... it's a bad omen. Owls don't fly during the day." Jinni dropped her gaze. "I, uh, I'm sorry."

Nicky suppressed a sharp flare of irritation. "Gianetta?" Tiny puffs of smoke still rose from the bush.

"I sat her on the ground in the shade of my truck. She's too stoned to get up." Still subdued, Jinni glanced behind Nicky. "She doesn't look good. Her face is really red. and she's howling about how the cuffs are too tight and she's going to find a lawyer and sue."

Gianetta's voice continued to echo off the rocks, but it was vague and metallic, like it came from an old transistor radio.

"Good luck with that." Nicky located her hat and sunglasses. She dusted off the hat and snugged it back on her head. After examining the lenses—no scratches—she slotted them in her pocket. "Fire-Sky Pueblo is a sovereign nation. She'd have to get permission to sue from the tribal council."

A pall of gray hung in the air. Nicky's focus shifted back to the burned bush, its charred branches sticking up from the piled sand. Rising curls of smoke morphed into flitting gray-feathered birds—tiny owls?—that circled up the cliff face. She leaned back to follow their flight and staggered.

"Sergeant Matthews?" Jinni grabbed her arm.

Nicky closed her eyes and pressed her hands against pulsing temples. The birds continued to fly behind her eyelids. "Pretty sure I breathed in a little too much smoke. You okay, Officer?" She blinked her eyes open.

"I held my breath."

It wasn't funny, but Nicky couldn't help chuckling. "The smoke changed into flying feathers." She swept a hand up, fingers fluttering.

Jinni straightened. "Sergeant, that's another thing. The feathers Ms. Green was using? Most of them look like turkey dyed to resemble eagle, except...."

A feather materialized and twirled in front of Nicky's face. She took it from Jinni's hand and stared. Over a foot long, it was pure white from quill to three-quarters up the vane, where it changed to a ruddy brown.

"I think that's real," Jinni said. "And unless Jean, er, Gianetta has a permit—"

"Possession of an eagle feather is a federal crime with a fine of twenty-five thousand dollars." Nicky sighed and ran her fingers over the feather's stiff edges. She suddenly felt drained and disappointed. "After you get Gianetta booked, call Conservation about the eagle feathers. Ask for Franco Martinez. You know who I'm talking about?"

"The guy who recently transferred to the pueblo from DEA. Yeah."

"If some of these are eagle, Gianetta really will have to call her lawyer." Nicky propped her hands on her hips. "Contact a tow company to pick up her car and request a search warrant. In the meantime, I'll do an inventory." An easy and perfectly legal method to see inside Gianetta's car before the warrant was approved.

"You're gonna stay here?" Jinni asked. "By yourself?"

"I need to make sure the effects of whatever this is are completely gone before I get behind the wheel." The tiny gray birds were still fluttering in her peripheral vision. "And Officer Sundry? We're going to have a talk about what happened with this arrest. Do you understand?"

"Yes, ma'am." Jinni had paled again.

They placed a sputtering Gianetta in the back of Jinni's vehicle. Nicky held a bottle of water to Gianetta's lips while Jinni advised her of her rights. In the cool of the air-conditioned truck, Gianetta's color was better, although she was flushed from the heat.

As the two women drove away, Nicky studied the burnt bush. No more feathered smoke-birds rose in the air, which meant the odd hallucinations of the seer's sage had disappeared. Time to get to work on the inventory.

She grabbed a bottle of water from her unit, glancing in the rearview. Brown eyes, faintly bloodshot from the smoke, stared back from an oval face that had been mistaken for Native more than once by tourists visiting the pueblo. She tipped her head and grimaced. Soot coated her straight black hair, and her ponytail had slipped sideways. She fixed her hair, motions quick and efficient, and dusted the ash off her palms. When she finished, she closed the door, and, water in hand, headed toward the jumble of rocks hiding Gianetta's bright pink car.

GIANETTA HAD PARKED her late-model VW Beetle behind two towering, triangular rocks that thrust out of the sand and seemed to glow in the blazing sunlight. Nicky tried the passenger's side door handle and yanked her hand away with a hiss. The metal was hotter than hell. Using the edge of her blouse, she popped the doors open and pushed them wider with her knee to let the super-heated air bleed out.

Inside, a tiny crystal hummingbird dangled from the rearview mirror, refracting delicate rainbows. Keys hung from the ignition, a slouchy leather bag lay on the passenger floor, and a large cardboard box was wedged behind the driver's seat. She checked her phone and sighed: 2:37 P.M. Hours before it would start to cool off. Small notepad and pen in hand, she dipped into the sweltering interior to inventory the purse and glove compartment, then turned her attention to the box in the back.

With the passenger seat inclined forward, Nicky hunched in the cramped space, the butt of her gun digging into her side and sweat gluing her clothes to her skin. Resting on top of the box's contents were more feathers tied with a leather thong, but she couldn't tell whether they were eagle or dyed turkey. Underneath lay smudge sticks resembling nothing more than giant joints. They smelled just as bad. A quick notation in her notepad reminded her to have them checked for anything illicit. She rummaged through the rest of the items, counting two terra-cotta smudge plates, two black-and-white painted bowls, half a dozen dream catchers, intricately beaded coasters and hair clips, a couple of small sand paintings, and a set of four place mats woven in Ganado Red patterns. All of the packaging bore the Fire-Sky logo—a masked face hovering over a stylized, smoking volcano—and the digital signature of the pueblo's marginally famous movie and television actor, J WhiteHawk. A folded receipt tucked in a book on animal tracks was time-stamped that morning.

Nicky blinked at the total. With that amount of money, she could buy groceries for a couple of months and *good* coffee, or catch up on some of her bills, or—

Her stomach flipped with worry that she quickly suppressed. She'd promised herself she wouldn't let her money problems interfere with work, but sometimes her head refused to cooperate.

With a jerky movement, she replaced the receipt and refocused on her task. She shifted on the seat, and the box tilted, rolling a small unglazed pot to one side and exposing a carved knot of stone. Nicky reached to grab it—and stopped, fingers curling away. The back of her neck tingled as she stared into the shadowy corner of the cardboard.

Exasperated, she shook her head. What the heck was her problem? The tow truck would arrive soon, and the inventory needed to get finished. She scooped up the stone and ducked out of the car into sunlight.

A delicately rendered black bear fetish lay in her hand, a grainy yellow substance clinging to the deeper cuts in the stone. She pinched her finger and thumb behind the carved shoulders and stood the little figure up in her palm. Astonished at the detail, Nicky found herself smiling. She'd never seen a fetish rendered this exquisitely, even down to tiny carved claws that pricked her skin. It was so different.

The bear shimmered in the stark light, and Nicky's smiled dropped. Prickles of unease ran down her arms. She lifted the fetish up—her face within inches, eyes unblinking—and stared.

Had it ... moved? No. It couldn't have....

Her gaze followed the swirl of stone-carved fur to the bear's tiny gem-red eyes. Sweat from her temple traced a path to the corner of her mouth. She touched her tongue to it, tasted ash and salt. A faint earthy scent mixed with smoke tickled her nose. The odor intensified, thickened. It soured into the stench of rotting vegetation, charred and putrefying. Nose stinging, eyes burning, Nicky curved her fingers over the bear to knuckle away blurring moisture. A bite of pain pinched her skin. She opened her hand and found a red mark. A sharp edge of the fetish had cut—

Footsteps slithered across the ground behind her. She jerked her head around, and the breath strangled in her throat.

The tall, narrow figure of a man stood at the edge of the towering stones, motionless. Ash covered his hair and skin and stained his clothes gray. He held a blackened club, his hand gripping, turning it, gripping. She met his stare, and every inch of her skin crawled. *His eyes*. They were ... were ....

Nicky spun. The stone bear flew out of her grasp and thunked hollowly against the metal of the car door. Even before it dropped to the sand, she'd pulled her gun, barrel leveled at—

Nothing. He was gone.

From behind the rock, sand rasped with the slide of his steps.

"Police! Show yourself. Now!" Nicky crept forward, gaze locked on the edge of the towering stones. She darted around the corner, gun up.

Nothing.

Movement flashed to her left. She swiveled, caught a glimpse. The gray man disappeared behind a cedar thirty yards away. Her mouth hung open. How had he...?

"Police! Stop right there!" She sprinted toward him, swung around the tree, sidearm braced ... and stared blankly at empty space. Palms slick on the butt of her gun, she juggled her grip to wipe one, then the other, on her slacks. The sun seared through her clothes and burned her tight knuckles. She pivoted full circle. Where the hell was he?

There. Fifty yards away, the man slipped behind the scraggly stand of cedars. From under the trees, two cows clumsily jolted to their feet, eyes rolling white. They moved away at a fast, jarring trot, dust puffing from their hides. When they halted, their dark, liquid gazes swung toward her.

Nicky smiled thinly. She knew what he was doing. Drawing her out into the flat, sunburnt landscape surrounding Hummingbird Mesa. Had he been watching all along? Seen something he wanted in Gianetta's car? Determined to stop his stupid game, she marched to the trees, her boots crunching on rock and dirt, gun clasped in her hands.

He wasn't there.

Hot, sweaty, and pissed, Nicky stepped between two cedars, using their feathery branches as cover. She slotted the gun in her holster and yanked the bottle of water from her pocket. Her unit, bright white in the sun, hummed, engine running. Its interior would be a welcome chilly cocoon. Was *her* vehicle his target? Was he circling around to steal it? She palmed her keys and pressed a button. Lights flashed, and the low hum of the engine cut off.

"Good luck with that, jack-hole." Nicky took a drink and wiped a sleeve over her brow.

Sunlight flashed off metal. Her gaze swept the desert, burned ashen gray by drought, and came to rest on a saddled horse moving aimlessly across the bleached landscape. Shimmering heat magnified its form as it wavered in and out of focus. There was no rider.

Nicky tracked the horse as she unclipped her cell phone. "Fire-Sky Dispatch, this is two-one-three, over."

"Fire-Sky Dispatch, copy."

"Do you have the bulletin on the man from the ranch outside of M'ida Village? Missing person filed a couple days ago."

"Er, yeah, yeah. Uh, let's see. Here it is. Name's Seneca Elk. Twenty-three age, five-nine height, one-sixty weight. On horseback. Last known location, uh, Black Mesa."

Two mesas and five miles north of Hummingbird. No wonder they hadn't found him.

"There's a saddled horse, no rider, about a mile west of Hummingbird Mesa. I'm going to investigate. Away from my vehicle, available by portable." Poised to report the weird man she'd been chasing, Nicky hesitated, now unsure of what she'd seen.

"Ten-four, two-one-three. Do you need ten eighty-two? Over."

"I'll call if needed. Two-one-three, out."

Nicky strode back to her unit. She grabbed a couple more bottles of water out of her cooler, slotting them in her front pockets, and added nitrile gloves and extra cuffs to her duty belt. At the VW, she found the stone bear half buried in the sand. It hadn't gotten up and walked away.

She smiled at her foolishness. A few whiffs of hallucinogenic smoke had affected her more than she'd realized. Fetish tucked back in the box, she put the keys on the seat for the tow-truck driver and tugged her ball cap lower. Nicky scanned the scorched field once more and trudged into the heat after the horse. Time to find out what had happened to its rider.

CHAPTER TWO

Nicky crossed into the barren landscape, the horse's image quivering in the rising waves of heat. The dryness of the air evaporated sweat from her body almost immediately but didn't cool her. Nor did it help that the refraction of light off denuded ground took the shape of sparkling blue playas. With each step forward, they drained away to form another transient mirage in the distance. Illusions of moisture in the absence of the summer monsoons.

What she wouldn't give for the water to be real. She'd fall into it face-first and let it suck the heat and sweat from her body. Nicky uncapped a water bottle and finished it off. Then she twisted it into a compact ball and stuffed the collapsed plastic back in her pocket.

The horse had moved out of sight behind a peninsula of rocks, but a trail of tracks churned the ground around her feet leading into the start of a narrow slot canyon. She knelt and outlined one of the shod hoof marks. They mixed into, onto, and were obscured by the double half-moons of cow tracks. Paralleling the freshest prints, she skirted crumbling rocks and dried brush at the mouth of the canyon. Two cracked, gray fence posts wrapped tightly with oxidized strands of barbed wire had been thrust into the brush. Iron eyebolts had been hammered into the stone. Probably part of a gate once used to block off access. A bent and rusted metal sign lay facedown, half buried in the dirt. She toed it over.

EV ME AL CO MIN ION

KEE OU

The KEEP OUT she got, but the rest? Time and age had scoured away the paint. She snapped a picture, then headed inside the gap between rising cliffs, ducking into the shade that darkened one side of the dry streambed. As she trekked, the walls rose ten then twenty feet, graceful static curves shaped by wind and water. Behind her, the opening of the canyon slipped away in twists and bends. Sound quieted to wind and birdsong. The canyon narrowed, completely draped in shadows, and Nicky could almost touch both towering faces with outstretched arms.

A rush of breeze bearing moisture and the herby scent of vegetation touched her face. She hurried around another bend to halt and stare.

Tucked in a large dead-end curve of a striated red stone cliff, hidden from anyone who didn't penetrate deep into the canyon, grew a desert Garden of Eden, an island bounded by sandstone, its air dusty-fresh. Nicky breathed deeply, filling her lungs. Grass, trees, and shrubs crowded around a thicket of Gamble oak, New Mexico olive, and water birch. Scrubby stands of chamois and Apache plume trickled along the edge of the cliff face. Her gaze slewed up to measure the top of a single tall cottonwood, deep green leaves fluttering in the breeze. From a tangle of *Ephedra torreyana*—Mormon tea—a cactus wren scolded her with its distinctive *cha-cha-cha*.

The horse, a small chestnut gelding with socks and an irregular star, stood beside a clump of juniper, bridle intact, saddle askew, one stirrup twisted and chewed. Nicky pressed her lips tight. She'd held out hope the horse would lead her to the rider, but the animal's general air of abandonment wasn't a good sign.

Ears perked, the horse stared with bright, curious eyes. Nicky approached, slow and easy, voice soothing, and picked up a trailing rein. He was small—close to pony-sized, fourteen or fifteen hands. She did a quick check of his teeth. Young, maybe three years old. When she released his mouth, he dropped his face to her chest and heaved a huge, sighing breath. Poor guy. She scratched itchy spots and breathed in his pungent horsey scent, all the while murmuring. When he dropped his head to snuffle her pockets, Nicky chuckled. "I got nothing, buddy. No treats." She led him to the shade of the trees.

After tying the reins in a quick-release knot, she snapped pics of the rig: horned saddle, leather sporting fresh scratches, black-zippered nylon saddlebags with water bottle slots. She then uncinched and lifted off the saddle to check for hot spots. The horse shivered under the stroke of her hands. Nothing a good wash and brush wouldn't fix. Pivoting to scan the oasis, she frowned. Where was his rider? He could've walked out, but she'd only found horse and cow tracks in the dry wash.

With one final pat, Nicky headed toward the thicket for a more thorough search. She pulled off her ball cap and let the breeze comb through her hair as she breathed in the sweet scents of flowers, the metallic tang of water—

And the tickling stench of death and decomposition. Nicky slapped the cap hard against her leg. God, she hated that smell.

Her gaze swept over the ground. There. She slipped her sunglasses to the top of her head and squatted down to trace a notch in the U-shaped heel print of a cowboy boot. It didn't take an expert to see the prints were a few days old—edges soft, degraded by wind and time. They headed into the oasis but didn't come out. Not good. Tension she'd shed upon entering the oasis returned with force. If the missing cowboy was the source of the unpleasant odor, she'd need to thoroughly document the scene as a probable unattended death. Nicky dropped a short vinyl ruler by the boot prints and snapped pictures with her phone.

She stood, hands on her hips, and surveyed the area in front of her. Grass crushed by hoofprints and tree limbs arced over a cow trail that burrowed into the clump of olive. She tramped through, ducking low. The smell of putrefaction intensified.

A rhythmic *creak-creak-creak* and the faint splash of water made Nicky stop and cock an ear. She shifted direction, but a few paces in, sodden ground sucked at her boots. There must have been a spring or a seep—ciénega—for this much water. It was why the horse had stayed near the canyon.

She pressed forward and stepped into a wide clearing, fifty or sixty feet in diameter. A semicircular cliff met the ground, its concave sides creating a lip at the top like that of a bowl. The creaking sound intensified, and she tipped her head upward, shielding her eyes. Around the cottonwood, she counted half a dozen dead trees, their crimped gray branches tangled and broken. A derrick windmill reared up behind them, almost completely hidden, its anodized blades rotating in the breeze. Near the spindly metal legs squatted a galvanized oval stock tank, crystalline water jetting from a spigot into thick green grass.

But it was the large, cylindrical structure to the right of the wind-mill that drew Nicky's focus. A corrugated metal water tank camou-flaged in mottled green and gray paint sat across the clearing, the Fire-Sky symbol for water and wind—a clockwise spiral—daubed into its curving side. It stood ten or twelve feet high and at least twenty feet in diameter and its steel walls pulsed heat from the sun and pushed away lingering coolness. A ladder welded from pipe crawled up the side, its vertical rails curving over the flat top of the structure. And in the dirt was a single line of boot prints, edges still sharp enough to see the notch in the cowboy's left heel. They headed straight across the ground to the tank. There were no returning tracks.

A narrow platform, head-high and accessible from the ladder, jutted out from under a hinged door in the side of the tank. On the roof above the platform lay a soft, lumpish pile. Clothes? The metal door stood open about a foot, and from the interior came the echoing hum of thousands of flies. Black dots filled the air around the tank door, their buzzing raucous and shrill.

Nicky hissed out a breath. She'd probably found the missing cowboy. Maybe. Even when surrounding water was plentiful, curious rabbits, coyotes, even deer got into open tanks, panicked, and died when they couldn't get out. Although all the evidence pointed to her missing man, she had to check before she called it in. Wonderful.

She snapped more pictures, wishing a gas mask bulged in her pocket instead of the water bottle. As she approached the tank, gases of decomposition—cadaverine and putrescine—locked into specific olfactory receptors in her sinuses, an evolutionarily imprinted warning signal to leave the dead alone. Except she couldn't. She was trained to investigate the smell.

Which was why a managerial position at Lotaburger seemed more appealing with every step.

Once she was by the ladder, she slotted her phone away and eyed the narrow opening. Dang. She was really gonna do this. Had to confirm. At least she'd had the foresight to carry nitrile gloves. She snapped them on, grasped the rung of the ladder, and hissed at the metal's heat. Each step resonated hollowly as she climbed. When she was within arm's reach, she shoved the hinged door wide. A bolus of buzzing, angry insects seethed from the tank. Her stomach muscles involuntarily tightened as the concentrated stench of death roiled out with the flies. *Oh, God.* Nicky gagged. She curled in on herself, tamping down the churning bile that rose in her throat, panting shallowly through her mouth, knowing if she contaminated the scene by throwing up, she'd never hear the end of it from her fellow officers.

She garnered control of herself before she crawled onto the flat metal plate, shuddering and waving her hands sharply as flies pelted her blouse and skin. Lips pressed tight, hand over her nose and mouth, she stood and studied the jumbled pile of clothes on the roof of the tank. A stained cowboy hat lay on its crown, listing in the breeze. Jeans, their pockets half turned out, a red-checked shirt, and the leather of well-used cowboy boots half hidden underneath. No wallet or ID, but that wasn't uncommon. No need to take them. Lifting the edge of the jeans, she noted the notched heel of one of the boots. She took quick pictures, close-up and panoramic. A fly burrowed into her hair, buzzing furiously, trapped near her ear. She batted at it, shivering in disgust.

Ducking down, Nicky peered within, but the brightness of the afternoon sun didn't penetrate the murky darkness. She swallowed nausea-thickened saliva and pulled the door wider. More flies rushed out, but the bulk of droning insects had already dissipated. Crouching closer, she pointed her flashlight beam inside. The surface sparkled and gleamed with a purplish, oily sheen. Nicky measured the water level at only a foot below her. A second ladder dropped into the tank. She propped the flashlight on the lip of the threshold, stuck her phone through the doorway to click a few photos, then scrolled through the series of pictures. Nothing but tank walls and a dark opaque surface. Her light was angled too high.

Nicky pulled out the crushed plastic water bottle and placed it under the end of her flashlight. More photos, still no body. She frowned. From past experience, she knew the heat inside the water tank should have accelerated the production of decay gases, bloating the corpse and causing it to float. At least, that's what the abundance of dead-guy stench told her. Maybe he was stuck on the bottom. She inched forward and slanted her light downward, but it still didn't penetrate the blackness of the water's surface.

Nicky pulled back and compressed her lips. She'd have to put her head inside the frickin' tank. *Great.* She sucked in a lungful of untainted air before she grabbed the interior ladder's curved top and ducked through the opening. The pounding summer sun made the interior a humid oven. Greasy air coated her exposed skin, and her eyes stung. Fingers tightened as she leaned in, flashlight pointed into the water.

She suppressed a gasp. A body floated a couple of feet below the surface, obviously human. Pale arms stretched out like wings, chest dark, maybe covered with a black T-shirt. Her light played over the submerged corpse, but details were indistinct. Fly carcasses as big as raisins—some still struggling to escape their watery death—and water cloudy with puffs of disintegrating skin and tissue obscured Nicky's view.

Her face twisted in sympathy.

Poor guy. Probably wanted to cool off from the heat. Instead, he'd been reduced to cowboy soup.

CHAPTER THREE

NICKY SWUNG out of the tank and inhaled lungfuls of clean air, putting together the pieces of the puzzle before her. Maybe he'd been overcome by noxious fumes within the enclosed space. Or had he been caught up in something on the bottom? Stock tanks were notorious for the detritus people and nature deposited in their depths. Wire, old tires, and tree limbs could snag an unwitting swimmer. Had that happened here?

Deciding her crouch was too precarious, she knelt, clasped the top of the ladder with a gloved hand, flashlight in the other, and leaned farther into the tank to scan below the surface. Nothing stood out. A drifting raft of flies crawling over who-knew-what made her turn her head in disgust.

She needed to call Dispatch. Get a team out here to retrieve the body. Suddenly impatient with herself, Nicky yanked back. The full water bottle in her pocket caught on the tank's opening. Her anchor hand slipped on the ladder, and a sharp protrusion tore into her gloved palm. Pain shot up her arm. Reflexively, her grip loosened, fingers slipped.

Nicky teetered forward on her knees. Her hand tightened and yanked at the ladder. Instead of stabilizing her, it torqued her off-balance. Her horrified gaze riveted on the foul liquid before she plunged—arm, face, shoulder—under the surface. She dropped the flashlight, and it plummeted downward, illuminating the water in a garish white glow. But instead of blurring the corpse's face, the turbid water seemed to magnify his bleached and bulging eyes. Long hair undulated in a spidery halo. Tissue dissolved from a split in one cheek, fluffy bits that floated away in the gentle ripples. A light purple tongue protruded from his mouth.

Her flailing hand tangled in his hair. She jerked it back, setting the body in motion. The dead man's torso drifted closer, his ruined face gliding toward hers. For a brief moment, she stopped struggling. Filled with an overpowering sadness, she gently pressed her hand against his shoulder to stop his movement and stare into his sightless eyes.

And the face changed.

The ruptured cheek healed to smooth skin; the blue-yellow irises sharpened to a frightened brown. He stared directly at her, expression pleading, scared, before his eyes rolled back, leaving only white. His mouth opened—

Nicky screamed. Huge air-filled bubbles boiled upward. Oxygen depleted from her lungs, she involuntarily sucked in a mouthful of contaminated water. Her muscles shuddered in panic when she realized what she'd done.

With a surge of terrified strength, Nicky heaved out of the water and flung herself off the platform. She landed with a jarring thud in the sand below. Coughing, heaving, she staggered to her feet and stumbled to the spigot at the edge of the clearing. There, she dropped to her knees, dizzy with adrenaline. Fingers shaking, she stripped off the remains of her gloves, braced her hands on the ground, and ducked under the pounding torrent, letting it scour her skin, face, and shoulders. Hallucinations. It wasn't real. *Wasn't real.*

A shadow blocked the sun. A tall gray silhouette stood to one side, blurred by the rushing water. Her panic mounted as bile rose in her throat.

She scuttled back against the trough and pulled her gun.

CHAPTER FOUR

Nicky forced back a strangled cry. Crouched on her knees, she pointed her gun at the bulky form, backlit and rimmed by brilliant light.

The figure stood completely still, hands out with fingers spread.

"Nicky, don't—" The voice choked. "Put the gun down, sweetheart. Please."

The sight of her weapon jumped a tiny bit with each *thud-thud* of her heart.

"Franco?" She quickly scraped the hair from her face and knuckled her eyes. "You're ... not him." Profound relief coursed through her. Her finger unhooked from the trigger. She dropped her hand, weapon pointed down.

"No. Not him. Just me." Franco took a step, wobbled. He sank to his knees beside her and seemed to deflate.

She stared at him, drinking in the hard angles of his jaw and cheeks, a nose slightly too large and lips slightly too thin, on a face tanned by the outdoors and Hispanic heritage—although right now, his skin was pale. Three years older than her own thirty-two, he had more gray sprinkled in his hair than she did.

Straightening, he braced his hands on his thighs. "Nicky. I'm going to take your weapon."

Her gaze never left his as he disentangled her fingers from the gun and nestled it into his waistband. He tugged her into his arms, and she buried her face in his shoulder, head spinning. He smelled of sweat and dust and menthol. She shifted and rested her cheek above his conservation badge. Franco tightened his hold.

"And here I thought our first date went so well." His voice was strained.

Nicky gave a watery chuckle. "Yep," she said. "That'll teach you to take me to a baseball game when I don't know the difference between an inning and an out."

Five years ago, she'd sworn never to date another man who worked in law enforcement. But she recently realized she'd let one bad—okay, ridiculously awful—experience control her life, so she'd broken that vow for Conservation Agent Franco Martinez.

It was a silly rule anyway.

"You okay?" His lips moved in her hair.

Nicky nodded and disengaged, appalled and embarrassed by her complete loss of control. She leaned heavily against the trough, the metal cold on her back.

Franco shifted to sit beside her, shirt wet from their embrace. He dragged a bottle of water from a pocket in his cargo pants and handed it to her. She rinsed out her mouth, then drank half the bottle in one long swallow.

"Guess you found the missing guy," he said.

"Think so." Her lips quirked up into the semblance of a smile. "You're not going to believe this, but I fell into the tank with ... with the body. And ... and I lost it." She tipped her head back, stared up at the sky. "I'm so sorry, Franco." A sob escaped.

Again, his arms enveloped her. She lay her cheek on his shoulder. Wetness from the corner of her eye wicked into his already damp shirt.

"You didn't shoot me. I'm counting that as a win."

The words vibrated gruff and low against her ear. But as they faded, she felt a catch in his breathing. They silently rocked back and forth.

After a few minutes of quiet, Nicky spoke. "Why are you here?"

"Jinni Sundry called me on her way to the hospital with your perp."

"Gianetta?" Nicky latched on to the change in subject. She straightened. "What's going on?"

"Chest pains. Didn't even get her booked. Ambulanced and admitted to UNM Hospital overnight for observation. Jinni sent me pics of the eagle feathers and told me what happened with the salvia smoke. Said you got a snoot-full and were seeing stuff that wasn't there. That you didn't want to drive until you'd recovered. Thought I'd come check on you."

She raised her arms to gather up her hair but stopped. The heel of her left hand contained a long diagonal gash that bled sluggishly.

"How'd you get that?" Franco asked.

"Nail on the tank's ladder, I think. When I slipped."

He retrieved a wet wipe from a small black pouch on his duty belt and grasped her forearm. "Why don't you update me on the arrest and salvia while I clean you up. It'll take your mind off the sting."

Her teeth clamped together tightly as he dabbed the cut. "Not so sure about that." She explained about the fire, the smoke birds, the bear fetish, even the odd smell, but she withheld her vision of the man and the change in the drowning victim's face. Somehow, they were ... different. *Weren't they?* "I didn't think the effects would be that intense. Everything was so ... real."

"Its psychoactive ingredient is salvinorin A, which is a potent hallucinogen. People see vivid manifestations of things that aren't there—telescopic visions, the merging of living and nonliving objects. Dose and user dependent."

Nicky stared at him.

"Remember? I'm DEA, along with being really, really smart." His lips twitched. "And I Googled it before I came."

"Well, Agent Genius, it didn't seem like that much smoke." Nicky frowned. "Captain Richards can't know about the salvia." Her captain had a personal and professional vendetta against her because he thought she'd slept her way to her position. Plus, he was a total ass. "He'll mandate a drug test, use it against me, get me suspended." He'd go after her job, and she couldn't afford to lose her job. Not right now. Frustration and worry blossomed.

"Hey. I got your back, partner. You know that."

"Do I?" Nicky lifted her chin, emotions too close to the surface. "Like when you got me suspended?"

Franco's lips thinned. "You know it wasn't personal. And I apologized."

She didn't reply.

He released her hand with a sigh. "I think you need stitches, probably a tetanus shot. I'll drive you to the Fire-Sky Clinic after forensics arrives."

"No. Let's go to Albuquerque instead. Talk to Gianetta tonight. I'll get my hand checked out at the hospital."

"Okay." He held her gaze and nodded slowly. "Nicky? When you first saw me, who did you think I was?"

"No one. You just startled me."

She'd answered too quickly. Face suddenly unreadable, he regarded her for a lingering moment. Finally, he stood. "Want me to call this in?"

"No. I got it." Nicky climbed to her feet. Franco put out a hand when she swayed, but Nicky stepped back. She squared her shoulders and called Dispatch. "We'll need a horse trailer." Drawing in a deep breath, she walked toward the tank. The body's stench permeated the burning air, so similar to the odor at Hummingbird Mesa. Questions built in her mind.

Franco gestured at the lush oasis of trees, grasses, and flowers. "Is this place on the maps? It's otherworldly compared to the landscape outside the cliffs."

"It's got to be, but I've never heard about it. These improvements look pretty new, too. And expensive. We'd better wait for forensics at the mouth of the canyon. Let's get the horse." She sighed. "It's going to be a long evening." She stepped forward, but Franco stopped her.

"Nicky? Your gun." He extended it, muzzle down, butt first.

Her stiffness melted. She covered his hand with hers as she took it. "Thanks. I owe you."

"The Isotopes play again next Saturday." His voice ticked upward, almost in a question, and he smiled boyishly.

Nicky laughed, the sound echoing off the canyon walls.

CHAPTER FIVE

THE BRIGHT BULB of the gooseneck lamp burned white dots into Nicky's vision. The ER doctor mumbled an apology and angled it away from her face. He met her gaze and raised his eyebrows, his expression holding faint impatience.

Franco crossed his arms. "Quit stalling and give him your hand."

"I'm not stalling." Nicky kept her frown in place and extended her palm. She suppressed a wince as the doctor unwrapped a suture kit and positioned the needle driver. "I just don't like needles."

"Fights, fires, dead bodies. But you don't like needles." The doctor bent over her gashed hand, the fluorescent lights above glittering in the gray hair threading his temple. As he curled the needle through numbed tissue, the tugging sensation made her cringe. He glared at her. "Unh! Stop moving."

Maybe if she didn't watch. Nicky tipped her head up to Franco, eyes squinting against a headache. "My truck's still at Hummingbird Mesa."

"I had one of the uniforms drive it to the station."

"How will I get home? And get to work tomorrow?" Okay. There was a definite whine in her voice. She scowled and dropped her gaze to her hand again, only to look away as the doctor pierced her skin with a second suture needle.

"I live in Rio Rancho. Your house is in Bernalillo. It's on my way in both directions."

"No." She scrambled for an excuse. "After we talk to Gianetta Green, I'll need to head back to the rez and get a preliminary report to my lieutenant. I'll pick up my truck then."

The silence grew, filled by the hum of the ceiling lights, muffled voices, and a baby crying somewhere in the ER. Franco's face was stony, hands clenched, knuckles white.

"Whatever, Agent Matthews."

Her throat burned at the dry indifference of his response. Nicky pulled her gaze away, struggling to focus on something other than the hurt she'd caused. The doctor began to wind her hand in what seemed like yards of gauze.

"How long does this need to stay on, doc? I can't afford any time off right now." She held out a gauze-mittened hand.

"Overnight, but keep the stitches covered." He swung the tray table to the side of the room. "Let's get your prescriptions."

He slipped between the curtains of the alcove. Nicky followed, weaving down the crowded hallway. She nodded to a couple of Albuquerque police officers standing beside a scruffy, snoring man cuffed to a gurney and glanced with sympathy at a harried young mother holding the crying child. Franco stalked behind her, his presence heavy.

"Here we are." The doctor gathered a small sheaf of papers from a printer. Nicky held out a gauzy hand, but he gave them to Franco.

"I don't think swallowing that water will give you an *infection*"—the doctor made air quotes—"of what, I don't know, but if you have any stomach issues, call the clinic." He propped his hands on his hips and gave them an exasperated stare. "Why don't you two go home? And for God's sake, take a shower. Please. You both look—and smell—like death warmed over."

He pointed them toward the exit and hurried off.

"You know, it's not so bad once the smell saturates your scent receptors," Nicky said. "Besides, I like all that scruffy stubble on your chin and the dark circles under your eyes. Makes you look world-weary. Dangerous. Very Indiana Jones." She gave Franco a tentative smile. A peace offering.

Franco stared hard at her before his shoulders relaxed. He sighed as he scraped a hand over his chin. "You must be tired if you're trying to butter me up with compliments. You still want to question your perp?"

"Yeah. Who needs sleep?"

She headed for the elevators, Franco falling in beside her. They stepped inside, and Franco punched the button to the fifth floor. A man in scrubs hurriedly entered, took an audible sniff, and backed out.

At the nurses' station, they signed in and walked down the darkened hallway.

"Here's the deal, Nicky," Franco said. "I'll agree to take you to Savannah's for tonight, not back to the station."

"But it's farther to Savannah's."

He continued like she hadn't even spoken. "We'll stop by a drugstore and drop off the prescriptions first. I'll pick them up tomorrow morning on my way in from work."

"I ... I can't pay right now. I don't carry cash." Panic again grew in her chest.

"Later, then." He stopped outside Gianetta's room, grasped the handle to open it.

"No." She grabbed his arm and yanked her hand back with a wince. Her eyes burned. She must be more tired than she'd thought.

"Nicky? What is it?" His voice was soft, and a pucker of concern creased his brow.

He'd backed her up today, hadn't pressed her for answers, even after she'd pointed a gun at him. She could trust him ... couldn't she?

The temptation to confess was severe, to share her worry, the burden that hung over her like a sword.

"Franco." She cleared her throat. "I, um. I don't have the money—"

The door to Gianetta's room swung open, and light dazzled Nicky's eyes. A slim, petite woman in a dark red wrap dress and ridiculously high heels stood in the threshold.

"Well, well. Monique Matthews in the flesh. I heard you'd become a cop after you dropped out of law school. Or did they kick you out? I can never remember."

The voice slammed through Nicky's head. She was riven in place, ripped from the present and into the nightmare of a past filled with depositions and accusations and a deep, abiding shame.

"What? Nothing to say?" the woman asked. "Wait. Are you one of the officers who arrested my client?"

Her blond hair was longer, falling in waves to her collarbone. Perhaps a few more lines around her eyes, but they were faint. A smile stretched across the perfect oval of her face, but her blue eyes stayed cold.

"What a coincidence. Because I'm Ms. Green's lawyer, and she has very obviously been roughed up. I guess some things never change."

No. Some things had changed a great deal.

Nicky shook herself internally, broke the lethargy that had invaded her muscles at the sound of the woman's voice. She straightened her shoulders.

"Ruth. I didn't know you'd stooped to ambulance chasing. Business dropped off since we last ... visited?" Nicky's voice had started out strained but gained strength as she spoke. She caught Franco's raised eyebrows out of the corner of her eye. "I can't imagine the Randals were happy with the final settlement you drew up. Pity if they decided to go after you, too. Karma's such a *bitch*." The woman's expression flattened, and Nicky felt a twist of perverse pleasure. She gestured to the open door with a bandaged hand. "You are correct on one little thing, though. I'm the arresting officer, and I need to question your client."

A single eyebrow rose as Ruth tipped her chin up. The hint of a smile twisted her lips.

Dammit. She'd pushed too far. Ruth was going to refuse the interview. She scrambled for a way to—

Hand outstretched, Franco stepped forward, bumping Nicky out of the way.

Her mind blanked, only to quickly fill with a spurt of annoyance. She frowned at his broad back. "Hey—"

"Hi. Conservation Agent Franco Martinez from the Fire-Sky Pueblo. I'm working with Sergeant Matthews on this case."

Ruth's startled gaze swung from Nicky to Franco. She stared for a moment before extending her hand. He cradled hers with both of his.

"Your hands are like ice," he murmured. "We know it's late, but it would save us a trip if we could speak to your client. You'd be right here, Ms.—?"

"Jäger. Ruth Jäger."

"Yep. Right here, Ru—er, Ms. Jäger, to hear everything we say." He bobbed his head up and down.

Nicky blinked. *What the heck?*

Ruth's straight nose twitched, and she scrunched her face a tiny bit. Franco dropped her hand and put his up in a placating gesture while managing to step around her into the room.

"Sorry about the smell. Hazards of the job. We'll be in and out as quickly as we can, ma'am. I promise."

Ruth frowned but didn't protest.

Gianetta lay on the bed, swathed in a cotton hospital gown and light blue flannel blankets, her gray hair in a thick braid over her shoulder. She stared at Franco. He flashed a smile and bobbed his head again. Nicky slid past him to stand on Gianetta's left, not about to let this opportunity go to waste, even if she wanted to kick him in the—

"Ms. Green? I'm Agent Martinez, ma'am. Sergeant Matthews

and I'd like to ask you about this afternoon's events." Franco settled on Gianetta's right side, bookending her, and glanced at Ruth.

"I'll allow a few questions," she said slowly. "Go ahead and answer, Jean."

Gianetta's eyes and neck bulged.

Franco fumbled a notepad and pen from his shirt pocket. "Officer Sundry Mirandized you earlier today?" he asked. Gianetta nodded. "Why were you at Hummingbird Mesa?"

"To exercise my rights under the First Amendment. Freedom of religion." She stuck out her bottom lip and glared at Nicky. "Then *she* came and beat me up about it."

"You forgot about the fire, Gianetta." Nicky placed her bandaged hand on the metal bed guard. The woman's eyes widened. Good. A little guilt could go a long way in making a perp talk.

"Gianetta," Franco said. "You don't mind if I call you Gianetta, do you?" She dragged her gaze away from Nicky's hand and shook her head. "The feathers you used in the smudging? They were identified as golden eagle, a federally protected species," he explained as if to a child. "Do you have a permit? No? Can you tell me how you acquired them?"

"Nice try, Agent Martinez." Ruth smiled and waggled a playful finger. "Don't answer, Jean. Until I get my own expert to examine the feathers, that subject is off-limits."

Franco was being too nice. Giving them time to recover. Nicky decided to come in at a different angle, keep Gianetta off-balance. "The cardboard box in your car—"

"I bought all that stuff from J's store. I've been going to him—and *only* him—for years to help me with my spiritual journey." Her mouth trembled with a small smile. "He's a wonderful man and such a good friend to me."

"By J, you mean J WhiteHawk?" Nicky asked. "If he sold you the feathers, I'm sure I could speak to the US attorney and get you a deal."

"Off-limits," Ruth said.

"I would never betray J! Besides"—Gianetta sniffed and looked away—"I found those."

"It's a felony to collect—"

"We're finished with that topic. You still don't listen, do you, Sergeant Matthews?"

Nicky squashed her frustration and changed directions again. "Then let's talk about the smudge sticks. The one you were burning at the mesa contained seer's sage, which is a hallucino-genic drug. *Salvia....*" What was it called? Nicky caught Franco's eye.

"Oh." He furrowed his brows and stared at the pad in his hand. "Uh, *Salvia div-in-or-um.*"

"But it's not illegal in the state of New Mexico, is it, Agent Martinez?" Ruth gave Franco a coquettish smile, one eyebrow arched.

He grinned back at her. "No, Ms. Jäger. It is not."

"I'm sensitive, you know?" Gianetta pushed herself up straighter in the bed, eyes bright. "J gave me seer's sage so I could experience the spirits the way the ancient ones did. Reach the fourth plane of existence."

"The fourth plane of existence?" Franco asked.

"Where shapeshifter and animal spirits that inhabit fetishes dwell."

"Fetishes," Nicky repeated.

"I was moving in between the third and fourth plane when you came and arrested me. He was there. I know it. I sensed him." Gianetta stabbed a finger at Nicky. "You messed it all up."

"You said you bought all the stuff in your box from J WhiteHawk —only buy from him. The stone bear fetish in the box wasn't on the receipt," Nicky said.

Gianetta hunched her shoulder. She gestured at Ruth. "I told her I don't know anything about any fetish in my stuff. I'm telling you the same thing."

"Where did it come from, then?" Nicky asked. "Tsiba'ashi D'yini statutes on non-Native possession of tribal artifacts are clear. They will prosecute to the full—"

"Are you threatening my client?" Ruth asked.

"One more question, Ms. Green." Franco looked down at his notepad, then directly at Nicky. "You said, *'He was there. I know it.'* Was there someone else?"

Nicky's heart jumped. She cut him off, not wanting him to follow that line of questioning. "Ms. Jäger, you know as well as I the federal authorities will go a lot easier on her if she confesses."

"Stop. Outside. Now." Ruth patted Gianetta's hand and beckoned Nicky to follow. They faced each other in the corridor.

"Jean is a dear, sweet woman, so let me make this clear as glass. If you press charges against her, I'll file a police brutality charge against you."

Nicky's jaw clenched. "Why are you here, Ruth? Is she so rich you jump when she calls?"

"Is money all you think about? I assure you, Agent Matthews, this is about justice. Jean, uh, Green is a longstanding client of mine. Of course I came when she called." She pivoted and said over her shoulder, "You'll hear from me soon." Franco stepped out of the shadows, and she ran into him. "Oh!"

He grasped her arms, an apologetic smile on his lips, and dropped his mouth close to her ear. "Sorry, Ru—uh, Ms. Jäger." With a nod, he released her and headed toward the elevator.

Nicky followed, her gaze boring into his back. He punched the down button.

"You going to explain the aw-shucks-ma'am persona?" she asked, an edge to her voice.

"Flies and honey, good cop, bad cop. No need to further alienate her since you were doing such a good job at it."

His jibe stung.

The elevator door slid open. They stepped inside, and Franco pressed the button for the first floor.

"You and Ruth Jäger have a history," he said.

Nicky stared up as the floor numbers changed. "She was one of the attorneys the Randals hired for a civil suit against me after the judge threw out—" She firmed her jaw, but her voice still wobbled. "After he threw out the attempted murder charges." And still the repercussions haunted her life.

A strong arm wrapped around her shoulders. With a sigh, she pressed her cheek against him.

"I never understood that." His voice rumbled deep in his chest. "Janet Stone came into your house and attacked you. You were defending yourself."

"God," she whispered. "You smell so bad."

The elevator door dinged, and Nicky drew away and wiped her eyes with her shirtsleeve.

They headed out the automatic glass doors of the hospital and into the parking lot. Though the sun had set hours ago, heat radiated from the blacktop.

Franco unlocked his truck and opened Nicky's door.

"Sorry about the elevator," she said, voice gruff. "I really must be tired. Maybe you should take me home."

"I'll be *happy* to take you home. At least the whole night wasn't a bust."

She snapped her gaze up to him, only to realize he was waggling his brows and grinning; her alarm melted away. Leveling a finger, she said, "You're only dropping me off, not coming inside to see my etchings, Agent Martinez." Definitely *not* coming inside.

"Darn. But that's not what I meant. Gianetta's lying about the stone bear and feathers."

"No kidding."

He closed her door. Once he settled into his seat, he started the truck and switched the air conditioner to high.

"But she wasn't the only one lying. I think this is the first time Ruth and Gianetta have met. She kept calling her Jean." Nicky rubbed a finger against her lips. "Do you remember what Gianetta said when I questioned her about the bear?"

"That she didn't know anything about it and she'd already told her lawyer the same thing." He threaded the truck between parked cars and drove toward the exit. "How did Ruth Jäger know to ask about it? What the heck's up with this fetish?"

"I don't know. But it's a puzzle I definitely want to figure out."

"*We* definitely want to figure out," Franco put the truck in gear.

"Yeah," Nicky replied. "We. But we also need to understand why Ruth is here and what's in it for her. Because, believe me, Ruth Jäger never does anything unless it benefits Ruth Jäger."

Franco headed north on I-25. Neither one spoke much during the drive, Nicky giving him simple directions to her house. As the truck idled at the curb, he hopped out and opened the door, then the driveway gate to her property, triggering her motion-detector lights.

"You sure I can't pick you up?" he asked. "It's on my way."

"We have the sting operation at CampFire Casino tomorrow night."

"I could bring you home. After."

She gazed up at his face, stomach curling with a building heat. It would be so easy to invite him inside, confide in him. Let him into her life. He seemed to want that.

So easy.

Nicky skirted around him and through the gate, rolling it closed between them. "It's okay. I'll use my mom's car." She held up her injured hand. "This won't stop me from driving."

"Well." He cleared his throat. "Get some sleep. We've got a long night tomorrow."

She watched him drive away, taillights flashing red at the stop sign before they disappeared around the corner. Burying both relief and regret, she entered her empty house and headed straight to the shower, her thoughts jumping through her day. The metamorphosis of the drowning victim she'd already dismissed as stemming from the salvia, jumbled with panic. But the illusive man who'd led her to the horse? Something about that had a different feel. The more she thought about it, the more she was sure she'd had another vision —maybe.

Restless, unable to sleep, she made a quick phone call to a traditional friend on the pueblo who'd answered her questions in the past. When he agreed to meet her at the police station, she slipped in her mother's car and headed back to the reservation.

CHAPTER SIX

Nicky leaned against the doorjamb of Savannah Analla's office, surprised to find her best friend at work and on the phone. She caught her eye, and Savannah mouthed, *Dad.* Brushing back her straight dark bangs with an impatient hand, she pressed the phone against her ear and spoke.

"I'm leaving in a few minutes. No, you don't have to come. I'll get Nicky to walk me out." Savannah paused. She rolled her eyes behind round wire-rimmed glasses. "No, Dad, that Ryan Bernal guy isn't here." Frowning, she rubbed her index finger between her eyebrows. "I know. Yes. I know. Tell Mom I love her, and get some rest. I'll try to stop by tomorrow night. Okay.... Okay.... I'm hanging up now. Love you, Dad."

Savannah propped her chin in her hand and stared at the phone on her desk. "He's always checked on me, but it's been especially bad after his bypass surgery." She released an exasperated sigh. "He's so traditional. He thinks if I'm not married before he ... leaves us, he'll have failed me. Nothing I say or do convinces him otherwise."

"How'd his appointments go?" Savannah and her parents had

stayed at her aunt's in Albuquerque the past week for her father's doctor visits instead of driving back and forth.

"The doctor said his heart's holding its own. Still, it's only a matter of time."

Fleeting sadness etched Savannah's expression, and the glow from the computer screen caught the moisture in her eyes. It made Nicky's chest hurt. "I didn't expect to find you here tonight."

"A week away's put me so far behind. The paperwork is never-ending." Savannah was the Fire-Sky Public Safety Director's executive assistant. He liked to joke he couldn't run the department without her, but there was more than a grain of truth behind his words. "So *I* have an excuse for coming in to work. What's yours?" She leveled dark brown eyes on Nicky.

"I need to speak to Ryan—and you, if you can stay." Her stomach jumped. "You heard about what happened?"

"You arrested Gianetta Green again and found a body. Nothing stays secret on the rez." She tipped her chin at Nicky's bandaged hand. "What's the damage?"

"Three stitches."

Savannah sat back. "Your unit was in the parking lot when I got here."

"I drove my mom's car."

"I thought you dropped the insurance on it."

And the registration in a futile attempt to save money, but it had only slowed the growth of her debt. Nicky's gaze roamed the room. She shrugged.

"What's going on, Nicky?" Savannah's tone softened.

What wasn't? Nicky slumped against the doorjamb and rubbed the back of her wrist across her forehead. "To start, Ruth Jäger is Gianetta's lawyer."

Savannah's eyes widened. "Sometimes you forget how small this state is, metaphorically speaking. You all right?"

"I guess. It brings everything back." She paused. "I need to speak to Ryan about something that happened today."

Savannah frowned. "He said you'd called. Why?"

Nicky ignored the question. Savannah wouldn't like the answer. "You've seen him? Didn't you tell your father—"

"What Daddy doesn't know won't hurt him. And I don't care what my father says; he still isn't over his problem with Ryan and ... Santiago."

"Your brother died over ten years ago. Ryan freely confessed his part in it."

"I don't think my dad can forgive the drugs."

They were silent while Savannah packed up her satchel.

"Where *is* Ryan?" Nicky asked.

"Around somewhere. It's like, you know, he hovers. He's on night shift, saw my car and the light and came over to lecture me on the dangers of staying late at work—as if I haven't done it a million times before and I'm not at the police station." Her voice dropped into a low grumble. "He's exhausted from fires popping up all over the pueblo. When you're as tired as he is, you make mistakes, and in his job, he can't afford to. He could get hurt or"—she raked her fingers through her hair—"and my only influence over him is as a friend."

A faint scuffle outside the doorway put Nicky on alert. She surreptitiously glanced into the hall and saw Ryan standing in the shadows. He met her eyes and dipped his head toward her, staring hard. *Cripes.* He wanted her to say something, see if Savannah would ... No way this would end well.

Nicky drew in a breath. "You and Ryan could be more than friends. You know that."

Savannah shook her head adamantly. "It's not that simple, Nicky. My father ... You don't understand, but this is the way it has to be." Her lips pressed into a taut smile, but shadows darkened her eyes.

Nicky glanced into the hall. Ryan was gone. When she looked back, Savannah was staring at the doorway, her fingers tightly laced, something like grief etched into her expression.

"According to my dad, that canyon and ciénega where you found the dead body are haunted." Savannah's father was a cacique, a traditional Tsiba'ashi D'yini leader.

"What?" The hair on Nicky's nape prickled.

"They're not even marked on some of the pueblo maps. I heard Lieutenant Pinkett screamed at some of the traditional cops because they wouldn't go when you called for backup." She banged a drawer closed. "Don't they understand that one of these days someone's gonna get hurt if they don't do their jobs?" Savannah had been immersed in the pueblo's history, culture, and tradition her whole life. But for all her knowledge, she was one of the most nontraditional tribe members Nicky had met, and she had little patience for those who were. "Chief Cochin will fire their—" Savannah's eyes suddenly widened. "I need to tell you something."

"Hey, Nicky." Ryan's voice came from the open door. He handed her a cup of coffee. "So you had another vision."

Savannah slammed the satchel down on the desk. "*Seriously?* That's why you called Ryan?" She aimed her finger at him. "Stop encouraging her."

Nicky blinked. Tsiba'ashi D'yini didn't point. It was considered the height of rudeness.

Ryan frowned at Savannah. "Why can't you accept that Nicky might experience visions? See spirits and ghosts?"

"Because they aren't *real.*"

"Stop," Nicky said. "Please."

The room was quiet except for the ticking of the ceiling fan above them.

"I have food in the break room. We can talk there." Ryan nodded to Savannah but didn't meet her eyes. "If you'd like, you can come."

NICKY FOLLOWED Ryan through the wide threshold of the police station's break room, wrinkling her nose against the perpetual odor of stale coffee and burnt popcorn. Savannah trailed in after her, slim bare arms crossed, a frown on her pretty round face.

Ryan opened the microwave and pulled out a couple of glass containers, steam curling above them. He sat them on the large Formica table half covered in newspapers, old *People* magazines stacked amid well-thumbed *Police Beat*, *Bowhunting*, and *American Hunter* journals. To clear more space, Nicky pushed aside poorly folded, marked-up topographic and pueblo street maps. She wasn't even sure where they were normally stored anymore. Ryan pulled out two of the dented beige folding chairs and gestured for her and Savannah to sit.

After retrieving small glass bottles of Pellegrino—the only thing Nicky ever saw Ryan drink—he sat across from her and Savannah. Ryan's Jicarilla Apache heritage dominated his Swedish father's genetics, which manifested itself in clear hazel eyes and golden-brown hair. It was a mixture that sat well on him. His hair fell in a tidy braid down the middle of his back, the tied-off end brushing the large block-lettered FIRE printed in white on his dark blue T-shirt. He'd learned firefighting in the military and had returned to the pueblo about the same time Nicky had been hired at the police department. He was a fixture in Savannah's life, but she'd vacillated about taking their relationship further. In the past, he'd seemed content to wait, but the pueblo's Blood Quantum murders earlier that summer had shifted something within him. Lately, he'd been more aggressive about pushing Savannah into making a decision about the two of them.

Ryan broke off a piece of a chicken nugget, gently blew breath over it, and placed it in the spirit bowl on the table, following the pueblo tradition of offering food to ancestral spirits as a mark of respect.

Nicky peered into the containers. Ryan wasn't much of a cook, mostly heating up convenience food. "Chicken nuggets and ... what is that?" Something gloppy, with an odd grayish color and green specks.

"Mac and cheese?" he said.

"You used vanilla soy milk again," Savannah said.

"Coconut." Expression sheepish, he scooped up a dollop with the rest of his nugget. "It had a weird taste, so I added green chile. Try some."

"I'll pass." Nicky took a bite of a chicken nugget.

"This spirit," he said. "You've seen it before? Like Ánâ-ya Cáci. Wind Mother?"

"No." She waved her nugget. "Let me explain. Gianetta Green was smudging herself—"

"You can't smudge yourself," Savannah said.

"—and had seer's sage in the smudge stick. I breathed in a little too much, and the smoke started to look like little owls."

Ryan took a drink, his gaze never leaving her face. "Franco called me before he went out to find you. He had some questions."

"About what?" Nicky asked.

"About seer's sage." His eyes twinkled. "I've had some experience with hallucinogens in my misspent youth."

"How did you ever get into the Marines?" Nicky asked with a smile.

"He played the Religious Ceremony card," Savannah said dryly.

Ryan grinned. "*Salvia divinorum* is powerful but short-acting. Maybe fifteen to thirty minutes. You were out there for a while, which means you're either very sensitive or what you saw had nothing to do with the salvia and you want an excuse."

Leave it to Ryan to drill down to the core.

"Nicky. It's a gift," he said.

"Doesn't feel like one." She sighed, and they munched quietly. "What do you either of you know about fetish carvings?"

Ryan leaned back and crossed his arms. "Mostly sold as touristy pieces. Pretty stones made into any animal you can think of. Easy to collect and display. Different from the ones used in ceremonies on the pueblo."

"How?"

Ryan shrugged. "Just different. My father inherited six from his grandfather, who inherited them from *his* grandfather. They represent the sacred associations or directions: mountain lion for north; the bear with the west; badger, south; wolf is east; and eagle with the zenith. I've never seen the 'below,' or nadir fetish. It's wrapped in leather."

"Tell me about the bear fetish."

Savannah frowned. "They represent protection and healing. What's this all about?"

"Gianetta had a box in the back of her car. There was a bear fetish inside covered with this grainy dirt."

"Corn pollen. Serves as a bridge between life and death, animates the stone," Ryan said. "You feed tsa'atsi y'aauni corn pollen."

"*Tsa'atsi y'aauni*. Breathing stone?" Nicky asked.

"That's the literal translation." Ryan took a drink. "A better description is living stone or living fetish."

Nicky's breath quickened. Living?

"They're specially made, tailored to the possessor, although that's not quite right. Caretaker? Custodian?" He shook his head. "It's considered a mutual relationship if a person adopts a tsa'atsi y'aauni. Hard to explain."

"Not as hard as you think. This bear fetish. It … it drew me." She rubbed her thumb over a tiny bruise on her palm. Where the carved stone had pinched her. "I picked it up, and I think it … moved."

"Oh, come on, Nicky," Savannah said.

"If this fetish is as you say, the woman should not possess it," Ryan said. "No Tsiba'ashi D'yini would give or sell one to an outsider. They are sacred."

Savannah picked up a nugget. She broke off a bite and exhaled softly over it before placing it into the spirit bowl with Ryan's offering. "What did Gianetta say?"

"That she doesn't know how it got in her stuff." Nicky propped her elbows on the table. "I was holding the fetish when I saw this … this man. At first I thought Gianetta had a partner, but this guy was dressed traditionally. Tall, thin—gaunt, even. Completely gray. Hair, skin, clothes." She swallowed, mouth dry. "He'd show himself, then disappear around some rocks. I'd chase him, but he was always ahead of me. Luring me into the desert. That's when I saw the horse. I followed it and found the body in the tank."

"You think this spirit and he led you to the body," Ryan said.

Nicky hesitated over her answer. "Whenever I've seen ... visions or spirits in the past, they've always helped me."

"So has good police work," Savannah countered.

"Who was in the tank?" Ryan asked.

"Seneca Elk was reported missing a couple days ago," Nicky said.

Savannah pressed fingers against her lips. "That's the third brother within a year to pass."

"The Elk Clan are sacred fetish carvers for the tribe." Ryan shifted on his chair. "For the last sixty years, Gemini, Seneca's grand-father, has made tsa'atsi y'aauni for Tsiba'ashi D'yini."

Nicky furrowed her brows. "First the fetish in the car, then I find a deceased member of a fetish-carving clan. That's a weird coin-cidence."

"Was there anything else about the gray man you remember?" Ryan's expression was troubled.

"A smell like death. He held a black club." Nicky straightened in her chair. "At one of the recent village meetings, residents described a gray ghost or spirit that tried to lure them off. A Fire-Sky boogeyman. The town crier told everyone to stay inside at night. I think you mentioned his name once—Stone Warrior."

The sheepish look was back on Ryan's face. "I made that up to scare off that undercover FBI agent interested in Savannah."

"Oh, my God, Ryan," Savannah said.

But Nicky noticed she looked faintly pleased.

"Do you know who this spirit is?" Nicky asked.

Ryan nodded slowly. "The god of fire and those who have gone before us. The Hopi have a name for him—Masauwu. Skeleton Man. I think the one you saw is like that."

"What is he called by Fire-Sky?" Nicky asked.

He shook his head, and Savannah dropped her gaze. Although she felt a little pang of hurt, Nicky understood. Certain sacred traditions, ceremonies, and practices were not shared with non-Natives. And though Ryan had been raised on the pueblo, he was not Tsiba'ashi D'yini. He might not even know.

"I can ask my dad for details, what he can share." Ryan's father was also a cacique. "But I do know to see this god's face is a warning of death. Nicky, you need to get medicined."

"*This god* doesn't carry a club. It's a torch. At night, its fire can be seen in the distance." Savannah stood up abruptly, her chair scraping the floor. "Don't get medicined, Nicky. It's superstitious nonsense, like all of this. I'm ready to go."

"I'll walk out with you, but I need to stay a little while longer. Can I use your computer? Your screen is better than mine." Something nagged her about the ciénega that she couldn't pin down. Maybe a quick review of the pictures she'd snapped would help her figure it out.

"You know my login." Savannah hefted her satchel to her shoulder and headed out the break room opening. "You're still helping me set up the FEMA trailer on Wednesday. And both of you are coming to dinner on Friday." Both statements, not questions.

"Yes, and yes," Nicky said. For the last few years, almost every Friday night, they'd gathered at Savannah's. It was about the only tradition Savannah believed in.

"So long as nothing else goes up in flames." Ryan held open the door to the parking lot.

The night was velvety with warmth, and horns of a crescent moon glowed low over the western skyline, edging one side of the extinct volcano central to Fire-Sky culture with silver. Over its peak, flickering bolts of heat lightning expanded and died in the nighttime sky. So far, the summer had been nothing but long, hot, and very, very dry.

"What can I bring to dinner?" Nicky asked.

"Apples from your tree. I want to make empanaditas. Just drop them off at my desk. I invited Franco, too. And Nicky? When you're done here, if you want, you can come over and stay at my house. It's a long drive back to yours, and you left some clothes from ... before." Savannah's voice was tentative. "I cleaned the extra bedroom."

Warmth invaded Nicky's chest at the invitation. After the tension earlier that summer, she'd been worried their friendship was damaged, but Savannah had a huge heart.

"Thanks, but I've got to be in town for the autopsy, plus there's the sting operation tomorrow night."

Savannah stared at her. "What sting operation?"

"We got a tip a few days ago—you'd just left for Albuquerque—about a possible drug transport van doing a drop at the CampFire Casino truck stop. We're going to use that old semitruck at the bone-yard as part of our cover."

"Who is it? Who's delivering drugs to my pueblo?" Savannah's voice shook. "I hope you get enough evidence to bury them."

"Hey." Nicky placed a hand on Savannah's arm. "If they show up, we'll get them."

Savannah nodded, the lenses of her glasses cloaking her eyes. "Sorry. It's just that I'd do almost anything to protect—"

"Your People. I know. Me, too." She stopped at Savannah's car. "You had something to tell me?"

"Oh, yeah." Savannah blew out a long sigh. "It's about Jinni Sundry and what happened at Hummingbird Mesa." She stowed her satchel in the passenger seat. Ryan stood to one side, his face obscured by shadows. "She broke down crying after the ambulance arrived for Gianetta. Said she had to go to the clinic to get checked out because she'd breathed in tainted smoke and saw an owl. Indians and owls. That really ticks me off."

"What about Jinni?"

"It all came out. She's looking at reprimand at a minimum, but knowing Chief Cochin, she'll probably get suspended, if not fired outright. It puts everyone in danger because you can't depend on her.

And you know how Chief is right now. Zero tolerance for that kind of weakness in a female officer."

"What all came out?" Nicky asked.

"The reason she backed off from the Gianetta Green arrest." Savannah said. "Jinni's five months pregnant."

CHAPTER SEVEN

Nicky waved goodnight to Savannah and Ryan and headed back into the darkened interior of the Admin complex. Offices lined three sides of the single-story building—brass populating one corner of the structure and Human Resources, including Savannah and her boss, occupying the other end. The fourth wall contained a wide doorway that connected to the police station through the copier/break room.

A square corridor ran around the inside of the building, and at the center of the structure, the roof opened to the sky. Glass walls enclosed a green space about the size of one of the offices—almost like a human terrarium. The garden never seemed to get enough sunlight, and the plants inside were elongated and sickly. It wasn't creepy during the day, but at night the moonlight lit the spindly trees and vines, casting crosshatched shadows onto closed doors and pale walls. On the other side of the hallway, a light switched on in the break room, and the shadows grayed. Nicky only spared a glance as she walked to Savannah's office.

Mousing the computer awake, she logged in and pulled up Seneca Elk's missing persons report. It had to be him. Called in by his father after he hadn't returned from riding fence around Black Mesa.

Details were sparse, though. She mentally added more questions to ask his family after the official death notification.

Nicky transferred the photos she'd taken at the ciénega from her phone to the computer, brought them up as thumbnails, and paged through images of the trough and derrick. She jotted a reminder to contact Fire-Sky Tribal Resources about ownership, typed in descriptions of the metal sign, the horse and its rig, and the clothes piled on top of the tank.

Click.

She studied the photo of a single boot print, furrowing her brow. The edge along one side had been flattened, like someone had stepped across it. The impression was oval, elongated. Not a cow or horse. Not hers. The pockets had been turned out on the jeans. Evidence of a second person at the scene? Was this what had been nagging at her? She opened a panoramic view of the prints and enlarged the area to the left and right of the suspect track. Clicking on enhancement tools, she played with color, contrast, lighting....

And sat back in her chair with a sigh. Nothing definitive.

She grabbed her cell and queued up the phantom footprint, tapped a message to Franco, and hit send. Maybe a second opinion would help. Laying her phone down, she rolled her head around to loosen the tightness in her shoulders and scanned through more photos. Most of these would be supplementary, but the ones directly outside and inside of the tank might be important for a reconstruction of the young man's death. She dragged and dropped tank door pics into a file before she began to sort through the ones she'd taken of the interior.

Click.

The first picture was too dark to see anything inside the tank.

Outside the office, a light flickered in the hall and blinked out. Distracted, Nicky stared at the open doorway. Whoever had been in the break room must have left. Above her, the faint *creak-creak-creak* of the ceiling fan suddenly seemed louder. She tipped her head back, eyes following the circling blades. It hadn't bothered her before, but now it reminded her of the windmill in the ciénega. She refocused on the computer screen.

Click.

The next picture was time-stamped a few seconds later than the first. A liquidy sheen of blacks and purples gleamed greasy in the low light. She could just make out the water level at the back of the tank. A little better, but maybe one with the camera flash on....

Click.

Nicky reared back, hair standing up on every inch of her body. Her eyes watered, and a tiny whimper escaped from the back of her throat. Scenes from that afternoon sharpened like a knife to slice slowly down her chest. The flash of an owl's shadow, smoke swirling into feathers, a pollen-encrusted fetish that rippled in the sun. The face of the drowning victim, his eyes rolling white. *The eyes....*

Nicky swallowed thickened saliva. And the spirit man.

In the picture, he stood at the back of the tank, against the curved metal wall, waist-deep in murky water. Completely gray, as if ash dusted his clothes, skin, and long braid of hair. Under a lowered brow, he stared at her out of the computer screen.

Like the corpse, his eyes were completely white, the detail she'd forgotten. With trembling fingers, she pressed the mouse.

Click.

In the next picture, time-stamped seconds later, he was gone.

CHAPTER EIGHT

CampFire Casino and Truck Stop Sting
Tsiba'ashi D'yini Pueblo
New Mexico, USA

"WE GOT a white panel van pulling into the parking lot, heading your way. Cable company logo on the side. Over."

"Two-one-three, copy," Nicky replied, peering out the large front windshield of the semitruck cab. The target vehicle emerged out of the night and passed under one of the bright overhead lamps dotting the big-rig parking lot, stark red lettering on its side. It backed into an open area against the cinderblock wall that separated asphalt from the surrounding high desert, an area the Fire-Sky police operation had planned to be vacant. "Eyes on. Over."

She blew out a breath as she smoothed her blousy red top. Her fingers slipped over the bulge of her gun, snugged into a body wrap beneath her arm, and her heart rate steadied. She exchanged a glance with Franco.

"Jeez, look at the response," he said.

She whistled under her breath. Half a dozen men trailed toward the van from all directions. Major potential for complications.

"Drugs or hookers?" Nicky drew in a deep breath, grabbed the handle on the passenger's side door. "I'm out."

Franco laid a warm hand on her arm. "Be careful."

She met and held his eyes, the deep brown almost black in the low light of the cab. "I'll be fine." Nicky ran her injured hand over her hair. She'd covered her stitches with a large flesh-colored pad. They still ached but wouldn't interfere. "How do I look?" The brown wig she'd chosen bobbed at her chin and covered her earpiece. Heavy bangs fell almost to her eyes, and her makeup was garish and thick.

Franco grinned and waggled his brows. "Like sin on a stick. Me?"

"Like a disgusting old trucker ready for some action." Nicky inhaled deeply. "Except you smell too good." She brushed the scraggly beard stuck to his chin. "Gotta go."

Nicky opened the door and climbed out into the night. Heat and a nauseating mixture of diesel fumes and frying food from the nearby diner enveloped her. The resonant sound of engines throbbed over her skin. From a loudspeaker, a voice called, "Number five-eight-two, number five eighty-two, shower sixteen is open."

She tugged at her extremely short skirt—more like a stretchy bandeau—but it still barely covered the crotch of her boy shorts underneath. Her fingers swept the tiny microphone pinned to the inside of her blouse.

Time to rock and roll.

With a casual wave to Franco, she swaggered into the sea of parked semis, a prostitute on the prowl in the flickering orange-and-yellow neon flames of the CampFire Casino marquee.

A truck door slammed behind her. Franco stepped in front of the big rig—unrecognizable—a massive trucker with long hair and a graying beard. He made a beeline across the lot to become one more man in the crowd milling a dozen yards from the target vehicle.

Nicky strolled between large parked trucks in a roundabout route to the van. Most were quiet and dark, their drivers grabbing a few hours in their sleepers or killing time in the diner or casino, both open twenty-four hours. She tucked herself into a shadow on one side of a tractor trailer, the target vehicle in direct line of sight. Two Caucasian or Hispanic guys—hard to tell—hopped out, heads shaved, white tees, tattoos on their necks and arms. They lined up the waiting men. Franco stood second to last.

Her attention shifted back to the van. Light cut a line on the blacktop as the side door slid open. Stereotype number three hopped out, all baggy pants and white T-shirt. She could make out nothing more than dark lumps inside. One lifted a face, and Nicky's stomach fell. These guys had a van full of people—prostitutes? Or something worse, she thought grimly. What in hell had her team uncovered?

Sudden violent movement shifted Nicky's attention. Two of the perps shoved a trucker out of line, arms wildly gesturing. Idling engines obscured their voices. The trucker argued back until the driver lifted his shirt up.

Franco's whisper sounded through her earpiece. "Gun." The trucker hurried away.

Chatter filled her ear. "Move in. Get into position." Nicky rubbed a suddenly sweaty palm against her skirt and waited for confirmation that the rest of the team was in place. It was happening so fast. Her eyes darted around. Too many damn civilians.

One of the white T-shirts ducked into the van. When he stepped back onto the blacktop, he carried a tether. At his sharp yank, a slim woman with long black hair climbed out. He leaned into her, face close to her ear. After a few seconds, she nodded. The first man in line bumped his cell phone against one held by one of the perps. E-currency exchange. Sophisticated. Transaction complete, the leash was handed over. The trucker tugged at the girl and slipped an arm around her shoulders. They walked away, her steps dragging. Not prostitutes. A sick knot tightened in Nicky's stomach. When they'd planned the operation, they hadn't expected human traffickers.

She pressed against her gun, and it dug into the inside of her arm reassuringly. She slid deeper into the shadows as they passed, her jaw locked, throat tight. The woman hunched away from the john, head down, arms wrapped around her waist, and Nicky couldn't do anything about it without tipping off the perps. *Dammit.*

She marked the truck the man dragged the woman to.

Nicky's earpiece crackled. "In position. Waiting for go." Her team was ready. Heart pounding, she stepped out into the streetlight. The van drivers flanked Franco now. His hands were up, palms out, placating. The third trafficker handed off a tether to another trucker —this time attached to a slim young man.

"Not yet, Franco. Wait for me." She sauntered toward the line of men. As she got closer, the trafficker stationed at the van door turned to stare. Nicky caught his gaze and gave him a slow smile. His mouth moved, and she read his lips: "*Puta.*" He smirked, tilted his chin ...

And his eyes rolled white.

She stuttered to a stop, heart flipping in her chest.

The voice in her ear yelled, "Vehicles coming fast. God*dammit!*" Sirens wailed in the distance. The sound expanded, pierced the air, coming closer. "It's state police. Confirmation, state police." Nicky jerked out of her stupor.

The truckers in the line twisted toward the noise. A few backed away, exchanged glances. One broke, and they all ran. The people in the vehicle darted out of the open door and scattered into the maze of parked big rigs and shadows.

The trafficker by the truck grabbed a trailing leash and hauled a girl backward, shoved her inside, but panic stamped his expression.

"Police," Franco yelled, his gun leveled at the guy.

Flashing red and blue lights cartwheeled through the darkness, and sirens crescendoed. Black SUVs with dark-tinted windows screeched to a stop in a semicircle around the van. Men and women jumped out, guns drawn, yelling, screaming, "On the ground! On the ground!"

The guy by the van door bolted, and Nicky broke into a flat run after him. He was fast. Faster than her. She pushed harder, muscles burning. He dodged around one vehicle, and she lost sight of him.

She slowed and drew her weapon, her breathing harsh in her ears, and searched the shadows. One of the truckers opened his door.

"Police! Get back in your truck!" she screamed.

The door slammed as the perp's white T-shirt flashed to her left. He dashed down the narrow lane of trucks. A blurred shape appeared from behind a semi and tackled him to the asphalt. Nicky slid to a stop, quickly snugged her gun in her waist, ready to dive in and help, but Franco had the guy pinned. Dropping to one knee, adrenaline blunting the sting of gravel cutting into her bare skin, she cuffed the driver, searched him, retrieving his gun and a switchblade.

Nicky lifted his shoulder up until she could see his eyes. They were filled with defiance, bravado—and completely normal. Relief crashed through her. A trick of the light, that was all. She'd been mistaken.

"*Puta,*" he spat, and she let go.

Her gaze met Franco's, breath still coming fast. He grinned and rose to his feet, held out a hand to her. Nicky grasped his wrist, and he drew her up and into him. Hat and wig gone, the threads of gray in his close-cropped dark brown hair glinted in the overhead sodium lamps. He stood close, and his grin faded as she stared into eyes. Her thrumming blood heated.

"No time for this," she whispered.

"I know." His gaze dropped to her lips.

The guy on the ground wriggled, and they both stepped on his back to press him down.

She shifted nearer, opened her mouth to say something, anything—

"Freeze! On the ground! On the ground! *Now!*" Half a dozen shadowy men and women surrounded them, firearms drawn.

Nicky sucked in a breath. She backed away from Franco and raised her arms.

"We're Fire-Sky"—Franco started, but the guy behind him stepped close and pressed the barrel of a gun against his neck. Franco tipped his head away, fists and jaw clenched—"Police."

The guy leaned in, mouth in a sneer. "I said *on the ground*, asshole."

Nicky stared into the face of the man who pointed his gun at Franco. Her eyes widened in recognition. He'd been at the Fire-Sky Fiesta earlier in the summer. One of *his* bodyguards.

And with piercing clarity, she knew who was behind this clusterfark.

"Dax Stone." A hard shove on the shoulder staggered her. She twisted to send a narrowed glare at the woman behind her. "They know who we are, Franco."

"Hands on your head," a masculine voice ordered. Her gun and the perp's weapons were yanked out of her waistband. "I said *on the ground*." Nicky lay down on the asphalt, arms out, head turned to Franco. He lay on his stomach, spread-eagle. They twisted his arms behind his back, cuffed him, and dragged him to his feet.

The metal handcuffs were cold against her skin as they clicked shut. Rough hands helped her up and pushed her forward.

She and Franco strode back in the direction of the van and the flashing lights, followed by the herd of state police. Nicky spared a glance at the perp. The state cops dragged him along by his elbow, but he was otherwise silent.

"They took our bust," Franco said. "I'm gonna kill Stone."

Nicky hissed a furious breath between her teeth. "Not if I get to him first."

CHAPTER NINE

FIRE-SKY POLICE CAPTAIN Philip Richards's office was cold, as was the expression he directed at Nicky. Body tense, she tempered her breathing. The immediate summons by her superiors after Fire-Sky had untangled the casino sting from state police was billed as a debriefing, but it felt more like a trial. One where she'd already been declared guilty by association.

James Vallery, the Fire-Sky Public Safety director, tugged at the cuffs of his dress shirt and cleared his throat. "Sergeant Matthews, I'm sorry, but I have to ask you this. Because of your ... connection with Chief Stone, did you coordinate with him, call him, tell him anything—even inadvertently—about last night's sting operation?"

Nicky's teeth ground together. "No. I wouldn't."

"James, this is an inappropriate line of questioning." Luz Cochin, chief of the Tsiba'ashi D'yini Police Department, placed her hand on Vallery's arm. "Sergeant Matthews's relationship—"

"*Past* relationship," Nicky snapped. "I did *not* coordinate, did *not* call him, did *not* talk to him because I am neither personally nor professionally in contact with Chief Stone. And I *resent*—"

"Matthews. Your tone is insubordinate." Captain Richards's light green eyes were icy, and his thin mustache bristled. "Unless you want another reprimand in your file, you will address Director Vallery and Chief Cochin with respect. Luz, James, I apologize for my officer." He grimaced and stepped closer to his superiors. "Your inference, sir, is spot on, of course. Chief Stone and Matthews..."

Captain's voice dropped, and Nicky couldn't catch anything else. *Kiss-ass.*

Chest tight, she turned her back on the quiet conversation and plucked at her blouse. It was streaked with oil and torn, the white concealment tank top exposed. Her wig—a discarded, furry lump—sat on the end of Captain's desk. With a sigh, she removed the bobby pins and clips that held her hair in place. It fell down her back, slick and cool on her hot neck. The cloudless sky outside Captain's picture window glowed white on the horizon. Even though the sun hadn't risen, all signs pointed to another scorching August day.

Nicky stared, unblinking, one hand loose around the clips, fingers of the other combing rhythmically through the hair at her temple. There was nothing she could have done to save her operation. It was imperative she shed her churning emotions and find a way to salvage it going forward.

The scent of floral perfume mixed with cigarette smoke tickled her nose.

"Officer Matthews." Police Chief Cochin appeared at her side. "No matter what they say, you did a good job last night. Even at the end, after they uncuffed you, and you—" She clenched her fist, made a small punching motion, and winked. "If charges are pressed, I'll make sure they disappear. Sometimes we gals have to stick together against...." Cochin tipped her head toward Captain and Vallery. The men's voices rumbled in conversation, low and indistinct.

"My team's still out there, Chief." Nicky gestured to her torn blouse and thigh-skimming skirt. "When we're done, I need to change—"

Captain's office door opened, and Dax Stone, chief of the New Mexico State Police, strode inside. He towered over everyone, a charismatic presence with movie-star looks: a perfectly proportioned build with wide shoulders and a trim waist; perfect wavy black hair with silver threads, a little too long so it could fall carelessly over his smooth, wide brow; and perfect white teeth, which flashed in a huge grin.

Nicky rolled her eyes.

Cochin's attention shifted, and she sidestepped away from Nicky. Vallery and Captain straightened.

"Luz! It's lovely to see you, and don't you look charming. Blue is so pretty on you." Dax grasped both her hands and bent to kiss her cheek.

"I was attending a show at Route 66 Casino in Laguna when I was called in. You stirred up quite a bit of trouble on my reservation, Chief Stone," Cochin responded, her tone light. "I'm sure you have an excellent explanation for state police interference last night."

"Of course, of course." He patted her shoulder as his attention slid away. "And James! How are Patricia and the kids? Your daughter's at State, right?" He shook Vallery's hand. Dax gave Captain a perfunctory nod. "Richards."

Nicky's lips twisted. The two men had a past, and Dax had little respect for her captain. Neither did she. It was one of few things they agreed on.

"Darla's majoring in animal science." Pride warmed Vallery's voice and lit his mild blue eyes. "Patricia's fine. And Janet?" He inadvertently met Nicky's gaze and ducked his head.

"Doing okay, she's doing okay. We take it day by day. She has lots of support." Dax shook his head, the picture of a devoted husband. "All I can do is love her."

Nicky couldn't contain her snort.

Dax spun on his heel. "And Sergeant Matthews," he drawled, gaze intense.

"Chief Stone," she responded. "You and your crew crapped all over my sting operation. Care to share the hows and whys?" Nicky kept her expression impassive as she stared up into his handsome features.

Behind Dax, Richards's face was apoplectic. If his eyes bugged out any farther, they'd fall on the floor. Vallery rubbed his forehead, and Chief Cochin smirked.

Dax chuckled and flashed a smile over his shoulder. Damn him; he was enjoying this.

"Care to share *how* and *why* you knocked Officer Archibeque on his butt?" he asked. "After all, he let you go."

"Like he was doing me a favor." Nicky scoffed. "The why? He cuffed me, took my weapon, and he's an asshole. The how?" She leaned toward him and held his gaze. "Men always underestimate a woman's strength, Chief Stone." She stretched her lips to bare her teeth in the facsimile of a smile. "But you already know that."

A dark flame lit his eyes. "How perceptive, Sergeant. Hate 'em or love 'em, for some men, women are their Achilles's heel." His gaze roved up and down her body. "This is a new look for you. I like it."

He turned away from her.

"Gentlemen, Chief Cochin. Before I came in, I was on the phone with the governor. She knew about this operation in advance and approved it. She and I are of one mind on the eradication of human trafficking throughout the great state of New Mexico."

"Cut the campaign speech, Chief Stone," Cochin said, but she moderated her words with a smile. "Why did you interfere?"

"We saw your operation on the National Criminal Intelligence Resource Center and realized you didn't know what you had. State police felt it was in the best interests of all parties to intervene."

"You mean in *your* best interest. You brought a reporter," Nicky said, anger bubbling again.

"And the cameraman got some great footage of you comforting that poor young woman after you extracted her from under the trucker," Stone said.

"We put our operations on NCIRC for deconfliction reasons,

Chief Stone," Vallery said. "Your people barreling in like that was dangerous. Guns were out."

"That's why we disarmed and cuffed your officers, James. It was part of our operational plan," Dax said. "Look, you don't have the complete picture. This was our first big human trafficking hit in over a year, ever since that van flipped on I-25 last summer."

"That van was traveling over a hundred miles an hour and weaving in and out of traffic because state police were in pursuit. They should've backed off," Nicky said. The van had rolled on Fire-Sky right-of-way, and she'd been there for cleanup. Her throat constricted. There'd been children.

"A tragic incident." Dax dropped his gaze. After a moment, he sighed and met her eyes. "We got a tip on this cargo and destination, checked the IRC, and had to move fast. We believe Chen Cano and the Albuquerque Crybabies are involved."

Captain Richards's chin jutted. "We keep his gang members and their drugs off this reservation."

And that was a puzzle, Nicky thought, because Captain could hardly tie his own shoes.

"Why do you think Cano's involved?" Cochin asked.

Dax extracted two baggies from his pocket and handed them to Vallery. Cochin and Captain stepped in close.

"What am I looking at?" Vallery asked.

"The drivers weren't only selling flesh. They were transporting that. Since *Breaking Bad*, drug traffickers have really been pushing their brands for marketing purposes. Cano's gang sells drugs with ground-up gold. Thinks it makes his product upscale. His logo? A stamped gold leaf. It's been flooding the I-25 corridor from El Paso up to Denver. The van was filled with it."

"So were some of the people inside," Nicky added. "They were forced to swallow dozens of balloons. Franco Martinez, our DEA liaison"—she earned a hard stare from Dax at the mention of Franco's name—"rode along to University Hospital with the victims. He'll be our direct contact when the drugs are … retrieved."

Vallery handed the bags to Nicky. One was filled with a white, powdery substance. Held up to the light, it glittered. The second baggie held a small pinkish-orange balloon with the gold leaf stamped into its skin.

"Why would the drivers jeopardize Cano's operation by stopping at the casino?" Nicky asked. "Tsiba'ashi D'yini is past Albuquerque. The woman I removed from the big rig thought their first stop would be Denver."

"Our best guess is the drivers were freelancing," Dax replied. "We took the two we caught to lockup in Albuquerque for processing, and the Feds are coming in this afternoon to question them. If Cano is behind the drugs and human trafficking, and I can close it all down...." He smiled.

"The US Senate seat will be yours," Cochin said under her breath.

"Chen Cano is vicious," Nicky said, her voice hard. "And because of your little stunt with the TV crew, all of Albuquerque knew about this bust five minutes after it happened. He'll off those guys to protect his operation. And what about the driver who escaped? My people are searching—"

"Give me some credit, Sergeant. I made sure the two in custody have extra guards and are kept sequestered." The cell phone buzzed in Dax's pocket. He slipped it out and stared at the screen. "Excuse me."

Vallery gestured Cochin and Captain Richards closer. Nicky cocked her head to listen. "Stone's a manipulative bastard, but I'll talk to him, make sure Fire-Sky gets half credit—"

"*Fuck.*"

"Dax?" Nicky pivoted, startled.

"The van drivers. After booking, they were placed in a segregated unit." He raked his hand through his hair with shaking fingers. His face was almost gray. "They were found in their cells, throats cut, hands severed." His mouth set in a grim line, he focused back on Nicky. "Sergeant Matthews, I need the third man your people are searching for. Now. State police will take over."

CHAPTER TEN

THE MIDMORNING SUN blazed down from a white sky, its harsh light bleaching the sand and stunted plants in the surrounding desert a beige monochrome. Desert scrub rolled under a wash of heated air as the helicopter continuously circled above, sniper hanging out the side. Nicky blinked gritty, tired eyes from behind her sunglasses. The long night of the truck-stop sting had dragged into the next day with no end in sight.

The thumping overhead made it hard for her to hear the state police lieutenant.

"This search is State's baby now, Sergeant. Your chief volunteered your people as backup and backup only, so you can best help me by staying out of it. I have three more units en route. Lead them to the staging area. We won't need you after that." The black-clad officer tugged off his peaked hat and swiped a hand over a dripping forehead. "Can it get any hotter?" He slid into his vehicle and started down the dirt track that T-ed north from the two-lane paved road, tires kicking up billowing clouds of dust.

Nicky climbed inside her running truck, grateful for the cold air pumping from the vents. She grabbed a bottle of water from the cooler on the passenger seat.

It wasn't long before cars with black bodies and white tops flew toward her. She hit her lights and picked up her comm.

"Two-one-three, Fire-Sky Police. Follow me, State. When we arrive at the staging area, park on bare ground. Over."

She turned her truck down the dirt road, and the cars trailed after her, eating her dust. The road through the brush and cedars was potholed with washout depressions from past rains. Her SUV had clearance, but the interceptors were made for freeway chases—fast and low-slung. They fell behind as she bumped along a maze of dirt tracks. After fifteen minutes, she topped a low rise overlooking the staging area for the search. Heat trembled off the state police trucks, and vans parked near the command center trailer. White canopies set up for shade billowed in a breeze, cases of water stacked on folding tables underneath. A firetruck and EMT vehicle branded with the distinctive Fire-Sky FER medallion—Fire, EMS, and Rescue—paralleled each other to one side. Nicky made a wide U-turn and parked next to the firetruck to wait for the cruisers.

Ryan walked toward her SUV. Bulky beige turnout pants did little to hide his tall, lean form, and his black T-shirt molded the sinewy muscles of his arms and chest. He'd twisted his golden-brown hair into a braid that fell down his back.

Nicky set her brake and opened the door, Ryan's words echoing in her head: *To see him is a warning of death.* Like the corpse in the tank, the trafficker's eyes had rolled white. Now that man was dead, his throat cut. Was there a connection?

"Hey, Nicky. What's the whole story?" he yelled over the vibrations of the chopper, his eyes scanning the scene.

"Dax Stone showed up last night with an entourage at the casino sting, and the perps and victims scattered. One of the drivers escaped." She waved her hand. "This is the result."

Ryan shook his head. "That guy's a disaster. I don't understand why you ever got involved with—"

She gave him a look.

"Sorry," he said.

The helicopter swooped away, and the vibrations diminished.

"Not one of my best decisions." Nicky followed the chopper from behind her sunglasses. "Where is everybody?"

"Walking the rim of the arroyo. We've already had to treat a couple guys for sunstroke."

"Where's Dax?"

"Where else? Up in the 'copter." His attention shifted behind her, and he jutted his chin at the crawling dust trails. "Who's coming?"

"State police, but the road's too rough for their cars." The wind swirled the hair of her ponytail over her face. She brushed it away. "I need to talk to you about something that happened at the sting last ni—"

Faint pops of sound made her duck. Ryan crouched beside her, eyes wide. The helicopter veered hard right and swung around.

"Shots fired! Perp's in the arroyo," someone yelled and pointed skyward.

The incoming state police cars hit their lights and sirens. Within seconds they swerved into the staging area, tires spewing skeins of dirt and sand in their wake, and jerked to a halt atop a thick patch of dried grass and weeds.

"No!" Nicky straightened and waved her arms. "Don't park there! Move your vehicles!" She and Ryan bolted toward the cruisers, but the officers were already out and running into the desert.

Nicky grabbed a door handle, pulse thudding in her throat as she yanked the door open. She knelt on the front seat, groped the ignition —no keys.

Air rushed out of the cab with a *whomph*, and heat scorched her legs as the hot undercarriage and muffler ignited the grass and brush underneath. She slammed the door and stumbled back. Flames boiled from beneath the car. Ryan scrambled away from the third unit as it was engulfed. He grabbed her arms.

"You okay?" he asked.

"Yeah. Go."

He sprinted to the firetruck.

Black smoke rose in waves, fire shooting high above the cars. Nicky backpedaled to her unit as the firetruck drew closer to the burning vehicles. Licking flames ran through the dried grass toward the fluttering canopies. One of the firefighters grabbed a handheld extinguisher and stopped its spread. A gas tank exploded.

More pops echoed in quick succession, followed by a single loud crack. Nicky jerked her head up. The helicopter hovered in the distance.

"Subject down. All units, subject down," said the voice over her radio.

Eye on the helicopter, she jogged over to the lieutenant in charge and waited for an assignment.

What a complete disaster.

CHAPTER ELEVEN

UNDER THE YELLOW PORCH LIGHT, the grape tomatoes glimmered like dull pinkish-orange eyes in pots along the walled front patio. Nicky's shadow stretched black on the cement. The rest of her home and the fields around it were dark. It would be hours until the sun would even tinge the sky gray over the Sandia Mountains, east of Bernalillo. She set her purse beside the door and pressed her back against the rough stucco, her Glock gripped tight in both hands. Ready.

The front door stood open an inch, and a rich aroma seeped out of the kitchen window. Annoyance welled up to swamp her apprehension. There was an intruder in her house. And they'd made *coffee*.

Releasing her left hand's grip on the gun, she flattened her palm and pushed at the door. It swung on oiled hinges and knocked against the wall; bells hanging from the inside doorknob jangled discordantly. She waited for a reaction to her announced presence.

No response. Neck craned, she peered into the empty foyer, then sidled through the threshold. Maybe they'd already left. The porch light from outside extended down to the end of the hall and into the den near the kitchen. It gleamed on a pair of dark shoes and traveled up black trousers, only to end at the bent, splayed knees of the man sitting on her sofa. His torso and face were in shadow.

Nicky jerked her head back inside the hallway. *Not* gone. Her heart beat a tattoo in her neck.

"Police. Put your hands where I can see them," she ordered. The sound echoed off bare walls, faded until silence reigned.

The legs shifted. "Lucy, I'm home!"

Shock stiffened her spine. Nicky ground her teeth and pointed the gun down along her leg. She slapped on the hall light.

"*Dammit*, Dax. I almost shot you."

He raised his arm to shield his face and groaned. "Turn it off."

"Not your house," Nicky snapped.

Scooping up her purse, she shoved her gun inside and slammed the door behind her, the bells jingling again. A cheap alarm system that only worked if she was home. She flipped the lock—which was loose—and marched into the kitchen to switch on overhead fluorescent lights, relishing Dax's second groan. He slouched on the sofa against the far wall, head resting along the back. His arm now covered his eyes.

"Are you drunk?" The half-filled bottle of very good bourbon by the coffee can answered her question. "Why are you here, and how did you get in?"

"I climbed the fence." Each word was carefully enunciated. "Then I jimmied your lock. Why is it cops always have the cheapest locks?"

"Because we're paid crap." She peered into the empty can. "You son of a bitch. You used up all my coffee." Nicky grabbed a mug from the cupboard and filled it. She crossed glazed Saltillo tiles until she stood in front of Dax. "If you drive drunk, I'll arrest your ass. Here. Drink the last of my coffee. You're out of my house as soon as you're sober. Where's your unit?"

He sat up straight and winced. His hair was tousled, he hadn't shaved, and wrinkles marred his blue silk dress shirt. How was it he still looked handsome as sin? She pressed the mug into his hand. His *left* hand. The gold wedding ring glinted in the light.

"If Janet finds out you're here—"

Dax waved his free hand. "She won't. Her shrinks have her too drugged up to even know what day it is." He sipped the coffee and wrinkled his nose. "What? No sugar ... *sugar?*"

An old joke. One he'd used when they—

She cut off that thought.

He hitched a half smile, and one very bloodshot eye winked at her. "You know how I like my ... coffee. Hot and sweet."

"Oh, for God's sake, Dax—"

"Hey! Don't make that face. It'll freeze that way. Come on. Sit." He clumsily patted the cushion next to him.

Nicky propped her hands on her hips. "Where's your unit? If someone sees—" She breathed deep. "I don't want anyone to see it and get the wrong idea."

"You mean you don't want that Boy Scout DEA Conservation Agent Franco Martinez to see it." Dax's voice held an acid edge. He sipped his coffee and eyed her.

Nicky kept her face impassive.

"No comment? Okay. Let's talk about my unit. I sent my driver to the twenty-four-hour Walmart to buy you some food, Goldilocks. The big bad wolf arrived, and there's no porridge. There's no *nothing*. Your cupboards are bare. As is this room." He swept his arm in an arc in front of him. "I don't remember your home being so empty. What the hell's going on?"

Her lips pressed tight. Figured he'd flip it back on her. He was good at that.

Wait.

"What? You sent Kevin Archibeque to buy me *groceries?* He knows about...? He's *seen* my house? Dammit, Dax. That guy hates me. He'll blab—" Nicky ran her hand over the top of her head, snagged her ponytail band, and tugged it out with a shaking hand.

"Your secrets are safe. He owes me big-time."

Nicky rolled her eyes. "I knocked him on his ass at the truck-stop sting. *And* humiliated him when Janet threw coffee in my face at the last Feast Day."

"But I saved his pension. He would've lost his job if I hadn't appointed him as one of my bodyguards. The CampFire casino sting? Redemption for him after that ill-advised pursuit and crash last year. He saved people this time."

"Dax—"

"He's loyal to me, Nicky." He put his coffee mug on the sofa table and reached for her, his fingers encircling her wrist. Brows knit, he twisted her palm to the light, studying the black line of stitches. "What happened?"

"Hazards of the job. I'll heal." *I always do.* She tensed against his grip. "Let go." He didn't and tugged. Nicky hissed out a breath and sat beside him on the lumpy cushions. She wiggled to find a comfortable spot.

His fingers laced with hers, and he squeezed gently. "I thought I gave you enough money—"

"You didn't give me anything," she bit out. "You owed me because of what you did, what Janet did."

He ignored her. "But you obviously didn't tell me about all your debts, did you? Foolish pride, Nicky. You didn't ask for enough."

"Not enough to be perpetually in your debt, you mean. I got what I needed. A chance to pay off my law school loans, *and* a spot in the Police Academy, which I consider the most important part of the settlement."

"And mandating treatment for Janet, after … what happened. She got help."

Her snort was loud in the empty room. "You still can't say it. She tried to *kill me.*" Nicky swallowed the knot in her throat. "And the help isn't working based on the fact she attacked me again this summer." She lifted their linked hands and opened hers, but he held on. "What's she going to do if she finds out—"

"She won't," he said flatly. "I knew you sold some of your grandmother's furniture to pay your lawyer. But I don't remember it being ... everything."

Nicky scowled. He just wouldn't let it go. "The initial retainer was ten thousand dollars. I didn't have that kind of cash. So yeah. I sold the table and chairs."

"Eighteenth-century Spanish colonial? It was worth way more than ten K."

She did yank her hand away then and shifted to sit at an angle, arms crossed over her chest.

"What about the other stuff?" he asked.

"Gone."

"Why?"

"You know why. Your in-laws went after me in a civil suit because I defended myself against your murderous wife."

He raised a finger. "At the time, fiancée."

"Whatever. It's not cheap to be accused of attempted murder." She rubbed her hand over her forehead. "I had to take out a second mortgage. The monthly payment is more than I make without over-time, and there's a balloon payment due at the end of the year."

"Janet was spiraling out of control back then. Paranoid. Delu-sional. Did you know that?"

Nicky opened her eyes wide. "I figured it out when she tried to stab me with an icepick. I'm kinda smart that way."

Dax chuckled, but his expression was grave. He appeared to have sobered up some.

"She never would have—could have—testified against you. Her parents would've paid you a lot more if you'd held out."

"I wanted it done."

"How much do you owe?"

"None of your business."

"Twenty-five thousand."

"Did you go through my mail?" Her whole body blazed with outrage.

"I'll write you a check, right here, right now. No one else has to know."

"I'll know." Nicky pushed off the sofa and strode to the kitchen, bracing her arms against the sink. She was tired, and she wanted Dax gone.

"Janet's parents bought the seventeenth-century cabinet that used to sit against that wall. I loved that piece," Dax said. He'd come up behind her. "Paid four thousand for it. After the settlement was signed, they took an ax...."

Nicky closed her eyes. Her breath stuttered.

"And chopped it into pieces. Then they had a bonfire." Hands caressed her upper arms, and his warm, boozy breath tickled her neck. "Nicky. Let me pay your bills."

She yanked away from him and spun around. "*You son of a bitch.*" She meant it this time. "Why did you come here?" Dax had a reason for everything he did. "What do you want?"

His eyes sparkled. "I made a mistake marrying Janet. You would've made a much better senator's wife." He brushed the hair from her cheek.

She jerked away. "Except I didn't have any money. Or the right connections, did I?"

The silence between them stretched. Then his lips twisted into a half smile. He shrugged. "Too bad."

Nicky eyed him warily as he sauntered to the living area and picked up the coffee mug. He took a drink and grimaced. "I came for a shoulder to cry on," he said matter-of-factly. "The human trafficking case at the Fire-Sky truck stop—"

"Which you *stole* from us."

"—ended up being an almost complete clusterfuck. Almost." A knock sounded on the door. "Archibeque with your groceries."

He turned, and she grabbed his arm to stop him.

"Almost?" she repeated.

He grinned.

"I've asked the governor to make me the director of her Human

Trafficking Task Force. This is my chance to make up for the, uh, problems that cropped up last year due to that crash. And, of course, with this recent operation." He tilted his head and stared down into her eyes. "I'm here because I need your help on a ticklish investigation."

"Body count too high to be elected senator?" Nicky dropped her hand from his arm. Her gut churned at the thought of the gossip and innuendo if the press found out she and Dax were working together. She'd barely survived the publicity after their affair had blown up in her face. "My superiors already think I tipped you off for the sting. This would only confirm it. There's no way in hell I'm helping you."

The knock sounded again, louder. The door handle rattled. "Chief Stone?"

"Don't you want to know why I need you, Nicky? How *this* would make me beholden to *you*?"

Damn him for knowing how to press her buttons.

"I'm listening." She wondered how quickly she'd regret her curiosity.

"One of the drivers from the sting talked before he was killed in lockup. To me. Only. No one else was there, and there's no recording. He wanted protection against Chen Cano and was willing to bargain."

"How'd that work out for him?" Nicky said.

"Chief Stone!" Archibeque pounded on the door. The bells jounced against the wood.

She sighed. "Tell me before your lackey wakes the whole neighborhood."

"I need you because I can trust you to keep this quiet. Because the driver said Cano cut a deal with someone on Tsiba'ashi D'yini Pueblo for information on patrols and operations. *Your* pueblo." His expression was tight, but his eyes glowed. "And I want you to find out who that is."

CHAPTER TWELVE

FROM HER BACK PATIO, Nicky's gaze traced the top edge of the Sandia Mountains. The sun wouldn't be up for another hour, but the air held residual heat carried over from the day before.

Mug of coffee in hand, she sat, bare legs curled beneath her, on a chair that wasn't particularly comfortable or attractive—a wide wrought-iron affair coated in thick Pepto-Bismol-colored paint. She'd helped her grandmother refurbish it one summer vacation over twenty years ago. They'd spread newspapers out on the concrete pad under the breezeway, and with the scent of fresh-cut alfalfa on the warm air, they'd painted and chatted about school and boys and a hundred other things. When they had finished, drips of pink spotted shoes, clothes, and the bare skin of their legs and arms. And after the paint dried, both had signed it with a marker—she in block letters, her grandmother with the flourish of an artist.

When Nicky's father had broken her mother's heart for the last time with his extramarital affairs, Nicky's mother had found solace not with her only child but with her career, leaving Nicky in the care of her grandmother. Nicky had thought that after her father died, she and her mother would grow closer, but almost twenty years later, nothing had changed. Unless there was a problem, her mother rarely came back to New Mexico between travels. So, growing up, Nicky's grandmother had replaced both her mother and her father, but now she was gone, too.

The only thing Nicky had left was her grandmother's house.

Nicky rubbed her thumb over the armrest. The signatures were gone, faded to nothing. What would happen to the chair if she lost her home, a home that had belonged to her family for five generations? Would it be sold to pay off her debt? Or dumped at the curb?

No. She'd work her ass off, take every second of overtime, scrape together the money. She'd made an appointment later that morning with the mortgage officer at her bank to ask for more time, to find some way—

Her gaze swept the shadowed acreage behind the house. A small field of alfalfa, two large pecan trees, a tiny grove of fruit trees—peach, cherry, and McIntosh apples she needed to pick for dinner Friday—and an empty corral and pasture shelter. Weeds choked the ground, products of the most recent flood irrigation. She'd ask her neighbor to mow next time he had his tractor out.

Lips against the rim of her mug, Nicky inhaled the coffee's bitter aroma. Her eyes closed on the burn of tears. Oh, God, she couldn't lose this.

To clear the tightness in her throat, she sipped the coffee generously provided by Dax. At least he'd furnished her with a suitable alternative to her swirling thoughts: Chen Cano, the leader of the most vicious gang in Albuquerque, had made a deal with someone on Fire-Sky to move drugs and human victims safely across pueblo lands. It was difficult to wrap her mind around this information, but there was no question. She had to investigate.

Nicky swept up her phone. Her finger hovered over the contact number for a few hesitant seconds before she pressed it, her stomach jumping as the ring pulsed in her ear.

"This is unexpected. Good morning." The deep, growly voice tickled her arms with goose bumps.

"I hope I haven't called too early."

"Nope," Franco said. "Just sitting on the back porch with the paper, drinking my coffee."

"Me, too. Well, the coffee part." She stared into her cup before a thrum of hummingbird wings drew her gaze to the feeder.

"How's your hand?"

"It hurts, but better." Nicky paused, not sure where to start. Through the phone, she heard the scrape of metal against cement.

"This isn't a social call, is it?" he said.

She traced the flight of the hummingbird as it whizzed away. "I sent you that pic of the boot print at the ciénega. We didn't get a chance to talk about it because of the truck-stop sting and its, um, aftermath."

"That's polite. Three men dead? I would have called it a cluster —" His breath hissed over the line. "Sorry. I know you and Stone...." His voice was stiff, stilted.

"That was over a long time ago." She clutched the phone, feeling a niggle of guilt. It was over, but that didn't mean Dax still wasn't in her life and useful to her. She just didn't think Franco would understand, and now was probably not the right time to talk about it. "But about the boot print."

"You, uh, you don't think you might have done it? I mean, you were pretty—"

"What? Oh. No. I took those pictures before."

"Then I could be convinced someone stepped across the track. You think this person was at the water tank after Seneca died?"

"Maybe. Or when he died."

"You mean witnessed his death?"

Nicky bit her lip. "Or helped it along."

"Murder? All we have is a single ghostly footprint and turned-out pockets on his jeans. More likely someone found the body and didn't want to report it, so they tried to erase themselves from the scene. It's feasible."

"I guess." She sighed and sipped her coffee.

"I heard two of Seneca Elk's brothers died this past year. Suicides, right?"

"Yeah." Nicky shifted on her chair. "It's just so weird, and my police radar keeps pinging. Three brothers dead in such a short period of time? I'm going to pull the case files and review them."

"If you'd like a second set of eyes, give me a call."

"Actually ... I have information from a source, and ... and I need to talk to someone I trust about it." Nicky wiped a bandaged thumb over the rim of her mug. "You."

A pause stretched between them.

"Me. Okay." Franco cleared his throat. "Go ahead."

"My source intimated that Chen Cano has cut a deal with someone on Fire-Sky. For operation and patrol information along the I-25 and I-40 corridor."

A low whistle sounded through the line. "That could explain why none of his transports have been busted for over a year."

"Chief and Captain figured after the debacle last summer, Cano must have changed his trafficking corridors," Nicky continued. "But if someone's tipping him off, it's possible he's still using the same routes."

"This Cano guy is ruthless. DEA has the Crybabies linked to the Coahulian Cartel, and they make those thugs look like Boy Scouts."

"It's just weird that someone on the pueblo would do this. I've liaised with a lot of their police forces and councils the last five years, and few come to mind who would put themselves before their People."

"There could be other motivations," Franco said. "Like money."

"'*We are poor ... but we are free. No white man controls our footsteps.*'"

"What?"

"Oh. Just a quote. From Sitting Bull." Nicky took a sip of coffee and grimaced. It needed more sugar.

"Why weren't they tipped off about our sting operation?"

She'd asked Dax the same question. The answer he'd given chilled her.

"My source said Cano's gang had been given the all-clear the week before. They didn't expect us to be there."

"Because we moved the sting forward a couple days."

"But why wasn't that information passed along?" Nicky rubbed her thumb over her lips. "Franco, I think someone's leaking NCIRC deconfliction reports on our operations. Not only are state police seeing our interdictions, but the Crybabies are getting alerted, too. Someone in law enforcement has to be a part of this arrangement. Not gonna lie. That makes me queasy."

"Who has permissions for the database?"

"I'll download access history. Franco? This stays between us for now, okay?"

"Are you asking me to help you?"

She clutched her phone tighter. "I don't think I can do this by myself."

He was silent for what seemed a very long time. She squeezed her eyes shut. She'd pushed him away so many times, it would serve her right if—

"Okay," he said.

She expelled a slow breath, feeling suddenly lighter. "Maybe when we ... maybe ... we can get together ... after we have our info, and...."

"That sounds great." His reply caused her stomach to flutter. "You coming in today?"

"No. I'm busy this morning, and Savannah wants some help decorating a FEMA trailer after lunch. There's a new computer teacher starting classes for the kids on Monday." Nicky trailed a finger over a wrought-iron scroll. "You'll be at Savannah's for dinner on Friday?"

"Wouldn't miss it. But I'll probably see you before then."

"Probably." She relaxed back in the chair. Light scored the top of the mountains like a jagged fringe of white-gold lace. "Sun's about to come up."

"Yep. My backyard has a great view. Yours?"

"Yeah." The first rays caught and sparkled ruby red in the sugar water of the hummingbird feeder.

"Hey, Nicky. Let's watch the sunrise together."

CHAPTER THIRTEEN

Nicky counted the number of boxes stuffed in the back of the old white Suburban baking in the sun outside the FEMA trailer. The nearest trees were bushy cedars at the farthest end of a scraped dirt parking lot edged with boulders.

"*All* of this stuff goes inside? For goodness' sake, Savannah, it's a hundred degrees out here."

"Yes, but it's a dry heat. How are your stitches?"

"Better." Nicky held her hand out, palm up. "I took some ibuprofen for the pain."

"Then stop complaining and start unloading," Savannah said. She hoisted a cardboard box into her arms. "I've got water and Diet Pepsi in the fridge, and I've turned on the AC. The trailer should cool down—"

"Never?" Nicky picked up a box of computer paper and headed up the short flight of stairs. She shouldered through the door, Savannah behind her. The air was cooler inside—not saying much—and contained a faint chemical smell that made her nose wrinkle. "This isn't one of those Hurricane Katrina asbestos trailers, is it?"

"Not asbestos. Formaldehyde. And no." Savannah dropped her

box on a Formica countertop and sighed happily. "Full kitchen for the summer meal program, a community washer and dryer through that door. Bathroom with a shower over there."

Simple computer tables lined the walls in what once was the living room. Corkboards were already pinned with Keresan words and phrases: *Dzii k'ui kədyeekuya?* ("What are you doing?"); *Sium'eegume ts'idyaadrani* ("I am reading.").

"Looks good, doesn't it?" Savannah grinned, the tiny gap between her front teeth giving her smile a girlish charm. "Brand-new computers will be installed this weekend for classes starting Monday. Come on. Only a million more boxes to move." She skipped down the stairs outside.

"Aren't you worried about break-ins? It's pretty isolated out here." The closest village, Chirio'ce, lay about a half mile to the northeast of the trailer along a narrow paved road.

Savannah hefted a brand-new microwave. She passed it to Nicky but didn't meet her eyes. "Council hired a caretaker. Didn't you see the RV parked around back?" She grabbed another box, and Nicky followed her up the stairs. "I'm just so happy this language grant was funded and that I helped write it," Savannah continued. "Not a lot of kids are even exposed to Keresan anymore. Only our elders speak it fluently, and it's our heritage."

"You should be pretty proud of yourself," Nicky said.

"You can't tell I am?" Savannah shot her a smile and waggled her eyebrows. "I mean, it's so different, so hands-on when compared to the tribe trying to preserve its legacy by building museums and heritage centers. Dad calls them cultural zoos. I mean, I don't agree with a lot of what he says, like no women may hold positions in kiva or tribal council because of tradition, but he has a point." She slipped her box next to Nicky's on the kitchen countertop and started to unload food into the cupboards. "My whole life I've heard him rant about how non-Indians are McDonaldizing our food and making us fat and diabetic, warping our perceptions about the roles of men and women, and bringing drugs and alcohol and addiction. The last one with good reason, considering."

Nicky nodded. Savannah's brother had been high when he'd stepped in front of a train his senior year of high school. Although he'd saved his girlfriend, he'd been killed.

"If Dad could build a wall around our land to keep all the bad out, he would." Savannah sighed. "His heart's in the right place, but he sometimes forgets there's bad within, too. Cultures and traditions aren't static, no matter what some people on the pueblo believe." She straightened. "I've always been an advocate of extracting best practices."

"Cultural appropriation. That's a hot-button issue."

"Right? Be careful about who makes your burritos and fry bread. Still, look at Luz Cochin. She's this close"—Savannah held her index finger and thumb about an inch apart—"to being elected first woman on tribal council. That never would've happened a generation ago."

They trudged back outside to the SUV.

"Speaking of traditional, I need a cultural expert to examine some evidence from a case," Nicky said. "An unusual stone bear fetish. Do you think I could ask your dad? He's helped the police with artifacts in the past, but with his health and all...."

"Are you kidding? I'm sure he'd love to consult." Savannah hefted the last box into her arms and started up the steps. "Can you get the groceries from the back seat?"

Nicky grabbed as many bags as she could and followed.

"One more trip and that should do it. I'll go." Setting her box on the counter, Savannah hurried back out the door and down the steps.

Nicky leaned her hips against the counter and let her shoulders slump. It was difficult keeping up a facade when all she wanted to do was curl up in the corner. The bank had been a waste of time. She was nowhere nearer to saving her home than she'd been.

"Hey." Savannah slid more bags on the counter. "You okay?"

Nicky straightened and met Savannah's worried gaze. She considered blurting out the painful truth. Instead, she fixed a smile to her face. Savannah was her best friend, but to use their friendship to save her home was something she couldn't do.

"My hand hurts a little." She adjusted the bandage, pressing against the throbbing wound. "That's all."

"There's a first aid kit in one of the grocery bags," Savannah volunteered.

"Thanks." She rummaged through one bag but only found cans of commodity tomatoes and beans.

"So, um ... I need to tell you something."

"What?" Nicky moved to another bag, pulled it open—and froze. A huge bag of Flamin' Hot Fritos lay on top. "Savannah." She kept her tone even. "Who's the caretaker?"

Savannah wrinkled her nose. "Well...."

The door to the trailer burst open, and a thin figure, dark hair sticking out in all directions, stood in the threshold. Rumpled and dusty, he was dressed in black canvas trousers short enough to show an inch of tube sock above tattered black Converse, and his creased button-down shirt might have been white at one time. He blinked at them through BC glasses. The planes of his face had filled in since the last time Nicky had seen him, and his once pasty-gray skin now held a slight tan.

"Howard? The tribe hired *Howard Kie* as the new caretaker?" Nicky's voice spiraled.

The room was silent except for the shush and hum of the air conditioner. Howard scratched his nose and sniffed.

"On my father's recommendation. He's been staying with my parents until the RV's ready." Savannah's overly perky voice grated on Nicky's ears.

"Haa'a." Howard gave Nicky a sweet smile. "Hey."

She closed her mouth with an audible snap.

CHAPTER FOURTEEN

"Right on time!" A thin, wheezy voice followed Howard into the trailer as Savannah's father clunked up the stairs. Robert Johnson Analla—RJ—grabbed the jamb and caught his breath. He towered over Howard like a giant scarecrow.

"Guw'aadzi, N'aishdiya." Savannah greeted her father and bustled to him, eyes down, head dropped slightly forward. In Fire-Sky culture it was disrespectful to meet an elder's eyes for longer than a few seconds, even if he was your father. RJ ducked his chin in acknowledgement of Nicky's presence, his smile widening.

"Nicky! You're looking well…. Uh? What happened to your hand?"

"A little cut." She stepped forward and gave him a quick hug, hiding surprise at his thinness. "I'm glad to see you, Mr. Analla. I wanted to ask for your help. I have an artifact, a fetish, found during an arrest. I've never seen one like it before. Could you come into the police station and take a look at it?"

"I'd be happy to, happy to. It's good to know I still have some value in life, even if some people only want me to stay home and rest. It's like I'm dead and buried already."

"Dad, I never—"

"Actually," Nicky said, "Savannah reminded me you've assisted the police in past cases like this one." A small white lie, but if it helped her friend....

"Oh. Of course." He sniffed and bestowed a frown on Savannah. "Just as manipulative as her mother. Always telling a sick old man what to do. It's no wonder I have one foot in the grave."

Nicky blinked. "I ... I didn't mean, I don't think—"

He waved a dismissive hand. "Tell Savannah when you need me, and I'll drive in with her."

"Thank you, sir, I certainly will."

He hobbled past, and Nicky leaned toward Savannah to whisper, "Sorry."

"Don't feel bad. He works in guilt like a master potter works in clay. Besides, that wasn't meant for you." She tapped her chest right over her heart and hurried to RJ's side.

"Dad? Come sit, and I'll get you a bottle of water." She hovered at her father's elbow as he ambled across the room. "It's too hot for you to be running around like this, too easy to get dehydrated—"

"Heem'e. Enough, daughter." Mr. Analla brushed away her helping hand and lowered himself into a plastic chair, falling the final inches with a grunt.

Nicky studied him from under her lashes. His wide shoulders stretched like a hanger for an oversized suit. His face, a masculine version of his daughter's, showed sharper cheekbones, the lids sagging over his eyes and making them look small and tired.

"Stop babying me," he grumbled at Savannah. "The doctor said I need to get out, walk around. It decreases the swelling. And I was glad to help this young man. We had a fine talk on the way over. Isn't that right, s'a-muh'dyi?"

Nicky's head jerked to Savannah, who met her gaze and responded with a tiny shake of her head. Mr. Analla calling Howard *s'a-muh'dyi*—my son—had enormous implications in Tsiba'ashi D'yini culture.

"Haa'a. Dawaa dza. It was a good conversation." Howard wiped two fingers over his upper lip. What Nicky had originally thought was a streak of dirt was actually a thin mustache of maybe ten total hairs on each side of his nose.

"Good! Good! See, Savannah? He could teach Keresan. A good traditional man. Pull that chair over here." He gestured to Savannah. "Howard, ai shdyə ch'uguya. Sit down there."

Howard sat and draped one leg over the other, an inch of bony shin showing above his sock. He folded his hands in his lap and stared around the room.

"Water for both of you," Savannah said. A tiny furrow crept into her forehead. "Dad, ch'awaasa sranasrka?"

"You know I always wake up with a headache, but I feel better seeing my favorite daughter."

"Your only daughter. Howard? Say hello to Sergeant Matthews."

"Hin'a. I never got to thank you for saving my friends in the Sacred Caves, because I had to go to rehab instead. Those guys said I was recovered so long as I don't drink." He smiled, and it lightened his features, making him look younger than his almost thirty years. "I'm glad to be home."

Hair and cheesy mustache notwithstanding, this was the most coherent Nicky had ever seen Howard Kie.

"You're going to be caretaker here? That's a very good job, Howard." Nicky hesitated. "Have you ever interacted with young children?"

Mr. Analla frowned. "He's had a background check. And the council has issued him a pueblo driver's license. Sovereignty, Sergeant."

"Yes, sir." The driver's license information was a bit of a surprise, but tribal council had that authority. "So long as he doesn't stray off the reservation. Do you have a car, Howard?"

"Haa'a. It's junk, though." Howard yawned and smacked his lips.

"Taken care of, son." Mr. Analla gave him a hearty backslap that almost knocked Howard from his chair. "Daughter?"

Savannah extracted the key fob to the Suburban from her purse and handed it to Howard. "It has the keys to the trailer, too."

He scrunched up his face and stared at the keys before lifting his eyes with an expression Nicky could only describe as puppy love. "Would you show me how to drive it?"

Savannah stepped back. "Uh ... now? It's really hot outside." She hurried to the kitchen to lift a box of pepperoni pizza Hot Pockets out of a grocery bag. "Aren't you hungry? I was going to make you a snack. There are Flamin' Hot Fritos, too. Why don't you go and explore the RV for a few minutes? I'll have everything ready when you come back."

Howard's eyes lit up, but whether it was for his new home or because of the corn chips, Nicky didn't know.

"Hin'a." He ambled to the back door.

Mr. Analla pushed to his feet. "I'll go with you."

"Dad, no."

RJ ignored her and followed Howard down the back stairs, hand tight on the rail.

Savannah let out an exasperated sound. "He won't even use the access ramp." She plugged the microwave in and tore open a box of Hot Pockets, obviously avoiding Nicky's gaze.

"S'a-muh'dyi? Son? Is your dad matchmaking?" Nicky grinned. "Savannah and Howard, sitting in a tree, k-i-s-s—"

"Knock it off. Do you know how uncomfortable this has been?"

"Not for me. I'm having a blast." She rocked back on her heels.

Savannah popped a Hot Pocket into the microwave. "Dad's his AA sponsor and recommended him for the job. He's the one who got the council to issue the tribal driver's license—Howard's got something like nine DUIs—and they've loaned him the truck and paid his insurance. Dad can be so persuasive sometimes. Where'd you put that bag of Fritos?"

"Why is this upsetting you so much? Howard's a little weird, but—"

"A little weird? It's like he's from another century or something in his traditions. He's full-blooded Tsiba'ashi D'yini, fluent in Keres, and he sees more visions and spirits than ten of you on salvia. And"— Savannah scraped her fingers through her hair and met Nicky's gaze —"Dad's using his heart problems to play the grandfather card." She narrowed her eyes. "What?"

"I'm just trying to picture your and Howard's baby." Laughing, Nicky deftly batted away the wadded-up ball of trash Savannah threw at her head.

The back door sprang open, and Howard assisted Mr. Analla into the room. Savannah's father was sweaty and pale, and Nicky rushed over to help him to his chair.

"Dad, I *told* you." Savannah pressed another bottle of water into his hands. The microwave dinged, and she hurried back to the kitchen, shaking her head.

"I'm fine. Too hot out there, that's all." He peeked out from under his brows. "Still, I don't think I'll be able to take Howard into Albuquerque to shop for new clothes. Maybe you should do it, daughter."

Savannah froze in the process of handing Howard a plate with the Hot Pocket and Fritos. "Uh...."

"You can take my car, and I'll take Howard's truck. Oh. And where's the paperwork for the Suburban? It wasn't in the glove compartment."

"On my desk in my office," Savannah said.

"I'll get it on my way home, then. Give me your key. You're coming for dinner tonight, haa'a? Bring Howard. That way he can pick up the truck." Mr. Analla slapped his hands on his knees. "I'm glad that's settled. Howard?"

Howard bobbed his head enthusiastically and brandished the Hot Pocket. "Your daughter is an amazing cook."

"She makes dinner every Friday night for her friends. I'm sure she'd love to have you attend. Then you can really see what a wonderful cook and housekeeper Savannah is. It's a puzzle why she isn't already married."

Nicky covered a smile with her hand. Completely outmaneuvered.

Under her breath Savannah said, "He's not done yet. Wait for it...."

Mr. Analla patted his chest and blinked teary eyes behind his glasses. "I just hope this old heart lasts long enough so I can hold a grandbaby before I die."

CHAPTER FIFTEEN

Nicky stopped in the doorway of the break room. Jinni Sundry slumped in a chair, staring at a Styrofoam cup half full of muddy coffee. Her round face was pale and her hair faintly disheveled. She toasted Nicky before she took a sip.

"It's not decaf. I needed high octane after"—Jinni closed her eyes and breathed deeply—"after the chief got through shredding me into little pieces."

"Sorry I couldn't be here to support you." Nicky stepped inside the room and leaned her hip against the countertop. "As soon as I came in this morning, I was called out on a five-year-old who brought a butter knife to day care. It was coated with dried frosting he wanted to share with his friends, but they have a zero-tolerance policy. I wish they had common sense instead."

Jinni smiled. It was half-hearted, polite.

"What's the damage?" Nicky asked.

"One-month suspension without pay, starting Monday. Desk duty till then." Voice gruff, she said, "I guess you know I'm pregnant. And, uh, I want to apologize for what happened with Gianetta Green."

Two officers walked into the room, laughing. After pouring themselves coffee, they settled at the other end of the long table and started a low-voiced conversation. This wasn't a good place to talk.

"Officer Sundry? You don't go on shift until ten, right? I could use your help."

She led Jinni out to the parking lot and nodded at the silver Mazda 3.

"This your car?" Jinni asked. "I never see you drive anything but your unit."

"It's my mom's. She lets me use it when she's traveling. I've got permission to store it at the Muuk'aitra warehouse. Could you take my unit and follow?" She handed her keys to Jinni. "We can talk on the way back."

"Muuk'aitra is pretty far out. What if you need your mom's car for something?"

"I let the registration and insurance lapse, so it's better if I don't have access." Nicky clicked the key fob, and the little car beeped in response.

Jinni climbed in the driver's side of Nicky's Tahoe. "Mountain or freeway route?"

"Freeway's shortest."

They drove in tandem out of the parking lot and north on I-25, taking the first off-ramp and heading west toward dark green mountains. The warehouse was nestled on the south side of a narrow valley. Jinni turned in past the vacant guard shack and headed to the back of the complex, where she parked. Nicky left her car running as she punched in the code to the enormous garage door. It ground open slowly, chains and gears clattering. She directed Jinni to close it after her, then drove into the cavernous space.

Nicky exited the Mazda as the segmented overhead door shuddered down with a deafening rattle. It boomed as it hit the cement floor, the sound fading slowly. Quiet crept up on her until she could hear herself breathing.

"This place gives me the creeps," Jinni said. Her voice echoed hollowly. She walked to the spot where Nicky had parked the car. Because of the haphazard placement of other stored vehicles, it was quite a distance from the bay door.

The stuffy air in the warehouse smelled of gasoline and dust and a faint sweet, rotten scent, as if an animal had died somewhere in the walls. High above them, a single overhead fluorescent mount flickered against the gloom, which was undiminished by hazy plastic skylights coated with accumulated dirt and pine needles. Nicky wondered when the warehouse roof had last been cleaned.

Wan light outlined bulky heaps of discarded office furniture, jumbles of old manufacturing equipment, and stacked boxes heavy with stored files and documents. The back of the huge garage was so dark. The walls melded with the blackness and seemed to disappear. Nicky rubbed her prickling nape and silently agreed with Jinni. This place was a little spooky.

Shaking off unease, she popped open the hatchback of the Mazda and retrieved the canvas cover. Jinni helped her spread it over the car.

"It's haunted, you know," Jinni volunteered. "The boneyard outside, where they store all the DUI wrecks? I heard the spirits of those who pass in the accidents wander and cause mischief. One of the night-shift officers got pushed. Had to take medicine. You need protection to come here."

Nicky slipped a magnetized key box beneath a wheel well before she tucked the cover around the front bumper. "I have a gun."

"Won't work against lost spirits." Jinni pulled an object from her pocket. "Corn maiden carved from deer antlers. It represents strength and wisdom."

A creamy white fetish about two inches long and detailed with tiny beads of turquoise lay in Jinni's palm. With black lines for eyes and its robe inlaid with onyx and coral, it was a work of art. She closed her fist and pressed it against her belly. Now that she knew, Nicky could see a bump.

"My baby's a girl. Found out a couple weeks ago. Father's married. I don't even like him much anymore."

Nicky said nothing.

"Chief Cochin said because of my baby I put everyone at work in danger. That everything's filtered through my pregnancy." Jinni blinked, and a tear splattered on her cheek. She caught it with the side of her fist, the little fetish clutched inside. "She's right. When I realized Gianetta Green was burning seer's sage, all I thought about was the baby. Then the owl's shadow happened." She shivered, eyes bleak. "I mean, you could handle that lady, but what if the situation was really dangerous? Or what if after my baby's born, I get hurt or killed because of my job? What would happen to her?"

"You're not alone, Jinni. Women go through this, ask the same questions. Have you talked to Officer Simpson? She's got a couple of kids. A lot of the men in the department have children, too. I'm sure they can give you advice on how to deal with your situation."

Jinni snorted. "Men? They don't have the same pressures at work, especially not from brass." She gave Nicky a curious look. "What will you do when you get pregnant? When you have a daughter or a son at home?"

"I hadn't thought—"

"Well, you should. I think you'd make a great mom, Sarge. A momma bear if you had kids. Maybe that's the fetish you should carry. Zunis believe the bear is a spiritual guide, and with your, you know ... visions...." She smiled fleetingly before her brows knit. "What's wrong? Your hand hurting or something? You keep rubbing it."

Nicky curled her hand into a fist. "No. It's fine. The stitches itch—"

Metal clanged in the darkness behind them. She jerked her gaze to the back of the huge space, heart pounding.

"There shouldn't be anyone here," Nicky whispered. She unsnapped her ASP baton. "I'll check it out."

Jinni stayed still, staring into the darkness. Her hand cradled her belly again.

Nicky peered into the shadows, alert for any sound or movement.

She walked soft-footed to the corner of a single-story office built in the middle of the warehouse. Along the back wall, jumbled piles of car parts—dented fenders, crushed doors and tailgates, dashboards, and car seats—were stacked high and deep. She reached for her flashlight and grimaced. Gone. At the bottom of the ciénega tank. Waiting until her eyes adjusted, she skirted a tower of tires. Her foot kicked something, and hollow metal scraped cement. She followed the sound and picked up a dented hubcap.

"Sergeant?"

"I think I found our noise," Nicky called.

Jinni trotted over.

"See? They're stacked on top of the tires. It must've slipped and fell." She pointed to other hubcaps scattered on the floor.

"Or the spirits did it because they want us to leave."

"Well, I don't think we should let them drive us away." Nicky perched the disk on top of the tires. "Sets a bad precedent."

Jinni shivered. "Don't say stuff like that."

She and Jinni fell into step and headed for the door leading to the boneyard outside. Nicky locked it behind them and drew a deep breath of fresh air. Wrecked vehicles were parked around the yard. She found one of her old units, shot full of holes during a confrontation on Scalding Peak earlier that summer.

Jinni handed her the keys to her SUV, and they climbed inside. Before she started the engine, Nicky said, "I'll talk to Chief Cochin about your suspension. A month seems like overkill. Let's see if we can get it down to a couple of weeks."

"That won't be necessary." Jinni's decision was emblazoned on her face. Nicky's stomach dropped.

"Officer Sundry. Jinni. Please. Take the week to think this over. You're a good cop. Don't throw away your—" She pressed her lips shut, appalled at what had almost slipped out.

"Don't throw away my career for a child?"

"That's not what I meant. You'll be put on light duty until the baby's born. It's not much different than an injury, like when Officer Garcia rehabbed his knee."

"My pregnancy's like a disability? You're not making this any better," Jinni said. "Look, I need to take control of my life. I pretty much live paycheck to paycheck. Frankly, I can't afford my suspension or to take time off after the baby is born. And we don't get paid after we use up our PTO and go on FMLA."

How was taking control choosing to lose something as vital as a job? Nicky almost choked on panic at that thought. Even though she might lose her home, she wasn't dragging another person down with her. But it was none of her business, right? Except....

"You're Zuni, not Fire-Sky. Don't you live on the pueblo? Non-pueblo members only have access to housing if they work for the tribe."

Creases formed between Jinni's brows. "I didn't think of that."

"Then you need to." Nicky's phone chimed. Grateful for the interruption, she read the text.

Parking lot videos from the sting operation available. Headed to casino to view. Will need you there at noon.

"It's Chief Cochin," Nicky explained. "I'll talk to her."

Jinni made a derisive noise. "You know how perfect she's trying to be right now. First woman elected to the Fire-Sky Tribal Council—how does she say it?—since the Creator's genesis of the Tsiba'ashi D'yini People. That's a lot of pressure. You can try, but you won't budge the chief from her decision." Jinni splayed her hand across her abdomen. "My baby has to come first. Over my job. Over me."

CHAPTER SIXTEEN

WHEN IT CAME DOWN to it, comfort food served the same purpose in every culture.

Nicky smiled her thanks as the waitress slid her order on the table. Chief Cochin picked up her fork and cut into her enchiladas. Behind Cochin, geometrically patterned wool rugs decorated the walls of Baabaa's restaurant. Fake adobe bancos painted in warm browns and reds gave the dining area a homey, cozy atmosphere—just like Grandma's, if her kitchen happened to be in a casino. The air-filtering system screened out the worst of the cigarette smoke and dampened the ringing cacophony of the slot machines.

She sighed inwardly. The last few days had been unsettling, to say the least, and she had yet to broach the subject of Jinni Sundry's suspension with Chief. She wrapped her bandaged hand around her fork and dug into calabacitas and stuffed sopapillas.

"Do you want me to call Chief Stone?" Cochin dabbed her lips. "Or would you like to do it? I know you're in contact with him, no matter your denials. You're a smart woman and excellent police officer. He's too valuable a resource for you not to cultivate him, even with your, um, past association."

Nicky's face heated, food congealing in her mouth. She'd ended her disastrous affair with Dax ages ago, yet people couldn't seem to let it go.

"We keep in touch, but it's rare and purely professional," she replied. "And I didn't tell him about the sting operation." But she had texted Dax about the casino parking lot videos right after she'd dropped Jinni Sundry at the station. He hadn't answered her back yet.

Cochin raised her eyebrows. "No need to get defensive. I believe you. Why else would you download the deconfliction database logs except to find out when his office accessed your operation?"

Nicky picked up her iced tea to avoid answering. That had been one reason for the download. She'd also needed it to see who'd signed into the NCIRC system at Fire-Sky. The snitch in Dax's Chen Cano investigation was probably on the list.

Time to change the subject.

"I spoke to Jinni Sundry this morning, and she gave me the details of her suspension," Nicky said.

"What she did was unforgivable. By hiding her pregnancy, she put you and every officer she works with in danger. If a man had done something similar, he'd be disciplined in the same way. I can't give preference because of her sex."

"She can't afford to lose a month's pay, Chief."

"We have protocols, Sergeant. If she'd reported her pregnancy, I could have put her on desk duty. Instead, she decided to hide her condition." She frowned. "Like everyone wasn't going to find out eventually. I get so tired of women doing stupid things like this. It makes us all look bad."

"She made a mistake."

"And it will cost her. Twenty-five years ago, I was one of the first women on the Fire-Sky police force because it was *mandated*. Do you know the kind of sexist attitudes I had to put up with?" Cochin met Nicky's gaze with defiant brown eyes. "Not one of my male colleagues thought I received my position because I was qualified.

They all believed I got it because I had breasts. I had to be twice as smart, twice as motivated, and ten times tougher than a man. I never complained, never took advantage, and I *never* cried. I followed the protocols when I became pregnant with my kids. My husband, who gives me strength and guidance, was traditional Fire-Sky, which meant I had two jobs. I had to run my household, raise my children, cook and clean"—she leaned toward Nicky, mouth tight—"because God forbid that man lift a finger to help." She straightened and breathed deep. "This is a patriarchal tribe, Sergeant. Women have very specific roles. Roles that don't give them any larger authority. That will all change with my election to the tribal council, the first woman in both oral and recorded history."

"But Jinni will have to quit because she can't afford—"

"The power on this reservation is watching for missteps. If I didn't come down hard on Officer Sundry, it would've been held against me."

Nicky clamped her jaw shut, frustration spiking. When her phone chimed with a new text, she dug it out of her bag, only to fumble it from her bandaged hand. Cochin picked it up and glanced at the screen. Eyebrows raised, she passed it back to Nicky.

"I've always been impressed by your intelligence and drive, Sergeant. You remind me of me at a younger age." Cochin jutted her chin to the cell phone. "Don't get caught in the past. We don't live there anymore. And don't let a pretty face divert your attention. Especially one who uses people and doesn't give back anything in return." She tucked her napkin under the corner of her plate and stood. "I'll take our vouchers up to the cashier."

As the chief walked away, Nicky lifted her phone and stared at the screen. Dax.

Hey, babe. Got your text.

Babe? *Seriously?* And Luz Cochin had seen it. So much for "rare and purely professional."

Her phone chimed again. Franco. The odd sense of guilt roused a spark of anger.

Autopsy finished on tank drowning victim. Identity confirmed —SE.

Seneca Elk.

Out on poaching call for rest of day. Want to be in on family notify. Tomorrow morning?

Nicky tapped in a terse *Yes* and hit send. Her phone chimed again.

You okay?

Fine, she texted back.

But it was a lie.

She was playing with fire by trying to hide Franco and Dax from each other on the Cano investigation. She just hoped she wouldn't get burned.

CHAPTER SEVENTEEN

Nicky hadn't slept well. Her neck and shoulders ached, and she and Franco had hours of driving ahead of them that morning: the Elks' ranch for the death notification on Seneca, then over the mountain to J WhiteHawk's store to ask him about Gianetta Green and the eagle feathers.

"Why are you so chipper?" Nicky hunched in the passenger seat of Franco's unit.

"Because I get to drive, grumpy," Franco said, a half smile on his face. "How's your hand?"

She flashed him a frown. "Fine."

"I get it. You like to be in control. But let a guy do something nice for you every once in a while." His smile ticked higher as he leaned toward her. "You're welcome."

Nicky's lips twitched. "Thanks for driving, Franco. And for bringing me coffee." He'd snugged hers in the console next to his. One packet sugar substitute, no cream, but she ached for some real sugar that morning. She needed the energy boost.

"There. That wasn't so hard," he said.

"Now that the caffeine's kicked in, I guess not."

"Any updates on the search for the Chen Cano mole?"

"Not really." She gave him her sparse information.

He reciprocated before he said, "I have some info on the ciénega. Only gossip, though. The tribe took it off the maps because it's contaminated. Some rancher back in the late forties dumped a bunch of chemicals in it. A beef with the government about boundaries between his land and tribal land. Then he shot himself, right there, next to the spring."

"Probably why people think it's haunted." Nicky knotted her brows. "What kind of contamination?" She'd fallen into the tank.

"Don't know, but everything looks okay now. I'm still waiting for Tribal Resources to call back about the tank and windmill. Maybe whoever placed them cleaned the ciénega up." He cleared his throat. "This notification we're doing. I heard tribe members won't speak of the dead. Instead, they say things like 'those who have gone before us.' Why?"

"I've never asked," Nicky said. "But we can't do that—use euphemisms. Even 'he passed away' can mean something different to different cultures. I heard about an officer in Albuquerque who told a family their son was in a better place. The mom asked how long he'd be in jail."

Franco cocked an eyebrow at her, lips curving into a skeptical smile. "Is that really true?"

"Well, if it isn't, it ought to be." Nicky grinned.

He chuckled before they fell into a comfortable silence.

The mountain range west of Scalding Peak traced along a sun-bleached sky. Nicky adjusted the AC vent. Midmorning and already damned hot outside, heading up toward a predicted high of over a hundred degrees.

"It's been a tough year for the Elk Clan," Franco said.

"Yeah. Cochise Elk's death around Christmastime. And Geronimo Elk's suicide." She stopped.

"The Fire-Sky cop?"

"I was first on scene." Nicky rotated her coffee cup in the holder.

"A couple months before, he began to act erratically. Lashed out at his family, became aggressive on the job. After the third complaint of excessive force, Captain placed him on administrative leave." She caught his eye. "He left two little girls."

"I saw the aftermaths of a couple suicides when I was deployed. Waste of good lives."

"Yeah." Nicky straightened in her seat. "Before we get there, I need to warn you about the Elk Clan."

He shot her a glance. "Warn me?"

"They live on the outskirts of the tribe both literally and figuratively. At the edge of the Jemez. Real pretty place. The patriarch, Gemini Elk, is Fire-Sky's official fetish carver. It's an important position, even higher than cacique."

"Gemini, huh? Seneca, Geronimo, Cochise.... I was sensing a theme."

"There's a fourth brother, Mangas. Gemini's grandsons are all named after famous chiefs. His sons after movie cowboys. I think Gemini's the only one left of his generation; they were all named for constellations. Makes for interesting grave markers. Seneca's father, Clint Walker Elk, lives on the ranch." She shifted on her seat. "There are no women at the compound. They leave."

"Why?"

She shrugged. "The ones I've talked to say they weren't born to be maids—or slaves."

Nicky scanned the open country. Other than the cracked blacktop road and power lines strung from short wooden poles, there were no signs of recent human habitation for miles—only rock houses, their roofs collapsed, and skeletal windmill derricks, blades bent or missing.

Franco guided the truck up a winding, narrow road carved into the side of a mesa that tongued out into the plains below.

"They're all outlaws," Nicky continued.

Franco raised his brows. "That's pretty old-school."

"There's a long list of crimes attributed to the Elk Clan—both on and off the rez. In alphabetical order: cannabis possession, discharging a firearm within village limits, disorderly conduct, petty theft, public intoxication, reckless driving, simple assault, vandalism, trespass."

"Trespass, vandalism." At her look he said, "Alphabetical order. I'm not a fan of the firearms charge, but most of that's kid stuff."

"And when they happen on the rez, it's dealt with by the elders over in M'ida Village. Fines, reparations, no jail time. The next list isn't so innocent. They've been picked up for domestic violence, check-kiting, poaching, cattle rustling, even horse theft. But I have to admit, they've kept off the radar the past couple of years."

"Poachers are scum of the earth."

She hesitated before answering. "A lot of tribe members believe conservation laws shouldn't apply to them. That this is sovereign land and it's their right to hunt and fish whenever and wherever. Enough of the tribal council privately agree, even if they disagree publicly."

His fingers flexed on the steering wheel.

"Fire-Sky police haven't been able to lay a hand on any of the Elks because they're the last fetish-carving clan," she said.

"So? A lot of the artisans on Fire-Sky make fetishes. I've seen them at the fiestas." Franco negotiated another switchback, and the tires of the truck squealed faintly on the pavement.

"Ryan says the Elks' fetishes are different somehow. They're used for special ceremonies and hunts."

As they topped the ridge, the blacktop ended with a thump, and the truck shuddered across a washboard dirt road. Around them was a stretch of grassland that undulated gently. It rose toward the side of a mountain covered in a towering wave of conifers. A red-tailed hawk dropped in a graceful curve before rising currents lifted it from below. Nicky tracked its path across the sky. In the Fire-Sky culture, hawks were symbols of courage but also represented a warning of danger. She shifted, suddenly uneasy.

A long single-story homestead sat at the end of the track, its porch running the whole length of the house. At least a half a dozen trucks were parked haphazardly around it, some ancient, paint oxidized by age and the elements, others slick and new, jacked up high, their exteriors dulled by a layer of dust. Scattered behind the house were outbuildings and corrals. Older wooden barns and sheds, their patina declaring their age, mixed with newer structures, the ground around them scraped clean and raw.

Nicky sucked in a sharp breath. "Look. Behind the house."

Almost hidden by a screen of deciduous trees and brush, a cylindrical metal tank squatted next to a windmill. Nicky snapped pictures with her phone through the tinted glass of the truck.

"I think we have the answer to who developed the ciénega," Franco said.

"But where did they get that kind of money?" she murmured.

"If there's that many Elks, per capita distribution comes to mind. Didn't each tribal member receive up to ten thousand dollars this year?"

"Tribal sovereignty might let them off the hook for misdeeds, but it comes at a price. Most of these guys have lost their distribution privileges."

"No kidding? Maybe they sell a lot of fetish carvings."

A ragged pack of dogs and collared hounds poured out of the yard and streaked toward the truck. Franco slowed to a crawl as they ran and barked alongside.

"Hunting dogs. For bear, cougar, who knows what else." Franco's tone was grim.

"Some of the Elks guide during the season," Nicky said.

"Well, it's not hunting season. Those dogs are probably wreaking havoc on the mountain. They need to be penned." Franco stopped his unit behind a gap in the trucks and let it idle. "At least ten guys on the porch." He bit off an expletive. "Are all of them armed?"

"See what I mean?" Nicky said. Adrenaline spiked her heart rate. "Outlaws."

Franco's jaw clenched. "We're not going out there. These guys are hostiles. We need to call for backup."

"Careful with your language. I know *hostiles* has a military meaning, but the connotation's derogatory here, especially from an outsider. Besides, they didn't shoot me last time. And Franco?" She thought of Jinni and gave him a steady stare. "Cops have to take chances or we aren't doing our jobs."

Nicky stepped out of the truck and into the hot morning air.

CHAPTER EIGHTEEN

NICKY CLOSED the car door at the same time Franco did, the muffled thuds loud in the silence, as were Franco's footsteps. He stood silently beside her, arms crossed, intimidating in dark wraparound sunglasses. A united front. Men on the porch shifted, eased back a step.

Good.

None of the Elks said one word of greeting. Even the dogs had gone quiet. Though she kept her expression neutral, Nicky rested the heel of her hand on the Glock at her hip, her index finger touching her gold shield, but it really wasn't that much of a comfort considering the waves of animosity issuing from the dozen or so men in front of her. What the hell was this show of force all about? This was a death notification, nothing more.

"That guy's holding a Winchester 1873 carbine." Franco's voice was low, close to her ear. Awe filled his tone. "Do you know how much they're worth in good condition?"

Her gaze settled on a middle-aged man, rifle cradled in his arms, its wood knocked and dinged by use but with beautiful patina, the barrel almost blue in the harsh sunlight. That gun would never be slotted in a glass case to gather dust. For these men, their cadre of personal weapons defined them, almost like fingerprints.

Funny. They'd found no guns with Seneca Elk's body.

Roy Rogers Elk stood unsmiling at the top of the steps, his face deeply tanned and lined, long gray and black hair loose. He was slight, medium height. His shoulders sloped under a dark red plaid shirt buttoned to his throat. It was tucked into jeans held up by suspenders that snaked over a small paunch. Unlike some of the younger men present, he didn't wear sunglasses to hide his eyes.

The sun burned Nicky's neck, and a hot pine-scented breeze ruffled her hair. It stirred the dirt at her feet into tiny dust devils. The windmill behind the house creaked to life, the sound faint and distant.

Her lips twisted. All that was missing was the theme song to *Hang 'Em High*.

Nicky hooked a thumb in her duty belt and cocked her hip. "Hello, Roy. I'm here to speak to—"

"We already know." His voice was rough from a lifetime of cigarettes.

"Got to be official. Clint inside?" Nicky dropped her hands and walked to the bottom of the steps, Franco at her shoulder. She placed her boot on the first tread.

"Gemini doesn't like women in the house."

Nicky continued her steady, deliberate climb up the steps until she stood next to him. Bloodshot eyes, brown irises clouding with cataracts, stared into hers. A hazy whiff of alcohol exuded from his body. She read grief in the tired lines of his face.

Nicky softened her tone. "Just because you don't want to hear what I have to say doesn't mean it'll go away."

The man's throat worked. "First Cochise, now Seneca. It's been ... hard on him." He propped his rifle against the porch rail, and the rest of the men gathered closer. They leaned their long guns beside Roy's, silent except for the shuffle and scrape of their boots and brush of their clothing.

"You forgot about Geronimo," she said.

A voice spat, *"Traidor."*

Nicky met the hard gaze of Mangas Elk. Unlike most of the men surrounding her, she had to look up into his eyes. About to snap out a reply, she paused. Mangas's skin was gray and his eyes swollen and red. She didn't like the guy or his attitude toward authority, but he was grieving.

"Geronimo was your brother, too, Mangas."

He hefted his rifle. "This has more loyalty than that pig did."

A wave of heat spiraled through her at his disrespect toward a man and police officer she'd admired from her very first day on the force. She shoved her sunglasses to the top of her head and held his stare for stretched-out seconds. Only when his eyes slid away did she allow her simmering anger to drain.

The wood-framed screen was closed, but the front door behind it was open.

"May I go in?" she asked to no one in particular.

Roy grumbled, "Gemini's gonna have my head."

She extended her hand toward the door, only to pause. A small figure crouched behind a rusty patio chair. A boy, maybe eleven or twelve. He didn't look at her; instead he wore a vague smile. Hazel eyes shot with tiny shards of blue gazed vacantly through the jean-clad legs and booted feet surrounding him. His hair was light brown, slightly wavy, and woven without a part into a thick braid. He wore a grubby, oversized white T-shirt, blue jeans, and square-toed cowboy boots. His round face was almost … pretty. Smooth skin, feathery eyebrows, lashes long and thick and tipped with gold.

Nicky knelt and gentled her expression.

"I almost didn't see you there." She kept her voice soft. "How've you been, Dyu'ami?" With careful fingers, she tugged at his braid. He stared over her shoulder, his expression unchanged. "I hear you're starting a new computer class. I know you like computers. Your teacher, Mr. Parker, told me." He blinked and his head tilted, but there was no true acknowledgement in his face. Nicky made a show of looking around. "And where's Diya? She loves you very much, so she has to be nearby."

Nicky heard the tap-tap of toenails on wood, and Dyu'ami's dog sat down beside her. Eyes cloudy with age, Diya laid a pointed muzzle frosted with gray on Nicky's thigh. Nicky scratched small floppy ears and ran her hands through the ruff of fur around her collar. Diya's eyes closed, and she gusted a sigh.

"I need to go inside now, Dyu'ami." She gave the dog's reddish coat one last pat. "It was nice to see you." With a gentle hand, she tucked a loose strand of hair over his ear. She rose, and her gaze dropped to his dusty boots. Across the wide, scarred planks were half a dozen crude wooden carvings—bear, horse, buffalo—spaced precisely from smallest to largest. She frowned. Had they been there a few seconds ago?

The men on the porch had been silent throughout her interaction with Dyu'ami. But now one murmured, "Damn. He doesn't let anyone else touch him but Gemini."

Franco held the door open for Nicky, and she stepped into the house. It was only slightly cooler than the porch. The room smelled of cigarettes and sweat, burnt food and spilled beer. The bare wooden floor was scuffed and the upholstered furniture dull with dust. Tables held a multitude of plastic cups, stained paper plates, and food and candy wrappers, some of which had spilled to the floor. Two men sat on the sofa at the back of a large room—the grandfather and patriarch, Gemini Elk, and his son Clint.

Nicky and Franco approached the sofa and faced the two men. The officers waited as the men's kin, their boots thunking hollowly, gathered to stand around them.

"Clint?" Nicky said.

The younger of the two men stood slowly. In his mid-fifties, he was at least a foot taller than Roy, but otherwise similar in looks and shape. He used a balled-up handkerchief to wipe at his eyes. Gemini stayed seated, refusing to acknowledge her. He never did. She'd often wondered if he was on the autism spectrum, like Dyu'ami.

"Clint," she repeated. "I'm sorry to inform you your son Seneca is dead."

His eyes closed and his face crumpled, shoulders shaking in sobs. He keened a long, grief-stricken moan, and the Elk men joined together in his cry. The sound echoed and amplified in the crowded room.

A small, grubby hand slipped into hers. Dyu'ami stood beside her, dog hunched at his legs. His expression was still vacant, seemingly unaffected, except ... his fingers trembled. A high, mournful wail issued from his throat.

Nicky held his hand tightly and blinked back tears.

CLOUDS OF DUST rose skyward behind a phalanx of pickup trucks. One by one, they hit the blacktop road and disappeared over the side of the mesa as the Elk men—except for Clint, Mangas, and Gemini—headed into Albuquerque to pick up Seneca's body for burial. Dyu'ami played a handheld game, legs hanging over the edge of the wooden porch, Diya asleep next to him, snoring faintly. Some of the other dogs lay scattered in shade under a large tree in the yard or bumped and growled beneath the stoop.

Clint lowered himself into a red metal chair. Mangas towered behind him, arms crossed, a scowl on his face. Gemini had disappeared into a private part of the house before they came outside.

"You could have requested an ambulance to bring Seneca back," Nicky said.

"We knew when you found the horse what must've happened. Been preparin' for a burial ceremony since then. We honor him this way." Clint nodded at the settling dust. His voice wobbled, and the faint, sweet smell of liquor stained his breath. "He drown? An accident?"

His eyes almost pleaded with Nicky, which was ... odd.

"An accidental death by drowning can't be wholly assumed when there are no witnesses. We'll do a more in-depth investigation," she said. "Our working theory is that he went into the water to cool off and tainted air inside the tank caused him to get dizzy and pass out. Do you think this wasn't an accident? Both of his brothers committed suicide. Was Seneca depressed?"

"I should've gone after him." Clint bowed his head. "Should've gone."

Nicky knelt in front of him and lightly touched his knee. "Clint? I know this is difficult. We can do it at another time."

He waved a gnarled hand still stuffed with his handkerchief. Half of his pinky was gone, and his ring finger bent in a frozen kink.

"Now or later won't matter. Won't change the fact that Seneca's gone. You both found him?" He addressed his comment to Franco.

"Sergeant Matthews did," Franco replied. "I was in the area when her call came in."

"Checking brands, cow ranger?" Mangas said under his breath.

Nicky drilled him with a stare. She stood. "Your original missing persons call had us searching a few miles north."

"That's where we thought he'd gone," Clint said. "We got a herd of about fifteen head scattered around Mishtyətsi K'uuti. Black Mesa. Must've drove 'em over when he couldn't find water."

"Your brand's the Rocking E? Most of the cows around the slot canyon had that brand," Franco said. "Some didn't."

Mangas bristled behind his father. "You accusing us of something, cowboy cop?"

Franco took a step toward Mangas. Testosterone fumes from both men rose to suffocating levels. Time to divert.

"What's going on with your hands, Mangas?" Nicky asked.

He thrust his chin out, and red climbed in streaks up his cheeks.

"I'm next."

"Next what?" she asked.

"Official fetish carver, now that Seneca's ... gone." His eyes sheened with moisture before he blinked it back. "The tools are sharp. So are the stones." He held up hands so cut up, he could've been in a knife fight.

"You don't appear too happy about it."

"He's just started, so he'll cut himself a lot until he gets the hang of it. *If* he gets the hang of it," Clint said. He laid his own gnarled and damaged hands across his thighs.

"Looks like you might have trained to be official fetish carver, too," Nicky said.

"Nah. Horse bit this off." He splayed his fingers. "Busted this in a fight, thirty, thirty-five years past. Never got it fixed. Wouldn't have mattered, though. Gemini wasn't interested in giving up power until a year ago. He chose my boys 'cause I'm his youngest son." His eyes slid away, and he shifted in his chair. "That's the way of it. With Geronimo and Cochise gone—and now Seneca—Mangas is next."

Nicky rubbed her lip with a finger. The man's body language was off. Was he lying about something?

"Why'd Seneca go out alone, Clint?" Nicky asked. "It's been hotter than hell, and that's rough country."

"Aw, he lit out hoppin' mad. Had a big fight—"

Mangas's hand dropped to Clint's shoulder. His father pressed his lips together.

"A big fight? With who?" she asked.

"You know how full of juice Seneca is. He'd pick a fight with the wind if it stayed still long enough."

"What was it about?"

"Don't remember. Only that Seneca was mad, and it's always better if you stay out of his way when he's like that. I tried to call him that night, but he didn't answer."

"We didn't recover a phone," Nicky said. She glanced at Franco.

"Must've slipped out of his pocket on the ride. He's always losing his phone. Was." Mangas blinked rapidly and dropped his gaze away.

"Could we get his number? And if you find his phone, could you give us a call as soon as possible?"

They exchanged information.

"No one followed him?" Franco asked.

"He's done this before, a couple months back. Came home fine after a few days. His temper's always been bad, but he was on a real tear since Cochise passed." Clint's throat worked. "You try to keep 'em safe, to make sure their lives'll be better than yours. Then they're gone. No father should have to see his sons die before him." He blotted his eyes with his handkerchief.

"Do you want to stop?" Nicky asked. "We only have a few more questions, but some of them aren't easy."

"No, no. Ain't nothing going to bring my boys back. They're with the Creator and their ancestors now."

"Do you know if he took a wallet or ID with him?"

"What for? Wasn't going anywhere but the range," Clint answered.

"It's in his room," Mangas said.

"Could you describe the guns he took when he left?" The question was a gamble. She held her breath when Franco shot her a sharp look.

Clint scratched his chin. "Can't say as I know. He busted out of here in a hurry. But after Cochise died, Gemini gave him the Winchester 1886 with the brass breach and a pearl-handled Colt Lightning Storekeeper. He was pretty proud of them. That what you found?"

"No," she admitted.

"Those are some valuable guns to be carrying out on a trail ride," Franco observed.

"To us, their value lies in our heritage, not their price on eBay," Mangas said. "Our father took Seneca's guns off a Texas Ranger who strayed mightily out of his jurisdiction. A big man. Like you."

"Your father?" Franco glanced at Clint.

"An ancestor." Mangas sneered. "We don't think of time as a linear construct, Ranger."

"Mangas, maaku," Clint said sharply. "He's on the computer all the time, reading that crap. We'll call when we figure out what Seneca was carrying."

"Do you know if he took any alcohol or drugs with him?" Nicky asked.

Clint's eyes narrowed, and his mouth hardened.

"Alcohol, maybe. He was over twenty-one. But my boys don't do hard drugs, you hear?"

"'*Will we let ourselves be destroyed in our turn without a struggle,*'" Mangas said, "'*give up our homes, our country bequeathed to us by the Great Spirit, the graves of our dead and everything that is dear and sacred to us? I know you will cry with me, "Never! Never!"*'"

Nicky stared back and forth between the two men. She hadn't been expecting such a hard pushback when she'd asked about drug use.

"'*Return your sword to its place, for all who will take up the sword will die by the sword.*' Matthew twenty-six fifty-two," she countered. "Who are you quoting, Mangas?"

"The great Shaawanwaki Chief Tecumseh. Do you think we're stupid? Some dumb Indians you can trick into copping to a crime?"

"I asked because alcohol or drug intoxication might explain why Seneca drowned in chest-high water—"

"We're not gonna give you any excuse to come tear up our ranch, looking for drugs or taking our guns."

Nicky raised her voice. "—in a tank no one knew existed in the ciénega. A tank and windmill exactly like the one behind this house. Did you get permission from the Rangeland Natural Resources to erect it?"

Mangas stepped around the chair and stared down into Nicky's eyes, his own black and fierce. "You don't get it, do you? The US government may have put boundaries up to keep us contained, but we are Tsiba'ashi D'yini. We'll do whatever we want on *our* land, and the law and tribe can go fuck themselves."

CHAPTER NINETEEN

FRANCO'S UNIT dropped over the mesa lip and hugged the road cut into its side.

"That went well," he said.

Nicky chuckled. "Textbook. Sure seemed to hit a nerve. Maybe I shouldn't have pursued the drug angle so hard, but a bunch of those Elk boys have been popped in the past for illegal narcotics. With the condition of Seneca's body, I doubt they'll find anything on a tox screen." Her stomach tightened. Seneca's bloated face swam like a vision in her head, morphing alive, frightened brown eyes begging, mouth opening to ... what? Scream? Ask her for help before his eyes rolled white? "Interesting about the fight," she said.

"Best guess, he and Mangas went at it," Franco replied. "Maybe some of the damage to Mangas's hands was clumsiness with carving tools, but his knuckles were pretty swollen. It'd be nice to know what it was about."

Nicky twisted in her seat to face Franco. "You think Mangas followed him to the ciénega and drowned him?"

"Those guys seem more crimes-of-passion jack-holes. I could buy one of them pulling his gun in a rage, but to hold his brother under-

water until he's dead is stone-cold. It takes a long time to drown someone. Not like the movies."

The truck reached the bottom of the mesa, and he accelerated
along the straight two-lane road.

"The gun question was a good call," Franco said.

"Only if he took them with him when he left. If the guns were
there, if they were taken, it could have happened after he drowned."
Nicky stared out the windshield. "Maybe we should've pressed them
about the guns."

"Wouldn't have mattered. The only way we'll know if Seneca
took those or any other guns with him is if they tell us they're missing.
And if he didn't...." Franco shrugged. "We still have nothing but an
accident."

Nicky grunted in acknowledgement. They reached the main
road.

"Which way?" he asked.

"Right and past M'ida Village, then right again through Dyaitse
Pass. J WhiteHawk's shop's on the other side of the mountain, almost
directly behind the Elk ranch as the crow flies. You filled up with gas
this morning?"

"Yep."

"Good. It's about an hour-and-a-half drive." She let out a long
breath. "Dang. I meant to show Clint or Gemini the bear fetish from
Gianetta Green's car, but once Mangas started quoting Tecumseh, I
knew we were done."

"A real 'live free or die' moment." He cast her a glance. "What
was your biblical outburst all about?"

Nicky stared out the window. "It was quoted at me when I
decided to go to the police academy. Seemed appropriate."

"I'm guessing someone wasn't a fan of that decision."

"Yeah. Someone," she said quietly. "Anyway, Mangas is the only
member of the family with a militant edge. He's built up a lot of
hatred for authority, especially law enforcement."

"Can't say I blame him. If someone tried to take what was mine, I'd fight like hell for generations, too."

"Then you'd be fighting Native Americans. Their land first. When would it end?"

Other than sending her a glance under lowered brows, Franco didn't answer.

He slowed as they drove by the village. They passed a jumble of boxy adobe homes with pitched roofs interspersed between a few old pink and mint-green stuccoed storefronts. The town trickled to the edge of a mesa, single-wides and horno ovens placed haphazardly in scrubby land. The layer of air directly above the rooftops bristled with a field of old antennas and satellite dishes. A rectangular church with carved wooden doors sat perched on the highest point of the town, a large space behind it given over to the cemetery.

"Did you believe Mangas about Seneca's cell?" Franco asked once they were near the town's outskirts.

"I don't know why he'd lie."

"We'll need to get a warrant to dump the phone."

"Yeah." Nicky let out a frustrated breath. "It felt like Clint was lying about something, too."

"The drug angle?"

"Maybe. But he started getting antsy when he explained the fetish-carver succession." Her head suddenly throbbed, and she pressed her fingers into her temple.

"I have some aspirin in the glove box."

"Thanks." She extracted a couple of pills and swallowed them with leftover coffee. "Clint made it sound like becoming fetish carver was inherited after the guy ahead of you dies." A chill raised goose bumps over her arms, and she slanted the cold air vent away.

"You mean like killing off the favorite son to take his place?" Franco gave a low whistle. "Speaking of biblical, *that's* pretty Old Testament. Three out of four brothers dead in less than a year. Who was the eldest?"

"Geronimo, followed by Cochise, then Seneca." Nicky

exchanged a glance with Franco. "They died in the same order as their birth, oldest to ... well, Mangas is the youngest."

"Maybe we should check the tribal registry to see how succession has worked in the past."

Nicky drew in a deep breath, hoping it would stop the gnawing worry in her stomach. She picked up her phone to call the cultural center.

CHAPTER TWENTY

SUNLIGHT THROUGH TOWERING pines cast a rhythmic strobe of shadow and light over Franco's unit as he drove through Dyaitse Pass. Headache receding, Nicky picked out stripes of hot blue sky between trunks.

"I counted at least a dozen trees that looked ready to fall into the road," Franco grumbled.

"Since the warehouse shut down, the pass isn't kept up like it used to be," Nicky said. "I normally go east around the mountains, but it's a backtrack from the Elks' compound."

Franco slowed as he passed a small slide of dirt and rocks. "This guy WhiteHawk's not a tribe member but lives on the reservation. I didn't think they allowed that. He's a movie star?"

"And TV," she said. "Claims his father was Tsiba'ashi D'yini. Apparently, WhiteHawk got fed up with the Hollywood lifestyle and opened his store a few years ago. According to his autobiography—"

"His *autobiography*? You a fangirl or something?"

Nicky playfully pushed his shoulder. "Let's try this again. According to *Savannah*, who has read his autobiography multiple times and gets an autograph whenever she sees him, his family was Bitterroot Salish, and he was born and raised on the Flathead Reservation in Montana. After his mother died, he drifted down to Fire-Sky but never found out who his father was, although Savannah believes he must be from her elemental clan."

"Why?"

"WhiteHawk always wears earrings made of mother-of-pearl—the stone designation for the Water Clan," she said. "He ended up in LA in his late teens and started working as a model and stuntman. He had a solid acting career but drank or snorted most of his money. Divorced, no kids. Cleaned up a few years ago and approached Fire-Sky Tribal Council. Asked if he could open a business on the pueblo with his residuals."

"Why'd he pick Fire-Sky over Montana?"

"No family left in Montana, and it's warm here most of the year."

"Try ridiculously hot."

"Says the man from southern Arizona who did three tours in Afghanistan."

Glimpses of a large light-colored building flashed through the tree trunks.

"That's where we're heading?" Franco asked.

The road ran down to a sprawling warehouse complex, its flat white roof dotted with rows and rows of bubbled skylights. It was surrounded on three sides by forest, but the front faced a narrow grass-covered valley.

"Yes. That monstrosity was the brainchild of the tribal council as a way to get manufacturing jobs on the pueblo. Didn't work. Too remote. So now it's four point five acres full of jack-crap nothing." She hesitated, thinking of her mom's car. "Well, that's not exactly true. One of our automotive boneyards is here."

The road continued downward, paralleling a chain-link fence topped with three strands of barbed wire. Overgrown landscaping was brown and dry, the only color circular pops of blue morning glories woven into the fence and stunted clusters of orange-red Indian paintbrush scattered by the side of the road.

Franco slowed his unit as they passed a large sign peppered with bullet holes.

MUUK'AITRA MANUFACTURING COMPLEX

TRADITION, SUSTAINABILITY, TRIBAL BETTERMENT

A TSIBA'ASHI D'YINI PUEBLO COMMUNITY-OWNED ENTERPRISE

PURSUING OPPORTUNITIES THAT STRENGTHEN THE PUEBLO AND

ITS ECONOMY

FIRE-SKY DEVELOPMENT CORPORATION

EST. 1995

Nicky pointed to the open security gate. "In through here.

Franco turned and drove by an unmanned guardhouse into a crumbling parking lot that stretched to the back of the complex, the warehouse bordering it on the right. On the left, a single-story mini-mall with a red metal roof ran about 150 feet along the perimeter fence. Three older-model trucks sat near the first storefront. Franco parked his unit by a white pickup with the license plate WHT HWK and reported their location to Dispatch. Nicky stepped onto the sidewalk. An air-conditioning unit on the roof hummed.

"What is this place?" Beside her, Franco studied the darkened storefronts.

Two marquees, the plastic dirty and cracked, hung along the roof edge: BAABAA'S DINER and, farther down, FIRE-SKY MINI-MART. A canted sign in the diner's door announced it was closed. Scattered piles of dried leaves and pine needles littered the concrete sidewalk, and the dusty windows and peeling paint accentuated the pervasive emptiness and decay.

"The tribe planned to employ upward of five hundred people. Because it's so remote, they built retail space for a coffee shop, sundries—stuff like that. There's only one occupant now, J White-

Hawk Outfitters and Supplies. This store—or his website—is where Gianetta bought the paraphernalia I found in her car."

"What does the *J* stand for?"

"Don't know. He apparently modeled his stage name after that actor A Martinez."

"The guy from *The Cowboys*?" At her headshake, he said, "The John Wayne movie."

"I thought he was on *Longmire*."

Bells on the door of the shop tinkled as a man and woman hurried out, climbed into one of the vehicles, and left. The shop door had barely closed before three young men, all wearing ball caps and hunting camo, did the same. One carried a bulging plastic grocery sack, which he dropped with a thunk in the open bed of a primer-gray Ford. They swung into the cab with the grace and strength of youth, crowding onto the bench seat, and the truck started with a grind, the engine skipping as it rumbled to life, fan belt squealing loudly. The guy in the passenger seat leaned his elbow on his open window and mad-dogged Nicky as they backed out of the parking lot. She stared back, face impassive.

"Must do their own work," Franco commented. "Are we chasing WhiteHawk's customers away?"

The door opened again, and a middle-aged man, face ducked under the brim of his cowboy hat, limped quickly to the final old truck. He glanced up at Nicky and froze a second before nodding. She recognized him as a resident of Ruby Crest, one of the pueblo's villages. Like the others, he didn't linger.

"WhiteHawk deals in USDA commodities," she said. "Tribe members sell or trade what they don't want or need for extra cash. It's not exactly legal."

"So selling federally protected eagle feathers would be right up his alley."

"There've been rumors, but nothing ever sticks."

Franco made a noncommittal sound. "How do you want to do this?"

"I've met him a couple times, so we'll start friendly. See how he responds."

Nicky tucked her sunglasses in her pocket and opened the door. Bells jangled against the glass, and the air that brushed her skin was cool and tinged with sage and mint.

Nothing much had changed since she'd last been inside. At the back of the store, a hallway led to a restroom and a door marked EMPLOYEES ONLY. A rack of DVDs stood in the far-left corner, topped with a hand-labeled sign that read, J WHITEHAWK FILMS AND TV. On the wall behind it was an old poster of a much younger, chiseled, and lanky WhiteHawk modeling men's underwear in a Calvin Klein-like pose.

The whole left side of the shop was hung with photos of hunters kneeling next to trophy deer, elk, bear, and cougar kills, racks of survival and hunting gear, and taxidermy animal heads in heartbreakingly lifelike poses. On the right-hand side, a long glass showcase housed jewelry, pottery, knives, feather bundles, and shrink-wrapped smudge sticks. Nicky's stomach tightened at the army of carved stone animals inside.

J WhiteHawk stood in the middle of the shop, feet spread, arms crossed, and a faint smile on his lips.

"Sergeant Matthews. Welcome." His deep, velvety voice slid sinuously up Nicky's spine.

In his late forties, WhiteHawk was tall and lean, his shoulders straight and wide. His face wasn't conventionally handsome; instead it was rugged, with a bold nose and squared chin. His eyes were a light cinnamon brown—an unusual color Nicky always found herself wanting to study—under dark brows, skin deeply tanned. Black hair threaded with silver was pulled away from his face into a traditional bun on his neck, and round iridescent earrings covered his earlobes. He wore a chamois shirt, sleeves rolled to his elbows and muscles flexing under the smooth skin of his forearms. A huge Bowie knife was strapped along his hip. Faded camouflage trousers fell over a pair of well-used moccasins.

And the guy absolutely oozed charisma.

"Mr. WhiteHawk." Nicky extended her hand to shake his. "This is Conservation Agent Franco Martinez."

She scrutinized the interplay between the two men. About the same height, they sized each other up with posture and stance.

WhiteHawk shook Franco's hand. "How can I help you, officers?"

"We arrested a non-Native over at Hummingbird Mesa a few days ago with ceremonial supplies bought from your store." Nicky handed WhiteHawk the plastic bag with the receipt recovered from Gianetta Green's car.

He tugged a pair of black-rimmed glasses from his breast pocket and slipped them on. Jeez. The glasses made him even *more* appealing.

"Ah, Gianetta. One of my best customers. Wants to be Native in a big way."

"We've chased her off the pueblo more than once in the past few years," Nicky said. "But this time was different. We found a box in her car. Everything inside it was on the receipt." She held up the plastic bag with the bear fetish. "Except this. Could you tell us about it?"

He peered at the bag, shrugged. "I didn't sell her a fetish. Never have."

"But is it one of yours?" she pressed. "It's pretty distinctive. Maybe she ... took it."

WhiteHawk's laugh was deep and rich. "Gianetta doesn't need to *take* anything. She's got more money than she knows what to do with." He waved an arm at the glass case. "My fetishes are mostly for tourists, although I do have a few expensive ones I sell online. Nothing like that, though."

Franco held out another evidence bag. "She was using these juvenile golden eagle feathers to smudge."

"I did sell her a smudge bundle specially blessed by a medicine man from Jemez Pueblo." WhiteHawk took the bag and turned it over in his hands. "But it didn't include any eagle feathers."

Brows furrowed, he walked to the outfitter wall. An intricately beaded ceremonial spear was mounted horizontally about a foot from the ceiling. Large brown-and-white feathers tied with a leather thong dangled from one end. WhiteHawk stretched to touch a cut piece of leather. He held the plastic evidence bag up. The feathers matched in size and color.

"Would you look at that? Gianetta must have cut a couple of these off while I was in the back packaging up the rest of her stuff." He shook his head, single eyebrow cocked. "Some people...."

Nicky walked over to the wall. She pressed up on her toes, but her fingers were still two or three inches below the tips of the feathers. She dropped back down. "Yeah. Some people. But how did she reach them? I mean, she's all of five feet and change."

He shrugged, but his expression carried a subtle smirk. "Where there's a will."

WhiteHawk was such a charming liar. Smarter than anyone in the room. Excitement trickled under her skin at catching him out.

"Mr. WhiteHawk," Nicky said, "we'll need to see your tribal and federal permissions and permits for the feathers on the spear, and we'd like to examine the rest of your feather bundles."

WhiteHawk handed Franco the evidence bag, dipped his hands into his pockets, and rocked back and forth on his heels.

"Oh, I'm sure you already know I've never submitted any paperwork," he said.

Nicky smirked back. *Got him.*

"But, Sergeant," Franco interrupted, "don't we need a warrant?"

Startled, she whipped her head around and met his eyes. "If Mr. WhiteHawk gives us permission, we don't." He knew that. "Besides, those feathers are in plain view."

Franco pointed at the feathers tied to the spear. "Those aren't real. I mean, they're real, of course, but they're not eagle."

Nicky's gaze shot to the feathers, then to WhiteHawk's face.

WhiteHawk gave her a half smile. "Dyed turkey. Impressive, Agent Martinez."

Franco straightened his shoulders, eyes bright.

Like a big, stupid puppy.

"Also, Agent Martinez is correct on another point—you'll need a warrant to search the rest of my shop because I won't grant permission. I'd like everything to be official and aboveboard. I have a reputation to uphold in the community."

Nicky blinked at WhiteHawk, her mind scrambling.

"Mr. WhiteHawk, that's not the only reason we're here," Franco said. "Ms. Green's smudge stick was laced with a hallucinogen. *Salvia divinorum*. It's not illegal in the state, but...." His tone of voice was apologetic.

"Call me J, Agent Martinez." WhiteHawk grinned.

Franco grinned back. "Thanks, J. Call me Franco."

Nicky almost gaped.

"I don't do drugs anymore, Franco, not even the more innocuous ones like seer's sage. A life lesson hard-learned." WhiteHawk's expression was beautifully grim. "A Medicine man gathers and assembles the materials for my smudge sticks from the native flora found on the pueblo. If they were laced with salvia, you'll need to talk to Gianetta."

"B-but Gianetta, she said—" Nicky spluttered.

"Lawyered up, I'm afraid," Franco replied. He lumbered in front of Nicky, so close she had to step back. "Hey, do you outfit off the pueblo? I drew for bull elk in section twenty-one, down in the Gila. First rifle hunt in October." Franco and WhiteHawk turned their backs on her.

"Most of that section is wilderness. Do you ride?" WhiteHawk asked.

"I was stationed in the backcountry of Afghanistan. We got around on horses and donkeys."

Heads together, their deep voices rumbled back and forth. Nicky stood there, left out and flat-footed.

The doorbells jingled, and a couple of young boys darted into the shop, followed by a woman in her early thirties carrying a heavy plastic bag. The kids galloped to the glass case and pressed their noses against it, but the woman stopped short when she saw Franco's uniform. She swung the bag behind her, eyes wide.

"You've got a customer. Let me get my card," Franco said.

He hurried out of the door. The bells banged against the glass.

"Sergeant Matthews?"

She swiveled around. WhiteHawk stood too close. Nicky held her ground and angled up her chin. His brown eyes were flecked with gold.

"A police officer's salary doesn't go very far. Even with extra hours and overtime shifts." His smooth voice flowed over her, making the hair on her arms prickle. "If you ever come up short...." He handed her his business card, the printed phone number marked out by black ink and another number written across the bottom. "And I really didn't sell those feathers to Gianetta."

Nicky stared at the card, gut churning.

Without another word, she barreled out the door, passing Franco on the threshold. A wall of hot, dry air blanketed her bare skin. She breathed in deeply to replace the freezing air in her lungs with the purifying warmth surrounding her.

Funny. She still felt cold.

The doorbells jounced, and Franco was next to her, his hand warm between her shoulder blades.

"Hey. You okay?" He wasn't the slobbering fool anymore.

"I'm fine."

Suddenly his touch burned like fire through her uniform. She threw off his hand and pivoted to face him.

"Actually, no. I'm not. Just what the *hell* were you doing in there?"

CHAPTER TWENTY-ONE

THE STORE BELLS JINGLED AGAIN. "Everything okay, officers?" WhiteHawk asked. He straddled the threshold.

"Fine." Franco straightened to his full height. He crossed his arms and stared down his nose at her. "PMS-ing or something."

Nicky narrowed her eyes to slits. "Get back in your store, Mr. WhiteHawk. *Now.*"

The man's face darkened. He opened the door wider and took a step toward her.

Franco flapped a hand and flashed a reassuring smile. "I can handle her, J. Go see to your customer."

WhiteHawk's gaze darted between them. He nodded slowly and went back inside.

Franco grabbed her arm and tugged her away from the store, leaning down to whisper, "He's probably still watching. Resist a little. I'm trying to be obnoxious."

"*Trying* to be?" She yanked at her arm, but he wouldn't let go. "Dammit, Franco, you undercut me. Made me look like an idiot in front of WhiteHawk."

He pulled her to the far side of his unit before she broke free of his hold.

"He set us up with those feathers. They were fakes—good fakes—but it was too easy. He must have known we were coming, because the whole spear and cut leather was a trap. Think of the publicity if we'd arrested him and came up with nothing."

Lips pressed tight, she stared at him as she processed his statement. "They weren't eagle feathers?"

"No."

Nicky swept her gaze back toward WhiteHawk's shop. She dragged a shaky hand over her hair and flipped her ponytail. When she met Franco's eyes again, her chest twisted. His expression had softened. Confused and unbalanced, she wanted to step into his arms for comfort.

And it scared her to death. What the hell was wrong with her?

Franco reached to open her car door.

"WhiteHawk might still be watching," she warned.

He nodded and walked to the driver's side. Once Franco started the truck, he switched the air conditioner to high, letting the interior cool as his unit idled. He snagged a water from a small cooler in the back seat and handed it to her.

"Drink," he ordered.

She took a swallow. It helped clear the tightness in her throat.

"WhiteHawk wouldn't have anything illegal in his shop," she finally admitted. "He wouldn't be that careless."

"No. Let's get something to eat. It'll make you feel better."

He backed out the truck and started to turn toward the gate.

"Wait. I need to go to the boneyard at the back of the warehouse."

She didn't explain, and other than raised eyebrows, he didn't ask.

Franco drove the truck slowly along the side of the vast metal structure, past padlocked doors and dry, overgrown landscaping. At the end of the building, he stopped in an area littered with the crumpled husks of wrecked vehicles. They both got out, and Nicky stared past the fence. The wind soughed gently through the branches of the thick forest of conifers that ascended the mountain. A track snaked into the trees, wide enough for a four-wheeler. Her shoulders relaxed.

"PMS, Franco? Really?" Her voice was mild now. She walked to the warehouse door and punched in a code. The overhead light switch was directly inside.

"Sorry about that." He stopped a few feet in. "It stinks in here."

"Dead squirrel in the wall?" She meandered toward her mom's car. "Tell me what I missed with WhiteHawk."

"He doesn't like women," Franco said matter-of-factly. "A real misogynist. Been around guys like him all my life. Sports, military, law enforcement—they're collection points. You learn to pick them out because their internal animus toward females can send an operation into a tailspin real fast."

"Savannah said his relationship with his mother was glossed over in his autobiography."

"He's a fountain of misplaced rage. His mom held him too much or too little."

A slow smile stretched Nicky's lips. "Okay, now all you're doing is quoting Garland Greene from *Con Air*."

"Great movie."

"Macho porn," she quipped back. "Misogynist? Animus? Big, complicated words for the friendly goof I saw in WhiteHawk's shop."

Franco's lips hitched into a half smile. "You should see my dumb jock. Or my stupid redneck. They've been called brilliant."

"I forget sometimes you're trained for undercover work."

"It's its own kind of acting." He hesitated. "I stepped in because you read him wrong. But he read me wrong, too. He wanted to be the smartest guy in the room, so that's how I played him. It's how we'll need to play him in the future."

Nicky tugged her bottom lip. "You think he's dirty?"

"Yeah, but you saw how Gianetta acted when we brought his name up in the hospital. If he is, I doubt she'll give him up. In fact, I wonder if she was the one who called to warn him."

"Me, too." She grabbed a handful of car cover. "Would you mind helping me with this? Of all the stupid things, I left some apples for Savannah in the car. I don't know where my mind is lately. The spare key's in a magnet box in the wheel well."

"Why's your car here?"

"It's been broken into a couple of times, so I asked for permission to store it at the warehouse."

They rolled the canvas back, and Nicky knelt and blindly reached underneath. "It's not here." Had she accidentally taken it home?

He squatted beside her and palmed his belt. "My flashlight's gone." He frowned. "I swear I had it at the Elks."

Nicky smirked. "Check your pockets."

"I'd know if it was in my pocket." Franco stood and dipped his hands into his khakis. He pulled something out and held it up to the meager light. "An antler disk. How did you know?"

"I didn't know what specifically would be in your pocket, but when you said your flashlight was gone, I suspected Dyu'ami Elk traded."

Franco's eyebrows shot up.

"Swapped something that catches his fancy with something he's found or made," Nicky explained. "It's happened to me a couple of times."

"Is this you?" He held the disk out to her. On one side, a face was etched in delicate scratches. "It's pretty good."

"He's a pretty amazing kid."

"What's up with him?"

She smoothed her finger over the disk. "Autism. The story is Gemini woke up one morning and found Dyu'ami on the porch with a typed note saying he was Elk Clan. Gemini took to him right away, said from then on, this was his grandson. They did a paternity test and, sure enough, he's related. He doesn't speak and no name was on the note, so Gemini called him Dyu'ami, after the most famous Tsiba'ashi D'yini chief."

"He was abandoned? How old?"

"Seven or eight."

"He could have been a kidnap victim. The state or federal authorities didn't step in?"

"They tried, and the tribe threw every lawyer they had at them. Do you know the history of Indian schools? Indian adoptions outside their culture?" she asked dryly. "Genetically, Dyu'ami is Fire-Sky. No way they'd let the authorities remove him. And as much as I don't like the Elks, Gemini loves that boy and takes good care of him. Besides, if his mother abandoned him, he's better off without her."

He stared, brow knotted. She hadn't meant to sound so bitter and defiant.

"What happens when Gemini's gone? He's in his eighties."

"Hopefully the rest of his clan or the tribe will step up." Nicky put her hands on her hips and huffed out a breath. "I don't have a key with me. I'll have to come back late—"

Franco lifted the latch to the passenger's side door. It opened, and the console light popped on.

"I locked it," she said.

"Here are the apples." He passed her the sack.

She hefted it. "Did any spill out?"

"I don't see—" He stilled. "Nicky, did you leave a wooden box on the floor?"

"No." Hair prickled on her nape. "Not another rattlesnake, is it?" She tried to inject a note of humor in her tone, but her hand slid to her sidearm. During the Blood Quantum murders earlier that year, she'd found a rattlesnake in her unit. Quick thinking by Franco and Ryan had saved her from a nasty bite.

"Too small."

He picked up the box and shook it. Something clunked against the sides. They exchanged a look. Slowly, he lifted the lid, then handed the box to her. She tipped it, and a stone—a carved owl, no bigger than her thumb—dropped into her palm. It was covered in grainy yellow pollen. She stared at it for a few tense seconds before her hand curled around it.

"What is it?" Franco asked.

"It's a fetish. Someone left a fetish in my car."

CHAPTER TWENTY-TWO

"HAVE YOU BEEN HERE?" Nicky's voice echoed in the cool, high-ceilinged gallery of the Fire-Sky Isgaawa Cultural Center and Museum, an unexpected stop before lunch. The curator had called on their way back to the station, saying he'd already retrieved Nicky's requests.

"First time," Franco replied.

A few tourists stood quietly in front of glass-encased pedestals holding incised polychrome pottery and ancestral black-on-white bowls, some whole, some carefully pieced together from collected potsherds. All were beautifully illuminated from above.

"Pieces by Fire-Sky artists are included in the exhibits," Nicky said. "Most of the newer stuff's for sale."

Franco slowed as he passed an intricately etched, monochromatic pot. He let out a low whistle. "Over a thousand bucks. I think I chose the wrong career."

Nicky led him around a curved wall made of stacked ocher and brown stone and into a hallway ending in a glass double door. A sign read, LIBRARY AND ARCHIVE: ENTRY RESTRICTED.

She pushed inside, and a bewhiskered head atop thin shoulders popped above the circulation desk. Fluffy white hair—including the semicircle of a beard—completely surrounded the man's face. The lack of a mustache gave him the appearance of a gentleman firmly entrenched in the nineteenth century. Nicky grinned. Nothing could be further from the truth.

"Nicky!" Faded blue-gray eyes twinkled behind tortoiseshell glasses. He hurried around the desk and gave her a tight hug, patting her enthusiastically on the back. "I was so excited when you called." He whirled to Franco. "Ah! And this is your partner?"

"Franco Martinez, Dr. Dean MacElroy, head archivist and curator, and marathon runner extraordinaire. He holds the over-sixty record for the Fire-Sky Mountain March."

"Pleasure." Dean stuck out a wiry arm, the white cotton sleeve of his dress shirt rolled up to his elbow, his narrow tie askew.

"Franco's working with me on the Elk Clan case."

"Yes, yes. The tragic death of, what? The third brother? I read about it in the *Dzeeni W'aachən'i*. The *Talkative Tongue*."

He rushed back around the desk, reached underneath, and heaved out a stack of three old books.

"Tribal registry." He gently flopped it open. "This page starts the Elks. Some very good pictures attached. This"—he placed his hand on a second book—"is a photo compendium of tribal, clan, and family heirlooms. About, oh, a dozen years ago, the council had their own 'Antiques Roadshow' at the Sruisiya Community Center." Dean chuckled, the skin around his eyes crinkling like a pleated fan. "Plenty of pictures of old rifles and guns in there. And this one contains clan photos going back over a hundred years. I bookmarked a few pages." He rubbed his hands together. "Now, I've got to run to a meeting about our next exhibit. Wedding and fertility vases! Leave everything on the desk when you're done. And Nicky, don't be a stranger."

"Thanks, Dean. This is great." She gave him one more hug, and he dashed out the door.

"Does he ever slow down?" Franco asked.

"As long as I've known him, he's gone a hundred miles an hour."

She leaned on the counter and peered at the large rectangular pages of the tribal registry. Franco settled in beside her, radiating warmth. Her stomach flipped. With effort, she stayed still, suppressing the urge to use their proximity as an excuse to press closer.

"So, what's the big deal about this book?" he asked.

"It's the official record of the tribe's membership, close to three hundred years old, but it stretches back further because of meticulous oral histories. Even now, youngsters memorize lineages at their grandparents' knee," Nicky said. "Keeps tradition alive."

Spidery handwritten names, birth and death dates, and occupations changed from the original Colonial Spanish to English and Keres in the last hundred years. Photos taken for Smithsonian monographs and treatises were affixed to the pages—faded brown tintypes and cabinet cards of stiff tribal members in traditional dress. Nicky never liked those pictures. They reminded her of Audubon's paintings of birds and animals, stuffed and posed to entertain a distant audience.

"Those early priests sure liked their *begats*. See anything interesting?" Franco asked.

"Lots of deaths, especially women in childbed." She grimaced and flipped to another page. "Here's Dyu'ami. Father and mother unknown, but he's in the list of Gemini's grandsons."

"None of Gemini's—what?—five sons claim him? He also has three daughters. Could one of them be the kid's mom?"

"Dyu'ami had a Y chromosome test. He's Tsiba'ashi D'yini through a male line."

"Gemini have an illegitimate child?"

"Not just him. Any of his brothers. He denied it, but he could be lying or doesn't know." Nicky trailed her finger down the list of names.

"No one's marked as fetish carver other than Gemini," Franco noted.

"I doubt the church allowed it before. Suppression of traditional customs ran rampant even into the nineteen eighties. Here." She tapped the page. "Gemini's grandfather Welcolm lived into his late eighties. And his great-grandfather Simón, early nineties. Maybe their position allowed for better food or something. You see how the tribe takes care of the Elks now."

"Doesn't seem to be stopping the deaths. Look. Simón and Welcolm were sons of the youngest son. Confirms what Clint said."

"Gemini's older brother died in his teens. Huh. No cause of death, only the date. I'll make a note to ask Dean if there's any significance." Nicky took a close-up of the information. "Let's check the clan photo album."

She opened to the first ribboned page.

"'Elk Clan, elemental clan Earth, circa 1944,'" she read. "Here's Gemini. Wow. Except for the dark hair, he looks a lot like Dyu'ami." She opened to the next flagged page and found a black-and-white wedding party photo from the *Talkative Tongue*. "'Gemini Elk and his new wife Elizabeth Shiochee from the Little Badger Clan, elemental clan Sky.' Look at their clothes. This must be right after the traditional ceremony."

"The woman to Elizabeth's left isn't Fire-Sky. Her dress and ornaments are different."

Nicky bumped his shoulder and caught his eyes with a smile. "Good catch." She scanned the accompanying article. "'Her Pend d'Oreilles maid of honor traveled south to celebrate the joining.' The name means 'hangs from ears.'" White shells dangled down from her head and over her shoulders.

"Ryan's been schooling me on Fire-Sky culture and traditions. He says outsiders tend to lump Native Americans in one big pile."

"Including some of the outsiders in the Fire-Sky Police Department," Nicky said dryly. "Let's check the heirloom pictures."

Franco opened the book to the first ribbon. Faded color photos covered one page.

He tapped a picture. "Here. Gemini's holding a Colt Lightning

Storekeeper and a Winchester 1886 with a brass breach, both 1877s. The ones Clint identified as Seneca's."

"Elk Clan treasures they'd want back. If he did take these weapons with him, maybe they were recovered before his body was found." Nicky raised a brow and met Franco's gaze. "There's a couple of problems with that theory, though."

"Yep," said Franco. "Who retrieved the guns, and why didn't they report his death?"

CHAPTER TWENTY-THREE

From her home in Bernalillo, Nicky zipped north onto I-25, on her way to work for more Saturday overtime hours. Her commute to the border of the reservation—the freeway crossed through tribal land—took about twenty minutes.

An old boundary sign caught her eye:

Welcome to the Fire-Sky Pueblo
Tsiba'ashi D'yini
INDIAN LAND
NO WOOD XAULING
NO XIKING NO SXOOTING NO FISXING
NO TRESPASSING EXCEPT
BY PERMISSION OF TXE
GOVERNOR OF TXE PUEBLO
VIOLATORS WILL BE PROSECUTED
DO NOT LITTER

No one could tell her why only some of the *h*'s were replaced with *x*'s. Or why the tribal governor would give permission for trespassing.

She flipped a switch on the console.

"Two-one-three, Fire-Sky."

"Two-thirteen," a flat, feminine voice replied.

"Good morning, ma'am. Ten-eight in district, I-25 at the two-five-eight exit."

"Ten-four, zero-seven hundred hours. Good morning, Sergeant. Following Captain and Chief to the meeting with the governor?"

"No, ma'am. Overtime shift and paperwork."

"Never ends. You see the fire over on the left side after the turnoff?"

"Fire?" Nicky answered sharply. With the late monsoons and everything tinder-dry, a wildfire across the reservation would be devastating. She accelerated down the off-ramp and sped under the freeway bridge, heading west. Her unit crossed the railroad tracks on the other side with a rapid double thump.

Smoke snaked above the scrub brush to gather in an opaque brown-black haze above. It pulled into a smeared contrail higher in the air. The fire had obviously burned for quite some time.

Dammit. Hair prickled on her arms.

"Copy, Dispatch. Has FER been notified?" she asked.

"Yes, two-thirteen. Fire, EMS, and Rescue notified. Both Chief and Captain called it in separately a few minutes ago. ETA ten minutes."

"Are Captain and Chief on scene?"

"Nope. Couldn't be bothered," came the flippant reply.

Her jaw clenched. "Two-one-three en route. I'll wait for FER arrival. Dispatch, and out."

Nicky yanked the truck left onto a paved side road that quickly turned to dirt as it wove in and out of the flat, scrubby lands. Her unit surged, pressing her back in her seat as she hit the accelerator. She was pretty sure she knew where the fire had originated.

Green Meadow Springs was an unincorporated area that in no

way, shape, or definition resembled meadows, springs, or green. Surrounded on three sides by reservation land, it was filled with old trailers, junked cars, and individuals who didn't want anything to do with law enforcement. Cockfights, nonpermitted structures, and potential meth labs abounded. It wasn't unusual for tires and other piles of debris to be set alight, resulting in the greasy black smoke Nicky could see in the distance.

But as she topped a hill, the smoke suddenly resolved into a trailer fire. Her unit slithered to a stop on a wide dirt clearing in front of the structure. She set her brake and quickly studied the scene.

A small shed to the left of the actual fire was already a black husk of twisted aluminum—probably the origin. But flames had jumped to the larger structure, a mobile home attached to more permanent construction that ran its length.

Two men futilely sprayed the fire with a garden hose. About a dozen people, some still in pajamas, cups of coffee in hand, gathered nearby to watch. Large swaths of desiccated grass and weeds blanketed the ground between the hodgepodge of derelict residences, the perfect tinder to spread the fire to the rest of the community.

Nicky radioed Dispatch, then stepped out of her unit. Not yet eight in the morning and it was already hot. Sweat prickled under her light body armor and across her forehead, only to be instantly dried by the start of a wind kicking up. Not good.

One of the men dropped the hose and ran up to her. About fifty, stocky, and bowlegged, he had a face creased by hard living, his brown eyes bloodshot. He reeked of stale beer and turpentine and wore a wrinkled chambray shirt, jeans, and work boots splotched with white paint. A cigarette hung between his lips.

"Is everyone out?" She hurried toward the fire, the scent of smoke acrid and heavy.

He took a long drag on the cigarette and threw it on the ground. Nicky stopped and stared at him. He blinked back, then glanced at the still-smoking butt before he mashed it into the dirt.

"Sorry," he mumbled. "We think so, but...."

"But?" Her heart raced. They were close enough that the heat watered her eyes. Nicky circled around to the far side, away from the fire. "Who lives there? What happened?"

"Luna and DeLeon Guerra, 'cept he's up in Santa Fe Main. They got a couple of kids. Luna paid me—I'm Larry Chris—and Buddy, er, Milton Trelivas over there"—he gestured to the man with the garden hose—"to paint the house and trailer. We were mixin' the paint in the shed, and it caught fire." His paint-spattered fingers burrowed into a breast pocket for a crumpled pack of cigarettes. "Don't know how." He lit one up, cupping his hand to shield his lighter against the gusting wind.

"Really?" Her response was clipped. She couldn't help it. "You're sure the mom and kids are out?" Nicky walked along one side. The windows were barred, a precaution against theft in a potentially lawless region. Thick black smoke billowed over the top of the house, but the fire didn't seem to be spreading that rapidly along the structure.

"She left before"—he waved the cigarette—"to drive her niece somewhere. Pretty sure she had the boy." A curtain moved, and a child's sleepy face peeked over the sill, his cap of straight black hair mashed up on one side. He patted a fat little hand against the glass. Larry Chris stiffened beside Nicky, cigarette stuck to his upper lip. "Jesus. Guess not."

Nicky's knees felt watery as she met the child's eyes through the dirty pane of glass. She grabbed the bars and yanked futilely. Fingers scrabbling, she searched for a way to open the window, but the bars were too close together to pull the child through.

Bolting to the front door, she twisted the handle. Locked. Wisps of smoke trickled from under the triangular piece of siding that held up the roof. She almost dropped in horrified realization. There was a pitched roof over the house. The trailer's real roof was probably flat, which meant the area above it was open—the perfect space for the fire to hide, expand....

Explode.

She had to get the kid out *now*. A fake fern stood beside the door. She knocked away the pot. Prayed for a key underneath. Nothing.

Steps thumped beside her. "Luna left us these." Cigarette Man dangled keys. She reached for them, and they slipped from his hand. They jingled as they hit the porch. "Sorry."

He bent, arm extended, in her way—

Nicky, fingers clawing, snatched them up. Her hands shook as she unsuccessfully tried the first, the second—the third key undid the lock. The faint whine of sirens caught in the wind, then disappeared. Still too far away. Now thick smoke streamed from the crack above her. She yanked open the heavy metal screen door, unlocked the solid door behind it, and shoved it inward. A tabby cat darted out between her feet. Nicky spared it a glance as it raced away. Larry Chris stood frozen behind her, his eyes wide.

"Get off the porch!" she screamed.

He ran, and everything inside her shrieked to follow him. Nicky thrust it down deep in her chest, ducked low to avoid the dark gray air congealing above her, and stepped inside. The air was breathlessly hot, and a subdued rush of sound pressed down from above. She stood in a large living area, the metal wall of the trailer cut away to expand into the built-on kitchen on the opposite side. A long hall ran down the middle of the house, hazy with smoke. From the window's placement, the child's room had to be behind the kitchen.

Nicky tasted chemicals. She coughed and pressed her sleeve over her mouth and nose. Her eyes watered and blurred as she ran down the corridor and opened the first door she found.

The toddler stood in a crib, hands pressed against the window, head turned toward her. He smiled. The room, thank God, was clear of smoke.

"Hey, sweetie." Her voice shook slightly. The child wobbled toward her on the squishy mattress and held out chubby arms. Nicky quickly wrapped him in a blanket, covered his head, and tucked him against her chest. A loud *whoosh* from the rear of the trailer stuck her feet to the rug. Aghast, she stared through the doorway. Smoke boiled down the hallway lit orange by flames. By opening the front door, she'd fed the fire. Her rational mind vied with bitter fear.

Run. *Now.*

Nicky clutched the child tighter, dodged left under the smoke and heat, and charged into the living room. She burst outside, stumbled, and fell into the yard and the arms of a khaki-suited fireman. A yellow helmet and breathing apparatus covered his head and face. Someone took the baby as the man dragged her away from the house.

Stumbling, she peered over her shoulder, eyes streaming. Flames blasted from the roof and out the front door. A few seconds more and ... and....

Her knees melted, and black spots marred her vision.

The fireman yanked off his headgear.

"No, Nicky, don't think about it." He pressed the breathing mask over her face. "You're safe. The baby's safe."

Another firefighter appeared. "Anyone else inside?" His muffled voice was insistent.

Breathing, coughing, Nicky rasped, "Unknown."

She hadn't checked any other rooms, couldn't. What if there was another kid? *What if...?* Her smoke-caused tears became real. She looked up at the man who held her.

Golden-brown hair topped worried hazel eyes.

"Ryan," she whispered.

"Keep breathing. I got you."

CHAPTER TWENTY-FOUR

THE HARRIED DOCTOR at the Fire-Sky Health Center clinic—Nicky didn't catch his name—pressed the cold head of the stethoscope against her back, directly above her body armor. Goose bumps peppered her arms, and she suppressed a shiver. Why did they always have to keep these places at refrigeration temperatures? Ryan stood just outside the curtains by her request.

"Now give me a deep breath. Good. Again...."

At the end of the third and deepest breath, she barked a cough, and the doctor yanked out his earpieces.

"A little irritation. You'll be fine." He turned to tap on the keys of his laptop.

Nicky shifted on the bench, paper crackling beneath her, and tucked her hands under her thighs. "You never answered my question about the little boy."

A high-pitched wail penetrated the room. Her chest tightened.

"Nothing wrong with his lungs," the doctor replied. "I'm sending your prescriptions to the pharmacy—something to soothe any breathing irritation and for the headache you complained about."

"I didn't complain," Nicky said. She stared unblinkingly at a gap in the curtains. Why wouldn't the kid stop crying? Why wasn't anyone comforting him? She hopped to the floor and grabbed her soot-stained blouse, suddenly desperate to calm the baby.

"Okay, Officer. We're done here." The doctor, laptop in hand, exited the alcove.

"You dressed?" Ryan stepped into the room.

"Could you hand me my stuff?" Nicky, her attention focused on the crying baby, gestured at the plastic bin holding her duty belt, cuffs, sidearm, phone, and everything she'd emptied from her pocket —keys, owl fetish, wallet.

Ryan scooped up the fetish. "This is a tsa'atsi y'aauni. Where did you get it?"

"Someone left it in my mom's car. I know you said not to keep a fetish or kachina if you don't know who made it, but...." She shrugged.

"Then why do you carry it?" He handed her the fetish, and she slipped it into her pocket before she again worked the buttons on her blouse.

"Because it feels right, I guess." The baby's cries were louder now, more agitated. Her fingers shook.

Ryan crossed his arms, his expression grave. "When they are done properly, the maker prays and sings, and his emotions are caught inside the creation. They settle the caregiver's spirit. If this was left for you and it feels good, keep it with you. It will protect you." He thrust out his chin at her and frowned. "It probably did today."

Heat flared at his tone of voice. "I don't want a lecture, Ryan."

A nurse slipped into the space, bouncing the sobbing child. "You said you wanted to see him—whoa!" The baby lurched, chubby arms reaching out to Nicky.

She scrambled toward him, blouse half buttoned. The nurse transferred the child to Nicky, and she cuddled him close, the knot in her chest loosening. He tucked his head on her shoulder, and his sobs dwindled to hiccups. Nicky swung her hips, rocking and swaying. With a murmur, the nurse left.

"They cleaned him up," she said. "I'll get him all dirty again."

Ryan stepped closer. He brushed a hand over the little boy's head. "I don't think he cares."

"What's his name?"

"Han."

"Like Han Solo?"

"Han Guerra. His mother's on her way."

Nicky shot him a narrow-eyed glare, her anger once again bubbling up. "She left him. He could have—"

"No. His mother didn't leave him alone. One of the neighbor kids was watching him. He was asleep, she ran to go home to grab her cell phone ... Nicky, let me take you home. You've already had a long day and it's not even ten."

She hugged the baby closer. "I'm fine. I need the overtime hours."

"You're exhausting yourself."

"Like I'm the only one. You should see the circles under your eyes."

"Ten fires in two weeks." He scrubbed a hand over his face. "We've suppressed them, but if one gets loose ... Fire chief's canceled all leave, and I've been pulling doubles." Ryan drew in a breath. "Nicky, we have to talk about today."

He wasn't going to let it drop. "Fine."

"What you did was incredibly heroic and amazingly stupid, especially after...."

"What? After I saw that gray spirit-man? To meet him is a warning of death, isn't that what you said? Well, I didn't die. And neither did this child." And while Ryan was here and she had his attention, "And what's the deal with the white eyes? Are they somehow linked with death, too?" Her words poured out faster. "Because this little guy didn't have them, and he was in way more danger than that gang member at the sting—"

"*Stop*. You need to hear this. That fire. A few seconds later ... if you'd been trapped...." Ryan cleared his throat, tried again. "If you'd been trapped, would you have been able to—"

"But I wasn't."

"Listen to me!" His voice was sharp, and the baby stirred in her arms. "That fire spread so quickly, you might not have succumbed to smoke inhalation first. You could have burned. It's an agonizing death. I've seen it, had buddies..." He sucked in a huge lungful of air. "Your weapon, Nicky. Would you have had the strength to ... do what needed to be done under those circumstances? Not only for yourself, but for the child?" His eyes glittered with emotion.

"I know you carry a gun."

"So do you. Could you do it?" His gaze was steady. "Because if the answer is no, don't ever, *ever* run into a fire again."

"But we're trained to run toward danger." Nicky rubbed her cheek on the toddler's hair. The little boy sighed in his sleep and snuggled closer, and she never wanted to let him go. "It's who you are. It's who I am."

"I know," he said quietly. "And it scares the hell out of me."

The nurse stepped through the curtain. "I hope you don't mind, but some of the staff want pictures of you and the baby. And there's someone out here who wants to see you." She called over her shoulder. "Officer?"

Franco jerked the curtain aside, jaw rigid, shoulders tense. "What the *hell* do you think you were doing? For God's sake, Nicky, you're not Superwoman. You could have been—" His voice choked.

Nicky glanced at him then looked away, blinking hard. Franco's eyes were glazed with moisture—and something else she wouldn't put a name to.

"Why is everyone yelling?" She slid a trembling hand over the baby's head.

"This the little guy you saved?" At her nod, he stepped closer and with a low, rough voice said, "Do you know how good you look?"

Nicky's throat constricted, and she closed her eyes.

Franco's warm lips brushed her forehead. "Nicky, there are some things a woman isn't physically strong enough to—I mean, a woman shouldn't, can't—"

"*What?*" The warmth she'd felt only moments before evaporated like a drop of water on a burning-hot skillet.

"Now who's yelling?" Ryan muttered, but at the sight of Nicky's glare, he retreated.

Smart man. Not like the idiot standing in front of her.

"We need to have a talk about the danger you continually put yourself in." Franco stopped, blinked, and took a half step back. "Uh, Nicky?"

The curtain zipped open, and a young Hispanic woman darted inside, face blotchy, eyes swollen with tears. She screeched a sob and fell on Nicky and the baby. The child woke with a start, and the woman snatched him into her arms.

"You did this. You saved him. Gracias a Dios, thank you! I owe you a life debt for rescuing my son. Remember that." The boy let out a wail, and the woman pivoted to one of the nurses now gathered in the room. "Está bien?"

As the staff reassured the boy's mother, Nicky grabbed both Franco's and Ryan's shirt collars and dragged them closer. A blaze of heat ran up her neck.

"Both of you, listen." She ground out the words. "Don't you *ever again* treat me, Savannah, or *any* woman like we're some fragile flower, shocked and surprised when we act decisively."

Ryan's eyes widened, and Franco's brows shot up.

"Men *always* underestimate a woman's strength." Dropping her hands to her hips, she stared back and forth between them, teeth clenched. "And you two should know better."

Franco opened his mouth.

"No. Don't say anything." She finished buttoning her shirt. "Now. I'm going to take some pictures with that sweet little boy because I'm damned proud of what I did. So, suck it."

CHAPTER TWENTY-FIVE

NICKY STARED at the medical diplomas hung on the sky-blue wall of Julie Knuteson's office, her friend and contact at the Albuquerque Office of the Medical Investigator—OMI.

Cold metal slid across the skin of her hand, followed by a tug with the forceps.

"And, done. I love a number eleven scalpel blade for stitches. Cuts like butter." There was a satisfied edge to Julie's voice.

"Thanks," Nicky said.

"I appreciate you taking your Sunday afternoon off to come in for my little show-and-tell. Working on a live patient is a bonus." Julie turned Nicky's palm to the lamp. "This healed really fast. You'll have a scar. Keep it covered for another week at least."

Nicky leaned back in her chair. "Franco expressed doubt about the healing skills of a pathologist."

"That cutie. What does he know?" Julie's tone was indulgent. "You slept with him yet?"

"No." Heat shot up Nicky's neck. "How's Brian?"

Julie's expression told her she wasn't fooled by the change in subject. Yet she stripped off her glove, held out her left hand, and wiggled her ring finger. The large diamond sparkled in the fluorescent lights above them.

"Engagement's back on. I'm chalking up dating a psychotic killer after I dumped poor Brian as a rebound relationship. Maybe I'll write a book: *In the Arms of a Modern-Day Frankenstein.*" Julie shuddered and sobered. "Guess I'm lucky to be alive. Anyway, I'm supposed to meet Brian downtown for dinner tonight, so let's get back on topic." She tipped her head to the side and gave Nicky a brilliant smile. "Thanks for the Seneca Elk autopsy. I love, love, love me some bloated, melting drowning victims."

"I found him, which wasn't all that pleasant, either." And drank contaminated water. And saw Seneca's scared face in her nightmares.

"After he dried out a little, it was a quick, gooey autopsy, even though identification took a while. Sorry I couldn't be more conclusive about cause of death, but since no one saw him drown, I had to put *undetermined*." She shrugged. "You said he might have recently been in a fight? Unfortunately, osmosis and hypotonic conditions caused his cells to swell and lyse. Tissue sections showed massive damage, but no definitive bruising. Tests aren't back yet for drugs or alcohol, although I doubt we'll find anything for the same reasons."

"Was there anything that could indicate a struggle?"

"Not really." Julie stared at her. "You're thinking this wasn't an accident?"

"We're working on the theory someone else was with him at some point."

Julie hummed and nodded before she bustled over to a glass cabinet filled with antique medical tools and utensils that resembled instruments of torture, but there were a few bottles with old-fashioned labels: QUAKER BITTERS FOR DYSPEPSIA & BLOOD; TINCTURE OF CANNABIS INDICA, U.S.P.; THOMAS ECLECTRIC OIL FOR ALL THAT AILS YOU. She plucked out a widemouthed, black-lidded specimen jar.

"This is what I wanted to show you." She handed Nicky the jar. "Those were in Seneca Elk's stomach."

Nicky held the bottle at eye level and shook it gently. Immersed in clear liquid, a handful of creamy, almost translucent stones tinkled against the glass, one as big as a marble and another ...

"Is one of these rocks shaped like a ... gummy bear?"

"Yeah. Guess so." There was a note of surprise in Julie's voice.

"What are these? Were they on the autopsy report?" She'd read it but couldn't remember anything about rocks.

"I had no conclusions. People eat weird things. I think that's what we're seeing here." She hesitated and shrugged. "There's even medical terminology for it—*pica*."

"I've heard of it."

"Yeah? Comes from the Latin for *magpie*. In adults, it's usually associated with mental illness or anemia, but not always."

"But don't people get other kinds of stones in their body? Like gallstones?"

"Kidney stones, bezoars, otoliths. Gastroliths are found in some animals, but they eat rocks for a purpose, like in bird gizzards. The ones I found in Seneca are more like gastroliths. That's why I think it's pica."

Nicky put the jar on Julie's desk and took a photo with her cell, but the final product wasn't great. The surrounding glass and glare from the overhead lights distorted the stones.

"Do you have better pictures?"

Julie sat down at the computer and tapped the keyboard. Nicky sat next to her, eyes on the screen.

"Why didn't you call me about this?" Nicky asked.

"I didn't think it was important, but this morning I was shooting the breeze with one of the other pathologists. You know, shop talk. Bizarre ways people die. Who'd caught the worst autopsy recently. Seneca definitely qualified for the last one." She scrolled through a series of gruesome photos.

"Cops do the same thing, except with callouts and arrests."

"I bet. Here they are. Roll through while I finish cleaning up."

The stones lay in a line spaced precisely from the smallest to the largest. The odd-shaped one was at the end. Nicky straightened at the strange tingle of déjà vu.

She clicked the mouse. The next photo was a close-up of one of the three smaller stones. A second click and the two larger stones filled the screen. Leaning closer, she studied the bumpy one. It really did look like a stone gummy bear. She hit the print icon, and the color printer hummed to life.

Julie continued, "I brought up the pica and the stones, and our new pathologist perked up. I don't know if you've met him yet. Tomás Greenberg? He was hired to replace David Saunders after"—she exchanged an eye-rolling glance with Nicky—"you know."

Nicky nodded. Until earlier that summer, she'd grudgingly worked with Saunders, who'd been a medical examiner at OMI. She'd never trusted him, with good cause. But he hadn't deserved to die the way he did.

"Anyway, Tomás said he had a case around Christmas from the Fire-Sky Reservation where he'd found small stones in the dead man's sinuses. A suicide."

Nicky swiveled to stare at her. "Who was the suicide?"

"Cochise Elk, Seneca's brother. Maybe it's genetic or some weird mental illness that runs in the family."

"Huh. I'm gonna choose door number two, Monty. Most of the Elks seem to have serious problems with authority and women, bordering on pathological." She paused. "You said you *think* this is pica. Why wouldn't it be?"

"Here. Look." Julie clicked through a few more slides and stopped on a close-up of the marble-sized stone. "See this area? How it's not smooth like the rest? That type of patch is on all of the rocks—exactly the same topography under a microscope. Like these rocks were ... *attached* to tissue, like this area was some kind of ... I don't know ... umbilicus."

Nicky chewed her lower lip and stared at the picture on the screen. "Could you do me a favor? Could you get these analyzed?"

"Sure. I know a guy at New Mexico Tech who could do it."

Julie picked up the jar of stones and held it up to the light. Her brow puckered.

"That's weird." She gently swirled the glass.

"What?"

"I pulled five stones from Seneca's gut. Now I count six."

CHAPTER TWENTY-SIX

Nicky stood at her desk, hands on her hips. Some jack-hole had stood a flashlight in front of her keyboard. A blue nitrile glove covered the end, fingers inflated with trapped air. Well, at least the middle finger was.

Good morning, Monday.

She peeled the hot-pink sticky note off the metal shaft:

Since you crapped up a crime scene and lost your flashlight, Captain asked me to get you a new one.

No name, but she knew who'd written it. Manny Valentine was one of Captain Richards's crew, officers hired by the pueblo but all connected to the New Mexico State Police. They'd formed a tight group, an old boy's club who had each other's backs and pretty much no one else's.

Nicky stripped off the glove, slotted the flashlight onto her belt, and scanned the busy police station, contemplating her second major problem of the day. Manny Valentine had been the first cop on scene at Cochise Elk's suicide, and she wanted to question him about the case.

Why couldn't her job ever be easy?

She found Valentine at the break room table, lounging back in a chair, coffee in hand.

"See you found your new flashlight."

A searing flare of anger blurred Nicky's vision as she seriously contemplated wiping the smirk off the man's face with her fist. Then she blinked, taken aback by the amount of rage that had swept through her over something so stupid.

But whatever had flashed over her features must have sobered Valentine. He straightened in his chair, a crease between his brows. Lieutenant's morning briefing started at seven-thirty. She had about fifteen minutes to extract something useful from him.

Nicky purposefully held his gaze a few beats longer than was comfortable. The man was a bully, and she'd had enough experience to know how to handle them. He actually started to squirm before she broke eye contact and poured herself coffee. Her hand hovered over the artificial sweetener before she grabbed the real sugar. Extra energy for her little chat with Valentine.

She sauntered across the room to loudly drag a chair over the linoleum and sit down across from him. They both squared their bodies, elbows on the table. An officer walked into the break room, glanced at them, pivoted, and left quickly.

The topographic maps had been pushed to one side, and yesterday's *Albuquerque Journal* was spread out and open to the sports page. A spirit dish sat at the far end of the table.

"Why are you always such a dick to me, Valentine?"

His smug sneer returned. "Am I? Or is that all you think about, Matthews?"

Walked right into that one. She took a sip of coffee, hoping the caffeine boost would help clear her head. Maybe she should grab a donut. She'd skipped breakfast because of an upset stomach.

"I need to talk to you about Cochise Elk's suicide."

"What about it?" He picked up his coffee. The cup shook the tiniest bit.

"You were first officer on scene and filed the report."

"So, read the report." He slid back his chair and made to stand up.

Her hand shot out and grabbed his wrist. In all their past confrontations, she'd never touched him or vice versa. Maybe that was why he didn't pull away. A powerful surge of energy zapped through her, and it felt good. She tightened her grip before she slowly uncurled her fingers and let him go.

"Sit down, Officer Valentine."

He sank in his chair, face brick red.

"I've read the report. I want your impressions."

"I don't remember."

"Try."

Nicky stood up and got a donut. She offered the box to Valentine. He stared at her, lips thinned, then examined the box's contents and snagged a maple bar. Figures. She hated maple bars.

He took a bite, beige icing flakes getting caught in his mustache. "When I got there, the vic was in some trees behind the house."

"Did anyone go with you to the scene?"

"No. I made them point out the area and went alone. But it was already contaminated because a bunch of those goddamned Elks had already cut him down."

"What did you find?"

"You saw the pics."

Nicky stared at him.

"Laid out flat on his back, arms by his side, charred rope around his neck, the skin of his torso and face blackened by the fire. He'd used gasoline. The container was nearby. Rest of the rope was tied over a tree branch. Best I could tell, he'd slipped on a noose, climbed onto a crate, and set himself on fire. Guess he really wanted to get the job done." Valentine's voice had lowered until it was difficult to hear. He took another bite of his donut.

"So, they saw the fire and ran out...."

"Not until they heard screams. His father thought Cochise had gone out for some purification ceremony." He waved his half-eaten donut. "Everyone interviewed said Cochise had been acting strange."

"How?"

"Outbursts, fighting—more than usual," Valentine replied. "Woke up screaming, banged at his head with his hands, complaining about headaches. One minute he'd be babbling, the next he'd stare off into space, and no one could get his attention."

"How long had he been acting strange?"

"Couple months."

Nicky ran a thumb over the bandage on her palm. "The tox report indicated drugs and alcohol in his system. Could he have gotten hold of something tainted?"

"The family wouldn't say. Clammed right up when I asked."

"Why didn't you file a warrant for his medical records?"

"What for? I'm not like you, Matthews. I don't drive the BIA and FBI crazy with unnecessary warrants and what-ifs. I'm efficient."

If by efficient he meant lazy.

"The death was an obvious suicide. What are you looking for?" he asked.

"I don't know yet, but three brothers dead—Geronimo, Cochise, Seneca—in less than a year. Both Geronimo and Cochise, possibly Seneca, acting erratically."

"You think their deaths are related?" He made a rude noise. "These guys were self-destructive dumb-asses. Whole family's messed up."

One of the day-shift officers stuck his head through the doorway. "Hey, Lieutenant's ready for briefing."

Nicky and Valentine stood, glaring at each other.

"One more thing, Officer Valentine. Did you see anything or anyone that seemed out of place? Maybe something you didn't put in the report?"

Like the gray man she'd seen in her photo? Or what she'd experienced at the tank? A chill cut through her.

His brow furrowed then cleared.

"Yeah. That kid. EMTs had taken the body, lights dismantled, everyone was gone, and he appears out of the trees like a ghost. Scared the shit out of me. I flashed him with my light and asked him his name. Didn't say a word. Just held out his hand."

Dyu'ami, Nicky thought.

"He wanted to give me a fetish, but I know better than to take stuff like that. They'd accuse the police of stealing—again." He snorted. "Then Old Gemini showed up, and they left." He ran his fingers over his mustache, wiping off the icing flakes. "I remember thinking it was so dark, that kid could have been out there the whole time. So, we done here?"

At her nod, Valentine dumped the rest of his coffee in the sink and started for the squad room.

Nicky quickly finished her donut, topped off her coffee, and settled into the back of the room, only half listening to the lieutenant.

There were too many similarities between the Elk brothers' cases. All three of them acting erratically before their deaths. Cochise and Seneca with stones in their body. She wasn't sure about Geronimo, but maybe there was a way to find out.

After the briefing, she hurried out to her vehicle and headed to Geronimo's descanso.

CHAPTER TWENTY-SEVEN

Nicky's unit bumped through dried hummocks of grass, a billow of fine soil boiling up around her truck. There was no road out to the place where Geronimo Elk had committed suicide, and she hadn't been to the site since that day. She scanned the valley, burned gray and tan by the drought. All she had was the remembrance of Scalding Peak's silhouette and the surrounding vista as she'd stood by his car a year earlier.

Metal winked in the distance, and Nicky steered left, bracing herself as she drove through narrow ruts carved by the hooves of cows, horses, and deer. The descanso that marked the place where Geronimo died stood out on the flat plain, the silvery cross decorated with bright plastic flowers. She slowed her truck to a crawl, and the tail of grit behind her drifted into fine particles. A good, hard rain would cleanse the air, but a light drizzle would cake everything it fell on with mud. Adobe rain, they called it.

No one she'd asked knew who had placed the memorial. It wasn't the Fire-Sky police or

tribal council—Nicky had checked. Perhaps the Elk family, though Geronimo's widow was adamant they hadn't.

Nicky swept up the bunch of red carnations she'd bought at a Fire-Sky mini-mart on the way. The heat magnified their spicy scent, and her nose twitched. She walked to the descanso, knelt, and laid the flowers at the foot of the cross. There was no writing on it, no date, no name. The slab had been poured into a circular iron mold, flush with the earth, a common base for descansos. The second step of the tier was also circular, the edge of the metal frame crimped over the cement. The cross stuck up from the middle.

Nicky took a deep breath and started a slow walk around the marker, eyes on the ground.

Geronimo had placed his gun barrel under his chin. He'd been... unrecognizable. Would she find them? Creamy stones like those Julie Knuteson had removed from Seneca's stomach? Like those found in Cochise's' sinuses? Head down, focused, Nicky spiraled outward in ever-widening circles, mechanically wiping the sweat from her face. Though she bent to examine a few rocks, she found nothing similar.

Then, about twenty feet out, she spied a series of flat stones, half buried in soil baked by the sun. She swept the sole of her boot over a rock, caught and unearthed it. Rectangular, brown red, like those used to chink stone walls. She kicked at a second one. The same. A quick search showed none of the rocks in the vicinity matched. These stones must have been brought to the site. Nicky prodded areas covered with dirt and sand and found the flat stones had been placed in a complete circle around Geronimo's memorial.

Nicky stood at the back of the descanso. Her gaze drifted to the shrine, and she narrowed her eyes. *What the...?* She hurried back and dropped to a crouch. On the lowest tier of cement, rocks were piled into a small pyramid. She touched the single stone at the top and yanked her hand back when the structure crumbled.

Dammit. She hadn't meant to—

Nicky sucked in a breath. A black bear fetish, tiny spearhead attached to its back with a thin strand of twisted gut, peeked out from under the dislodged rocks.

She took a series of pictures before she hurried back to her truck to grab zipper bags from her evidence kit.

Her phone rang, piercing the quiet. She glanced at the screen, surprised she had a signal. Dean MacElroy from the cultural center.

"Father Dean," she said.

"Hello, Nicky. Not Father anymore. I gave that up when I married Maureen, God rest her soul. I'm calling because I found the answer to the question you left me about cause of death for those ancestral Elk Clan members. There's a list of dictates for the book, but I couldn't remember where I'd read them. My mind isn't what it used to be."

"Stop fishing for compliments. I think it's one of the seven deadly sins."

"Thou shalt not fish?" He chuckled. "Anyway, I found the instructions. It appears the priests who started the registry requested two causes of death be left out of the book to keep the records spiritually pure."

"And those causes are?" Nicky squinted at the light glinting off the descanso's metal cross.

"Suicide. And homicide."

CHAPTER TWENTY-EIGHT

It was dark when Nicky stopped her unit next to the huge black SUV sitting in front of her house. She rolled down the passenger window and exchanged a long look with Kevin Archibeque, Dax's driver. Archibeque curled his upper lip the tiniest bit. What an ass. She sighed deeply and swung into the gravel driveway.

Light glowed from the kitchen window, and the front door to her home was cracked open. Again. Nicky pushed it open and stepped into the hall. The whole house smelled delicious. Her stomach growled.

And the doorknob felt ... sturdy, tight in her hand. She flipped on the hall light and studied it.

"Dammit, Dax," she called. "You can't keep breaking into my house like this. Is this a new lock? Did you really have a new lock installed?"

Dax walked into the hallway, wearing a purple-and-green plaid apron over his uniform. Lifting the heavy black bag from her shoulders, he pecked her cheek. "Stop whining. I got your text and decided this would be the best place to talk. Quiet. Private. On the downlow."

"Yeah, because no one will notice the big black cop car in front of my house." Nicky scrubbed the spot of his kiss with the back of her hand. "On the down-low? Really? Wife out of town?"

"You're being childish. Come on. I made dinner."

Nicky stopped, hands on her hips. "What's this?" Her bag rested on one of two new ladder-back chairs tucked under a small table set with flatware and mismatched plates from her pantry. Ridiculous in the apron and enormous oven mitts, Dax placed a steaming, bubbly casserole on a trivet in the middle. She shifted her bag to the floor and dropped heavily onto the chair, smothering a yawn.

"You needed a real table," he said. "Let me get the salad."

He settled across from her as she drank iced sparkling water from a purple metal cup. She had a stack of them in all different colors, inherited from her grandmother, but hadn't used them in years. When she was six, she'd scraped the paint off the rim with her teeth to mark this cup as hers. She'd told Dax about it back when they were together and felt herself softening toward him. Not good.

"I want all the keys to the new lock." She scooped chicken, creamy sauce, and vegetables onto her plate. "If I find you in my house again, I'll shoot you."

"Locks, plural. I had the side and back door changed, too." He fished his hand into the front pocket of his trousers. "Every key. I promise."

"What do I owe you?" Nicky tucked the keys by her plate.

"Nothing." His mouth seemed to droop, but the light was dim, so she couldn't be sure.

"Hmm. Now why don't I believe you?" Nicky took a bite of food. It was really good.

Dax spooned casserole onto his plate.

"Okay. How about information? What do you have on the Chen Cano snitch?"

"Not much other than I think whoever's leaking is feeding NCIRC deconfliction reports to their contact. But it's not easy getting records without raising red flags and Chief Cochin is already suspicious of me asking. I'm meeting—" She clamped her lips shut. She'd go through the deconfliction reports after Dax left since she was meeting with Franco the next morning to discuss their progress. Dax didn't need to know that. She wasn't sure how he'd respond. "I've been really busy. I don't know how much time I can devote to this project."

He crumpled his napkin, laid it on the table, and leaned forward. "Then let me give you some incentive. We've found a website—hidden, with a darknet address. Chen Cano and the Crybabies have an illicit marketplace set up—Mercado Měishí, the Market of Delights. Customers can purchase anything with cryptocurrency. Guns, explosives, drugs, sex, slaves. You can buy torture. Murder." His lips pinched tight. "There are ... video clips of horrible things."

Dear God, he was a manipulative bastard. She laid her fork down, appetite gone. "You shut down the site?"

He held her gaze for a long moment.

"Didn't you?" She reached across the table and grabbed his wrist. "Dax."

"If I shut it down, Cano will know he's being surveilled. Besides, it'll pop up somewhere else with more layers of security. It's a small advantage we need to exploit." Dax laid a hand over hers. "I need you to trust me with this, okay?"

"Trust you." Nicky scoffed. She tugged her hand away.

"Don't let your personal feelings about me, our past—anything—interfere with how we do our jobs."

"I've seen how you do the job."

"The CampFire Casino raid?" He shrugged. "Sometimes you have to do the hard thing to get the biggest payoff."

"You're okay with people getting hurt or killed for a headline?"

"No. But taking down the entire operation justifies the sacrifice." Dax's face softened. "You never liked playing the long game. You're all about running into the fire."

Nicky swallowed and dropped her gaze. She hated this type of compromise.

"I need you to double your efforts. Find who's behind these leaks. I've got to go." He stood, untied her grandmother's apron, and draped it along the back of his chair. "You were out of food again. And coffee. I stocked up."

Dax headed toward the front door, phone in hand. She followed. He stopped and turned at the threshold.

"Nicky. Let me help you out. No strings. I promise."

"No." She was shaking her head even before he'd finished. "I'll do this myself."

"Then you'd better hurry. You don't have much time left, do you?" Dax opened the door, and a wave of warm air surrounded them. He strode into the courtyard, phone already pressed to his ear.

CHAPTER TWENTY-NINE

THE WAITRESS SLID a plate of scrambled eggs, bacon, and hash browns in front of Nicky. Butter melted atop pancakes stacked on a smaller plate. Franco sat across from her behind a huge Denver omelet smothered in green chile sauce, a frown on his face.

They'd asked for a secluded booth in the back of a generic breakfast chain in Rio Rancho. Sunrise was at least an hour away.

"We can shut down Cano's website," Nicky said. Damn Dax and his political compromises. "I have a contact in FBI Cyber Crimes—"

"No. We can't shut it down."

Lips pressed tight, Nicky fixed her coffee—two packets of sugar instead of sweetener for a blossoming headache—and took a sip. The burn of frustration and worry simmering in the pit of her stomach would be harder to get rid of.

Franco's expression softened. "I hate it, too. But we'll need to keep that site under wraps as long as possible. Once the Feds figure out what's going on, they'll crawl all over it and we'll lose our edge."

It was almost ironic that he and Dax both thought the same way, wanted the same thing. She searched Franco's gaze. How would he react if he knew about her partnership with Dax, a man he held in contempt? She wanted to be upfront and honest, but he wouldn't understand her tangled relationship with her former lover. She wasn't even sure she did. But if she lost Franco's help, lost his support....

Something akin to panic jumped along her skin. She ruthlessly suppressed it and forced a smile. "And you know how badly the Feds can mess things up on the rez, DEA Agent Martinez."

His lips curved in return. "That would be funnier if it wasn't true." He forked a bite of his omelet, gaze on her face.

"Then we have to find out who's tipping off Cano," she said. "It's our best shot at getting inside his operation. What have you got?" She didn't want to go first. Didn't want to lay out what she'd found in the deconfliction logs last night. That might make it real.

A large tablet lay at his side. He handed it across the table.

"NCIC criminal analysis maps of the I-40 corridor between Gallup and Albuquerque, and I-25 between Socorro and Santa Fe. A friend of mine put together all arrests from the past year connected with Chen Cano's gold-leaf brand. Launch the 'CA map Albuquerque Only.'"

Nicky opened the interactive map. Pink dots, each representing a drug arrest, dropped like rain onto the displayed satellite image of the city. Pulses of color blossomed before fading away.

"Waves of arrests occur when Cano's drugs hit the streets, then slow until the next shipment," Franco said. "But there's no specific schedule, no pattern—like drugs arriving at the beginning of each month to take advantage of paychecks or welfare distributions."

"Random," Nicky said. "Not easy to track. I'll cross-reference the Fire-Sky deconfliction logs to see who accessed the database before peak arrests. Whoever did could've tipped Cano's gang off to operations, could be our leaker."

Her hands tightened on the tablet. What if the dates confirmed her suspicions? Appetite gone, she pushed her plate of half-eaten food to the edge of the table.

"Sounds good. But what I really want you to see are the CA maps of the reservations lining the freeway corridors."

Nicky swiped the screen. There were half a dozen files. "Which one?"

Plates out of the way, she propped the tablet on her empty coffee cup and shifted down the banquette so he could sit. Franco's arm slid along the back, and he angled his torso toward her. He smelled of soap and a faint woodsy aftershave, and radiated warmth. Nicky hadn't realized how cold she was until then.

"Here's an overview of the reservations and the freeways." His voice was deep and low, his lips close to her ear. "This time, the drug arrest circles won't disappear." He hit play and, once again, pink drops rained on the screen.

The results were breathtaking—but only if you didn't understand Indian Country.

"Except for Green Meadow Springs, which is private land, there are no arrest overlays for Cano's stuff on any of the pueblos," Franco said. "I was pretty confused until I ran controls for domestic abuse, robbery, DUI. All three CA maps showed the same thing. No crime in Indian Country, and we both know that's not true." He shifted to stare into her eyes, his thigh pressed along hers. "So, why?"

"Some tribes don't share criminal convictions with NCIC. It's a sovereignty issue. They don't want the Feds in their business. Considering historical precedence, they have a point, but I think it's shortsighted. I've pushed for disclosure, and Chief Cochin supports my efforts. It would result in access to more federal resources and targeted interdiction, but the Fire-Sky Council won't allocate the funding." She blew out a sigh. "Hopefully, once Luz Cochin is elected to Council, she can change that."

"I knew it was too good to be true, but it got me thinking," Franco said. "For the past year, there've been very few arrests associated with Cano's drugs on Fire-Sky land, right? Even though the sting and these maps proves he continues to transport and sell in the region. This could point to a motive for our collaborator."

"What?"

"Protecting his or her People from narcotic exposure. Some kind of agreement or contract. Cano keeps his drugs off the pueblo in exchange for information on police operations."

"But it also means the continued trafficking of drugs and victims. And what about the people affected by the drugs that get through?" Heat suffused her neck and face as anger grew, driving away the chill. "In Gallup or Albuquerque or Denver or anywhere else?"

"Maybe that was a compromise our snitch was willing to make."

Chest tight, Nicky stared at the screen as it replayed the blossoming drops, leaving the Fire-Sky Pueblo clear of color, as if caught in a drought of crime. Like playas in the desert, it was an illusion.

Franco's arm dropped over her tense shoulders. He hugged her, briefly pressing his cheek against her temple. Nicky closed her eyes. Some of her anger dissolved, but she purposefully left a tiny fire kindled.

He released her and moved back to the other side of the table.

"You've downloaded the deconfliction database logs?" he asked. A manila file folder lay near a rack of syrups.

"Yes, but I had to go through Chief Cochin to do it. Told her I needed it for case review. I'm not happy about lying to her, and I don't know if she believed me. Since I'm not certified, she wouldn't give me access to the digital files for legal reasons."

"The NCIRC program can't be accessed remotely?"

"It's not set up that way because of the potential for abuse. What happened with state police when they busted our sting was bad enough. Imagine if the targets of an operation are notified and meet the police with guns drawn?" Nicky opened the folder and handed a stapled sheaf of papers to Franco. "This is what I have. Spreadsheets for the past year. On average, two to four total log-ons per day, minimal users, all passworded. Police and Conservation, lieutenants and up, including Director Vallery, Captain Richards, and Chief Cochin. I spoke to my lieutenant about Captain's usage and found out he opens the website every morning before briefing."

She'd left one name unsaid: Savannah. Nicky stilled as he read over a spreadsheet. The waiter came by and silently topped off their coffees. Franco took a sip, flipped the page, paused, flipped it back. The corners of his mouth tightened.

Finally, he spoke. "Nothing fell out?"

She didn't answer directly. "We don't even know if the deconfliction records are how Cano's being tipped off. The CA maps aren't correct, so keeping drugs off the rez might not be the reason for the collaboration."

"But everything fits. I mean, if this alliance does keep Cano's drugs off the pueblo, what better way to punish the Crybabies for reneging on a deal than to bust them in the act? To *not* tell them about the sting operation. It's just...." Franco shifted, brows knit. "This gang is vicious. Why haven't they retaliated against the collaborator for loss of revenue? Unless the informant was absent or somehow unable to tip them off."

Nicky licked dry lips. He was thinking out loud. And coming too close.

"Or it has nothing to do with the deconfliction database." She flashed him a glance and quickly dropped her gaze at the intensity of his stare.

"Maybe," he said, voice low. He pushed the papers away and sighed. "Let's hold off on the deconfliction files right now."

Some of the tension flowed out of Nicky at his shift away from the database.

"Based on criminal analysis maps, Chen Cano's been moving product from Mexico to Albuquerque and beyond with relative impunity for about a year," he said. "What happened before that?"

"Police, including state and tribal, were popping one or two shipments a quarter. Last summer, during a chase on I-25, five human trafficking victims were killed in a crash. After that, drug activity dropped off on the pueblo significantly. Since the crash coincided with Captain Richards's zero-tolerance policy for drugs on the rez, he thinks his program's the reason. But I've always felt like something was off."

"Why?"

"Because we've had operations like Richards has implemented in the past. Once the police let up, the drugs flood right back in. Only they haven't this time. It's like a … a protective circle surrounds the pueblo, which is ridiculous." Nicky rubbed absently at her palm. The scar was barely noticeable. "Richards is also parlaying his success into a super-secret consulting business everyone knows about."

"If he's our snitch, this could be about money and ego for him," Franco said. "Who else?"

"Chief Cochin. Like a lot of places, addiction is a scourge in Indian Country. An aggressive drop in drug crime under her watch can only enhance her reputation for toughness. Motives—power? Historical context?" At Franco's raised eyebrows, Nicky clarified, "First woman ever elected to tribal council."

"What about Director Vallery?"

"He's well-respected on the pueblo. Combating drugs could mean more grants, higher salaries. Other than that, I can't come up with a specific motive except money. Same with the lieutenants."

"Cano paying for information. Does Fire-Sky monitor its employees' bank accounts or spending?"

"Yes. The pueblo instituted background checks every five years for all employees because of the temptation of all that casino cash. Mine's scheduled later this summer."

"What's the process?"

"They hire an outside firm, so no conflict of interest even though Vallery and Cochin review the final reports. They audit arrests, complaints, bank accounts, look for anything odd or out of place. A couple years ago, one of our officers was fired because of a domestic he didn't report. Another had to go to rehab for a drinking problem."

"But if Vallery and Cochin view the final reports, there's still a possibility of a cover-up if one of them is our informant. What if I use my DEA contacts to examine their finances?"

"With what probable cause?"

He shrugged, and Nicky caught her breath. Every time she thought she knew him, he stepped out of the box she'd fit him in.

"I don't want to cross that line, Franco."

He nodded but didn't look happy. "The crash last summer. You said drug arrests on Fire-Sky dropped off after it occurred."

"It could be the inciting event. Timeline's right." Nicky chewed the inside of her lip. "Two of the five who died were kids, so it was all over the news. It didn't have to happen, either. State police got aggressive and wouldn't back off."

"Did the guards or driver talk?"

"The driver was killed. Another man jumped the median to the other side of the freeway. He was hit by a car, but he got up and ran into the desert. He was never found." Nicky swirled her coffee and stared at the rippling black surface. She raised her eyes and froze. Franco's gaze stabbed into her.

"Savannah has access to the deconfliction database." His voice held an edge. "Did you think I wouldn't notice?"

Her eyes widened. She hadn't distracted him. *He'd* distracted *her*. Sat next to her, comforted her, led her through a series of questions to lower her guard.

Manipulated her emotions. *Just like Dax.*

Anger spiked, but she shoved it away. Lips twisting into a smile, she waved her hand dismissively.

"That's nothing. We funnel her our official operation e-mails. Place, time, participants." Nicky craned her neck and touched one of the rows on the page, only to curl her fingers away. Her hand was shaking. "She accesses it for her morning meeting with Vallery. So what?"

Franco flipped to the next page and tapped it. "But she's also on late at night."

Nicky took a breath to calm her roiling stomach. "We all work late to catch up on paperwork."

His eyes narrowed. He shuffled through the papers. "There's a missing sheet."

The cold was back, settling deep in her core. With stiff fingers, she withdrew a single piece of paper from her file and handed it to him. Franco's gaze moved over the page, and his mouth flattened. She swallowed as he brought hard eyes up to meet hers.

"Savannah was off the pueblo the week before the sting operation," he said.

"Her father had a series of doctors' appointments and tests at the VA. They stayed with her aunt in Albuquerque, but she was back the day before—"

"Why'd you hide this? Do you suspect Savannah?"

"She loves her People."

"Enough to tip off Cano and keep drugs off the reservation?" Franco's shoulders dropped. "Have you talked to her about this?"

"No."

"Then *we* need to talk about Savannah."

The kindle of flame she'd kept burning inside flared at his words. "No."

"She has access and motive and—"

"*No*. I won't—" Nicky choked, face hot. "Savannah's my best friend. She's *your* friend."

"Her brother *died* because of drugs."

"Then maybe her dad and mom are behind this, because it *devastated* them, too!" Across the restaurant, heads swiveled. "Maybe it's a *huge* family conspiracy, and her whole clan is in on it!"

"You said the system is passworded. How often are they changed?"

Nicky blinked, startled by another swing in topic. She answered automatically: "The IT department assigns our computer rights and passwords. Changing anything is an administrative process."

"So, an immediate global password change would probably tip Savannah off if she's Cano's collaborator."

Her jaw dropped. He'd done it again. Jerked her around like she was some kind of puppet.

"No kidding," she said. "You get a gold star."

His brows snapped together. "Knock it off. I don't believe Savannah's involved, but we need to figure out who is. We need to do our jobs, and lately you've been unpredictable and overwrought, and—" Franco clamped his lips closed.

"And *what?*" Her voice shook. "Not only am I *physically* not strong enough to do my job, now I'm not *emotionally* strong enough, either?"

"I didn't mean—" He wiped his hand over his mouth.

She sat, unmoving. When he didn't say anything, didn't apologize, *didn't take it back*, she slid out of the seat, threw a precious twenty-dollar bill on the table, and left.

CHAPTER THIRTY

NICKY'S PULSE pounded and the acrid fumes from the cars and trucks in line for gas stung her nose. Standing at the pump, she peered around the large truck blocking her unit from view of a knot of men in front of the mini-mart. Laughing and high-fiving, they milled around a parked pickup truck.

Her phone chimed. She glanced at the screen and swallowed. Just the man she needed, even after she'd stormed out of the restaurant, even if what he'd said about her emotions struck a nerve.

Even if what he'd said was true.

"Franco—"

"Nicky, we have to talk."

"Stop," she ordered. "Listen to me. Has tribal council designated a special hunt or stalk?"

There was a brief silence.

"Nothing till September."

Next to her, the pump clicked and gurgled as it filled her vehicle. Seven-thirty in the morning and it was already hot under the canopy. She wiped her forehead with the back of her hand.

"Remember those three young guys who mad-dogged us at

WhiteHawk's last week? They're at the Little Aquita Gas and Go, decked out from head to toe in camo, truck bed full of a dark brown animal with fuzzy branched horns."

"Antlers, not horns. Deer or elk. The fuzz is velvet." Franco's voice held an edge. "Nicky—"

"By the size of the *antlers*, I'd say they have a large elk. They haven't seen me yet." The metal nozzle made a loud clack as it automatically shut off. She drew it from the side of her unit and slotted it into the gas pump with a clatter.

The man in front of her watched the hunters as he filled up. When the green nozzle in his truck clicked off, he turned. His eyes widened as they met hers.

She leaned toward the guy and mouthed, *Leave*. He nodded, finished his transaction, and hurriedly climbed into the dark blue pickup. Nicky got a face full of black smoke as he gunned the engine.

"How far out are you, Franco?"

"I just exited the freeway onto tribal land."

Twenty-five minutes away. Goose bumps swept her arms as the truck in front of her drove away. She was exposed to the celebrating crowd. One man caught her eye, stilled, then hurried into the store. Others rotated and saw her. They scattered. She climbed into her vehicle and started it up.

"Nicky." Franco's voice was sharp. "Did you call for backup? Call now or get the vehicle license number and let them go. If they poached that elk, they're armed." He paused. "These guys won't be intimidated by you. They don't—won't—respect a female cop."

A female cop. Nicky's face and neck flared with heat. She squeezed the phone.

"Really? Well, guess what? I'm getting pretty used to that."

She terminated the call, tossed her cell into the passenger seat, and started her unit. Tires squealed as she angled hard right and parked behind the elk-filled truck to block its exit.

By the time she secured her vehicle, only the three guys she'd seen at WhiteHawk's remained.

She keyed her mic to Dispatch.

"Two-one-three, Fire-Sky. Start me an eighty-two. Little Aquita Gas and Go."

"Ten-four. Backup direct and en route. ETA fifteen minutes. Agent Martinez called it in. Fire-Sky, two-one-three."

Damn Franco. Her breath hissed between clenched teeth. He didn't think she could handle these jokers.

"Forty-nine?" Dispatch asked.

"Three male suspects." She relayed the license plate. "Large elk in their truck bed. Possible poaching."

"Ten-four."

Nicky signed off and sized up the suspects. She tracked movements, expressions, but especially, she watched their eyes. They glared at her SUV, leaned in to talk to each other, all of them shifting from foot to foot, bodies twitchy. The short one on the end—the one in moccasins—would bolt as soon as she opened her door. The middle one in the Raiders ball cap? He'd give her the most trouble. He was the one she had to control.

She pushed a button by the steering column, grabbed her keys, and slotted them in a deep pocket in her slacks. Her unit stayed on, blowing cold air.

Nicky stepped out onto the pavement, movements slow, purposeful, every sense awakened and sharp. With deliberate fingers, she unclasped the snap on her ASP baton. This close to the bed of the truck, she was struck by the sweet stench of blood and the uriney, musky odor of fur. But the smell hadn't turned. The animal hadn't been dead for long. Sunglasses on, eyes hidden, she examined the scene without alerting them to her intentions. Stepping forward, she ran her fingers over an antler tine, the waxy velvet prickling.

Shorty—the one she'd predicted would run—stayed put. Nicky felt a twinge of disappointment.

The men exchanged a series of quick glances before Raiders Cap took a half step forward, chin thrust out.

Yep. She'd called that one. Nothing but grief. Excitement prickled.

Nicky measured the distance across the pavement. Maybe fifteen feet. She stood in the V of their truck bed and the driver's side of her unit. Trapped if they decided to rush her. Her heart pounded, throbbing to the tips of her fingers. She widened her stance, relaxed her lips into a half smile. Her right hand tightened on her ASP.

"Hi, guys. Sergeant Matthews with the Fire-Sky police. May I see your hunting licenses?" Her voice sounded appropriately calm to her ears, but her already-tense shoulders tightened further.

"We found it on the side of the road," Raiders Cap said. "Hit by a semi. We could use the meat, so we took it."

He was Native but not Fire-Sky. The cadence was off.

The little guy squeaked and bolted. His friends flinched, heads snapping around to follow his retreating back. The second guy cursed softly.

She grinned. A little off on her prediction, but she'd take it.

"Then I'll need your collection permit," she said. "Any big game —whole or parts—found on the Tsiba'ashi D'yini Pueblo may not be possessed without the permission...."

Nicky blanked.

Panic bit as she frantically searched for the words. "Without permission from...."

"We're not from around here," the second guy said, his voice cracking. He looked at his buddy. "Give her the elk. We got the money."

"Shut up, Willy," snapped Raiders Cap. His lip curled as he eyed Nicky up and down. "Start the truck. This won't take long."

At his boast, her panic cleared, and her focus sharpened. "Without permission from the Tribal Conservation Department," she finished. "Money? What money?"

She caught Raiders Cap's eyes and braced. With a bellow, he charged.

Nicky freed her ASP and snapped her wrist. The baton deployed parallel to her right leg, and she swept it up tight to her shoulder in one smooth motion. He was close, eyes wild. She torqued using her hips, torso, and shoulder, whipped the ASP, and caught him in the left arm, her strike powerful. He staggered, his scream high-pitched. Without pause she swung again, this time at his thigh. He toppled, rammed her into the side of her unit. His right hand scrabbled, tearing at her clothes. Off-balance, she brought the ASP down across his back, but the blow fell with only half its force. He snaked an arm around her waist and flipped her with wiry, stomach-swirling strength. She crashed to the ground, him on top of her. Pumped with adrenaline, she felt no pain, no fear, only fight.

Nicky bent her knees and thrust hard with her feet to free herself, but his torso covered her, their legs tangled. His right elbow pinned her left shoulder. She brought the butt of her ASP to the side of his head. It glanced off his cheek.

"Start the truck!" he screeched and scrambled to his knees, straddling her. His left arm hung at his side.

She smiled grimly, twisted, and whipped the ASP into his arm again and again as she bucked and writhed under him. His right fist swung. Blood tanged in her mouth, but she didn't stop swinging the ASP. He arched, cringing away from the blows. With a powerful surge, she bucked him over her head and burst out from beneath his thrashing legs. A knee caught her temple. Stars sprinkled the air, and her bones jellied. Dazed, she rolled unsteadily to her hands and knees, lifted her sagging head. He inched away, turned....

Their eyes clashed. Unblinking and still, she stared at him, drew strength from his pinched expression, the fear in his face. His gaze wrenched away. He resumed his retreat, but the motion was disjointed, ineffective. Exhilaration flooded her muscles, sweeping away inertia. She snatched cuffs from her belt and scrabbled to the crawling assailant. She could take him, could beat him. Nicky grabbed his useless left arm, bent it behind his back, and snapped on a cuff. He jerked and tried to roll, so she jammed his hand up his spine. His neck arched, and he let out a howl.

"Right arm out to the side!" She shoved his cuffed hand higher, one knee buried into his lower back, the other grinding in the oil-blackened pavement, using her whole body as leverage. "Now! I'll dislocate your shoulder!" She pressed her advantage, and he screamed again.

He slid his arm in a stuttering circle across the rough pavement. Nicky grabbed his wrist, rotated it back, and clasped on the second cuff with a snap.

She'd done it. She'd fought and won, by herself. Her captain, Valentine—all those jack-holes in the department who'd ever doubted her, who thought she'd gotten her job because of who she knew, not what she could do. She'd done it without them.

And Franco.

Nicky pushed to her feet and stepped away from the man on the ground. Her senses came back online as the rush of adrenaline receded. She tasted blood on her tongue. Her skin stung from abrasions and the scorch of the sun. The smell of frying burgers and gasoline assaulted her nose, and the high, whining squeal of a fan belt sounded over the grinding rumble of a truck engine.

Her eyes widened until they burned.

The truck. The second guy.

"Don't move." His voice was thin, on edge. "I ... I have a gun."

CHAPTER THIRTY-ONE

"UNCUFF HIM." The boy's voice shook.

A haze of anger blurred Nicky's vision. Anger at her carelessness. Anger at these bozos for their stupidity. And white-hot anger that a *kid* held her at gunpoint in a situation she should have controlled from the start.

If I hadn't been trying to prove something, she thought.

Her back was to the second guy and his rifle, her Glock inches from her fingers.

"I can't do both," she replied.

"What?" Confusion laced his voice.

The man on the asphalt moaned. He'd be in a world of hurt from his ASP-whooping now that his adrenaline was wearing off.

ASP-whooping. Her lips hitched.

"You said, 'Don't move.' I can't uncuff him without moving." She kept her voice steady, reasonable. "May I turn around so I don't have to yell over the engine?"

The fan belt took that moment to squeal loudly, emphasizing her request as eminently practical.

"Okay, but don't try anything or I'll sh-shoot you."

She surveyed the scene as she rotated. No bystanders outside, but a dozen people pressed their noses against the glass panels of the mini-mart. She and the gunman paralleled the front of the store. Nothing behind him but open parking lot, a large dumpster, and miles of scrub forest.

Nicky focused on—what was his name? *Began with a w. Will? Willy. That's it.* Willy stood less than ten feet away, the rifle's large bore a deadly black eye. A .30-30 or a .30-06. Carved wooden stock, darkened with age and the patina of countless hands. Bluing intact, the barrel held a rich gray finish. The kid handled it like he'd been born with it in his hands—

Her eyes narrowed.

—and trained never to muzzle a person. First commandment of firearm safety: Don't point your gun at anything you don't intend to shoot. He'd angled the barrel to the side and down because he didn't want to shoot. Calm settled over her.

She met his eyes and gave him a soft smile. Her lip burned as the split cracked open.

"Your rifle. It's old. Was it your father's? Your grandfather's?" she asked.

"Shut up! Uncuff him. Now." There was a thickness to his voice. He blinked rapidly.

"My husband has one his dad gave him," she lied. "His favorite, even though he has half a dozen others. Shot his first deer with it. A little four-point buck. Said the recoil knocked him on his butt." A story she'd once heard Ryan tell. Nicky chuckled and cocked her head.

The air sang with the faint cry of sirens.

Holding his gaze, she said, "You never forget your first, right?"

Slowly, his fingers lost their white knuckles. His thumb caressed the wood beneath it. He gave her a tremulous smile and nod before his face crumpled. Eyes closed, he let out a single sob. Tears streaked down his face.

"My grandfather's. I shot my first deer with it, too. I was nine."

He opened eyes swimming with moisture. "Now I'm gonna lose it. 'Cause of that elk." The barrel dropped.

"Probably." She didn't want to lie to him about this. If convicted, everything would be confiscated, including the truck.

"He'll be so sad," he said.

The door to the store cracked open, and a woman peeked out. Nicky met her gaze and shook her head. The woman ducked back inside.

"I'm gonna step around this guy on the ground. I want you to hand me the gun. He taught you firearm safety, your grandfather?" She eased closer. Sirens screamed now. Willy tensed back up, licked his lips.

"Willy. Give me the gun. I don't want them to shoot you because they think I'm in danger."

Tires squealed and doors slammed. She kept her gaze on the kid's face. Smooth skin except for a hint of dark fuzz over his lip. He couldn't be more than sixteen years old.

Nicky wrapped her hand around the forestock. It was hot from the sun.

"Let go, Willy."

Franco crouched behind the front of the pickup, his gun trained on the boy. He must've pushed his unit to the limit to get here at the same time as backup. A second movement. Officer Cyrus Aguilar sidled around Franco's shoulder, gun out, black and deadly.

"Please," she said.

With another sob, Willy released the rifle. Bellows of "Down on your knees! Hands on top of your head!" sounded from behind him. The boy complied, and Nicky stepped back as Franco and Aguilar rushed in to cuff him. She secured the weapon. The single bullet lay in her palm, and she sucked in a ragged breath.

"You all right?" Franco asked. He knelt beside Raiders Cap, his expression taut, face white. Aguilar stood behind Willy, one hand on his shoulder.

Nicky touched her lip with one finger, the bullet wrapped tight in the others.

"The guy on the ground resisted," she said. "There's one more. He ran."

Willy choked out, "Ma'am. I'm so ... so sorry. It was just, the money—"

"Stop." Nicky stepped forward, rifle tucked under her arm. She wouldn't let him get into any more trouble. "You have the right to remain silent...."

CHAPTER THIRTY-TWO

NICKY HAD CLEANED up and had pictures taken of her lip, the darkening bruise on her jaw, and her hands. Her hair, wild and disheveled after the fight, was smooth again, brushed back into a neat ponytail.

Franco stood across from her in a narrow, low-ceilinged corridor lined with three solid metal doors. The linoleum was white down the middle but yellow gray along the creases where it met the scuffed cream wall. Nicky flashed him a glance from the corner of her eye. Body tense, his fingers hooked into his belt. She'd expected a lecture from him about her behavior, but he hadn't said anything, and she was grateful. Not that she didn't deserve one. She'd been reckless and stupid, and this encounter could have ended so much worse.

"Officer Aguilar called," Franco said. "He's at the Fire-Sky Clinic ER. They're taking pictures of the guy who assaulted you. He's pretty bruised up from the ASP."

A penny was adhered to the floor with multiple coats of wax. She dragged her gaze up to the papers in her hand, shuffled them around in the folder before she spoke.

"The guy at the clinic is Joseph Hopinkay, twenty. Address in

Grants. The kid with the gun is his cousin, William Hopinkay—Willy. He's only seventeen."

"Willy's in interrogation room three," Franco said. "He hasn't called for a lawyer, and he's pretty emotional. We should start with him. He'll be the easiest."

"No." Her reply came out too sharp. Nicky took a breath. "No. Let's start with the one who ran away." She curled a page to the side and read, "George 'Toad' Chester from Milan." Hand on the door-knob, she finally lifted her gaze high enough to look at Franco directly. Her stomach flipped at the coldness of his eyes. "You coming?"

He held her gaze for a long time before the tension seemed to ooze out of him on a long sigh. "Yeah. Right behind you ... partner." His voice was rough.

Partner. Nicky swallowed, relief weakening her knees. God, she'd needed that. The trust he offered to her was a balm.

She gave a jerky nod and turned the handle, the scrapes on her knuckles burning under a sheen of antibiotic ointment.

The room, small and square, smelled of stale body odor and campfire smoke and looked exactly like ones she'd seen on every TV police drama, except these walls were painted a pleasant calming blue instead of institutional green. On the other side of a heavy metal table sat George Chester, chin thrust forward, lips twisted in sneering bravado. But as Nicky met his gaze, he blinked rapidly and twitched on his chair. His round face did resemble a toad's, with a full, mobile mouth and wide-set eyes. A thatch of straight black hair fell over his forehead.

Nicky asked the uniformed officer standing inside the door to wait in the hall. She tugged out a chair and sat. Franco lounged against the wall on her right. She'd take the lead, let sympathy and empathy fill her questions. Disarm and soothe in a hostile atmosphere. She tried to become the woman in the perps' lives: mother, sister, daughter, girlfriend—whether they loved or hated that person.

Franco would step in if her connection failed, if they wanted a buddy instead, and she'd back away while he took lead. It worked for them. Professionally, they were good together.

Her thoughts shied away from the personal.

"George, you've been read your rights and can stop this conversation at any time. But I'd really appreciate it if I could ask you a few questions—"

"We found that elk on the side of the road. Hit by a truck." George's voice had started loud but fell low by the end. He hunched and dropped his gaze.

After the arrest of the Hopinkays, he'd been found walking down the road, about a mile from the Gas and Go, drenched in sweat and out of breath. It hadn't taken much to get him cuffed and into the back of Franco's air-conditioned unit. Willy had been in the back of hers.

"Side of the road, huh? Let's circle back around to that later." From her folder, she slid a large photo in front of George. In it, he stood in a burned clearing, blackened tree trunks in the background, his hands wrapped around the elk's antlers. He was so short, the crown tines almost came up to his shoulders. George sniffed and stared down at the picture, but his lips curled into a tiny smirk. The little SOB was proud of the elk he and his buddies had poached.

"That's a nice animal," she said. "You don't see many that size. Right, Franco? The one you got last year..." It was an out and out lie he needed to fill in. He hadn't been on Fire-Sky Pueblo last fall, but undercover in Arizona with the DEA.

"Only a four-by-five, but the meat was good." Franco stepped forward and nodded at the picture. "That's a monster. Six-by-seven? A real trophy. Did you shoot him?"

George's face shuttered. "I told you, we found him by the side of the—"

"Come on, George," Nicky cajoled. "We have the GPS coordinates and social media posts. Where do you think we got this picture?"

"I've sent one of our conservation officers up to the location. There'll be evidence at the site, whether it's blood or the entrails from field-dressing," Franco said.

George's gaze skated to Franco, but if anything, his smirk deepened.

"Anyway, you're not really the one in trouble, especially if you didn't shoot it. The Hopinkays, though. Resisting arrest, assault with a deadly weapon." Nicky tsked. "They have way more to gain by cooperating. If they decide to talk, I'm afraid they'll pin this on you if you don't tell us what happened first."

Smirk gone, George's Adam's apple rolled as he swallowed. His eyes swiveled back and forth between Franco and her. "No. I, um..."

"They're cousins. They'll protect each other. Why'd they bring you along? As a scapegoat in case they got caught?" Nicky pitched her voice soft, sympathetic.

"I track! I ... I'm a better tracker." George stopped.

"Tell us about the money." Nicky flipped to a page in front of her. "Nine hundred dollars in small bills, split between the three of you. Someone paid you to kill the elk."

George blinked rapidly. *Bingo.*

"You were gonna drop off the carcass?" asked Franco.

"Right." George scoffed. "Like anyone would give us money *before.*"

Nicky exchanged a glance with Franco. That was a good point.

"We saw you at WhiteHawk's Supplies," Franco said. "Did he order the animal?"

"That's not why we go there. We get different government cheese out at Halona:wa Idiwan'a—at Zuni—but my grandma loves the stuff from here, so we come to buy it sometimes. That's all."

"You drove all the way from Milan to buy cheese?" Nicky flavored her tone with skepticism.

"Not just cheese. We bought—" He stopped again.

"Fetishes?" Nicky arrayed a second photo beside the one of the elk. There were seven fetishes in the picture. Two bear, three cougar, and two elk.

"I bet you bought three elk fetishes. One for each of you. Will we find the third buried at the kill site? Tucked in the heart?" Nicky leaned over the table, her face close to the young man's. "These aren't state charges. They're federal. You killed the elk on Fire-Sky sovereign land. That means jail time if you're poaching for money. Does your mom have the cash for bond? How about to pay a lawyer?" She sorted through the photos she'd stacked in the file, letting him stew. When he finally squirmed in his seat, she leaned forward again. "George. Why should whoever paid you get off scot-free? That's not fair. Tell us and I'll talk to the assistant US attorney assigned to your case, get her to lessen the charges. Think of your family."

She pushed one more picture in front of him. Two women stood in a tan landscape below a turquoise-blue sky. The younger one, in a pretty flowered dress, had her arm around a shorter figure in black, graying hair tied up in an elaborate bun.

"You're a good grandson, George." Nicky's voice softened again. "Your grandmother, when she finds out, she'll be ashamed. These animals are sacred to the Fire-Sky People, and you're shooting them for money."

George's face was brick red now. He'd folded his lips tightly and stared at the picture.

Nicky let out a long sigh and thrust her chair back, the scrape grating in the quiet room.

"Agent Martinez, you said Willy Hopinkay was in room three? Let's offer him a deal instead. George obviously doesn't care enough about his family."

Franco opened the door.

"Wait!" A sheen of sweat glistened from George's brow. "Y-you won't find the elk's guts at the site. That's what they wanted."

"Sure. The people who paid you wanted elk guts, not the head." Nicky pushed to her feet. "Let's go, Martinez."

"No! Really. I ... I mean, it still had to be a trophy elk, a six-by-six or better. That's why we posted the picture. If they approved our kill, we'd get the money. Joe had the instructions. He handled everything."

"Instructions?" Nicky asked.

"Yeah. Field dress on a tarp and load all the elk's insides into a cooler with ice. We didn't even know if they'd accept our ... our ... until they gave directions to a drop site. We left the cooler at a mailbox. Inside it, there was a paper with more directions. It sent us to another mailbox with the money."

"Where are these mailboxes?" Franco asked.

"I ... I don't know. I wasn't driving." He slumped, his face falling. "I need that money. For my grandmother's diabetes. Those strips, you know, to test her sugar? They're expensive."

Nicky let the silence stretch. Finally, she reached across the table and patted the young man's hand. "We'll see that your grandmother gets some strips. You did the right thing, George."

His cheeks pinkened, and he gave a tiny nod.

"Now, I need you to write down the type and size of cooler, and any other information about—"

The door of the interrogation room swung open, and high-heeled shoes clacked sharply against the linoleum.

"You will stop this interrogation immediately, officers. I wish to confer with my client. George, put the pen down and don't say another word."

Dressed from head to toe in a deep red, her blond hair glinting in the fluorescent lights, Ruth Jäger met Nicky's startled gaze before she swung her leather bag on top of the table.

CHAPTER THIRTY-THREE

THE INTERROGATION ROOM door snapped shut. Nicky stood flat-footed in the stuffy corridor, jaw cocked in astonishment, George's file clamped in her fingers. "*Ruth Jäger?* First Gianetta Green, now this?" She held out one hand toward the door. "What the heck?"

Franco's eyes crinkled into a smile, but he said nothing.

"I mean, Gianetta—some of her charges are serious because of the eagle feather and the unknown provenance of that fetish," Nicky continued. "But an out-of-season elk?"

"And assault on a police officer," Franco reminded her. "This could be about you."

"Before Gianetta's hospital room, Ruth and I hadn't seen each other for over five years. Why now?" She couldn't make the connection.

They walked slowly down the hallway, and Nicky glanced through the window into the third interrogation room. Willy Hopinkay sat inside, head on his arms.

"Maybe this kid knows," she said.

The officer guarding the door opened it for her and Franco. She threaded around him and inside the room. The young man lifted his head, his eyes red-rimmed.

"How are you doing?" Nicky slid out a chair and sat.

Willy wiped his cheeks. "I ... I called my mom. She ... she said she'll call a lawyer and then drive out here with ... with my grandfather. They don't have much money. I don't know where they'll stay."

Nicky caught Franco's eye. "Call Savannah. See what she can arrange."

"You'll be okay with him?" At her nod, Franco left the room, phone already to his ear.

"Willy? Who's the lawyer?" Nicky asked. "Do you know?"

"He's out of Gallup. He's A:bachu—Navajo—and helped me and George before. When I was fourteen, we kinda took a car that didn't belong to us." He lifted dark brown eyes to her face. "He negotiated with the guy who owned it 'cause he was our clan. We helped him around his ranch for a few months to make up for what we'd done."

"What about Ruth Jäger?"

Willy shook his head. "Please. I know I did wrong, but can you just give the rifle back to my grandfather? It was his grandfather's, and he has stories, and he said I was to add my stories, and I messed it all up. I don't care what happens to me. I'll go to jail, but the rifle—" He blinked, and tears splattered his cheeks. "I was stupid to bring it. Stupid. Did you see the scabbard?"

"It's beautiful," said Nicky. "But you should be more worried about yourself."

He shook his head again. "No. The *scabbard* is important. It was beaded by my grandfather's grandmother. Will that be taken, too?"

"Willy, it's *you* who's important." She leaned forward, hands clasped. "If you cooperate, tell us who hired you—"

"I don't know. Joe handled it."

Cool, fresh air tainted with expensive perfume rushed into the room. Nicky twisted in her chair, then stood, her stomach dropping. Franco stepped inside, followed by Ruth. *Dammit.*

"Sergeant, you will cease this interrogation immediately." A tight line circled Ruth's lips. "William? I'm your lawyer, Ruth Jäger."

Willy's brows knit tightly. "But Mom said she'd call—"

"Hush." Ruth's voice was gentle. "We'll talk as soon as these officers leave." She stared pointedly at Nicky.

When Nicky and Franco stood in the corridor, he asked, "Did you get anything?"

"He said Joe was the one who handled everything. What'd Savannah say?"

"She'll get them rooms over at the boardinghouse near, uh, Little Mijito's Car Wash and Day Care. There's really such a place?"

"In Salida. They do a great job on upholstery."

Franco's chuckle was interrupted by the chime of his cell phone. "Yeah, Pep. What'd you find?" His face turned serious as he listened. "I'll be right up."

"What?" Nicky asked.

"He's at the GPS coordinates we got from these jack-holes. Looks like they poached more than one animal." His jaw hardened. "They left a bunch of gear and tents, so they were definitely heading back up once they delivered the elk to a processor. We need to search their camp. Can you call for a warrant?"

"I'll have it before you're there." She checked the time. It was after noon. "Did you get lunch?"

"I'm still pretty full from breakfast." He paused. "Nicky. About what happened this morning—"

"Not here."

He caught and held her gaze, but she couldn't read his expression. "Okay. Keep me updated."

As he walked away, she called after him. "Did you check Willy's rifle into the evidence room?"

"Yep. It's in the end gun locker, along with the scabbard. Why?"

"No reason."

CHAPTER THIRTY-FOUR

NICKY SHUT the driver's side door of her unit and took a deep breath. The smell of scorched wood seasoned the air even though a stand of healthy green conifers lined the gravel logging road and ran up the steep, rocky incline behind her. The passenger door closed, and Ryan rounded the truck's hood. The call from Franco for them to meet him up at the Hopinkay's campsite had come right after Nicky'd finished lunch.

Franco stood in the shade of overhanging bows at the edge of the dirt, hands on his hips. Black soot streaked his khaki-and-olive uniform.

Nicky snugged her POLICE ball cap on before cocking her thumb at the man next to her. "I had to wake him up, then he slept the whole drive."

"Sorry, buddy." Franco clapped Ryan on the shoulder. "I owe you one."

Ryan smiled. "No worries. I haven't slept in so long, I hardly miss it."

"We've all been there," Franco replied. "The Hopinkay's camp is about a half mile west of here, over that rise of trees."

"They shot more than just the elk?" Ryan asked.

"A doe for camp meat and a small bear," Franco said. "We'll add that to the charges. Down this slope is where they got the elk. What George Chester said was true. No entrails at the site, although why someone would pay for a cooler full of elk guts ... What a waste." Jaw tight, he scrubbed a hand over his short hair. "I want to show you the hunting shrine Pep found. Got water?" When she and Ryan nodded, he led the three of them into the spruce and pine forest.

Within a hundred yards the scent of burnt wood sharpened. The landscape folded upward as Franco guided them to a short ridge that topped out on a narrow mesa.

They stopped to catch their breath. Scorched shrubs and singed grasses stretched before them. Nicky took a drink to wash away the soot that coated her throat. Dark clouds were again gathering north, anvilling high and promising rain. Too bad they were probably a hundred miles away.

"This fire occurred a few weeks ago," Ryan said. "We classified it as a light-to-moderate surface burn—a miracle it wasn't worse considering the lack of monsoons this summer. It essentially cleared out the underbrush and blackened bark on the trees. No endangered structures, so we monitored, but that was about it. Not surprising we missed the shrine."

Nicky swung a booted foot over a clump of grass, and the black stalks shattered. The sour stench of char made her nose burn.

Franco appeared to be scanning the horizon when he asked, "So, Ryan, if I wanted to know more about the Fire-Sky god of the dead and fire, could you tell me?"

Nicky, swigging more water, choked and coughed. Ryan thumped her back until she straightened. She glared at him and said in a low voice, "You *told*?"

"I may have had too much to drink," Ryan said, a smile playing around his mouth.

"You don't drink." Clutching the water bottle to her chest, she inhaled a calming breath, curious. "Is there more? Can you tell us?"

Some of the Tsiba'ashi D'yini histories were sacred, passed down orally and unknown to outsiders.

"This one? Yeah."

"We got half a mile or so," Franco said. "Good way to pass the time." He headed toward the other side of the mesa, she and Ryan beside him. They descended into fire-singed forest, boots crunching in the detritus.

"I spoke to my father," Ryan said.

"So who didn't you tell?" Nicky said dryly.

He laughed. "He said this could be shiwanni. The spirit of this man—Seneca Elk—becoming a rainmaker, on his journey to pay respects to White House. Did he draw you north?"

"No, west. Toward the ciénega."

"Then I believe the one you saw is who we talked about. The god of death and fire. He is also known as '*the one whose touch destroys.*' They say he is kept away by rituals of fire, although at night, he sits and tends his own campfire or carries a torch. Savannah was right about that." Ryan caught Nicky's eye. "They also say that one day, long ago, there were unknown footprints near the village. The chief and People were frightened and gathered together to talk about what they'd seen."

Nicky's heart thumped. The footprint across Seneca's boot track. The one they couldn't account for.

"The chief decided to approach this unknown creature with ceremony and smoke, and the village people made prayer feathers as offerings. Then the chief called for volunteers. Four brave warriors stepped forward to carry offerings and approach the fire. It was a terrible duty, this path into the unknown. No one knew if the offerings would be accepted or if the warriors would return alive." He paused. "I told you that to see him is a warning of death."

"Gianetta said something when we arrested her. That her ceremony couldn't be interrupted. If she didn't finish, more would die." Nicky licked dry lips, tasting ash. She wiped her sweaty forehead, and her fingers came away gray. "Seneca was one of four brothers. Three are dead, but only one by fire—Cochise."

"Four is a sacred number," Ryan said. "And four must approach the fire. Maybe Cochise and his offering weren't accepted."

"What offering?" Nicky asked.

"I don't know," Ryan said. "But if you've seen this god, you may have been chosen as a warrior. The offering is something you'll need to figure out."

White, powdery cinders veiled the air, kicked up by Franco's steps. The late afternoon sun illumined the glittering swirls that defined each beam of light as it filtered through the pine boughs above them.

"What about the white eyes?" she asked.

"Some depictions of this god show him with white eyes, like that of a marble statue. But that makes sense." Ryan glanced at Nicky. "Physiologically, eyes become more white and opaque during the first couple of days after death."

"Corneal clouding." Something she'd observed a number of times, especially if a body wasn't discovered immediately.

"My father believes that if the living show white eyes, it is the same as seeing the god—a warning of death." Suddenly, Ryan veered away. "Franco. Nicky. Over there."

Nicky started after him, but Franco grabbed her wrist. Startled, she whirled toward him, her breath coming fast.

"'A warning of death,'" he said, repeating Ryan's words. "At the ciénega. Did you see this man? Is that why you were so afraid?"

"No. The salvia. Hallucina—"

"Don't lie," he said. "And don't underestimate me."

Franco released her and turned away, shouldering through branches.

A bough snapped, and Nicky flinched. She hurried through the trees, finally catching up as she trudged into a gently sloped clearing. The thick bunch grasses—western wheatgrass, big bluestem, tufted hair grass—were now black and curled. Ryan ducked under a tree trunk arched so severely, it touched the ground on one side.

"A marker. Ones around these mountains designate water or hunting shrines. The old stories say they have the promise to tell us more, but no one knows what that means. The meaning's been lost." He patted the tree.

"The shrine's at the edge of this clearing." Franco pointed to a tumble of stones at one end of the open space.

Ryan tramped to the spot. Nicky gave Franco a wary glance and followed.

"I knew it." Ryan's voice held a quiet note of triumph. "This is an amuma ochani. A prayer shrine. It is tsityu. Sacred." He squatted down near a short circular wall about five or six feet in diameter, stones spalled and crumbling, one edge of the circle stacked with larger rocks. Inside lay a concave, debris-filled pit. "I remember going to one as a kid, setting up shuhuna y'aauni and hish—hunting fetishes and white shell—to petition for help to catch deer. But as the Old Ways disappear, so does the knowledge of these places. Amuma ochani hidden by time exist all over the mountains and in the canyons."

"The Hopinkays and George Chester shot the elk a quarter mile west of here. I found this shrine when I tracked them." Franco wandered around the stone perimeter.

Ryan swept his hand over the shrine. "In the middle, you would drop corn during t'iitra—the spring—and the war chiefs would visit and predict whether rain would be plentiful or scarce depending on growth."

He beckoned Franco and Nicky to the stack of larger stones before he knelt, laid his hands on top of the rocks, and closed his eyes. His lips moved soundlessly. As Ryan prayed his offering, connection swept through Nicky, settled her. She wanted to hold on to it, so she closed her eyes to pray to a different god than Ryan.

Maybe.

The breeze shirred through the pines. Loose needles dropped

with tiny patters. Birdsong and the cry of a hawk echoed in the distance.

"Franco, Nicky." Ryan's voice was soft. "Help me with the stones."

They dissembled the tumble of rocks and stacked them to one side. At ground level, they uncovered a flat, round stone. Ryan worked his fingers under one side until he could lift it. Sunlight filled the cavity in the earth.

"Looted." Ryan's tone was flat.

Franco stood. "I have one more thing to show you. Step in my tracks."

He led Nicky and Ryan single file to a trail covered in a thin layer of soot. He stopped and motioned for them to come up beside him.

"The elk came through here. See the black spots on those leaves? Dried blood. Three sets of footprints from our poachers. Tread patterns match up to those boys' shoes. But look at this."

The sharp, clean edge of a single boot print was gone, one side pressed flat by a treadless, elongated oval.

He raised his head and stared into Nicky's eyes. "Someone's stepped over it. Just like at the ciénega."

CHAPTER THIRTY-FIVE

THE STATION ROOM was practically deserted, most of the officers out on patrol or in the break room eating lunch. Paperwork from ongoing cases had taken up most of her morning, but Nicky couldn't get Willy Hopinkay's interview from the day before—or the confiscation of his grandfather's rifle—out of her mind. She tapped in her password and opened Willy's file on her computer. As soon as the evidence photo of the Winchester Model 1894 and beaded scabbard loaded, she hit print. Her stomach growled again, so she opened her desk drawer and grabbed the baggie with her sandwich, an apple, and a bag of grape tomatoes from her plants on the front patio.

"You've been avoiding me," Savannah said from behind her, voice laced with accusation.

Nicky stilled. It was true. She hadn't seen her friend since Friday night's dinner, afraid the guilt would show on her face for suspecting Savannah was Chen Cano's contact.

"I've just been busy," she finally replied.

Savannah walked around the desk and propped her hip against the front. "Have you seen Ryan?"

"Yesterday. When we investigated the poacher's camp."

"He's been avoiding me, too." Savannah frowned and crossed her arms.

Anger flared. Nicky slammed her hand down on the desk. *"I'm not avoiding you."*

Savannah blinked and paled. She suddenly looked ... lost.

Nicky sat back abruptly, shocked at her outburst. What was she doing? This was her best friend. "I really have been busy."

"I know, but ... are you okay?"

Nicky's chest tightened. "Yes. And I'm sorry."

Savannah nodded but wrapped her arms around her middle. Her next words were stilted. "I, uh, heard about what happened Saturday at Green Meadow Springs. I wanted to talk to you about that mother's life-debt vow. And about what's going on with Ryan." She drew in a breath. "And me. In Fire-Sky culture, if you save someone's life, they must '*clear your path of rocks and break the branches that obscure your vision.*' I don't know how that's interpreted as a life debt, but Ryan said I owe him after ... after ... what happened on Scalding Peak this summer." She hesitated, lips tight. "But that's not the worst of it. My dad says I owe my life to—get this—Howard Kie."

"That's ridiculous. How does your dad figure that?"

"I don't know, but it always comes back to what a nice, traditional, unmarried Fire-Sky Indian Howard is."

"You did spend quite a bit of time with Howard, getting him settled." Nicky forced a smile, wanting to lessen the tension. "Have you been over since then? Has he cooked you dinner yet? I can see it now. Candlelight, two plates, and pepperoni Hot Pockets served with a side of Flamin' Hot Fritos."

Savannah's cheeks flooded red. "Stop harping on Howard. Please."

Taken aback by the emotion in her friend's voice, Nicky nodded. "Okay." Her thumb rubbed at the healing cut on her palm.

Savannah's eyes followed the motion. "Still hurts?"

"Not really. Julie Knuteson took the stitches out of it on Sunday."

"I guess you have been busy." She gave Nicky a real smile, and the stiffness between them finally seeped away.

"She had some information about Seneca Elk's autopsy. He ate rocks. It's a disorder called pica. And when Cochise was autopsied, he had rocks in his sinuses." Nicky leaned her elbows on the desk and propped her chin in her hand. "But you know what's weird?"

Savannah snorted. "All of it?"

"No kidding. One of the stones in Seneca's gut was shaped like a gummy bear."

"Could it have been a fetish?"

Nicky sat back. "You think he might have eaten a fetish?"

"The Elks are a fetish-carving clan."

"Do you know why the Elks' fetishes are different?"

Savannah grabbed the chair from the closest desk and sat across from Nicky. She leaned in, voice hushed. "It's mishtyətsi. Black. A secret. The technique passed down to those worthy of the knowledge. Like some of the sacred ceremonies are passed orally from war chief to war chief, or cacique to cacique. I do know that to receive one of their fetishes requires a major ritual with fasting and singing."

"Why can't another clan be given this fetish-carving privilege? The Elks wield it like a weapon whenever they get into any trouble with the law." Nicky clenched her jaw. "All the tribal council does is slap their hand and blanket them in tribal sovereignty." Anger and frustration boiled over again. "I really get tired of the sovereignty crap."

"For all its problems, sovereignty is vital to the tribe." Savannah frowned. "It's our right."

"But it's not fair when one person gets treated differently under the law than another. It breeds resentment and makes the pueblo seem capricious and unjust."

"To who?" snapped Savannah. "The outside world? To *your* world? To a country that tried to wipe Indians off the face of the earth? That only granted citizenship to Native Americans—people whose ancestors settled this land thousands of years earlier—in 1924?"

"What the hell, Savannah? How is 1924 *my* world? How can I be blamed for things that happened before my grandmother was born? I'm saying when someone sells drugs or gets a DUI, there should be consequences that are fair and equitable. No one, whether it's *my world* or *your world*, should get off because of how much money they make, or their last name, or what clan they belong to. It perpetuates class systems and cultivates outlaws like the Elks."

Mouth mulish, Savannah shook her head, the blunt-cut edge of her hair brushing her chin. "Every state has its own laws and its own penalties for different crimes. Why don't the Tsiba'ashi D'yini People get that privilege? Sovereignty is about justice, not an ever-changing set of rules. It protects us, allows us control of our lives, our culture. You don't understand—"

"Oh, I understand privilege. I ran smack into it with Dax and Janet and her parents. I'm still dealing with the repercussions." Bitterness permeated her tone.

A phone rang in the distance, and voices drifted out of the break room.

Savannah finally broke the silence between them, her words almost a plea. "Don't you see when sovereignty might be necessary? Maybe because someone thinks they're doing the right thing? I mean, people shoot and kill intruders in their home—that's homicide—and yet they get off. Or when a law is broken because someone is young and stupid? Or grief-stricken? Or because of an addiction, maybe to alcohol? It's to give them another chance."

As suddenly as its onset, Nicky's anger disappeared. "Are you talking about Howard?" She kept her voice low. "Or your dad?"

Savannah reached her hand across the desk. "Dad took my brother's death so hard. Santiago was to be a cacique, a Tsiba'ashi D'yini leader. If the tribe hadn't intervened, helped when Dad was arrested for driving drunk, he wouldn't be alive today. I'm sure of it. Since then, my father's dedicated his life to the pueblo, done so much good. I can't say anything bad about sovereignty rules."

Nicky sighed and grasped Savannah's hand with hers. "We did get a little off track, didn't we? All I really wanted to do was ask whether you and Howard wanted a large wedding or were going to elope."

Savannah squeezed her fingers hard.

"Ouch, ouch, ouch!" Nicky tugged her hand away and shook it.

Savannah's lips twitched into a smile. "One of the real reasons I came to talk to you was because of your text yesterday. You need my dad tomorrow?"

Nicky nodded. After she'd left the poacher's campsite, she'd sent Savannah the request on her way back to the station. "To look over the artifacts we've gathered on a couple of cases. See if he has any insight to their origins. Turns out, the three poachers had fetishes, too."

"These are the guys you fought with?" Savannah touched her own lip, her gaze dropping to Nicky's. "How are you feeling?"

"Sore. But I handled everything." Nicky winced internally at the defensiveness in her tone. "Thanks for helping with Willy Hopinkay's mother and grandfather. They're at the boardinghouse in Salida?"

Savannah nodded. "They'll stay until Willy gets bail."

"I need to head over after lunch and chat with them again."

"Before you go, I need a favor. They had another hellacious fire last night at Green Meadow Springs. With casualties."

Nicky frowned. "I didn't hear about it."

"State police and Valencia County Fire and Rescue took the lead once the bodies were found." She smoothed down her skirt and flicked Nicky a glance. "You know how Ryan gets when there are burn deaths. Would you eat lunch with him? Make sure he's okay?"

"Why don't you go talk to him?"

Savannah scrunched up her nose. "He might have come over to my house on Sunday, and ... we might have had another fight."

"What was it about this time?"

"Not important." She paused. "Nicky? Are we okay now?"

"Sure."

"Good. Ryan's at the fire station."

———————

NICKY SWUNG OPEN the front door of the police station and trotted outside. Heat and sunlight practically scalded her exposed skin, making it itch. Sweat trickled down her back before she'd crossed halfway into the sticky parking lot that linked Fire, EMS, and Rescue to her buildings.

The two-story, hanger-like structure that made up FER gleamed white in the sun. Beds of xeriscape plants tidily arranged among creamy rocks bordered the cement path to the dark-tinted glass doors. Nicky wrapped her fingers around a metal door handle only to yank away with a muttered curse. Pressing her hip against the push pad, she waited as the doors hummed open.

It was blessedly cool inside the cavernous space that served both FER and Conservation. High windows ran along the walls near the ceiling, and skylights glowed. The whole place was modern and energy efficient so that during the day few if any lights were switched on.

Ryan's slumped form sat alone at one of the long tables, dunking a tea bag into a steaming mug. A series of three glass containers filled with food were arrayed in a semicircle on the table in front of him, red plastic lids stacked to one side. A spirit bowl sat nearby with bits of food from lunch and breakfast.

"Want some company?" she asked.

Ryan tipped his face up. His normally bright hazel eyes were bloodshot with fatigue. He looked miserable.

"Sure." He jutted his chin to the orange plastic chair across from him. "Saw Franco. He came over to retrieve his favorite rifle. Said he was headed up to the poachers' camp again."

More FER personnel filtered into the room, speaking quietly, getting coffee, tea, or Pepsis from the industrial-sized stainless steel fridge. Some settled into groups around the tables or relaxed onto sofas and chairs. The flat-screen TV in the corner flickered on.

"What is it with you guys and your special guns?"

He smirked. "You know it's a metaphor, right?"

She rolled her eyes as she arranged her sandwich and fruit on the table. "That all Franco said?"

"No. But my mom told me if I can't say something nice...." The corners of his tired eyes crinkled into a smile.

"Not even gonna ask. It'll only tick me off." Nicky peeled open her sandwich bag and held it across the table. Ryan pinched off a piece, lips moving silently. He blew on it and dropped it in the spirit bowl.

"Peanut butter again? How old is that bread?" He pushed the largest glass container toward her. "Have some." A warm, savory scent wafted up. Her stomach growled.

"What is it?"

Ryan shrugged. "Chicken with noodles?"

Nicky peered inside the other containers. "Spinach salad with mandarin oranges? Berry cobbler?" She grabbed his fork and took a bite of the pasta. "You did not make this. Your mom? 'Cause no way Savannah—"

"Did she send you over?" His cheeks turned ruddy.

"Yeah. She's worried about you. Me, too." Nicky set the fork down, tempted to blurt out her suspicion that Savannah was alerting Chen Cano's gang. She wanted Ryan's insight. Decided against it. He had enough to deal with right now. "The fire last night. Was it bad?"

Ryan wrapped his hands around the mug of tea. "Two dead." A haunted expression carved his face. "Green Meadow Springs. Once everything cooled down, I did the walkthrough. A neighbor told us the men who lived in the trailer drank too much and smoked." He squeezed his eyes shut. "But when I examined the kitchen, the floor had a burn pattern indicative of poured accelerant. Every room did."

She pressed her hand against her mouth as his words sank in. His eyes opened, and Nicky read horror.

"There was no door to the last room. The interior—walls, ceiling, floor—was black. Furniture pushed away, the center of the room open, except...." Ryan swallowed, his gaze inward now. "Both men had been lashed to chairs with wire. They'd been doused with accelerant and set on fire."

He stretched one hand across the table. Nicky clasped it and held on tight. Ryan's worst nightmare, to be burned alive.

"Positive identification is pending, but the neighbor gave us their names." He tightened his grip. "Larry Chris and Buddy Trelivas."

"What?" Her eyes burned as she stared at him.

"The two men who started the trailer fire last weekend. The one with the little boy you saved. Someone murdered them—a brutal hit —and made no attempt to disguise it."

CHAPTER THIRTY-SIX

AFTER LUNCH with Ryan and finishing another hour of never-ending paperwork, Nicky skipped down the steps of the police department's admin building. Her thoughts were so focused on the arson murders in Green Meadow Springs, she'd almost forgotten to grab the picture of Willy Hopinkay's rifle and scabbard from the break room printer. Keys and picture in one hand, plastic grocery sack of apples from her tree in the other, she hit the sidewalk at a jog —and stopped in her tracks. Captain Richards and a knot of day-shift officers stood under the canopied area of the parking lot, backslapping, laughing, and gesturing toward a shiny silver Lexus. Brand-new. Sitting in Captain Richards's parking spot.

Savannah had told her the captain's salary when he was hired. No way he could afford a car like that. She hurried to her unit, slid inside its oven-like interior, and texted Dax. Maybe it wasn't such a bad idea to check the finances of their suspects in the deconfliction case.

This might clear Savannah. Nicky grinned as she drove out of the Public Safety complex and headed to the village of Salida.

THE ADOBE boardinghouse that housed the elder Hopinkays sat on the main road through Salida. Long and low, with pealed log posts holding up a bulky overhang, it had originally been built in the 1940s as a motor inn for intrepid travelers who'd braved rough western roads before the advent of the interstate system. Next to it, a trading post and garage from the same era had been transformed into a car wash and day care by village funds. Sounds of spraying water and children's laughter floated in the heated air.

Nicky shut her truck's door, stomach jumping. With the bag of fruit clasped in one hand and the printed picture of the rifle and scabbard under her arm, she expanded her chest on a long, calming breath. Her actions could come back to bite her hard if this encounter wasn't handled properly.

She walked under the shaded overhang and rapped on the door numbered with a brass five.

Mr. Hopinkay, Willy's grandfather, opened it and stood on the threshold in old leather cowboy boots, faded black dungarees held up by suspenders, and a crisp long-sleeved button-up. The scent of coffee and starch wafted through the doorway as worried brown eyes peered at her from under wrinkled lids. "Sergeant. Is everything all right? Willy and Joe?"

"They're fine. We should be hearing back on bail soon." Nicky held out the bag. "I brought you apples from my garden. And a case of water, in my truck. May I speak to you and your daughter?"

"My daughter is not here now. But we can talk." He accepted the bag and opened the door wide.

The boardinghouse room was scrupulously clean, even if its decor seemed from another age. Large, plain area rugs covered the wood floor, colorful blankets doubled as bedspreads and drapes, and the heavy furniture—a sofa and two chairs—were slipcovered with dark red fabric. In one corner, a Formica countertop held a sink, microwave, coffee maker with a half-full pot, and a tiny refrigerator.

A casserole dish, covered in aluminum foil, sat next to the sink, and an unopened box of pastries rested on a round table near the window.

"The Aklinne a'bo'yanne People have been generous. Coffee? There are sweet things, too." He waved a hand the color of walnut at the table.

"No, thank you." Nicky handed him the printed page. "I've, uh, come to speak to you about the guns Willy and Joe carried. Under tribal and federal statutes, they'll be confiscated and destroyed if your grandsons are found guilty of poaching and resisting arrest."

His suddenly sharp gaze scrutinized her bruised chin and split lip. "That lawyer, the woman, she explained this to us."

Nicky widened her stance and clasped her hands tightly in front of her. "Willy told me the history of his gun. How much it means to you, its place in your stories, your family. I, uh, I understand that. My grandmother left me heirlooms, furniture—many years old—for safekeeping, and her house. Five generations of my family grew up there, including me. I, uh, haven't been a very good steward." Saying it out loud was almost cathartic, even though it didn't mitigate the imminent loss of her home. "I don't want Willy to feel the way I do. It's—it's like a spiritual wound. It shadows everything." She ran her hand over her hair. "I have a way to get your family treasures back to you."

Mr. Hopinkay stared at her for a long time. She fidgeted under his gaze. Finally, he hobbled to a chair at the table and, using a hand on the back, levered himself into the seat. He smoothed the paper across the tabletop. Nicky's tongue worried her lip as she waited for his response.

"Would this way to get me the rifle be illegal? Get my grandsons or you in trouble?"

"Not your grandsons. Me? Not if you don't tell anyone."

The skin around his eyes crinkled, causing them to almost disappear, and echoing creases bracketed his smile. "You think this is so important—this rifle—that you would sacrifice yourself?"

"Yes, sir." Nicky frowned. "Isn't it?"

He slapped his thigh with one hand. "Let me tell you, young lady, I would love to have my rifle back, and my grandmother's scabbard."

Nicky opened her mouth to explain her plan, but he shook his head.

"Not for reasons you believe are important. That rifle is worth a lot of money. Money we don't have. Money my family needs now for the defense of my grandsons. If you got me that rifle back, I would sell it and not give it a second thought."

Nicky blinked, surprised. She'd had to do that, too. Sell her family's heirlooms to pay for her defense. But she felt like a failure for it.

"The more I think of it, the more I believe it's my fault for putting such value on this gun. It has warped my grandson's judgment so that he thinks he is worth less to me than an old piece of wood and metal. It was not like that for our grandfathers. In that time, after our Creation, the A:łashshina:we moved with the Earth, chasing the seasons." He draped an arm over the back of the chair, his gaze focused only on memories. "The People could not carry much, so they took on their backs only what was necessary, relied on their skills for food and shelter. It wasn't until some fine fool built a house that these worldly goods took on such importance." His gaze dropped and pinned Nicky. "You ever seen that TV show *Hoarders?* Well, we are all hoarders now."

"But, sir … your history, the stories associated with that gun. Willy's first deer, food it put on your table. And … and the love put into the scabbard by your grandmother. All that will be lost if—"

"Do you hear yourself, girl?" He swiveled and grabbed the box of pastries. "You think that after these are eaten, we won't remember the kindness of the one who brought them? That's important, not the thing. You melika and your need to write everything down or jam deshhuk'wa in a museum. You know, I visited President George Washington's house one time. They kept that poor man's teeth for everyone to see. If he was alive, would he want that? You talk about your family's history in the form of heirlooms and a building. Do you think if your grandmother could come back to this world and visit for one day or even one minute, she would choose to sit alone in that old house, surrounded by old furniture?"

Nicky looked at the old man, and her vision burned and blurred. She would give everything she owned, even years off her life, to see her grandmother one more time. To talk and laugh and ... Throat tight and aching, she closed her eyes.

Mr. Hopinkay was silent while she cried. When she finally dried her eyes, she held a damp, old-fashioned handkerchief.

"Thank you," she said. For so much more than the cloth tucked in her hand.

He nodded. "I learned just as much about myself. Now, if you really want to help my boys, explain why that fancy Santa Fe lawyer wants them to keep their mouths shut instead of taking a plea deal so the law can find the one who put them up to this."

CHAPTER THIRTY-SEVEN

TRAFFIC THROUGH SALIDA had picked up by the time Nicky left Mr. Hopinkay. Feeling lighter about her money problems than she had for a long time, she walked to Mijito's Car Wash and Day Care, dodging excited children as workers ushered them inside for after-school care.

A jingle of bells on the double glass doors announced her arrival in the sundries and coffee shop. She caught the barista's eye. An iced latte on a baking afternoon was an indulgence that used up precious funds, but Nicky justified it—poorly—by cutting back to twice a month. It helped that the coffee Dax had left at her home was delicious, but it would run out eventually, tempting as it was to let the grocery delivery continue. He did owe her for the mess he'd made of her finances, but she had to temper that with the fact that Dax never did anything out of the goodness of his heart.

She glanced at her phone. He hadn't replied to her text about her captain's new car.

Ambling around the store, Nicky examined kitschy souvenirs: brass sheriff badges with first names stamped across the star, tiny

New Mexico license plate key chains, and refrigerator magnets shaped like rattlesnakes, howling coyotes, and saguaro cacti. Boxed sets of aluminum six-shooters with white plastic grips were stacked on a shelf next to miniature bow-and-arrow sets. She picked up a pleather belt, its holster threaded through, and turned it over. *Hecho en China*. Her fingers smoothed across the glass-beaded design, her thoughts still swirling from her meeting with Mr. Hopinkay.

The barista called her name. She headed for the front of the store, and her gaze caught on a rack of J WhiteHawk movies and DVDs. As she paid for her drink, the bells jangled again, and Clint Elk hustled into the shop. His eyes opened wide and his feet seemed to stick to the floor when he saw her.

"Clint," Nicky said.

His face looked older, more lined and grayer.

"We buried Seneca," he told her. "Grave-guarding finished a couple of days ago."

"I heard."

He jerked his chin over his shoulder. "Got Dyu'ami in the truck. Takin' him to that new FEMA computer trailer." He studied her face closely, probably noticing the aftereffects of her fight or ... emotion. "That boy listens to you. Maybe you can talk him outta taking that damn dog with him. Just waitin' for the teacher to complain. Need to get him a snack." He skirted around her to the glass refrigeration unit.

Clint's truck was parked out front, the windows rolled down. Gemini sat in the passenger seat. Though she nodded to him, he stared straight ahead. Dyu'ami was in the back seat, arm around his dog, eyes vacant, lips in a faint smile. Diya stuck her head out of the window and grinned, tongue lolling. Nicky scratched her behind the ears, and her eyes closed on a big doggie sigh.

"Hey, Dyu'ami. How've you been, sweetheart?" She gently touched the hand tucked around Diya's neck. No response except a slight shift of his fingers. He was dressed in a starched plaid shirt and jeans, his golden-brown hair combed into a neat braid. "How are you liking school?" She carried on a gentle, one-sided conversation with the boy until—suddenly—Gemini got out of the truck and stumped around the hood to face her. Like Dyu'ami, he wouldn't meet her gaze.

"Give me back my Winchester and Colt." His voice was gruff, rusty, his lips twisted. "I know you police. You steal from us—keep whatever you want."

Nicky took a sip of her latte and eyed the old man. "What are you talking about, Gemini?"

"You kept the horse too long but had to give him back. I want the rifle and pistol you took from Seneca. They were my grandfather's. They're mine."

The doorbells clanged, and Clint rushed out.

"N'aishdiya, get back in the truck." He thrust a grocery bag at Nicky. She automatically took it. Curling a hand around his father's arm, Clint tugged on the old man.

"The guns. I want them back. And the tsa'atsi y'aauni. Tell her." Gemini jerked his chin at Nicky.

Tsa'atsi y'aauni. The Keresan term Ryan had used for the special fetishes.

"Seneca didn't have a fetish," she said.

"You *lie*. He was chosen. He would have kept his tsa'atsi y'aauni close, as an offering. Always.

"Shush, old man." Clint guided Gemini around the front of the vehicle. Nicky strained to listen to their continued conversation.

"None of your boys are good. They are all corrupt and sick," Gemini said querulously.

"And three of them are dead, no thanks to you. Get in the truck and hush."

Nicky stared through the open windows as Clint buckled his father back into the seat. Gemini was still talking, but the noise of the industrial driers at the car wash obscured his voice. She glanced at Dyu'ami. Eyes still vacant, he rocked back and forth, his soft lips tight. Diya had pressed her head into his shoulder.

"Hey, hey. It's okay." Nicky sat her coffee on the top of the truck and covered his hand. This time, fingers curled into hers. "Why don't we see what Uncle Clint bought you for your snack?" Anything to distract the boy from the upset and noise. Nicky let go of his hand and shuffled open the bag. "Cheetos. Yum. Do you like Cheetos? I do. Dr. Pepper. My favorite. A whole bag of gummy bears? If you eat all those, you'll get a stomachache. No fruit or veggies? Hold on."

Nicky patted his fingers and jogged to her unit, mind tumbling over Gemini's accusation. Even though it was on her list, she and Franco hadn't yet followed up on whether Seneca'd had guns when he'd taken off. And Seneca's fetish. *He would have kept his fetish close.* In his jeans pocket? They'd been turned out. Had whoever taken the guns stolen the fetish, too?

From her backpack on the front seat, she grabbed a plastic zipper bag of tomatoes left over from lunch. Clint waited for her by the driver's side door, expression tense, but she deliberately spoke to Dyu'ami first.

"These are from my home." Nicky held up the bag of a dozen small oval tomatoes, bright pinkish orange in the sunlight. "I'm going to put them with your snack, okay? And you'd better eat all of them or my feelings will be hurt." She ran a gentle hand over his hair and tugged at the braid, chest warming with a swell of affection for the boy. "Now you be good and learn about computers today."

With one last tickle of Diya's ears, she faced Clint and handed him back the sack of food.

"He worries about those guns of his," Clint said hurriedly. "Thinks they're gone, but we have the ones he's talkin' about. Gemini's getting too old to remember. Turns out, Seneca didn't take any guns."

"Really?" Head tilted to one side, Nicky bared her teeth in a smile. She didn't believe him. "Your father was pretty adamant. Tell you what, I'll come up to your ranch. You can show those guns to me so I can close out my report."

Clint's eyes widened. "Sure, sure. Give us a call so we know you're comin'."

He climbed in the truck and backed out of the parking spot with a wide turn. Nicky's latte tumbled from the truck's roof and splashed to the ground.

But she didn't care. Her gaze followed the big black vehicle until it dropped out of sight.

CHAPTER THIRTY-EIGHT

"I'll need to take them out to examine," RJ Analla said. Savannah had brought her father to work with her that morning for the fetish consultation. He sat at one end of the conference room table, a desk lamp placed near his shoulder, its bright light pointed at an evidence bag on the laminate tabletop. They were in a windowed conference room that bounded the squad room along one side.

"Would you mind using disposable gloves?" Nicky pushed the box closer.

"Of course, Nicky. I wouldn't dream of further contamination." RJ smiled and looked around the room at those gathered, their attention centered on him. His smile widened, and he sat up straighter. "I assume you've checked for fingerprints and other trace evidence?"

"Yes, sir. And that information has already been transferred to Ms. Jäger for the Hopinkay and Chester poaching—"

"*Alleged* poaching," Ruth interrupted.

Nicky cast a tight-lipped glance in her direction. Garbed in a turquoise wrap dress the color of her eyes, Ruth stood *way* too close to Franco. Nicky forced herself to look away, to hide the unwelcome jealousy she felt. Chief Cochin stood on the other side of the room, arms crossed, gaze alert.

"I didn't know other cultures used fetishes." Franco opened the glossy book RJ had carried into the room. He riffled through thick, colorful pages.

The bag crackled as RJ opened it and extracted an elk fetish.

"Yes. From ancient carved Venuses to large wooden totems to Christian holy relics. But this fetish was factory made." He held the carved elk under the light of the lamp. "Soapstone, easy to carve. Details laid in by hand." He tugged a round magnifying glass from his shirt pocket. "See here? The brown stain is blood. Those Hopinkay boys shot a big elk, right? They would have dipped this in the heart's blood."

"Could you explain why, Mr. Analla?" Nicky asked.

"To feed the spirits of the animals, make them more powerful. And to pray for success in their hunts." He put the stone elk away. RJ picked up another bag, opened it, and extracted a crouching mountain lion. Turning it over, he peered through the magnifying glass before placing it back. He did this with all the fetishes from the poaching case. "All of these are cheap knockoffs."

"How much do fetishes cost if they're made by a Native artist?" Franco asked.

"Depends on the stone, the size, and animal," Mr. Analla replied. "When they're carved in turquoise, I've seen them for upwards of five thousand dollars. More in Santa Fe galleries, especially if they're antique."

"And by antique, you mean...."

"Collected or looted, or an heirloom sold by a family who needed the money." His voice held disdain.

"A Tsiba'ashi D'yini hunting shrine was found in the vicinity of the poachers' camp. Could any of these fetishes be from that shrine?" Nicky asked.

Ruth frowned. "Why was I not informed of this?"

"We're still assembling our report." Franco smiled down at her.

"I'll personally make sure you get a finalized copy as soon as it's done."

Nicky refrained from rolling her eyes. Of course Ruth would get the report. It was part of discovery.

RJ pursed his lips. "These fetishes could be from a hunting shrine, but if they are, it would only show the ignorance of those who placed them."

"Would you elaborate, Mr. Analla?" Ruth asked.

"Factory-made fetishes don't contain the w'in'uska—heart—that which is put there by the fetish carver. Traditionally, these figures are"—he waggled his head back and forth, like he was trying to come up with the right words—"*custom* from the maker. If you don't know who carved it or the ... the *purpose* in his heart ... you should not keep it. It could be dangerous."

Nicky laid three more bags on the table. "What about these?"

RJ held up the baggie with the bear found in Gianetta's car. "This one ... this one is different." His gaze pinned Nicky. "It would not be found in a hunting shrine. It is tsa'atsi y'aauni."

"A spirit fetish?" Chief Cochin's face lost some of its color.

"The spirit in this stone is ... restless, angry." Mr. Analla turned the stone, still in the bag, over in his hands.

"It's the one from Gianetta Green's car."

"You handled it? Held it?" RJ frowned. "You will need to be cleansed, Nicky. Medicined."

Franco gave her a hard stare.

"Could you look at the other two?" Nicky asked calmly, but her neck prickled uncomfortably.

RJ stared at her, worry coloring his gaze, before he picked up the second bag and tugged out the bear Nicky had found at Geronimo Elk's descanso. "Another spirit fetish. The heart in this one does not seethe like the other, though it, too, is restless."

"It was found in a pyramid of rocks." She pushed a printed picture of the descanso toward him. "And beyond that, surrounded by a circle of stones."

RJ studied the picture. "The circle contained it, like the circles of stone that make up hunting shrines. The one who assembled the circle feared that the soul who inhabits this fetish is not at peace and could haunt them. This is especially true if the person coupled to a tsa'atsi y'aauni was taken in violence. Their spirit becomes trapped in the stone."

"Taken in violence?" Franco asked.

"Took his own life, or another took it," RJ replied. "Suicide. Or murder."

Nicky exchanged a glance with Franco before her eyes slid to Ruth Jäger. The woman's face was white and her expression blank.

"If you could examine the last fetish." Nicky pushed the final bag toward RJ. It was her little owl.

"This one is cruder than the last two, but it is still tsa'atsi y'aauni. It's young, immature, but ... something is *here*." He cupped it between his hands, brow furrowed. "They say as we grow old and the Creator takes our vigor, mutes our senses ... they say those pieces we lose wait in the heart of tsa'atsi y'aauni, wait to become complete again when the caretaker of the fetish leaves this world." Fleeting sadness etched his expression. He shook it off and frowned, shoving the bag away. "I'm surprised the owl is its tsa'atsi adyaashi—its animal spirit. In Fire-Sky tradition, the owl is evil."

At that, Chief Cochin snorted, and RJ pivoted his torso to glower at her.

"You disagree with me, k'uu."

Nicky raised her eyebrows. Not daughter, but k'uu. Woman. That wasn't very nice.

"I'd appreciate it if you addressed me as Chief Cochin, Cacique Analla." She softened her demand with a stiff smile. "Owls are only evil in a man's eyes. There's a different meaning for Tsiba'ashi D'yini women."

RJ hunched his shoulder away from her. "These last three fetishes are made in the old way, but by design; they are modern, not ancient. They would not be associated with your looted hunting shrine. As to their value, perhaps in the thousand-dollar range because of their rarity, but no true member of the tribe would sell these." His voice was adamant. "If you need more information, take them to Gemini Elk. He is most probably their creator."

"We can head over to the Elk compound after lunch." Nicky glanced at Franco, who nodded his assent. "Is there anything else you'd like to add, Mr. Analla?"

"Have you had someone cleanse the looted shrine yet?" RJ's eyes sparkled. He pushed against the tabletop, rising with difficulty. Franco hurried to assist and placed a hand on RJ's elbow to steady him. "If not, I would be happy—"

"Thank you, Mr. Analla. Ryan Bernal took care of it," Nicky said.

"Oh." RJ sniffed. "Him."

CHAPTER THIRTY-NINE

MEETING OVER, Savannah retrieved her father. Nicky, with Franco by her side, faced Ruth, who stood next to Nicky's desk, one manicured hand pressed against its edge. Her eyes glinted below delicately arched eyebrows.

"Well, I think we can eliminate Gianetta Green as a suspect in your shrine looting. She can hardly climb a single flight of stairs, much less clamber around the rugged countryside, digging up artifacts."

Her voice was a smooth contralto, pleasant but commanding. A voice Nicky had heard ad nauseam in depositions five years ago. Now it scraped every nerve to the point of screaming. Irritation built from somewhere deep in her core, setting her teeth on edge.

"You still can't explain how the fetish came into her possession," Nicky said.

"It doesn't matter. Based on your expert's opinion, that fetish is not some ancient artifact or tribal heirloom." Ruth hefted the strap of her leather satchel more firmly onto her shoulder.

"Then the shrine was looted by the Hopinkays and George Chester."

"Please. I just read your preliminary report." Ruth snatched it up from the desk and waved it under Nicky's nose. "Their footprints weren't found near the shrine."

"That means nothing," Nicky interjected hotly. "They could have scouted that area before the fire—"

"Sergeant Matthews." Franco's tone held a warning note. "This isn't the time—"

"If I were you, *Sergeant Matthews*, I'd be more focused on countercharges of police brutality during the arrest of those young men *and* Ms. Green."

"They resisted arrest!" Pressure built in Nicky's head with each beat of her heart. She couldn't let Ruth win. Not this time. Not ... couldn't....

Ruth leaned in close. Her exotic perfume slammed Nicky's senses. Her intense turquoise eyes, steeped in satisfaction and triumph, bore into Nicky's. "I've interviewed witnesses at the Gas and Go. I've reviewed the store's video of the arrest. If this goes to trial, your aggressive, confrontational attitude and the excessive force you used would be an easy sell to the jury." She smirked and drew back, her expression smug. "Oh, the times we live in. Perhaps, as part of the plea deal for my clients, mandated therapy for your issues will be required. I'm sure Janet Stone would appreciate that."

A red tinge surrounded Nicky's vision. Her body shook. Fists clenched into tight balls....

"Matthews. *Sergeant!*" Franco's voice, harsh and hard.

The room swam as the red receded. Franco stood between her and Ruth, hand clamped on her arm. She caught Ruth's shocked gaze over his shoulder; the lawyer's hand was clutching the collar of her dress, and her skin was even paler than it had been in the conference room.

"I have to be in Santa Fe in less than an hour," Ruth said. Her voice held the slightest tremor. She hugged her bag, holding it like a shield. "Franco. If you're ever up at the capitol, give me a call. We can grab dinner." With a quick staccato step, she hurried away.

"Wait." Nicky pulled away from Franco. The woman halted and half turned back. "Who referred you to Gianetta Green and the Hopinkays?"

From across the room, Ruth sent her a long look. Her smile built slowly, mockingly. She tilted her chin, smugness restored, then pivoted, almost bumping into Savannah, who'd made her way back in. Smile startled off her face, Ruth sidestepped and sped off.

"I should have tripped her on her ass. The nerve of her bringing up Janet Stone." Savannah scowled, following Ruth's retreat before she turned back to Nicky and Franco. "I called Mom. She took Dad home to rest. Too much excitement. But he wanted to know if he was helpful."

"I'd like to ask him about his reaction to the first spirit fetish." Franco glanced at Nicky and frowned. "He implied the, er, spirit or soul trapped in that fetish died violently, and because Nicky handled it, she needed to take some medicine."

"Get medicined," Savannah corrected. "That's his go-to as a cacique, and I've already told Nicky not to. As for the spirits-and-souls stuff, the men in my family say they have tee'e huwana'ani—faraway eyes. That they have visions and whatnot." She smirked and crossed her arms. "Do you know how psychics work? Or mediums? Fortune-tellers? My dad's the same. He pretty much reads the room and applies Fire-Sky cultural elements. You said you found Geroni-mo's fetish at his descanso? Surrounded by an infinite circle of rocks. I bet Dad told you whoever placed the fetish there didn't want to be haunted by its spirit."

Franco smiled. "On the money. Next time, we call you."

"Tip your waitress, I'm here all week." Savannah glanced at the large clock above the break room door and grimaced. "I'd better get back to my office and do some work. If you have any more questions for Dad, shoot me a text."

Franco crossed his arms and half sat on the desk behind him.

"What's going on with you, Nicky? I thought for a minute you were going to hit Ruth."

Nicky ran her hand over her hair. "I thought so, too. Thanks for stepping in."

He grunted, his gaze never leaving her face. "Did you see Captain Richards's new car? His consulting business must be paying pretty well, or ... what do you think? Is that purchase enough to convince you we should look into his finances?"

Mouth suddenly dry, Nicky flicked him a glance. "I've, um, already contacted my source about it. I forgot to tell you."

Franco's jaw clenched, and his chest and arms swelled with a long indrawn breath.

God, she was blowing it.

"Seneca Elk's phone records dropped in my inbox this morning," she said. "I haven't had a chance to go over them because of the meeting. And I want to cross-check them with Cochise and Geronimo's records. Do you have some time now? I've got snacks."

Franco gave her a searching stare, then exhaled a breath that seemed to deflate some of his stiffness. "You mean tomatoes from your garden."

Nicky opened a drawer and grabbed a baggie bulging with the pinkish-orange fruit. "They're never-ending, but I feel guilty about not eating them. I'll print everything out if you'll get coffee."

He studied her for what seemed like forever. "Sure. We can work in the conference room."

"Franco?" She touched his arm, held his gaze. "I really am sorry. I've been a little ... off lately."

"Yeah. That's one word for it." Franco strode toward the break room.

Throat tight, Nicky watched him walk away. She obviously wasn't forgiven yet.

IN THE CONFERENCE ROOM, they silently combed through phone records. Nicky munched a tomato, washing it down with a swig of coffee. Her gut suddenly burned. She grabbed two more packets of regular sugar, added them, stirred, and sipped. Much better. She bent her head over her laptop again, using the RISSIntel —Regional Information Sharing Systems—to cross-reference the phone numbers. She pressed the point of her pen on an unknown number Seneca had called dozens of times. It looked familiar.

"I've seen this somewhere before, but I can't quite...." She sucked in a breath. "Didn't WhiteHawk give you his business card?"

He tugged one out of his wallet. "Yeah. Pushing payday loans. He offered you one, too?"

Nicky's gaze flew to his dark brown eyes. They were soft with something like sympathy ... and understanding. When she and Franco had first worked together, she'd told him confession was good for the soul. Maybe finally owning up to him about financial troubles would soothe hers now. Nicky licked her dry lips, opened her mouth—

The phone number connection spun into her brain. Eyes wide, she grinned. "I know where I've seen this number." Nicky hurried into the squad room, Franco following, and pulled Gianetta Green's file off her desk. She opened it and tapped a page. "We'll have two visits to make this afternoon—WhiteHawk's store and the Elk ranch about those guns. We can take the freeway. It's faster."

CHAPTER FORTY

FRANCO SWUNG into the parking lot of the Muuk'aitra warehouse complex, and Nicky craned her neck to peer at the sleek pearl-white car parked in front of WhiteHawk's store.

"And here I thought Ruth had a pressing appointment in Santa Fe," she said.

"Like cops, lawyers have been known to lie." Franco parked the conservation truck in an empty slot. "Looks like she's the only customer."

"You know, WhiteHawk and Ruth Jäger keep popping up as links between the cases we're working on."

"Yup. So do fetishes."

"A spirit fetish shows up in the box of supplies Gianetta picked up from the store before she was arrested. WhiteHawk sold fetishes to the Hopinkays." Nicky's mind slotted puzzle pieces together. "Then, out of the blue, Ruth miraculously takes both Gianetta's and the Hopinkays' cases."

"Easiest explanation? She's here to ask WhiteHawk more questions based on Mr. Analla's information this morning."

"Stop. You're spoiling my fantasy of arresting her, although I have no idea for what."

Franco shot her a half smile. "I bet her foot is about the size of the tracks we found at the ciénega and hunting shrine."

"Right. Louboutin moccasins."

"What?"

"Never mind." Nicky climbed out of the truck, a manila folder tucked in her hand, and stepped onto the sidewalk beside Franco. "You gonna play the bumbling, misogynistic jack-hole again?"

Franco chuckled and pushed open the glass door, bells jangling as cool, sage-tinted air brushed her face. This time, Native American flute music played low in the background.

Nicky scanned the room. Ruth bent over a tray of turquoise bracelets, body stiff, profile tight. She didn't look up as she tried one on a delicate wrist. J leaned his narrow hip against the glass case, reading glasses pushed to the top of his head, impassive gaze roaming between Nicky and Franco. Today, his hair flowed loose around his shoulders except for a thin braid that started on his right temple, tied off with a string of dangling shells. Matching circles of shell covered his earlobes and hung from his ears. The tableau laid out before her was fake; Nicky was sure of it.

"I'll take this one," Ruth said as she admired the bracelet. "More questions, officers? No need to follow me. Next time, give my office a call." She trained cold eyes on Nicky. "My meeting was canceled, in case you were wondering. I thought I'd ask Mr. WhiteHawk a few more questions." Ruth fidgeted with the bracelet, turning it around her wrist.

Nicky strolled to the counter and looked at the tray of jewelry, taking her time. Out of the corner of her eye, she saw Ruth shift, heard her quickened breaths. Good.

"Actually," she finally said, "this isn't about you. We need to speak to Mr. WhiteHawk. Would you like us to step outside until you're done with your ... client, Ms. Jäger?"

A flicker of alarm lit Ruth's gaze before it was abruptly snuffed out. She squared her shoulders. "Still fishing, Sergeant Matthews? Mr. WhiteHawk is not my client. Now, I really do have to get back to Santa Fe." She nodded to WhiteHawk and brushed her body against Franco's as she passed, face tilted up to his. He held the door as she hastened through.

"She forgot to pay," Nicky said.

"Oh, I'm sure Ms. Jäger's good for it. Anything that interests you, Sergeant Matthews? I take trade." WhiteHawk's voice dropped. "And make loans."

Her pulse spiked, but she took a steadying breath. WhiteHawk didn't know about her financial troubles. When he'd offered her money, he'd somehow picked up on her distress. Like Savannah's dad, he'd "read the room." This time, he wouldn't rattle her.

"I have a friend who makes authentic jewelry." Nicky smiled as her gaze clashed with WhiteHawk's before he turned away.

"And you, Franco? Something for a special woman in your life?"

"Same friend." Franco caught Nicky's eye and winked.

WhiteHawk slotted the tray away. "So how can I help you today?"

"We have a few more questions." Nicky opened her folder and, across the top of the glass case, laid out three pages marked with lines of yellow highlighter. "As part of our investigation into"—Nicky paused for emphasis—"accidental deaths, we review the phone records of the victims. These are Seneca Elk's. We were able to identify all of the numbers except this one." She touched the first page. "It's from what's called a burner phone. Purchased anonymously, no link to a name or business. For example, drug dealers use them. The last outgoing call Seneca made was to this phone."

WhiteHawk slid his glasses over his eyes and bent to study the page. He straightened but said nothing.

"This second page is from Cochise Elk's phone records. Tragically, his death occurred only a few months before Seneca's. Turns out, he'd been calling the same number right before he died. Two deceased brothers, linked by the same burner phone. That piqued our curiosity, so we checked Geronimo's records." Nicky aligned the third page. "The same number popped up. And once again, the last call he made before he committed suicide was to this burner phone. Oddly, the phone was inactivated two days after Seneca's death." The practiced lines rolled off her tongue like she was a seasoned actor. Nicky tipped her face up to WhiteHawk's. "What do you think of all this?"

He shrugged. "I think that you know the phone belongs to me."

"You'd be right." Nicky laid the J WhiteHawk Outfitters and Supplies business card he'd given her the week before on Seneca's phone records. A handwritten phone number topped the one marked out by black ink. She then plucked another piece of paper from her file.

"This page contains a copy of your business card—one in Gianetta Green's possession—with the same phone number we found in the Elks' phone records. Underneath it are copies of your card found on Joseph Hopinkay and George Chester with the old number marked out"—she touched the line obscuring the print—"and a new number written above. The new number is also linked to a burner phone."

"And this is some kind of Perry Mason gotcha moment," White-Hawk said.

"You tell me. Why don't you start with burner phone number one?" Nicky couldn't hide the smugness of her reaction. Didn't want to.

"I use, er, 'burner' phones because they're cheap and easy to replace. Though you may be unimpressed by my celebrity status, I still have groupies and the odd stalker. Gianetta Green turned out to be a little of both." He stared out the front window, lips pursed. "After her arrest, she must have called fifty times. When Ms. Jäger contacted me about the case, I relayed my little problem with her client. She recommended I change my number. I changed my phone, too."

"See, Matthews?" Franco interrupted. "Just a coincidence J inactivated that phone around the time of Seneca Elk's death."

"As to these"—WhiteHawk tapped the page—"I still had a stack of my old business cards. Instead of wasting them, I marked out the old number and wrote in the new."

Franco nudged her in the shoulder. "I told you the explanation would be logical. You always overreact."

Misogynistic jack-hole, right on cue.

"Then I guess the Elk brothers must've been stalkers, too," she said. "Between the three of them, they made or received over a hundred calls using this old number in the last year. Could you explain your relationship with the three dead men?"

"Did you actually read my card? I run an outfitting business during hunting season. Those boys guided hunts. They called me about jobs."

"You want me to believe the night Seneca Elk rode out to move cattle, the very last call he made before he died was about a job," she said, her tone sharp with sarcasm.

"I thought it was odd, too." WhiteHawk smiled thinly, eyes cold. "In fact, both Cochise and Seneca guided for me last season."

"And Geronimo Elk?" Nicky asked.

WhiteHawk's smile grew a little nasty. "I once had a small part in *Law and Order*, Sergeant. 'Never ask a question to which you don't know the answer.' You worked with Geronimo, so you know he never guided hunts for me."

"Then what was the nature of your relationship with Geronimo Elk?" Nicky asked.

WhiteHawk crossed his arms. He stared from Nicky to Franco. "Business. Pawn and payday loans. But it developed into one of friendship and support, especially after his wife took his children away from him."

"What did you talk about during that final call?" Nicky asked.

"He'd been chosen to be the next fetish carver in his clan. The pressures of training and his family troubles were contributing to his depression, maybe even led to his suicide."

"Geronimo Elk's spirit fetish," Nicky continued. "We know it's similar to the one found in Gianetta Green's possession. Did he pawn it?"

"He never pawned any fetishes."

"How about Cochise or Seneca Elk?"

"No."

"So how did you come to possess a spirit fetish—the one you sold to Gianetta Green?" Nicky asked.

"Nice try, Sergeant. I didn't sell Gianetta that fetish. I'd never seen that fetish before you showed it to me."

She swallowed disappointment. "What did Cochise and Seneca pawn?"

"Oh, you'd be surprised at the artifacts and heirlooms many of the clans hold sacred."

"Guns?"

"I don't carry a license to sell guns." He brushed his hair back. The white shell of his earrings glittered in the light.

Nicky suppressed a gasp. She stared at him, arrested. *Pend d'Oreilles.*

WhiteHawk's brows drew together in a frown. He tugged at an earring. "You know, officers, you haven't asked me about their brother, Mangas. From what Geronimo told me, Mangas was bitter about the succession and lashed out by insulting Geronimo's wife. He and Seneca physically fought. Mangas wanted to be the tribe's fetish carver, and, with three older brothers ahead of him, he never thought he would. It ate at him." He smiled grimly. "Funny how things worked out, all his brothers gone like that."

Notes of the flute music died away.

Franco sighed. "Jeez, Matthews, I hate to say I told you so. We'll get out of your hair, J." He stretched out a hand to WhiteHawk. "I'll give you a call about my elk hunt."

"That'd be great."

Nicky gathered her papers while the two men talked, but her mind worked furiously. WhiteHawk's earrings. Coincidence could explain her startling conclusions, but she wasn't a strong believer in coincidence. Pieces of the puzzle started rearranging in her head—

"Ready, Matthews?" Franco threw over his shoulder as he headed to the door.

Pieces scattered, but there was one more thing. Nicky pivoted at the threshold.

"Mr. WhiteHawk? Both Geronimo and Cochise Elk had illicit drugs in their system when they died. Seneca Elk's blood work isn't yet available, but I wonder if he'll also be found to have drugs in his system. Would you know anything about that?"

"I told you, I don't use drugs anymore. When I did, I caused a lifetime of pain."

CHAPTER FORTY-ONE

"I asked you to call first." Clint hurried down the porch steps of the Elk ranch house, half a dozen barking dogs milling around his legs. Dyu'ami sat on the wood slats, elbows propped on the lowest rail, moccasined feet dangling over the edge, his gaze never leaving his iPad. Franco's black flashlight hung from his belt, and Diya lay next to him, her tail whipping back and forth happily.

"Sorry, Clint. I forgot. You remember Agent Martinez." Nicky ambled over to Dyu'ami and tugged his braid in greeting.

Franco nodded from behind his wraparound sunglasses, this time playing the silent, intimidating cop. He was almost worse than WhiteHawk with all the acting he did. At least he'd stayed quiet on the long drive from WhiteHawk's to the Elk compound, something she'd appreciated while she turned over parts of the case in her head.

"Is Gemini around?" Nicky asked. "Cacique Analla recommended we talk to him about some fetishes we found."

"I'll get him. Don't have much use for RJ, though. He's a kiss-ass." Clint trudged back up the steps. The screen door creaked as he opened it.

"And, Clint? Could we see that Winchester rifle and Colt revolver?" Nicky called. "The ones Seneca didn't take with him?"

The door clacked shut behind him.

Diya came down the porch steps and sat on one of her boots, and Nicky leaned over to scratch her ears. She kept her voice low so Dyu'ami wouldn't hear her.

"WhiteHawk was sure quick to throw Mangas under the bus, but it's not like this whole fetish-carving succession thing hasn't been bothering me," she said. "Especially if Seneca's death wasn't an accident."

Franco propped his shoulder against the railing and tucked his sunglasses on his ball cap. He leaned over and peered at Dyu'ami's iPad. Then he straightened and leaned toward her, his voice almost a whisper.

"Mangas was next in line, but to murder your own brother?" Franco shook his head. "The guy would have to be pretty messed up."

Nicky snorted. "Like the rest of his brothers? You know, I finally feel like we're making progress."

"Except on the poaching case. I still can't puzzle out why someone would pay for a cooler full of offal." Franco pointed to a spot on Dyu'ami's screen. "Press here."

Booted footsteps and muffled voices resonated from inside the house. Diya stood, stretched extravagantly, and wandered toward the large, shady tree growing in the front yard. Dyu'ami scrambled down the steps after her. Nicky smiled faintly as the boy hopped from one of the dog's footprints to the next as he followed, making it a game. He slipped his iPad into his shirt and, with unexpected agility, climbed the tree to nestle in the crook of two large branches about fifteen feet up. He pulled out the flashlight and trailed the beam into the limbs above.

The door opened, and Clint, rifle cradled in his arm, ushered Gemini out. The old man's scowling glance brushed Nicky before it settled on Franco. "Where are these fetishes?" he asked.

Franco fished the evidence baggies from a pocket in his cargo pants. The first one he handed to Gemini contained a cougar bought by the Hopinkays at WhiteHawk's store. The old man studied the fetish inside and shoved it back at him.

"Trash." He spat.

Franco handed him the second bag.

Gemini moved the fetish around, brought it close to his face. "Where'd you get this?"

"At Geronimo's descanso. Is it his *tsa'atsi y'aauni*?" Nicky asked.

Gemini nodded curtly and handed the bag to his son. Face gray, Clint stared through the plastic at the black bear fetish with the tiny spear lashed to its back. He looked at Nicky, his eyes pleading.

"Can I keep it? We need to pray over it. I ... I want his spirit to rest."

"I'm sorry, Clint," Nicky said. "You'll need to speak to Geronimo's wife about that."

Franco handed the third bag to Gemini. The old man manipulated the brown bear fetish in the plastic. And stiffened.

"Is this Seneca's spirit stone?" Franco asked.

"You kept it. Like you kept my guns." Gemini shook the bag in Nicky's face, spat at her feet. "Liars, all of you."

"No, N'aishdiya. Here are the guns." Clint held a Winchester rifle out to Franco and fished a Colt revolver from a holster at his hip. "See?"

Nicky met Franco's gaze in silent question. He shook his head. Clint was lying. The guns he held weren't Seneca's.

"Who's the liar, Clint?" Nicky dug a piece of paper from her hip pocket. She snapped it open and thrust it at Gemini. "This picture was in the Tsiba'ashi D'yini archives. These are the rifle and pistol Seneca took with him the night he rode off, not those." She swept her hand dismissively toward the guns Clint held. "Mangas followed him that night, didn't he? He took the guns. You're trying to protect him."

"No." Clint's face blanched. His eyes were dark with fear.

"Mangas killed Seneca because he was jealous of his brother. He wanted to be fetish carver." Gripped by sudden agitation, a black haze surrounded Nicky's vision.

"No, he never wanted that!" Clint shook his head. "He doesn't want it now!"

"Sergeant Matthews," Franco said. She ignored him.

"Mangas took those guns." She pointed at Gemini. "And Seneca's fetish. He sold them to WhiteHawk. That's how the fetish got into Gianetta's box. That's why—"

"Matthews!" Franco grabbed her arm and gave her a single hard shake.

Nicky jerked like she'd hit the ground. Blinking, confused, she stared into Franco's face. She'd lost control again.

"What's wrong with you?" he said, his voice rough.

Suddenly, Gemini appeared beside them. Gaze hard, he shoved the photocopy of the guns and the bag with the fetish into her chest. She reflexively clutched them.

"Seneca's bear fetish. It bit you, didn't it?" he said.

She thought back. She'd thought the bear had moved and clutched it tightly. "No. I held it too hard, cut my hand—"

"You fed this tsa'atsi y'aauni your m'aat'i. Your blood." His lips curled in his craggy, ancient face. Gemini lowered his voice to a growl. "You keep this fetish, k'uu. You have been infected. And you will bear final judgment."

CHAPTER FORTY-TWO

Nicky cradled her glass of Dr. Pepper as Savannah fussed around the kitchen. She opened the oven to check on red chile cheese enchiladas that smelled amazing, washed a spoon in the sink, carefully dried and put it away, then refilled the napkin holder on the counter that divided the kitchen from the den. She finally stilled, hands propped on the sink edge, and stared out the kitchen window.

"Franco's not coming tonight?" Savannah asked.

"No." Nicky hunched her shoulders.

Yesterday, after her confrontation with Gemini Elk, she and Franco had retreated back to his truck. He'd slammed the door and turned to her. "What's going on with you?" He hadn't waited for her answer, just started up the truck and maintained stony silence during their drive back. He only grew colder when she received a text from Dax saying that none of the personnel who had access to the deconfliction database—Cochin, the lieutenants, Savannah—had any odd payments to their bank accounts, and that Captain's car was purchased from consulting fees. Nicky had been relieved, thinking Savannah was cleared, until Franco'd said, "All that means is money's not the motive. It still could be about protecting the pueblo from drugs."

"Do you think Ryan will come to dinner?" Savannah's question knocked Nicky out of her reverie.

"I don't know. What did you guys fight about, anyway? You were pretty vague the other day."

Savannah slumped against the kitchen counter. "He wants us to start dating. I mean really dating, not just be best friends anymore."

"Dating someone who's your best friend. How awful," Nicky said.

"He says what happened up on Scalding Peak earlier this summer was a wake-up call. That he's waited long enough because who knows what could happen tomorrow. But, Nicky. What if ... circumstances, family pressure, tradition interfere, and it doesn't work, no matter how much we may want it to? Wouldn't that be worse? To lose someone close to you and still see them every day?" Savannah raised her hand and slid a finger under her glasses to wipe her eye. She rubbed the moisture with her thumb.

Nicky sighed. "Family pressure. Your dad."

"He says Santiago's drug use is Ryan's fault, and that it led directly to his death."

"That was a long time ago. I thought your parents made their peace with Ryan. When he came back to Fire-Sky and explained Santiago died a hero, not by suicide."

"I thought so, too. As part of AA, Dad had to deal with his anger over losing his son, but it's buried too deep. If Ryan and I—" Savannah swallowed. "Dad's heart's so bad. It could kill him."

Nicky circled the tip of her finger through the chill condensation on one side of her glass. "Ryan makes you happy, even when you're furious at him. Once your dad really gets to know him, sees he's not that stupid teenage kid anymore, that he's steady and kind and loves you, that he's traditional."

"Ha. Traditional. All I need is another traditional man in my life. Sometimes Dad's all I can handle." Savannah pivoted to the oven.

"And Ryan gets so caught up in his traditional side, he doesn't think of anything else. I *hate* that he encourages you about—" She sighed. "Nicky, nothing you ever see in your visions is real. It happens a lot to outsiders. They immerse themselves in the romance of a southwestern Indian reservation, get caught up in the landscape and history, and voilà! Spirits everywhere."

"Romance of the culture? Really? Well, here's some romance for you. This morning, I got called out to Margret and Ruben Gomez's trailer. They were both drunk—again—and Margret was on the roof —*again*—except this time she had a can of grease and was throwing handfuls at anything that moved, including me. I smelled like bacon the whole day. Got two marriage proposals."

Savannah's lips twitched. "How'd you get her down?"

"I didn't. Ruben apologized for calling her a *borracha gorda*. She climbed down—I'm gonna record that sometime because she is very nimble for someone of her size—and they both fell into each other's arms and started to cry." Nicky met her friend's gaze. "Working as a police officer quickly erases the romance, Savannah. I admit my visions could result from a tired mind, physical fatigue, or—"

"Salvia hallucination, heat exhaustion." Savannah peered into the oven.

"Whenever I've seen something in the past, it's been about *saving* someone, whether they're alive"—she took a deep breath—"or dead. What if this is about Seneca Elk? My subconscious telling me there was something wrong with how he died."

"Like what?"

"We have questions about guns Gemini insists Seneca carried with him—we didn't find them. His pants pockets were turned out like they'd been searched, and his spirit fetish wound up in Gianetta Green's car out at Hummingbird Mesa. *And* there was an extraneous footprint. What if someone else was there with him? Killed him, and took the guns and fetish?"

"Who? Gianetta?"

"Of course not. But it's too much of a coincidence. She had

Seneca's missing bear, and her arrest triggered me to find Seneca because the vision—"

"No. A manifestation of salvia and who-knows-what-else intoxication."

"Fine. A manifestation led me to Seneca."

"So how do you think the fetish got into Gianetta's car?" Savannah asked.

"I think whoever took it might have sold it and the guns to White-Hawk. Then he sold the fetish to her." Or WhiteHawk had taken them himself when he'd killed Seneca. But why?

Savannah was shaking her head. "You said it's a tsa'atsi y'aauni? In his biography, J said he opened the supply and outfitters shop as ... as redemption for past drug use. That, in the end, it would save him. If he did sell it and Gianetta talks, J could lose his store and get kicked off the pueblo."

Something tickled at the edge of Nicky's mind. "WhiteHawk's biography says his family was Bitterroot Salish and he was born and raised on the Flathead Reservation in Montana. You once told me because he wears shell earrings, you thought maybe his father was Water Clan."

"Pure speculation. Wishful thinking."

"Could he be Pend d'Oreilles?"

"Sure. The Confederated Salish and Kootenai Tribes include Salish, Pend d'Oreilles, and Kootenai People. Why?"

"An old picture I saw at the cultural center." Was that White-Hawk's connection to the Elks? The Pend d'Oreilles woman who was Elizabeth Elk's maid of honor?

"Nicky?" Savannah shifted and nibbled at her lip. "Remember when Dad practically invited Howard to dinner at my house?"

Immediately distracted, Nicky laughed. "I thought the enchiladas smelled like pepperoni."

"Funny. You know, Howard's not that bad. He's sweet, and ... and ... really smart." Savannah's face puckered. "His parents died when he was little, and he was raised by an uncle my dad said was

never there. Howard's been on his own too long and needs social-
ization."

"You make him sound like a stray puppy. I thought he went to
UNM and got a computer degree."

"He did, and that's why we helped him get a job working at the
FEMA trailer. He can fix any problem—hardware or software. I'm
hoping over time, he'll start teaching kids—"

"Since he's extremely childlike, it's a good fit if they don't bully
him because he's so weird."

"Howard's from an old and respected clan. He's full-blooded,
like me."

"I thought you hated—" Nicky blinked. "You're joking, right?"

Savannah dropped her gaze to the floor.

"Are you ... *dating* him? You said there were enough traditional
men in your life." Nicky couldn't stop the rise in her voice. This was
unbelievable. Savannah and Howard Kie? "Ryan's traditional, too."

"Let it go, Nicky. Ryan's not Tsiba'ashi D'yini."

"What difference does that make? You love who you love. Deal
with it."

"Yeah, that worked out so well for you and Dax."

A sharp pang stabbed her chest. Nicky swirled her glass of soda.
The ice had almost completely melted.

"Nicky. I'm ... I'm sorry."

"Why? It's true. Or it was." She tried to keep her voice flippant
and light.

"You don't understand the pressure I'm under. You're not Fire-
Sky."

"That excuse is really getting old, Savannah. I've worked on the
pueblo for over five years—"

"You think because you speak a few words of Keres and see some
stupid Fire-Sky spirits, you know us and our culture? Well, you don't.
Stop being so patronizing."

The screen door to the patio screeched. Nicky swiveled, and her
jaw dropped.

Howard Kie stood in the den. His hair, usually sticking out in every direction, was buzzed short on the sides and fluffed into a pompadour over his forehead. Instead of wrinkled gray trousers and a cheap Kmart polyester oxford, he wore black skinny jeans rolled above the ankle and an untucked red plaid, pearl-snap shirt. With his BC glasses and bright yellow high-tops, he'd been transformed into some kind of Native American hipster.

Nicky looked at Savannah and pointed at Howard. "Did you do that?"

Savannah lifted her chin. "Don't point. It's rude."

Nicky gaped at her.

"I knocked," Howard said. "Your home is very clean, Savannah. It smells tasty, but...." Lifting his nose, he sniffed the air and pinched his lips. "Uh-oh. I will need dyaami huuseni and sage."

"I don't have any eagle feathers, Howard, or sage." Savannah's voice gentled as she addressed him. "I do have peacock and some potpourri."

"Stop treating him like a child. He's your age. You went to high school together," Nicky said. Hands on her hips, she frowned at Howard. Through thick Coke-bottle lenses, Howard mooned at Savannah like some lovesick puppy.

"Why do you need the feathers, Howard?" Savannah asked.

He approached Nicky. She took a wary step back. His smile was sweet. "I need to look at your hand."

Reluctantly, she extended her arm. His fingers were a little clammy. He rolled her hand back and forth, and delicately touched the fading scar on her palm. Howard sighed.

"I was afraid of this. Although I am not a war chief or cacique, I must cleanse your house, Savannah, of sickness. The peacock feathers will have to do." He thrust his chin toward Nicky. "This cop has carried mishtyǝtsi gur'ar'aka into your home, a black demon."

Nicky snatched her hand away and scowled.

"Howard, Nicky didn't bring a demon into my house."

"You are correct, Savannah. Not yet. But as she sickens, it will come. I must cleanse your home with song and chase it off with sacred smoke or we cannot continue to date. It's too dangerous."

"Oh, yeah. This guy's a *much* better choice for you than Ryan and his talk of my visions," Nicky said.

Howard tsked. "If she doesn't get medicined, this blackness will kill her. She doesn't believe now, but she will once she's dead."

Nicky stared at him, struck. She sucked in a wheezing breath, slapped a hand over her mouth, and blinked against burning eyes. It didn't help. She doubled over, convulsing with laughter.

ONCE NICKY'S intense response to Howard's prophecy of her death ebbed, it left frustration, anger—*fear*—pulsing against her temples. She met Howard's grim gaze, then Savannah's anxious one.

"Are you all right?" Savannah asked tentatively.

Oh, no. No, no, no. She didn't want to talk about it, didn't want to think about it. Scooping up her keys, she marched out the front door and into the smothering evening heat.

"Nicky! Wait," Savannah called after her.

The sky to the west was an odd yellow gray as the last rays of the sun etched the horizon hard and black. Streetlights flickered, bulbs triggered by the growing darkness. A group of children whizzed by on bikes, followed by two older boys, sneakered feet slapping the pavement.

The motion detector perched on the edge of Savannah's roof glared on. A moment later, the door banged open as Savannah rushed out. Nicky stopped short and gaped at Howard's white Suburban. It listed drunkenly, and the passenger's side window appeared to be held up by ragged strips of silver duct tape. "Is that a snow tire on the back?"

"He might have had a flat when he bumped a sidewalk," Savannah said.

"The front bumper. It's bungeed on."

"You know those big rocks that line the FEMA trailer's parking lot?"

Nicky swirled around. "Has he been driving drunk? Because, I swear, I will suspend his license, tribal sovereignty be damned."

"No. He's just not a very good driver."

Nicky threw her hands up. "Instead of Ryan Bernal, you're dating Howard Kie." She pinned Savannah with her gaze. "Does Ryan know?"

Her friend stood in the middle of a large flagstone in the front yard. She clutched a covered glass container against her stomach.

"Why do you think we fought?" Her reply was barely audible.

Nicky approached her, feet crunching on the tiny rocks in the yard. She placed a hand on Savannah's arm. "Why are you doing this?"

"Ancestry. Tradition. Guilt for wanting the man who helped kill my only brother."

Nicky's throat tightened at the pain that colored Savannah's voice. "That's your dad, not you. He's using the past to manipulate you, and you're letting him."

Savannah raised eyes that might have sparkled with tears, but Nicky couldn't be sure. The lenses of Savannah's glasses hid more than Nicky ever thought they could.

"And you don't let the pressures of your past dictate your present actions?" Savannah asked. "You think I don't know what's going on? You're killing yourself over your grandmother's house."

Nicky dropped her hand and tipped her face up. Stars burned to life as she stared at the dark sky above her.

"Family matters, doesn't it? We're a lot more alike than you think." Savannah pressed the container into Nicky's hands. "Enchiladas. There's enough for breakfast if you add a fried egg."

Nicky looked from the food to her friend but said nothing.

Savannah sighed. "Ryan's too much like my father. He's too strong, too traditional. I love him, but what if I started to resent him like I resent my … my father? I can control Howard. And I like him enough, even if he's a little weird."

"You sound like a bad romance novel," Nicky finally said, her voice gruff.

"Romances are happily-ever-after fantasies. Another quote from my dad." Savannah's mouth lifted on one side in a halfway smile. "You take back control where you can, too, Nicky. You do it every day in your work." She stepped back, her face hidden in the shadows of the porch overhang. "You going over to Ryan's?"

"He texted earlier. Said he needed to speak to me."

"Could you not talk about this? It only upsets him."

"Goodnight, Savannah."

Turning away, she heard Savannah's front door close behind her with a muffled thud.

NICKY CROSSED the yard and stepped into the street.

Control.

Savannah had said they were alike because the past directed their present actions. That both she and Savannah had to extract control wherever they could.

Was that true? The world had dropped beneath her feet with Dax's betrayal so long ago. He still overshadowed her life because of her debt and the possible loss of her grandmother's house. The home she'd willed to Nicky, bypassing Nicky's mother, her only child.

Not that her mother cared. She hadn't even attended the funeral. Had been out of the country. Nicky couldn't remember where.

The house was an extension of her grandmother, and she'd swear her grandmother's soul was embedded in the walls. With an absentee mother and a father who'd left for God knows where, Nicky's anchor had been her grandmother, as had the house and all it contained. Antiques that reached back to great-grandparents and great-great-grandparents. She'd heard the stories—her family's own oral history.

Traced the initials a long-dead child had carved into a cabinet. Knew how the cedar chest in her bedroom—aromatic oils long faded—had been carried by wagon to New Mexico. Been so overwrought when she'd sold her family's heirlooms to pay for a lawyer, she'd likened it to the loss of a child.

Nicky hopped onto the sidewalk, navigating bunches of native grass growing in the cracks of the cement. Her shadow lengthened in front of her as she walked through the pooling light of a streetlamp. Two dogs barked from a backyard, one a quick echo of the other. She sidestepped a tricycle and cut between parked cars, her thoughts somersaulting.

Did possessions—her house, furniture, *things*—truly control her life? No. The emotions associated with them did. Decisions she'd made about her job and relationships were byproducts of a need to hold on to the past. Were they controlling her present and future, too?

Ryan's house was dark. He'd probably gone to bed, as exhausted as he was. She wouldn't disturb him. She laid Savannah's enchiladas on a patio chair and sat on the wooden bench swing fastened to the thick beams of the front porch. One foot pushed against the cement, and she swayed. The heat of the day bled away as night took hold. Moths flitted under the streetlight, bats and nighthawks periodically tearing a path through the flickering swarms. A window closed across the street, silencing the canned laughter of a television set. A person walked past, tiny Chihuahua on a heavy leash, cell phone pressed to one ear.

And Nicky sat and swung and argued with herself, running agitated fingers through her hair.

"Did I really become a cop because my life was spinning out of control? Because the law is black and white, and the rules ordered my chaos?"

"That's why my family made me join the Marines. And why I became a firefighter."

Nicky jumped and laid a hand over her thumping heart.

"*Dammit*, Ryan. You have *got* to stop sneaking up on people."

"I walked right past you." He sat in the chair next to her, dressed in a soft T-shirt and nylon shorts, barefoot, casserole dish on his lap. "Thanks for coming by."

"Didn't want to go home." She resumed her swinging. "You became a firefighter for control? I thought firefighting was more about the danger and excitement."

"You could say the same thing about law enforcement." He settled deeper into his chair. "There are a lot of rules when you fight a fire. Protocols. The danger is always there, but I think that's part of the control, too. Challenges no one ever thinks will defeat you because you train and train. Most injuries and deaths in our professions are because of dumb bad luck or operator error. Mistakes are the epitome of a lack of control."

She let the silence between them stretch before she asked, "Is that why you carry a gun?"

"Ultimate act of control, to choose the way you die. Sounds weird, but it's almost a comfort, especially when the way we want to live doesn't choose us."

The soft sounds of the night filled the gap in their conversation.

Nicky finally stirred. "You wanted to talk to me?"

"Yeah. That shrine Franco showed us? I couldn't get it out of my mind, so I took a look at the photos of other burns we've had this year. There was a bent tree in one of the pictures." He sighed. "I went out there this morning and found another looted shrine."

CHAPTER FORTY-THREE

NICKY PARKED her unit in the deserted admin parking lot at the Fire-Sky Police Department, flipped off the headlamps, and leaned against the steering wheel. After her talk with Savannah, and Ryan's revelations, her thoughts wouldn't settle. She'd been way too restless to head back home, and there was always plenty of catching up to do. It wasn't that late—ten o'clock. The monotony of paperwork would be a perfect distraction.

She grabbed the enchiladas before she locked up her truck and trotted up the stairs. Once inside, she started Savannah's computer, then headed to the break room to warm up her food.

"Hey, Sarge. You take a late shift?"

Cyrus Aguilar, a homegrown Tsiba'ashi D'yini cop, stirred a travel mug of coffee. His black braid hung down his back, almost invisible on the midnight blue of his uniform. His partner, Officer Gracie José, sat at the cluttered break room table and eyed Nicky narrowly. Her dark brown hair was wound in a bun, and her shirt stretched tight over her body armor.

"Paperwork. I'm gonna hide in Savannah's office." Nicky popped her enchiladas in the microwave. "Where is everyone?"

"Out on calls."

"Coffee?" she asked.

"Freshly brewed a couple hours ago."

They chatted while Nicky's food heated and she fixed herself a cup, adding sugar instead of artificial sweetener, hoping the hit of carbohydrates might quell her burgeoning headache.

"We're on patrol over in Little Aquita tonight. Not too crazy about that. I hear there's a black-spirit thing in one of the houses that refuses leave. War chiefs even did a blessing." Aguilar grimaced. "Have a good evening, Sarge."

He headed out the door into the quiet squad room. José followed.

"Officer José?"

She halted and looked at Nicky, her aspect flat, eyes cold.

"How's Jinni Sundry doing?"

"The tribe served her with an eviction notice."

"I didn't know." Nicky felt a tug of guilt. "Will she go home?"

"Back to Zuni? She's got nothing there. Or didn't you know that, either?"

Guilt evaporated, overwhelmed by a sudden flare of anger.

"Belay that tone, Officer. There are consequences for breaking the rules. Officer Sundry wasn't fired. She elected to resign her position." Nicky held Gracie's stare until the young woman dropped her gaze. "What will she do?"

"I offered to let her stay with me, but she's met someone, and, well ... she's pretty happy." Gracie shifted. "Sorry, Sergeant."

"I don't hold it against you for sticking up for Jinni. She's lucky to have a friend who supports her." Nicky wrapped her hands around her coffee cup. "Your partner's waiting. And Officer? Take care out there."

Once they'd left, Nicky gingerly drew the enchiladas from the microwave and sat down. The stiff topographic maps that littered the table ruffled and snapped as she swept them to one side. It was quiet in the squad room, the only sound a hum of fluorescent lights and a periodic sizzle from the coffee maker. She ate methodically, thinking.

When she was finished, she covered what was left of the enchiladas, turned out the break room light, and headed back to Savannah's office. She hadn't made any firm decisions about her home, but for the first time she contemplated taking control of the process by letting it go.

———

CRACKLES—LIKE rustling paper—penetrated Nicky's concentration. The sound traveled in through Savannah's half-closed office door. A light switched on, faint, distant, but other than the vague yellow glow, the hallway remained dark. One of the cops back from a call getting an endless cup of coffee in the break room. Nicky frowned and rubbed her hands together against the chill. Someone must have turned the air conditioner way down. Tucking her fingers under her legs to warm them, she ignored her discomfort and focused on the computer screen.

It wasn't until she glanced at the time that she realized another hour had passed. It was closing in on midnight, and she needed at least thirty more minutes to finish her report, but her bladder wouldn't wait that long. Nicky rose and felt pops down her back as she stretched out the kinks. She swung the office door completely open and stepped out into the hall—

A gray silhouette, face indistinct, stood in the glass-encased garden.

Her shoulders relaxed, and she cocked a half smile at her foolishness. Only her reflection, backlit from the desk lamp in the office. She massaged the gooseflesh from her arms and headed to the ladies' room, going the long way around to shake the stiffness from her legs. Her hand hit the door with a thump.

When she walked back to Savannah's office, she used the shorter route, her mind already on her unfinished report. Other than the light spilling out of the break room's wide opening, the corridor was dark. She quickly glanced into the room. An officer sat at the table, his gold badge standing out starkly against the midnight blue of his uniform. He was sorting through large sheets of paper—the topo maps—twiddling a red pen in his fingers, a cup of coffee at his elbow. She walked past and he looked up, did a double take, but smiled and raised his hand in greeting, then bowed his head, once more focusing his attention on the maps.

Nicky took four steps down the unlit hallway before her mind blanked. Leg muscles turned to water. She braced a hand against the wall to stop from sinking to her knees, heard a muted whimper. It took a moment to realize the sound had come from her throat.

Her nose and eyes stung. Her chest jerked. Breath came in gasps as her brain frantically tried to sort out what she'd just seen.

The man sitting at the table couldn't be in the break room, couldn't have smiled, couldn't have waved. Couldn't have—

Nicky gulped, desperate for air.

Couldn't have *been*.

Because Geronimo Elk had put the barrel of his service weapon under his chin and pulled the trigger. Because he was dead.

Something clattered behind her. Nicky wrenched her body around.

The red pen rolled slowly out of the break room and into the hall.

CHAPTER FORTY-FOUR

Nicky paced in Savannah's living room, head pounding, pent-up energy in her body screaming. Savannah, in her nightclothes and robe, perched on the edge of the sofa, her fingers worrying around a mug of coffee.

"Nicky, *please*. Sit down."

Nicky stopped, breath seething from clenched teeth. "Why isn't Ryan here yet?" She pressed the heels of her hands to her temples, swiped shaking fingers over her hair, and yanked out the band holding her ponytail. "I told him I needed him. Now. I told him."

"He had to go to his dad's. But Nicky, this isn't the way. You shouldn't—"

The front door of Savannah's home burst open.

"Got it," Ryan said. He tossed a bulging plastic baggie on the side table.

Nicky swayed on her feet, potent relief dizzying her.

"What's happened?" He strode to Nicky and grasped her arms.

She stared into his hazel eyes, his familiar face. But her throat was too tight, her voice caught inside. She needed to explain, had to tell him—

He shook her gently. "Nicky. Calm down." Ryan caught her in an embrace, hugged her tight. She hadn't realized how cold she'd been until then. Chill that penetrated deep to her core.

Another hand pressed into her shoulder. Nicky tipped her head back and met Savannah's gaze. Ryan untangled an arm and tucked it around her friend—their friend.

"My two girls," Ryan said.

Savannah caught her eye and winked. "God, that remark is so sexist."

Nicky chuckled. With a shuddering breath, she forced her body away. "I'm so glad you came." She bit her lip, her gaze swiveling back and forth between them.

"Savannah and I declared a truce. At least until dawn." Ryan's voice was gruff. He tightened his arms around Savannah before he let her go.

Nicky was glad he couldn't see the love and sadness on Savannah's face.

"But I'm pretty sure our negotiations didn't include—" Ryan pivoted to the door and sighed. "Dyeetya. Are you coming in or not?"

Howard Kie inched around the doorjamb.

"Howard?" Savannah clutched the edges of her robe. "You left hours ago."

"He's been parking his truck around the corner each night. He sleeps there," Ryan said.

"But, Howard. Why?" Savannah asked.

"Since I saved your life, I have a duty to watch over you."

"Since you ... *what?*" Ryan scowled. "You didn't go into that cave. *I* did."

Howard thrust out his lower lip. "You wouldn't have found her without *my* directions."

Ryan took a step toward him, and Savannah rushed to stand between the two men.

"I am not afraid of you, Apache diya," Howard said, crowding behind Savannah. Big talk, but Nicky was pretty sure he was using her friend as a shield.

"Well, you should be, druusishə dyeetya, because I'm about to kick your—"

"Stop it. Both of you!" Savannah pressed her hands against Ryan's chest. "Nicky! Do something."

"Are you kidding? I'm about to go make popcorn." Hand shaking, she picked up the plastic baggie. "What do I do with this stuff, Ryan? Burn it and inhale the smoke?"

Howard's head poked up from behind Savannah. "Medicine?" He scurried over to Nicky and snatched the bag out of her hand to examine it under the light. "This is a powerful mixture. You did good, Apache. This cop is very sick. I told her so, and she laughed at me."

"Why doesn't that surprise me?" Ryan murmured. He caught Nicky's eye. "You steep it in boiling water and drink the tea. There's more to the ceremony, but I need to know what happened. Did you see the gray-man vision again? The god of the dead and fire?"

"An *outsider* sees visions?" Howard's voice spiraled. "That's not fair."

"And ghosts. Seneca Elk," Nicky said.

Savannah scowled. "You practically had heatstroke when you found him, and inhaled all that salvia."

"And tonight, Geronimo Elk was in the break room at the police station. In uniform." Nicky couldn't seem to steady her voice. "He waved at me."

Ryan whistled. "Two brothers in the span of a couple of weeks? They're trying to tell you something."

"When I'd ... recovered enough to—" Residual terror shivered over Nicky, strangling her voice. "He'd marked those with a red pen." The topographic maps lay across Savannah's dining room table.

"You think a ghost did that? Come on, Nicky. Those maps are always on that table, and everyone marks them up." Savannah rubbed her arms. "And Geronimo was a manifestation of an exhausted mind."

Howard frowned and leaned toward Ryan. He notched his chin at Savannah. "Is that one always like this?"

"Yep," Ryan replied. "Not a traditional bone in her body."

"Huh. You would think, with her father and ancestry—"

"Stop talking about me when I'm right here."

The two men quickly bent over the table. Ryan traced his finger to a red circle.

"This mark. It labels the burned shrine near the poacher's camp. This one"—he tapped a second red circle—"is the one I told you about, with the second looted shrine."

Nicky nodded. "I think the marks pinpoint locations of other hunting shrines, more than the ones burns revealed."

"Because they're being looted, too?" Ryan asked. He shuffled between the maps. "I'll have to cross-check them with the past burns, but if this is real, someone is systematically stealing from Tsiba'ashi D'yini sacred sites."

"No wonder these ghosts are bothering you," Howard said. "But the god of the dead and fire is very serious. Savannah, you will start boiling the water. We need to bless and cleanse the whole place with k'uuchini waani."

Savannah dropped her head and moaned. "Not yellow smoke. I hate yellow smoke. It'll stink up my house for days. Wait. Cleansing's supposed to be done by a war chief, right?"

Nicky and Ryan turned on her. "No war chiefs," they barked in unison. Not after what had happened earlier that summer.

"That's why I brought Howard," Ryan said. "He has some training. He'll do the blessing."

"You'd better make sure she goes outside after she drinks that stuff, Ryan," Savannah said. "Way out into the desert. Once it's over, she can sleep it off in the guest bedroom."

"*Once it's over?*" Nicky said. "You're just going to smudge me, and then I drink tea. Right?"

Ryan and Howard exchanged glances.

"You must trust us." Howard stretched his lips into a smile that didn't reassure Nicky at all. "The Apache and I will guide and take care of you."

"Yep. It's all about trust," Ryan said. "Do you have an old T-shirt or something to change into?"

"Why?"

Savannah held up a hand. "Don't tell her. I want this experience to be a wonderful surprise. C'mon, Howard. Let's get the water boiling." She and Howard disappeared through the kitchen's arched opening.

"I'm in for it, aren't I?" Nicky asked Ryan.

"Big-time. But it's necessary. These ghosts won't leave you alone unless you're cleansed. But being medicined is more than just drinking the tea we brew." He hesitated. "Nicky? It might not work."

"I'm okay with anything that'll help." She let out a slow, shaky breath. "We still need to figure out what's going on. You'll check out the shrines marked on the map? Could you take Franco with you? Give him enough information without telling him about ... about...."

"He's not stupid, Nicky. You'll have to tell him at some point that you're—"

"Delusional? Crazy? That I have meaningful interactions with dead people and ancient Native American spirits?" She gestured wildly. "How can I explain when I don't understand it myself?"

Ryan took her hand and stilled its agitated motion.

"I've told you before, this is a gift. The gods and spirits chose you for a reason. You need to stop fighting your visions and embrace them."

"But Savannah makes a valid argument about the heat exhaustion, the salvia. Everything." She couldn't keep the edge of desperation out of her tone.

"You're afraid Franco will reject you. Is that it?"

"I ... don't ... it's...." She stopped. "He wouldn't be the first."

"Your mother's a scientist. People like her need a different level of proof." His fingers tightened. "And she didn't leave because of you. She left because your dad cheated on her."

She opened her mouth to argue when a loud metallic clatter from the kitchen jerked her head around.

"Put that down. Stop." Savannah's voice was sharp. "Go sit down. Sit!"

"I have a feeling that Howard's finding his goddess has feet of clay," Ryan said.

"That would be good for you, right?" Nicky studied his face.

He shrugged, his mouth tight.

"Ryan? How do you know Howard sleeps in his truck around the corner?"

Ryan met her gaze, and she bit the inside of her lip at the pain in his eyes. "He's not the only one who watches out for her, you know."

———

"I HATE YOU." A vicious cramp tore into Nicky's belly. She doubled over and heaved onto the sand.

Ryan rubbed gentle circles on her back. "I'm sorry, Nicky, but it's necessary."

She stumbled farther into the desert, hunched against the pain. Ryan stayed by her side, a steadying hand on her elbow.

"Necessary to poison me? God, please let me die." Agony radiated through her torso and down her limbs.

"Getting medicined cleanses your mind, your body, exorcizes your—"

"Lunch and dinner."

"Why else do you think Savannah sent us out here? It's an ancient, sacred ritual. There are paintings of shamans from hundreds of years ago, spewing—"

"Stop." She dropped to her knees in the soft sand as her stomach emptied again.

Nicky sat back, nose and eyes streaming. Ryan handed her a wet washcloth. She wiped her face and mouth and pulled in a breath, body as limp as the rag in her hand.

Bluish moonlight bathed the desert. Warmth lingered from the previous day, although dawn was minutes away. For miles in front of her, nothing was manmade. She could have been in another age, an earlier time. Pain retreated as the peace of the night seeped in. Nicky closed her eyes.

"Ryan. I think the Elk Clan is looting the shrines. They guide hunts all through that area."

"You'll have to have more evidence than 'I think.'" His voice rumbled, low and soothing.

"The grandsons have new trucks. They've constructed two expensive pumping systems and tanks. It has to be about money."

"Explain to me why a family of fetish carvers, for whom these objects are sacred, would desecrate shrines from our ancestors? This is not a trivial crime. The spiritual consequences can be grave, and it would result in banishment from the tribe. I've gone through banishment. It's not—" Ryan's voice caught. "Anyway. Why now? That family has been guiding and scouting for decades."

Nicky shook her head.

Big mistake. The movement triggered another wave of nausea. Ferocious pain cramped her insides. Stomach muscles contracted.

When it was over, she curled forward into a ball and stared at the sand. Her breath checked in her throat.

Horrible retching sounded in the distance. Footsteps crunched, coming closer.

"Ryan. Come get Howard and take him away from my house," Savannah said. "I barely got him outside, and now I have to hose off the patio. Why did you let him drink the rest of Nicky's medicine?"

"I didn't *let* him do anything. Said he hadn't seen any visions since he's been sober and thought getting medicined might help."

"You handed him the cup."

"Only to wash," Ryan said, placating.

"You are such a liar. You want him to look bad."

"Doesn't take much, does it?"

Nicky groaned. "I thought you two called truce until sunup."

Another choked cry echoed from behind her. Nicky's stomach cramped sympathetically. "Help him, Ryan. I don't want you to see me—" She moaned piteously.

"I already have, but all right. Stay here."

Nicky rolled her head and pinned him with a blurry glare. "Like I can go anywhere."

Savannah bent and put a hand on her back.

"Go ahead," Nicky said. "Say it."

"Hey, Nicky? About getting medicined? Told you so." Savannah gave her one last pat and marched off, her and Ryan's bickering voices floating in the graying dawn.

Nicky stretched out a hand. Her shaking fingers wavered over the stained patch of desert where a half a dozen small luminescent stones lay on the sand. She pinched one between her finger and thumb and placed it on her palm. They'd come from inside her. Just like Seneca Elk's.

But she hadn't eaten any rocks.

Nicky stared at the tiny stone. What the heck was going on?

CHAPTER FORTY-FIVE

Nicky slammed the door of her truck closed and hurried through the parking lot, tired and drained from being medicined, already five minutes late for her ten a.m. meeting with Julie Knuteson. Just to the west, the I-25 freeway wound its way through Albuquerque, the background hum and growl of vehicles chasing Nicky until she stepped through double glass doors into the soaring interior of the New Mexico Scientific Laboratories, the OMI's home.

Cool quiet enveloped her. Wavy canvases of the artwork *Outside, Inside* hung above the lobby, abstract explosions of color. Julie stood across the lobby with a wiry, casually dressed man of about thirty who was shorter than her by a couple of inches. Swallowing mounting apprehension, Nicky squared her shoulders and walked toward them.

Julie gave her a quizzical smile. "You look like death warmed over."

"Then I guess I'm in the right place," Nicky said.

The man beside Julie chuckled.

"Nicky, this is Dr. Aaron Vedec. Aaron, Sergeant Nicky

Matthews of the Fire-Sky police. Dr. Vedec is the chemist at New Mexico Tech who I contacted about Seneca Elk's stones."

Vedec brushed wavy black hair off his forehead. Gray eyes smiled, the skin around them crinkling with laugh lines.

"Thanks for coming up to Albuquerque, Dr. Vedec," Nicky said. He had a firm handshake, his palm dry with calluses.

"Aaron, please. No problem, Sergeant. My wife wanted to shop, and tomorrow I'm briefing a collaborator at UNM about what we've found." His Adam's apple bobbed with every word.

"So I wasn't wasting your time?" Nicky asked him.

Aaron grinned. "Not at all."

"He's got a preliminary analysis you have to see to believe." Julie practically bounced on her toes. "Come on. I've reserved a conference room."

Their shimmering excitement was contagious, and the unease blanketing Nicky since Julie's call to set up the meeting subsided a little.

Julie hurried toward a door behind the security desk, badged the lock, and tugged Nicky beside her as they headed down an apricot-painted corridor. "Remember the horrible mine disaster on the Animas River? The Gold King in Colorado?"

Nicky nodded. "That spill ran through the Navajo Reservation."

"It was all kinds of toxic." Julie punched a button, and the elevator door opened. "So the state hired clots of researchers to monitor pollution along the river."

"I'm part of a clot." Aaron sidled in beside them. "Our team is tasked with measuring contaminants in organic materials, soils, groundwater—study how it moves through the ecosystem over time."

Nicky leaned against the rail as the elevator swooped upward. "A perfect addition to the New Mexico Institute of Mining and Technology," she said, smiling.

"Did you go to Tech? Great school."

Nicky shook her head. "Graduated from State."

Julie ushered them down a wide hallway. Windows in the doors they passed framed sunny wet-science labs, light rainbowing through a myriad of glass bottles crowded above the benches.

The conference room had a projector screen across one wall, a laptop on the long table, and the aroma of freshly brewed coffee. Aaron, steaming cup by his elbow, clicked the mouse to start his presentation. A picture of Seneca Elk's stones flashed on the screen. Nervousness back, Nicky took a calming breath and a quick sip of coffee, grimaced, and added two more packets of sugar.

"When Julie asked me to analyze stones found in the stomach of a cadaver—and suggested pica—I figured this would be quick. Scan the rocks and possibly figure out where your guy picked them up before ingestion. We have a soil and mineral database of samples from around the region, so once we have an atomic profile and measure radioactive isotopes or military-industrial contamination—think trinitite and the Trinity Site, for example, or gypsum and White Sands—we can get pretty close to a geographic area."

Nicky nodded. Police had access to similar databases for minerals and soil composition.

"But when the data came back on these stones, we realized they were extremely unusual. Their metal and mineral content mimicked —" Aaron clicked to a new slide showing a sleek stack of instruments. "Sorry. I skipped over important explanations. We use this machine, a wavelength-dispersive X-ray fluorescence spectrometer, to quantitatively measure the elements in the samples." He clicked to a new slide, and a series of bar graphs appeared, labeled with periodic table abbreviations. "Ready? Here it is. The rocks you sent us exactly match"—he took a deep breath—"the percentage composition of minerals and trace metals found in the human body. Except for the chromium."

Both Aaron and Julie faced her, wide-eyed and beaming.

"Isn't that amazing?" Julie's tone was reverent.

"So amazing." Nicky sat forward, elbows on the table, hands clasped. "Except I don't understand any of it."

Aaron tipped his head back and laughed. "Sorry. Julie told me who your mom is. Since she probably had a hand in developing some of these instruments and techniques, I figured—"

"A reasonable assumption," Nicky said hurriedly. "And I did start out as a chemistry major before I switched to criminal justice."

"Didn't want comparisons with your brilliant mother." Aaron nodded sagely. "I understand."

Nicky took a sip of coffee, eyes on the screen. No. He didn't.

"Let me explain," Aaron said. "Most of our body mass—ninety-six percent—is composed of only four atoms: oxygen, carbon, hydrogen, and nitrogen. But we're made up of about sixty total chemical elements. A large percentage of those are considered trace or even rare. Based on their composition, we believe these stones are actually comprised of minerals and metals extracted from their host—in this case, your drowning victim."

"*Extracted?*" Nicky pressed laced fingers to her mouth.

New slide. Circles of porous gray materials filled the screen, almost like three-dimensional patterned doilies.

"Scanning electron micrograph of a tiny chip of the sample," Vedec explained. "All the specimens were structured like this."

"That looks biological," Nicky said.

"Yes." He clicked again. The latticed stone paralleled an analogous micrograph with a different pattern but the same lacy structure. "Your specimen next to corallites from *Porites lobata*, a common reef coral. If I didn't know better, I would've said your guy had been eating chunks of this."

"Maybe he was. Coral's used extensively in Native American jewelry," Nicky said, something akin to panic tinting her voice. Julie turned to study her, brows knit, but Aaron shook his head.

"Mineral composition's wrong. Besides, coral would dissolve away in the highly acidic environment of the stomach. The organism that created your stones extracted these elements, essentially acting like a mineral extension of its host."

"*Tsa'atsi y'aauni.*" What Ryan and RJ Analla had called the special fetishes. "Living stone."

"Living stone. I like that." Aaron sat back in his chair, grinning.

"Show her the gummy-bear rock." Julie turned in her chair. "Remember that one, Nicky?"

He clicked to the next slide. "I used synchrotron X-ray fluorescence microtomography to image the element distributions. This allows analysis of the three-dimensional structure with high spatial resolution." On the black screen, the creamy bear-shaped stone stood out starkly. Aaron manipulated the mouse, and the stone rotated and swirled on the screen. "The software allows me to colorize specific minerals. Zinc's an essential trace element that's super important in gene expression. This is how it's laid down in the stone." Thin spikes of blue color shafted into the structure, like spines of a porcupine. They stopped at a dark internal core.

"That's so weird," Julie murmured.

Aaron flipped through magnesium, iron, copper. "Even fluorine. Dental hygiene was important to Mr. Elk. Again, the ratios of the elements we found are exactly like those of the human body, except—"

"Chromium," Nicky said.

Click. Fluorescent purple dotted the structure.

"Chromium's believed to help with blood sugar regulation, but studies also implicate low levels of chromium in changes in mental health. There were *five times* the amount expected in these stones. This organism seems to have a predilection for it."

Changes to mental health. "Isn't chromium toxic?"

"And carcinogenic. A lot of the trace elements in our body—cadmium, arsenic, lead—are dangerous at higher levels. This organism chelated those, too."

"If this living stone leached out the chromium in Seneca Elk's body, how was he affected?" Nicky asked.

Aaron and Julie exchanged glances.

"If the organism was extracting chromium, his glucose regulation was probably off. He might crave sweets," Julie said.

"Like gummy bears." Even in the air-conditioned room, a bead of sweat trickled down Nicky's spine as she made the connections. When she and Franco had delivered Seneca's death notification, discarded candy wrappers had littered the Elks' living room. The day Gemini confronted her about his guns, Clint had bought a sack of gummy bears for Dyu'ami. Nicky stared at her heavily sugared coffee. She pushed it away.

"Ingestion of gummy candy could explain the shape," Aaron said. "Watch. I'm going to digitally peel the stone." The image shrank as outer layers disappeared until the white shape of a gummy bear was all that was left. "The core of this stone and all the others were hollow, probably because they're built on a whole or masticated gummy candy. I bet you could start with any carbon source and construct whatever shape you liked. The stomach becomes an incubator, a growth chamber. Candy, grains, wood—"

"Wood?" Goose bumps shivered across Nicky's skin.

"Cellulose is pure glucose if you have the right enzymes to access it." Aaron paused. "Julie said this guy's brother had stones in his sinuses when he was autopsied. That implies others in the family could be—"

"Infected." Nicky whispered the word.

"*Colonized* is a better description," Aaron said.

"Another brother complained of headaches before he committed suicide. Could colonization have been the reason?" Nicky asked.

"Anything said here is pure speculation," Julie answered. "But if neurologic levels of chromium were depleted, there could be behavioral implications."

"Mood swings, reckless behavior, aggressiveness? Violence?" This couldn't be real, couldn't be happening. She caught Aaron's gaze. "Does this organism pose a threat to people who are exposed?"

"If it did, someone probably would've seen it before," he answered. "I mean, the tribe's lived on that land for a long time. In fact, I bet this organism is associated with the reservation's geology."

"What?"

"Archaea and extremophiles. A whole domain of organisms that thrive in bizarre conditions we don't normally associate with life. I mean, this thing grows stones in the stomach, where pH can drop to one or two. Extremely acidic. What if this creature originally adapted to the extreme conditions of, say, a volcano? There once was volcanic activity all through this region."

"But wouldn't that mean extreme heat?"

"Hyperthermophilic archaea. Yes." He hesitated, exchanged another glance with Julie.

Nicky sat up straighter. Something was up.

"There are lots of other life-forms found in extreme environments," he continued. "Halophiles, acidophiles, alkaliphiles, organisms like *Cupriavidus metallidurans*—"

"Stop. You're just making up words now." Nicky kept her face and tone pleasant and firm, but her insides quivered, panicky. Deep breath. Cop demeanor, cop voice. "In plain English, what's going on?"

"The microorganism—bacterium or archaebacterium—that constructed these stones could have enormous commercial potential," Aaron said. "It has the ability to scavenge trace amounts of heavy metals and minerals and consolidate them into a neat little package. It creates rocks using minerals in its environment. And it grows fast."

"Remember, Nicky?" Julie touched her hand. "I found a *sixth* stone in the specimen jar after I took out your stitches. When Aaron analyzed that stone, the composition was different. It had extracted silica from the glass, as well as micro-contaminants from the preservative. It grew within a few days." Her eyes sparkled. "*A few days.*"

"This has huge implications in toxic-waste cleanup, like the Gold King mine." Aaron leaned forward. "Mix it with leachate, wait awhile, filter out the living stones, and voilà! Purified water."

Franco'd said the ciénega had been poisoned back in the 1940s. Nicky quickly pulled up the picture on her phone of the warning sign she'd found at the mouth of the canyon and filled in the lost letters: EV ME AL CO MIN ION. *Heavy metal contamination.*

"Except this organism can colonize humans," Nicky said. At the ciénega. She'd been infected. "Extract important elements from their brains, possibly driving them to suicide."

"And of course that's something we'll have to get a handle on and why we need to study it," Aaron replied soothingly. "I don't think you understand the value of this discovery. And since this thing was found on tribal land—"

"No. *Inside* a person." Knuckles white, Nicky laid her clenched hands on the table.

"But he was a member of the tribe, and that means the tribe could hold the patent on this organism or anything commercially derived from it. *Tons* of money if it ends up extracting minerals, and not only for cleanup. What if it can extract trace quantities of gold or platinum or—or rare earth metals needed for technology?" Aaron sat back, eyes suddenly hard. "Decades ago, *Thermus aquaticus* was found in a hot spring at Yellowstone National Park. Isolation of a DNA polymerase enzyme called *Taq* changed the way the whole world did science—polymerase chain reaction. PCR. The company who patented it made billions of dollars. Guess how much Yellowstone got? Zilch. I don't want that to happen to the Fire-Sky Indians. Look, once this information gets out, you'll have bioprospectors overrunning the pueblo, harvesting this organism without the tribe's permission."

"You have the stones," Nicky said. "Go talk to the tribal council."

Silence. Her gaze swiveled back and forth between Aaron and Julie.

Julie finally sighed. She grasped Nicky's forearm with a warm hand. "Because the stones were taken from a corpse, there was always the possibility of contamination by a disease-causing organism."

"You got that right." Nicky snorted. "You warned everyone who touched them to be careful?"

"Of course, but that's not quite my point." Again, Julie sighed. "I sterilized them with high heat."

"Me, too." Aaron shifted in his chair. "Burned away any possible organic contamination. Nothing living made it through."

"But you said the organism could live in extreme environments." Nicky stopped as Julie shook her head. "You *killed* whatever made the stones?"

"Yes. But we have a plan. Since both Seneca and his brother were colonized, we want to approach the Elk family, see if anyone else is infected. I know it's not ideal"—Aaron inhaled deeply—"but we need more stones to analyze."

"No, it's not ideal." Nicky's voice was flat. She stared blankly at the gummy-bear rock floating in the blackness of the screen. "You don't need to go to the Elk family for more living stones."

CHAPTER FORTY-SIX

NICKY SAT at her kitchen table, chin propped on her fist, body still, mind dazed. Orange-gold light from a setting sun filtered through the window over the deep kitchen sink, old-fashioned and white. It contrasted starkly with the faded red Textolite countertop edged in aluminum but matched the wood cupboards painted white so many times that they didn't close. An avocado-green refrigerator, a white stove. The cheap black microwave and coffee maker were her only contributions to the mismatched decor.

She turned her head in a desultory fashion and examined the attached living area. In newer homes, it would be called a great room, but there was nothing great about it. An ugly green sofa was pushed against the far wall, the matching chair angled ninety degrees on one side. Coffee and lamp tables bought from a secondhand store, no TV. All the lovely furniture—heirlooms handed down from one generation to the next—gone. Sold.

Funny. That didn't bother her so much anymore. After her talk with Grandfather Hopinkay, she'd come to an internal understanding about what she held dear in the past and what she should hold dear in her future.

Except now her future was in jeopardy.

She wished her grandmother really could come back for one day so they could talk about what had gone wrong in Nicky's life, and what had gone so wonderfully right. Grandmother would have loved Savannah and how she questioned and pushed Nicky. Their friend-ship wasn't perfect—how boring would that be—but they challenged each other.

Grandmother would have comforted Ryan, something Nicky wasn't sure how to do. Would she have encouraged him to move on? Find a new way, happiness without Savannah? Nicky knew it was her own selfishness—wanting, *needing* everything to stay the same—that made her hold back that advice. Was she that afraid of change?

Franco, Grandmother would have invited to dinner. She would have made him feel at home. And she would have encouraged Nicky to not be so alone anymore. Take a chance with a good man because life was passing her by.

Pain stabbed, and Nicky pressed the heels of her hands against her temples as her body reminded her she was sick, infected ... *colonized*. Her gaze dropped to the plastic baggie on the table and the tiny stones inside it. Stones from inside *her*. Elemental imbalances caused by an organism scavenging trace minerals from the body.

Was she staring at her death?

She hadn't told Julie and Aaron where she'd get more stones. Had absorbed their excitement, their outlandish predictions of money to be earned with patenting and licenses, feeling only a spark of interest. Infection explained her headaches, her emotional outbursts, her recklessness on the job. Just like Jinni Sundry, she'd hidden something that increased the danger to her colleagues and friends.

It all started to weave together. Geronimo's and Cochise's suicides, the discovery in the tribal registry of odd deaths in the Elks' family history. She needed to talk to a doctor, find a treatment or antibiotic or something before whatever was inside her took over her mind.

But … what if the doctor reported her? What if she was suspended? Deemed unfit and fired? Without a job, there was no way she'd salvage her home, no way to maintain control of her life.

No way out.

Breath ragged, Nicky closed her eyes against the despair that threatened to decimate her. Pressure pounded in her head, her stomach cramping in sympathy. Was this how it had started with Geronimo Elk? Spiraling thoughts? Physical pain? Her eyes stung with moisture as her hand dropped to her lap, dragged to her side. Blood rushed as her palm covered the butt of the gun. Warm, rough, the diamond-patterned grip was familiar, comforting. She wrapped her hand around it tighter. *So easy.* For her. For everyone else. Her finger pressed the release, and the holster pushed a hard knot into her thigh. The owl fetish in her pocket. Ryan had told her to keep it close. That it would protect her.

Almost unconsciously, Nicky's hold on the weapon loosened. She let go and slipped her hand into her pocket, curled fingers around the stone, and clutched it tightly. The pain suddenly dissipated, and warmth spread through her body, clearing her mind. She exhaled slowly, settled.

She couldn't let the organism control her. What she did as a cop was too important to risk putting her colleagues and her friends in danger. She'd fight it, wouldn't take the easy way out.

She'd make that doctor's appointment and deal with the consequences.

CHAPTER FORTY-SEVEN

Nicky slammed her unit's door with more force than necessary. Bright sunlight stabbed her eyes even through her wraparound sunglasses, adding to a burgeoning headache. Back to work Monday. Once again, she found herself at the tongued section of Hummingbird Mesa, its stepped layers of red-and-tan cliff ambling east and west into scrub-covered ground and barren fields. Residual heat radiated up from the sand and rock, doubling the morning's warmth. Clouds with dark blue-gray underbellies built over the mountains, huge and thick, balling one on top of another. Monsoons on the horizon. About time.

She looked west to the hidden canyon that led to the ciénega where she'd been infected. Sleep the last two nights had been fitful, but she'd woken up with a plan and called the clinic. Her first step on the path forward into the unknown.

"Gianetta." Nicky's boots crunched through rocks, dried and crispy grass, and stunted shrubs.

Gianetta Green stood at the foot of Hummingbird Mesa next to the large smudge of charred black earth. She wore a different kaftan, one splotched with bright pink and yellow roses, and held a chartreuse umbrella with a fringe. The scorched side of the cliff loomed behind her, a dark, static smear in the shape of a flame.

Nicky unscrewed the cap from a bottle of cold water and handed it to the woman, who drank down half of it. "Why'd you call Dispatch to report you were violating your restraining order and ask for me? When your lawyer hears about this, she's not going to be happy."

"I needed to talk to you. Figured if I showed up here, you'd come and warn me off—plausible deniability." Gianetta peered over her glasses.

Nicky sighed, lessons from her two years in law school bubbling to her lips. "You know the part in the Advice of Rights about what can and will be used against you? I'm duty bound to report anything you say that might impact your case."

Gianetta shrugged. She lifted her umbrella and gestured for Nicky to step under the shade. "I told Ruth Jäger I wanted to trade my information, but she refuses to barter with the US attorney. She's not interested in justice for me. She has her own agenda."

No surprise there.

"And I didn't call her—she showed up at my bedside in the hospital," Gianetta admitted. "I'd heard of her. Big name in Santa Fe. California transplant. That civil suit against you was her first in New Mexico. Since she couldn't prove you attempted to kill the Randals' daughter, I figure she took my case to get back at you."

Nicky's stomach curled as she listened, but she'd thought the same thing.

"The Feds don't care where I got the eagle feathers. They only want the money. Ruth's advice? Pay the fine. But twenty-five thousand dollars seems excessive, so I told her I knew something about that bear fetish in my box of stuff." Above them, the umbrella rotated slowly as Gianetta's fingers walked around the handle. "Ruth asked me about that bear *before* you and that hot guy came to the hospital. How did she know unless J told her? Sent her? That little bear must be very important, otherwise why was she asking about it? I said she'd better make a bargain or else. Oh, man, her face went white as a sheet!" Gianetta's whole body jiggled as she laughed. "It's all about that little stone bear. She's protecting J WhiteHawk."

"He did sell it to you."

"No, no, no. I never would've bought a ... a *used* one. They're special, made for one person only. For their spirit, their soul. Created in a way that transcends human understanding. They aren't carved, you know. They're organically cultivated with layers that mimic the multiple planes of existence but maintain an open home at the heart." Her face was animated, eyes glowing. "The maker infuses emotional peace and puts a sense of being into the finished creation. When you die, it becomes a resting place for your soul. A place to reside until rebirth in a more enlightened state. I wanted—want—that," she finished, her face wistful.

Most of what Gianetta said sounded like New Age gibberish, except ... except about how the fetishes were produced. In layers. How had J WhiteHawk learned the process?

"That day, the day you arrested me?" Gianetta continued. "He told me—maybe—he could have one created *specifically* for me. Had someone who could do it. I could even choose my animal spirit guide. But he said Fire-Sky traditions don't allow outsiders to have them, that he could get into a lot of trouble, so I couldn't tell anyone, even my friends. That it would be expensive. I told him I could pay, but he still said only maybe. I was so disappointed." She pointed the water bottle at Nicky. "That's why I think that boy put one inside my box."

Nicky jerked straight. "What boy?"

"The one at J's shop. The pretty-faced one who won't look at you."

Dyu'ami? "Was there a dog?"

"Yeah. Friendly old girl. J always ordered the kid into the office when, uh"—she leaned in—"*indigenous* customers drove up, and I mean barked orders at him. I felt sorry for the boy. Left him some candy a few times."

Nicky stilled. Gianetta gave Dyu'ami a gift. He would have felt bound to reciprocate.

"The kid was always playing with wooden animal toys," Gianetta said. "They were so detailed, so pretty. I asked J about buying one, but he said no."

Dyu'ami on the porch at the Elk compound, lining up his little carved animals. Nicky blinked. *Not toys. Templates.* Templates for *tsa'atsi y'aauni.*

"Then J would smile in that gorgeous way that makes all thought fly from my head."

"Oh, Gianetta...." Pity swept through Nicky.

"It's okay, honey. J's a manipulative bastard, but when you get to my age, it's nice to know you have some control over men, even if it's only monetary. I was one of his best customers. Gave me his card with his personal phone number. Called me a couple times when he had specials." She elbowed Nicky. "My friends were so jealous."

Nicky's mind whirred. WhiteHawk's burner phone. "After you were arrested, did you contact or call Mr. WhiteHawk?"

Gianetta snorted. "No. I told you I didn't want to get him into any trouble—then. But if J and Ruth Jäger are working together against *me*, I'll burn him—them—with no remorse."

WhiteHawk had lied about why he'd gotten rid of the phone.

Gianetta wiped her forehead with the back of her hand. "Do you think you can use any of this? Help me out?"

"If the boy gave you that fetish, there's really no way to prove it. He's autistic and doesn't speak."

"Just my luck. What about going after Ruth Jäger? I'd bet my butt they're connected. Ruth's from California. J worked in Hollywood. I mean, why's that rock bear so special?"

Nicky's mind cleared for an instant. Franco had said the same thing, back at the hospital: *How did Ruth know to ask about it? What is up with the fetish?* She had the answer now. *Because it came out of a dead man's pocket.* Gianetta's revelations and suppositions made perfect logical sense.

A flash of brilliant color caught her eye. She swiveled to look at Gianetta's car. The crystal bird hanging from the rearview mirror glinted rainbows. "Did WhiteHawk send you out to smudge Hummingbird Mesa?"

"He told me to go to the other side of the pueblo, but I found myself here."

Nicky stepped out of the umbrella's shadow, heart thumping. She slipped on her sunglasses, cleared her throat. "In the hospital, you said there was a man present when I arrested you. You really saw someone?"

Gianetta twirled the umbrella faster. "Of course. Didn't you?"

GIANETTA'S VW bumped over the rough ground and out to the dirt road that ran along a barbed-wire fence. Nicky's gaze followed the car as it left, her thoughts juggling Gianetta, WhiteHawk, Ruth, Seneca, Dyu'ami…. She couldn't put the pieces together alone.

Swiftly, she unclipped her phone and pressed in a number. It picked up on the third ring.

"Franco? Meet me at Savannah's. I'll explain when you get there."

As she snapped her cell back in its case, a black shadow crossed her face. The sound of a footfall slithered behind her. Chills passed through her body like a wave. Heart pounding, Nicky spun, her gaze riveted on the rocks where she'd first seen the gray man.

Nothing.

CHAPTER FORTY-EIGHT

NICKY PACED, but Savannah's den only allowed for four steps back and forth from the glassed patio doors to the kitchen. Franco sat on the round cushioned arm of a den chair, water bottle dangling from his hand. When Nicky had called and asked him to meet at Savannah's, he'd been with Ryan working out. Ryan leaned against the kitchen counter, munching grapes from a bowl. Both men were dressed in logoed T-shirts and black basketball shorts. They smelled of sweat and a sharp menthol deodorant that sat unpleasantly on Nicky's stomach.

"Dyu'ami was at WhiteHawk's without Gemini or Clint or any of the other Elks?" Savannah asked. She sat at the breakfast bar, scrolling through photos on her computer.

"I think so." Nicky rubbed her forehead. "She also said White-Hawk would order Dyu'ami into the back when Native customers drove up, like he was trying to hide him."

"Both Seneca and Cochise Elk guided for WhiteHawk," Franco said. "Maybe the rest of the Elks trust him to watch Dyu'ami. I mean, they leave him at the FEMA trailer with Savannah and Howard."

Ryan abruptly tossed his handful of grapes back into the colander. He slanted a glance at Savannah, who lifted her chin. Her hair fell back from her ears, silver and mother-of-pearl earrings dangling.

Earrings. Something niggled in Nicky's mind.

"If Seneca was chosen as fetish carver, he'd carry his tsa'atsi y'aauni. Always." Ryan's tone was adamant.

"That's what Gemini and Clint said. So where did Dyu'ami get Seneca's fetish?" Nicky asked.

"Either he brought it from home or WhiteHawk had it at the shop," Franco said. "And if Ruth asked Gianetta about it at the hospital, who else could have told her but WhiteHawk?"

"How did he find out about Gianetta's arrest?" Savannah asked.

"I heard about it the same day." Ryan shifted and shrugged. "I mean, it's not like it was a secret. Stuff like that gets passed around on the rez."

Nicky stared. He was blushing. "Find anything yet, Savannah?"

"No. I've searched every possible combination of Ruth's and WhiteHawk's names, and nothing's come up linking them except maybe this picture from some Hollywood party. See what you think." Savannah sat back, and Nicky, Franco, and Ryan crowded around her.

WhiteHawk, sweaty and pale, lines stamped on his face, stood in a crowded, darkened room, arms slung around two laughing, scantily dressed women.

Savannah pointed to a figure behind him, the face slightly blurred. "I think this is Ruth. It would at least place them together about a dozen years ago."

"But Ruth's a blonde. That woman has dark hair and much less, um ... up here." Face burning red, Franco swirled a hand around his chest.

Nicky and Savannah exchanged a glance before Savannah rolled her eyes. She muttered something in Keres that roughly translated to "Men are idiots."

Ryan snickered. "And you work undercover."

"You think J WhiteHawk had something to do with Seneca Elk's death," Savannah said. "Why? Weren't you focusing on Mangas Elk?"

"Yes, but Gianetta said the fetish was at WhiteHawk's shop a couple days after Seneca drowned," Nicky said.

"What possible motive could J have to murder Seneca Elk?" Savannah asked. "I thought you said Mangas fought with Seneca before. Why couldn't it have been Mangas?"

"It could have been—I mean, Mangas could have killed Seneca and taken the guns and fetish, and … and … Dyu'ami took the fetish to WhiteHawk's shop. But then why was Ruth asking about it? Why would WhiteHawk care if Dyu'ami put a fetish in Gianetta's box unless it linked him to Seneca?"

"Maybe Seneca figured out WhiteHawk was the one desecrating the shrines," Ryan said. "And WhiteHawk killed him to keep him quiet. Maybe."

Nicky spun around.

"I found two more looted shrines." Ryan nodded to Franco. "Told him about it at the gym, but I didn't tell him about the maps."

Franco narrowed his eyes. "You have maps to the looted hunting shrines?"

The room fell silent.

"Does this have to do with your … visions?" Franco asked.

Nicky's heart seemed to stop before it began to race. She cast a desperate glance at Savannah. Ryan stood next to her, their shoulders touching.

"We've kept your secret," Savannah said softly, "but others know."

Lips dry, Nicky's hand burrowed into her pocket and curled tightly over the owl. She met Franco's eyes squarely. "Geronimo Elk was in the break room Friday night. He marked the shrines on the maps. And when I found Seneca in the tank, his faced changed. Became alive again. He stared at me, begged me to help him." Her gaze faltered and fell to the floor.

"No wonder you almost shot me at the ciénega," he said. "And here I thought you saw the god of the dead and were going to die." His tone was light.

"I did see him," Nicky confessed. "He led me to Seneca's body." She leaned back, searched his eyes. "Seneca's death and ... and the looting, the spirit fetishes, the poaching. I think they're all connected. And I don't believe the gray man is bad. He and Geronimo and Seneca have been trying to help me—help us." She squared her shoulders, pulled in a deep breath. "I want to visit the site of Cochise's suicide."

Franco stared at her for what seemed like forever before he nodded. "We can go this afternoon, before we pick up WhiteHawk for questioning. But, Nicky, sometime soon, you and I are going to have to talk about all this ... and us."

Nicky held his gaze until hers burned. She wanted this. "Okay."

"Jeez," Ryan said, "it's about time."

Savannah high-fived him.

CHAPTER FORTY-NINE

Nicky leaned against the split-rail fence behind the Elks' ranch house, feeding sugar cubes to the little chestnut horse, the same one she'd found at the oasis. A murmur of masculine voices sounded behind her—Franco questioning Roy and Clint Elk about permissions to build the windmills and tanks at the ranch and the ciénega. He'd agreed to keep the Elks occupied while she snooped and would text her when he was done.

With a final pat to the horse's neck, Nicky ambled away from the corral and toward the copse of trees. A breeze stirred the blades of the windmill. It creaked as it turned into the wind. She pressed through the shrubbery, and immediately the dusty scent of the foliage was marred by the sour smell of soot. She stopped and surveyed her surroundings. Ahead of her lay a dimly lit opening hemmed in by thick undergrowth and domed by crosshatched branches. A blackened metal drum filled with trash sat on the far side.

Nicky crept forward and stood at the edge of a low barrier of leaf litter—maybe twelve feet in diameter—encircling the space. Her gaze lifted to the heavily scorched branch where Cochise Elk had hung after he'd set himself on fire. A lot of suicide attempts were a cry for help, but Cochise ... He'd meant business.

Fire-Sky police had arrived after the body had been cut down. Photos showed him flat on his back under the tree limb. She dropped her gaze. Directly below the branch, almost hidden in shadow, was a pile of rocks stacked in a conical pyramid.

Like the one at Geronimo's descanso.

Steps deliberate, eyes never leaving the pyramid of stones, Nicky walked the perimeter of the circle. Her boot rolled, and she squatted and picked away plant debris. Underneath the carefully piled litter were squared and precisely placed rocks. She brushed away more debris and revealed a trail of stones that enclosed the swept circle like a tiny wall.

A circle built to contain a restless or violent spirit.

The windmill's creak accelerated, and leaves rattled in a wave through the clearing. A spot between her shoulders itched. A footfall crunched, then another. Nicky pushed to her feet, hand sliding to her ASP.

"Who's there?"

Dyu'ami stepped out of the bushes, face down, Diya by his side. He wore a grubby white T-shirt, and both of his hands were deep in the pockets of his jeans.

Nicky breathed a quick sigh of relief. "Hey, sweetheart."

Diya crunched through the piled leaves edging the circle and approached Nicky, her tail wagging. Nicky dropped a hand to her ears and scratched.

"Did you see me and Franco drive up? I'm happy you came to see—"

Diya stiffened and growled as the leaves rustled behind Nicky. Another dog, black with pointed ears, darted into the circle. It pressed its nose against the pyramid of rocks, and one side collapsed. Dyu'ami released a high, keening noise. The black dog swirled, hackles raised. Diya's growls deepened, and she lunged away from

Nicky's hand, snapping and snarling. The second dog tucked its tail, and both animals crashed through the brush and disappeared.

Dyu'ami crouched and rocked, arms tight around his knees, his face turned toward the center of the circle and the toppled pyramid.

Nicky hurried over and knelt next to him.

"It's okay. They're gone." A twig was caught in his braid. He stilled as she untangled it. "I've messed your hair up a little." With gentle fingers, she smoothed the golden-brown strands behind his ear. "I'm sorry the rocks got knocked over. But they can be fixed." Nicky glanced at the tumbled stones and did a double take.

She dropped her hand and stood. Something orange-pink gleamed between the rocks.

Dyu'ami grabbed her wrist.

"What's inside the pyramid, sweetheart?"

Her phone chimed. *Dammit.* She grimaced and unclipped it. Franco. Nicky shoved it in her back pocket.

Letting go of her wrist, the boy stepped onto the dirt in the circle and stood for a moment, his breath rapid and shallow, before he continued to the center. He dropped to his knees, blocking her view of the broken pyramid. Methodically, he placed the stones in a neat row to his side. He stood and came back to her. Eyes downcast, he pushed objects into each of her pants pockets.

"Thank you." She slipped her hand into one pocket. Her fingertips smoothed over a small oval shape, cool to the touch. She pulled out the pinkish orange object.

"Dyu'ami! Did you save one of my tomatoes?" She smiled. "You were supposed to eat all of these, not—" Her voice caught.

Not a tomato. A balloon, about the size of a large grape. Nicky rolled it over. Stamped on its skin was a gold leaf. She'd seen the logo before in the captain's office on evidence Dax had presented to them. She knew what filled the balloon, knew its origin.

"Chen Cano," she whispered. "Dyu'ami, where did you—?"

With a gasp, she dug out Dyu'ami's second gift, scooping up her own fetish in her haste. Two stones stood in her palm. Her small owl and a hump-shouldered grizzly, each hair a sharp line, long claws defined, and its mouth full of sharpened teeth. *Cochise's spirit fetish.* The figures flickered—moved—in the dappled shadows. The branch overhead creaked, and her gaze shot upward. The air darkened, as if a cloud had passed over the sun. Her insides lurched, and Nicky staggered, perspective skewing violently. An image wavered above. A dark body swayed. A dangling foot jerked. Suddenly, she could smell the acrid stench of burnt hair and flesh, the sickening odor of death. A gust of wind, and the body twisted slowly....

No. Her head spun dizzily, and the clearing tilted around her. She reeled, dropping the fetishes.

"Di-did you see?" she jabbered. "Did you—"

The boy rotated his head and stared directly at her.

Nicky's breath froze in her throat. She stumbled back. Careened off a tree trunk, almost fell, lunged into the thicket. She ran, broke out of the brush—

"Hey!" Strong hands grabbed her. "Are you all right?"

Franco.

"We gotta go." Her voice was a thread of sound. *"Now."*

Nicky jerked away from him and hurried toward the truck. Franco called her, but she didn't hear what he said. Didn't care.

With shaking hands, she fumbled open her unit and slid inside. It was sweltering—air so hot, it was hard to breathe. But the heat didn't erase the chills that slid over her skin. She leaned her elbows against the steering wheel, dropping her head into her hands.

Dyu'ami's hazel eyes had stared directly at her before they'd rolled back in his head and become completely white.

Like Seneca's eyes in the water tank. Like the eyes of the god of the dead.

Marked for death.

CHAPTER FIFTY

"I EXPLAINED why I had to leave him." Nicky adjusted the strap of her external body armor, the rip of Velcro almost obscuring her voice.

She kept her face turned away from the social worker, who continued to badger her with questions. Yes, she'd left Dyu'ami instead of extracting him. Yes, she understood what danger the boy was in. No, she didn't think it was negligence. Why? Because it would have alerted the men on the ranch—if the Elks anticipated what was to come, Fire-Sky police could face heavy resistance.

Nicky's chest felt hollow because so much of it was lies. Pure, unadulterated fear had driven her to leave Dyu'ami, a cowardice that lashed her with guilt.

The men and women around her checked their weapons, pressed extra ammunition into magazines—voices low, attention focused, movements controlled and purposeful. Prepared for the worst, hoped for the best. An overwhelming show of force that would cause the Elk men to lay down their arms, no shots fired, nobody hurt.

"Those men," the social worker said, a woman in her early forties with a rounded chin and frizzy hair going naturally gray. "They're gun-ridden, violent, and your tribal council doesn't do a thing about it. How soon can you have the boy out? Because I won't get out of the car until it's safe."

Nicky knew this type of woman. An outsider, come to save the poor Indians from themselves, burning out in a few years because she wasn't appreciated and thanked enough.

Franco came into view, helmet in hand, even bulkier than usual in heavy tactical gear. He was briefing the canine unit officers. As they'd driven away from the Elk compound, Nicky had gathered her scattered control and showed Franco the drug balloon, stuttered out some excuse for how she'd found it. He hadn't pressed her about what had happened in the screen of trees, but he *had* provided her the pretexts she now fed the social worker about Dyu'ami—and had grabbed the wheel of the truck to stop her from going back.

"Remember, Dyu'ami works on a barter system," Nicky said to the social worker. "If you give him something, a gift, he feels like he owes you—"

"I read his cumulative file, Officer." Her lip curled as her hand dug into her purse. "We prepare for these types of contingencies just as much as you do."

Nicky clenched her jaw and leaned over to lace up her boot. "Chief Cochin will be in my unit as coordinator. You'll ride with us. Once I extract Dyu'ami, I'll place him with you." She glanced up. "Hey! No phones. We made that clear in the briefing."

The woman's finger hovered over her screen. "I have to tell my partner—"

"No contact with anyone about this raid. If I have to, I will take that away." In black from head to toe, Nicky pressed the intimidation factor. An undercurrent of satisfaction rolled through her when the woman tucked her phone back into her purse without comment.

Savannah hurried toward them and addressed the social worker.

"Everything is set. Dad brought the signed paperwork." She waved her hand to RJ, who stood in the break room's threshold. "My mom's at home, ready for Dyu'ami. Dad and I will stay here until you come back with him."

The squad room quieted as Chief Cochin called the assembled force for final instructions.

"Our first priority is to secure the scene, our second to extract the minor child. Sergeant Matthews will take point on extraction."

All eyes turned to Nicky. She nodded, but unease crept in as she searched the faces of the team. A couple of the traditional officers shifted restlessly. One dropped his gaze and scowled.

"Officer Gallegos. What's going on?" Nicky asked.

Gallegos glanced around the room. He licked his lips and finally met her eyes. "We go out and risk our lives, and for what? Only to have tribal council let them go because of the Elks' status as fetish-carving clan. I call that bullshit."

Nicky nodded slowly. "I understand, Officer."

Cochin scanned the room, face taut, meeting and holding the gaze of each of those present. "I'll make *all* of you a promise. If—when—I'm elected to tribal council, I will do my damnedest to apply the law so that no one on the pueblo feels as if special treatment is given to one clan or family over another. And, depending on what we find tonight, I will start with the prosecution of the Elk men."

Silence prevailed for a few moments. Then, with surprising swiftness, the strained atmosphere dissipated. Men and women stood straighter, chins up, mouths firmed.

"Then we're with you, Chief," Gallegos said. He leaned toward Nicky, his voice low. "Hey, Sarge? Thanks."

Mouth tight, Chief held Nicky's gaze, then nodded. She focused back on the room. "Okay, team, let's rock and roll."

CHAPTER FIFTY-ONE

THE CYLINDRICAL BATTERING ram splintered the lock on the Elks' ranch house door.

"Police! Police!"

Coordinated knots of black-clad figures rushed into each structure on the property. Weapon drawn, Nicky huddled behind her lead, steps short and tight, the three officers in front of her screaming directions and aiming sidearms at the men congregated in the living room.

"Don't move! Let me see your hands!"

Half a dozen men sat in the room, their hands rising slowly off their thighs, eyes forward. A quick scan showed Dyu'ami wasn't present. Nicky left the living area to travel with Officer Aguilar down the long hall.

"Room clear!" he said.

"Bedroom clear!" The twist in her stomach tightened when she couldn't find the boy in room after room.

"Got him!" Aguilar called. "It's clear, Sarge. Just the kid and the dog."

"Stand guard, Officer. This may take a minute."

Nicky stopped in the doorway and steadied her breathing. She dropped her Glock down to the side of her leg and sidled inside, flipped up the plastic visor on her helmet, and scanned. Curtains drawn against the night, no closet. The underbed space was too shallow to accommodate a person.

A single lamp rested on a heavy, battered dresser, glowing golden in the small room. Dyu'ami sat rigid on an unmade twin mattress, his face turned to the wall. Fear lanced through Nicky. She couldn't see his eyes, didn't know if they were still white.

But she wouldn't buckle this time, wouldn't let Dyu'ami down again. Nicky slotted her gun away and lowered to one knee.

Diya had her head in Dyu'ami's lap, and the boy's fingers twisted tightly in the thick fur at her neck. The dog's tail thumped a couple of times, and cloudy eyes rolled in Nicky's direction.

"Dyu'ami? Will you and Diya come with me? Please?" Nicky extended her hand and held her breath.

His lashes fluttered. He turned.

Clear hazel eyes slid over her face and focused on some distant point. She exhaled, relief slumping her shoulders. Dyu'ami slipped to his feet. Without releasing Diya, he held out a clenched fist. His fingers uncurled.

Nicky's owl fetish lay tucked in his palm.

"DYU'AMI OKAY?" Franco asked. He waited for her at the bottom of the wooden porch. They ascended side by side, and he ushered her into the house.

"Yeah. I left him in my unit with Chief and the social worker. Where's Ryan?"

"Still up the mountain."

"What the heck's going on here?" Nicky looked around the room.

About a dozen Elk men—from young to old—hunched on sofas and chairs, their hands zip-tied behind their backs, quiet.

"They knew we were coming. Everyone was sitting in plain sight. Hands flat on their thighs. None of them had any weapons. Not even a pocketknife." Franco's lips were tight. "Did you notice? No dogs. All penned. All their guns secured, none loaded. There'll be a thorough search for more drugs, but I doubt they'll find anything." His jaw bunched rhythmically. "Nicky, they knew we were coming. Savannah—"

She grabbed Franco's arm and jerked him back out the screen door to the porch. The night was pitch, stars and moon covered by clouds thick with rain, the only light twinkling white dots that outlined M'ida Village in the distance. She took a calming breath and faced Franco. "Don't even think it. Savannah wouldn't—"

Wood creaked behind her, and Nicky whirled.

From the dark reaches of the porch, Captain Richards strolled toward them, his compact figure garbed completely in black. He stopped in the rectangle of light shining through the screen, feet braced, icy gaze never leaving Nicky's.

"Officer Valentine," he said over his shoulder. "Report."

Valentine thunked to the door and pushed it open. "Everyone present secured, Captain, but they don't have IDs and aren't talking."

"All accounted for?" Captain asked.

"Uh, no, sir. We should have twelve, not including the kid. Eleven men in custody so far."

"Who's missing?" Captain asked.

Nicky's heart began to pound. She rushed inside and skimmed the faces. "Mangas isn't here." She quickly found Clint. "Where is he?"

"Gemini told him not to touch Dyu'ami." Clint's face was gray, and his breath stank of alcohol. "You made sure the boy's safe?"

"Yes. He's in my unit with the chief."

"That won't stop Mangas."

The knot in her throat hardened.

Clint looked at her with red, swollen eyes. "He knows the boy caused this. Knows Dyu'ami gave you the drugs."

Nicky hit the screen door at a run.

CHAPTER FIFTY-TWO

Nicky pounded down the rutted dirt road, stumbled, righted herself, and picked up speed. Against the darkness, stark interior light poured out of her unit's windows. Diya scurried around the truck's interior, scratching against the glass, barking frantically. Dyu'ami wasn't with her.

The passenger's side hood halted her momentum, her arms absorbing the shock. Franco slid to a stop behind her.

The social worker hurried around the truck, phone in hand, openmouthed. "What's going on?"

Breathing hard, Franco said, "You were told ... no phones."

She thrust it at his face. "RJ Analla texted me and asked when we'll bring the boy."

"Where's ... Dyu'ami?" Nicky gulped in air. "Chief Cochin?"

"Back at the house. The boy needed to go to the bathroom."

"We didn't see them." Panic tore through Nicky. She keyed her shoulder mic. "Valentine. Is Chief at the house? Over."

Long seconds ticked by.

"Negative," Valentine replied.

Pivoting sharply, she sprinted back up the road, Franco pounding beside her.

"Take the outbuildings," she said. "I'm going around back." Bypassing the house, she headed into the darkness behind it. The copse of trees was a blur of black against the rising mountain slope. Even the windmill's silhouette was obscured. She only knew its location by a growing creak of the blades. The wind picked up, and susurrations of leaves and branches ebbed and flowed.

Nicky slowed, breath loud in her ears. A moan sounded to her right. She flicked on her flashlight.

"Lights out! He has my duty weapon."

Cochin. Nicky switched off her light, but she'd seen enough. The woman sat on the ground, hand pressed against the side of her head.

"He came out of nowhere. Hit me," Cochin said.

"Where's Dyu'ami?" Nicky knelt next to her as she scanned the shadows, heart beating at a sickening rate.

"I thought all of the Elks were secured. Thought it'd be safe to—"

A single shot cracked.

Nicky sprang up and sprinted toward the trees, sidearm in her hand. She crashed through the bushes. An orange glow blazed in front of her, and gasoline fumes fouled the air. Mangas stood in the center of the swept circle, arms by his side, a scattering of *tsa'atsi y'aauni* fetishes in the dirt around him. Dyu'ami sat on the ground in front of Mangas, rocking feverishly, hands over his ears. No obvious injuries. *Thank God.*

Nicky aimed at Mangas, center mass. "Let me see your hands! Now!" she shouted. "Step back! *Back!* Do it!"

"No one wanted him, and *we* took him in." Mangas stumbled back from Dyu'ami, empty hands rising. Flames jetted from the trash barrel into the trees, devouring the leaves above. Shimmering reds and oranges outlined his silhouette. "*He's* why Seneca's dead. So Gemini'll choose *him*. Don't you understand? Now he's after me." Mangas's voice spiraled. "I won't succumb, so I brought him. He *has* to take my offerings or I'm next. *I'm next!*"

"I heard a gunshot. Where's the gun?"

He tipped his head back with a quick jerk.

Hands sweating, Nicky adjusted her grip, inched closer. She had to get Dyu'ami. "Arms above your head! The gun, Mangas!"

The blaze licked skyward, climbing branches, jumping from shrub to shrub. The air, lit bright as day, swirled with smoke. Heat radiated, increasing in intensity as fire enveloped the clearing. The smell of smoke turned rancid and sour....

Slowly, Mangas lifted his head, his expression a rictus of anguish, and his eyes—

His eyes rolled white. Nicky smothered a cry.

"I don't have it," Mangas yelled over the roar of the blaze. He swiveled his torso, gestured with his chin at the trash barrel. "I threw it in the—"

A shot shattered the clearing. Mangas dropped.

Nicky whirled, ears ringing, weapon pointed at Luz Cochin.

Chief held her backup gun in her hands. "I thought ... I didn't mean ... *Oh, God.*"

Nicky slammed her weapon into her holster and charged into the circle as branches cracked and flaming leaves dropped around her. She grasped Dyu'ami under the arms. Something hard bounced off her shoulder, and a black object slid across the dirt to stop near Mangas's hand. Nicky's eyes widened. *Cochin's backup gun.*

Dyu'ami twisted and broke loose. He lunged for Mangas, and Nicky grabbed him again.

Franco and Ryan crashed through the bushes. Franco hauled Chief back. They disappeared behind thickening smoke. Nicky bodily lifted Dyu'ami and thrust him at Ryan.

"Take him!"

Fire roared. Smoke burned her throat and eyes. She leaped toward the boiling cavern of flames, but vise-like arms clamped her shoulders and waist and dragged her back.

Nicky arched and twisted. "Mangas. We have to—"

"Too late." Franco's voice was grim.

The bushes around them were on fire. Embers rained from above. With one last glance at the still body, she turned away and dove through the flames, Franco at her side. They backpedaled away from the burgeoning heat.

"What happened in there?" Franco asked.

Cochin appeared at his side. "Mangas Elk committed suicide. Just like his brothers." She grabbed Nicky's arm and squeezed. "Isn't that right, Sergeant Matthews?"

CHAPTER FIFTY-THREE

"Hey. Wake up. I brought coffee." Carefully juggling two Styrofoam cups, Nicky closed the door, file folders and evidence bags clamped under her arm. Franco leaned against one wall in the small observation room, arms folded. He opened red, tired eyes.

"Someone sprang for donuts since it doesn't look like we'll get out of here until sometime next week." Nicky put everything down on the narrow countertop that ran along one side of the room. From her cargo pants pocket, she tugged a slightly squished packet stained with grease and offered it up. "Got you an apple fritter. Took out one of the night crew for it."

"Thanks." Like her, Franco had showered and changed into fresh clothes while the Elks were processed. "How'd it go with Dyu'ami?"

"Okay, I guess. Mrs. Analla and Savannah mothered him immediately. Cleaned him up, fed him, got him to bed. He was asleep when I left."

"Poor kid." Franco stretched. "Need an update?"

"Yeah. I got bits and pieces via texts, but the whole picture would be great."

"The Elks had a system in place to protect their property against wildfire. Ryan and a couple of the other guys tapped into it and put the fire out before it spread up the mountain. Now that things have cooled off, forensics is there to retrieve Mangas's body."

Nicky nodded. And forensics would give lie to Cochin's story of suicide. Still, she'd kept her mouth closed about the shooting. For now. "Find any drugs?"

"No one's found jack-crap. Plenty of time to hide or destroy evidence because of the tip-off." He rubbed a hand over the back of his neck, and his whole body seemed to shimmer with frustration. "Nicky?"

"Don't say it."

"Savannah knew the tac plan. She—"

"Stop."

"—had motive and opportunity. And her loyalty to Fire-Sky, her People."

Her gaze clashed with his. "Savannah knew how dangerous the situation was. The Elks could have met us with guns blazing. She would never do that. Never."

He sighed. "Her phones—personal and work—need to be added to the warrant. We've held this too long, hoping it could be someone else. If you don't do it, I will."

Nicky whirled away and stared through the one-way window. She suppressed a need to lash out at Franco. It was the organism inside her driving her anger, not the man or the situation. She'd tracked her swings in mood since she'd learned her fate—the spikes in rage, the descents into sadness and anxiety. Her doctor's appointment was today. No way she'd make it.

Her hands tightened to fists. Would she end up like Geronimo Elk? Was suicide the way he took back control of his life? Would she succumb?

Succumb.

I won't succumb. Almost Mangas's final words. He'd been the next one chosen as fetish carver, so he *must* have been infected. He'd

scattered fetishes and called them offerings. But Dyu'ami as an offering? Was this about the gray man, the god of the dead and fire?

Nicky focused through the window and on the men sitting at the
table. They'd put Clint in with Gemini, their strategy to play one off
the other, especially since Clint was close to breaking. It was a
gamble she hoped would work.

Clint's fingers rotated his coffee cup around and around, his
motion slow, perfunctory. Gemini's arms were crossed, chin resting
on his breastbone, eyes closed. *Gemini....* He might know how to cure
the infection. Excitement spiked her heart rate.

"They said anything?" she asked.

"No."

Nicky reached for the door handle. "Then let's ask them who
called and warned them we were coming."

CHAPTER FIFTY-FOUR

"MORE COFFEE, CLINT?" Nicky asked. She sat down at the table directly across from him. He appeared to have sobered up.

"Where's Mangas?" His bloodshot brown eyes searched hers, face creased with weariness. "And Dyu'ami? He all right?"

Clint was on edge, barely holding on. If he knew about Mangas's death, she'd never get the information she needed. She addressed the last question only.

"Dyu'ami's fine. He's been placed with a foster family."

Gemini scowled. "Who? Where?"

From behind her, Franco said, "We can't give you that information. Just know he's safe."

"Bah. Like he was last night?" Gemini said. "I heard the shots."

Clint paled even more, if that was possible.

"Let's talk about the raid," Franco said. "You were waiting for us."

Gemini grunted and looked away. "You had no right."

Nicky laid an evidence bag on the table, the drug balloon Dyu'ami gave her inside. "Oh, we had the right. We also have a warrant pending for your phone records, so we'll find out who called to tip you off. As a gesture of goodwill, why don't you tell us?"

"We don't know," Clint said. "Mangas took the call."

"On his cell?"

"No. Phone in the kitchen. He wanted to arm, wanted to fight against those who would come to take what's ours. But Roy said no. He took away his gun, and Mangas ran out." Clint pressed his eyes tightly shut, but lines of moisture seeped between his lashes.

"Selling drugs is how you paid for the tanks and windmills," Nicky said.

No answer.

"Are you working for Chen Cano and the Crybabies? Tipping him off about our operations? This is his mark." She tapped the logo on the balloon. "They're an extremely dangerous gang."

"Why do you think we keep our guns with us, k'uu?" Gemini snapped. "If he found out...."

Nicky stared hard at the old man. Puzzle pieces snapped into place. "Last year, one of Cano's transport vans crashed. A driver escaped, ran onto the reservation. He was injured and bleeding. He'd swallowed balloons like this one. Did you help him in exchange for the drugs?" She tapped the bag.

Gemini looked away.

Nicky's eyes widened at the realization. "No. You took the drugs he carried, didn't you?"

"Your idea," Clint said to his father. "Tell them, old man. *You* put us in danger."

Gemini frowned. Grudgingly he said, "Dyu'ami found this man near Hummingbird Mesa. Led me back to him. He was dead when I got there."

Franco pressed his palms on the table. "What did you do with the body?"

"Burned it."

"You never should have taken those drugs." Clint grabbed his head. "My boys—"

"Are trash!" Gemini said. "We agreed to sell those drugs for the good of the family. What'd your boys do? Stole. Used." He hunched down in his chair. "They got what they deserved."

Clint's chair scraped back as he pushed himself up to loom over his father. "They never shoulda been chosen! It was not their place. Now they have left this earth by their own hand, or—" He sagged.

Or what? Were murdered? Old wounds were being ripped and torn right in front of her. She'd gather her questions and wait.

Gemini stared straight ahead. "Those were not your words when I chose your sons as successor. You were fools. Being the tribe's fetish carver is nothing to covet." He held up his hands. The skin was scarred and stretched, knuckles thick, fingers stiff. "My hands are dead, my eyes dim. It drove away my wife, my daughters. You think I wanted that? You think I held on to this position because of the power? Dza. No one deserves this burden, yet our ancestors and tradition demand it. I am trapped by this life. Trapped in tsa'atsi y'aauni, like the dead."

"You sacrificed my children to protect Dyu'ami because you love him more than my boys. *He* should have been next, not my boys. *He* should have made offerings!" Clint fell heavily in his chair. "Now the choice is taken from you, N'aishdiya. Mangas will not be fetish carver." Clint bowed his head. "Because he's dead."

Quiet followed his stark words.

"I'm sorry, Clint." Franco stepped behind Nicky and placed his hands on the back of her chair. His presence steadied her.

"Clint's not your youngest son, is he?" Nicky stared at Gemini. "There's another son. Dyu'ami's father." She and Franco had speculated about another child, one Gemini either didn't know about or wouldn't acknowledge. His *actual* youngest son.

Gemini didn't flinch at the revelation, but beside him Clint nodded, suddenly calm. He wrapped a hand over his father's arm. "I've kept your secret, but I have no more boys to lose, N'aishdiya. They need to know because of Seneca's murder."

Clint looked back and forth between Nicky and Franco. "At first, we thought it was Mangas who killed Seneca. Seneca found a drug balloon in Dyu'ami's room. The boy, he's always takin' stuff. Seneca fed Dyu'ami that ... poison as punishment for stealing his drugs."

Nicky pressed her fingers against her mouth. Franco's hands gripped her shoulders.

Clint waved a hand, his gaze pleading. "Seneca boasted about it, thought it was funny. Mangas and he fought about the drugs. Both them boys took off afterwards. Mangas came home the next day. Seneca didn't." He swallowed. "But Mangas didn't kill Seneca. He didn't take those guns."

The silence fell, heavy and thick. "Who killed Seneca?" Nicky asked.

"I believe ... Dyu'ami's father. He came to get the boy that night. Dyu'ami stays overnight with him sometimes. Must've heard what Seneca did," Clint said. "Took revenge."

Nicky faced Gemini. "Who's Dyu'ami's father?" But she knew.

Gemini crossed his arms tightly. His eyes glared, but Nicky saw shame. She attacked from a different angle.

"You cheated on your wife."

"I loved Elizabeth," Gemini said.

"Your youngest son's mother was at your wedding. She was your wife's friend. Tall, pretty. From the Flathead Reservation in Montana. Bitterroot Salish, Kootenai. Pend d'Oreilles."

"She seduced me. I wanted nothing to do with her child." Gemini slanted a glance under lowered eyelids but pressed his lips closed.

"John Wayne Riva." Nicky had looked it up in his autobiography. "He changed his name when he became an actor to J WhiteHawk. He wears shells in his ears. Pend d'Oreilles. He murdered Seneca. Was it just for revenge? Or did J kill his brother so Dyu'ami would be one step closer to the position of fetish carver?" It all fit, made sense. The final phone calls between Seneca and WhiteHawk. And now that Mangas was dead—

A click sounded behind her, and she glanced over her shoulder. Officer Cyrus Aguilar beckoned to Nicky. She and Franco stepped outside and closed the door behind them.

"I'm sorry to interrupt, Sergeant, Agent Martinez, but I thought you'd want to know." Still dressed in his tactical gear, filthy with dirt and soot, he clutched a piece of paper in his hand, the expression on his face grim. "It's about the warrant you submitted for the Elks' phone records." He handed her the page. "The judge denied it at the request of the New Mexico State Police."

CHAPTER FIFTY-FIVE

THE STATION'S parking lot was deserted except for Cochin's vehicle. Nicky closed the passenger's side door of her unit. Gemini Elk sat buckled in, handcuffs removed. Franco dogged her steps as she walked to the driver's side. In the distance, thick clouds, heavy with moisture, crowded the morning sky. The breeze picked up, and the scent of moisture tickled Nicky's nostrils. There'd be rain later today, waves and waves of it.

"Gemini said he'll show me where Seneca hid the rest of the drugs." She climbed into the driver's seat of her unit.

Franco planted himself in the V of her open door. "Then wait for me. It'll take me thirty minutes to get Conservation's morning shift up to speed." He peered into the cab at Gemini and lowered his voice. "We need all hands for the Elks' inventory and to secure WhiteHawk's homestead and store after we pick him up." He paused, searched her face. "There's more to this, isn't there?"

"I need to speak to Gemini. Alone." And she needed to get to the Elks' landline. State police had actually done her a favor by blocking Fire-Sky's phone warrant.

Franco's mouth tightened, and she read fleeting hurt in his eyes. Nicky ground her teeth against a surge of guilt. Whoever said women were more emotionally fragile than men needed a knock upside their head. She took a cleansing breath then laid a hand on his cheek. Stubble tickled her palm, and her temper dissipated.

"When I have my answers, you'll get them, too. Please. I need your trust right now."

Franco stared into her eyes, and a flurry of goose bumps covered Nicky's skin. He covered her hand with his. "Got your back, partner. Go. I'll be up with the rest of the team in a couple of hours." He closed her door and sprinted toward the conservation building.

Nicky drove out of the parking lot and headed to the highway. She gave Gemini a sidelong glance. Funny how he rarely met her eyes. Rarely met anyone's. Just like his grandson. "Who left Dyu'ami with your family?" she asked.

Silence.

Nicky huffed out a frustrated breath. "WhiteHawk moved to Fire-Sky Pueblo within months of Dyu'ami. Did he know the boy was his son?"

"Haa'a. Yes. He wanted to see Dyu'ami. Said he'd rejected the child when the mother told him."

"Like you'd done with him."

Gemini turned away and stared out the window. Nicky clamped her teeth. She needed to shut up, take her emotions and bias out of this.

"Go on," she prompted. He took his time.

"I will fight him if he tries to take the boy away." The fierceness in Gemini's voice startled her. "My grandson belongs with his clan, with me. He thrives with us. When he first came...." The old man swallowed. "He was lost. I knew what he needed."

"Who's Dyu'ami's mother?"

Gemini shrugged.

"Dyu'ami visits his father at the store," Nicky said. "According to Clint, he stays overnight."

Gemini's laugh was harsh. "That man doesn't keep him long. Boy's got a mind of his own." He paused. "You worry about him."

"He's been through a lot. Abandoned by both parents." Something they had in common. Nicky clutched the steering wheel, shoulders stiff.

"My grandson understands sometimes you must let go. His w'in'uska is strong."

His heart is strong.

"You don't think much of WhiteHawk," Nicky said.

"He fools many people. He is conniving."

Nicky glanced at the old man and barely contained a snort. Another family trait.

"Clint's eldest son, Geronimo. You picked him as your successor."

"Haa'a." He shrugged. "It did not choose him. Or Cochise."

"It. The organism, the colonization."

Gemini shrugged again.

Face and neck suddenly hot, she hit the steering wheel with her fist. "That organism is deadly. You *sacrificed* them—"

"Dza. The tsa'atsi y'aauni brings a feeling of power, of strength. They coveted that."

Nicky's breath went shallow. She'd experienced the same thing. Invincibility in the face of danger. It stimulated recklessness, carelessness.

"Did not want to admit with jubilation comes weakness," Gemini continued.

"And instability," Nicky said. "Seneca showed the same signs, didn't he? Because of his family history, his death could easily have been ruled as accidental or even a suicide. WhiteHawk used the suicides of Geronimo and Cochise to hide Seneca's murder, didn't he?"

"Haa'a." Gemini's scarred fingers scraped over his brow.

Nicky drove the truck onto the road that arrowed straight toward the mesa. Black clouds hid the mountaintops. The morning had turned dark.

"WhiteHawk took Dyu'ami with him when he killed Seneca," she said, "and stole the guns and Seneca's spirit fetish." The moccasin print across the boot would fit that of a small woman ... or a young boy. And she'd seen Dyu'ami hop from one of Diya's footprints to another. He'd have thought it was a game. "Dyu'ami dropped Seneca's spirit fetish in Gianetta's box." The puzzle came together seamlessly. "No one knew WhiteHawk and Dyu'ami were father and son but you and Clint. Why?"

"That man's famous. Outsiders would come to tell this story to the world, bother Dyu'ami. But after Seneca's death, Clint told Mangas."

"And Mangas thought WhiteHawk would come after him." Instead, he'd been killed by Chief Cochin's bullet. Nicky shifted and dug into her pocket for her little stone owl, handed it to Gemini. "I think Dyu'ami left me this."

Gemini turned the fetish around and around in his fingers. "Dawaa dza. It is good. Filled with w'in'uska—the heart—and tsa'atsi of my grandson. It is ... peaceful. But it does not belong to your spirit. Another already claims it."

"But he gave it to m—"

"No." He pressed it back in her hand, and Nicky held it tightly. "WhiteHawk is training the boy to create spirit fetishes. It lives in Dyu'ami."

She shoved her owl back in her pocket. "How does the organism help make the tsa'atsi y'aauni?"

Gemini shifted to look at her. "It creates the heart of the stone, where the spirit lives. When it is ready, the fetish carver says sacred prayers as he lays in the fine details."

"You put the templates in your bodies? The stones grow inside your stomach?"

He snorted.

"Then how?" Her mind worked, piecing together more clues.

The elk in the truck. "You use the guts of poached animals. The organism extracts minerals from the tissues, and stones grow. You pay for the offal."

"Dza. The tribal council allows us to hunt when we have need."

"Then who—" *WhiteHawk.* The warehouse. Its smell. "He's growing *tsa'atsi y'aauni* somewhere inside the warehouse." She jerked her head to stare at Gemini. "You used the organism to clean up contamination at the ciénega, didn't you? That's where I became infected. That organism is deadly. How could you do that?"

Gemini scoffed. "Think, k'uu. I've lived with it. For the right choice, there is little effect. But you ... I have never seen it jump outside our clan."

"How do I kill it"—her voice wavered—"before it kills me?" Nicky angled her unit up the grade to the top of the mesa. She kept her eyes on the winding road, but she could feel the weight of Gemini's gaze.

"You've been chosen as a warrior. You must run into the fire."

"What?" Eyes wide, Nicky skewed him a look.

"They say the god of the dead and fire visits our clan during succession. During this time, they say four warriors must approach the fire to bring their offerings. If the offerings are accepted, the warriors are protected from the tsa'atsi y'aauni. I believe Cochise and Mangas were the first and second warriors. They were not chosen to survive."

"They were not sons of your youngest son. Was that why they died?"

"Maybe. But all four warriors have survived in past histories. I believe the offerings presented by Cochise and Mangas were not accepted because they were given in fear and selfishness."

Nicky didn't know what Cochise had offered, but Mangas had offered Dyu'ami's life in exchange for his own in what she considered a callous act of desperation. It was no wonder the god had not accepted it.

"Mangas's eyes. Before he ... died, his eyes turned completely white, like the god's eyes. And I've seen another man with white eyes who died. Dyu'ami—when Agent Martinez and I came to the compound before, his eyes rolled white. Does that mean he's marked for death?" Her voice dropped almost to a whisper.

"This sign is a possibility, but you saved my grandson from Mangas and the god of the dead and fire, I think. And Dyu'ami is truly the son of my youngest son. He might be chosen as the next fetish carver, but he has not been tested."

"Dyu'ami lived through the fire that Mangas—"

"That was *Mangas's* fire and *Mangas's* offering. Dyu'ami must present his own offering and *choose* to run through fire. If he survives, he will live peacefully with the tsa'atsi y'aauni, and I will train him as the next fetish carver for the Tsiba'ashi D'yini People."

If he survives. She steadied her breathing. "You were chosen. Did you...?"

"Haa'a. My brother. Tsa'atsi y'aauni made him act like my grandsons. When there was a fire in the school building, he ran into it. I followed and tried to save him but could not. I have lived with tsa'atsi y'aauni since then."

"Your offering? What was it?"

"I carried nothing as an offering."

"Then why?"

"I don't know."

The truck topped the mesa and bumped onto the dirt road leading to the Elk compound.

Gemini's gaze swung toward her. "There are two more who must run into fire to complete the succession, and you hold the tsa'atsi y'aauni inside you. I believe you are the third warrior."

"The third—? But ... I've run through fire." The state police vehicles, the boy at Green Meadow Springs, Mangas's death. In the last two, she'd barely escaped with her life. She raised a hand to wipe her mouth. Running into fires hadn't cured her so far. "There has to be another way."

"Geronimo chose another way," Gemini said softly.

A stark reminder of the infection's probable outcome. "But—"

"No. Those fires must've been a test because you didn't know." He pinned her with his gaze. "Now you know."

CHAPTER FIFTY-SIX

NICKY PARKED among a fleet of official vehicles: Fire-Sky police units and firetrucks, and half a dozen pickups, doors flung open. To one side sat an unmarked FBI sedan, its darkly tinted windows almost as black as the body paint. Behind the Elk house, a white awning was anchored against the rising mountain slope at the mouth of the fire-blackened copse of trees. Figures garbed in yellow hazmat suits moved between it and a van from the Albuquerque OMI.

Gemini sat quietly beside her, watching the activity. Nicky shoved their conversation out of her mind. She had a specific goal to achieve.

She keyed her mic and reported her location. Her jaw tightened when Chief Cochin responded, but she wasn't all that surprised. The raid and cleanup had left them short-staffed, and Cochin had a better vantage to direct operations from the station. Nicky had already deflected numerous questions about Mangas's attack on the chief, not all of them sympathetic, and they didn't know the half of it. After last night's debacle, Nicky wondered if Cochin's election was in jeopardy.

Dark clouds tangled in the trees up the mountain. She exited her truck and slipped her keys into her pocket; they clicked against the little owl fetish. Gemini waited for her. She clamped a hand around his upper arm before leading him to the front yard. Nicky caught a glimpse of Seneca's horse, ears perked, pacing along the split-log fence of a corral. The dogs, conspicuously silent last night, barked incessantly.

Officer Gracie José hurried down the porch steps toward her and eyed Gemini before reporting.

"Sergeant, Officer Flores searched the house with Shaq." The blue-heeler–border-collie mix was the pueblo's drug-sniffing dog. "He hit on a few spots—only residue, though. They're finishing up the outbuildings now." The barking intensified, and José grinned from a tired face. "Those other dogs sure don't like Shaq invading their territory."

"Mr. Elk here informed me that even our drug-sniffing dogs wouldn't find the cache, so I brought him in to show us the way. Where's the stash, Mr. Elk?"

He pivoted until he faced the tree and notched his chin. "Dyǝ. Up."

Nicky marched the old man under the canopy of leaves, Officer José beside him. About twenty-five feet up, a camouflaged canvas bag was lashed to a narrow bough.

Dyu'ami had climbed this tree one of the times she and Franco had been at the house asking questions.

AT LEAST A DOZEN police and firefighters milled in the yard, arguing logistics, while vehicles were moved and a firetruck brought around. Nicky left Gemini sitting on the porch steps and slipped inside the empty house.

A few lamps were on, but dark corners filled the disarrayed room. As she strode to the kitchen, a plastic wrapper caught her eye, and she scooped it up. Swedish Fish.

She pushed through a swinging door into the narrow galley kitchen and flicked on the light. Dishes emptied from cabinets during the search for drugs were piled high along the countertops. Pots and pans littered the floor. *Indian Country* and *Native Max* magazines covered a small table at one end of the room, and a door decorated with dusty red-checked curtains led outside at the other.

A faded yellow phone hung on the wall next to the refrigerator. Heart pounding, she lifted the handset. Besides the fact that she was tampering with evidence, Dax would know what she'd done as soon as he viewed the phone records. But she had to make sure.

Unsteady fingers hovered over the touch pad. She released the breath she held and pressed star sixty-nine. Three rings. It picked up with a muffled click.

"Guw'aadzi. You've reached the office of Tsiba'ashi D'yini Human Resources. Our hours are...." Savannah's voice chirped the recorded message.

Nicky listened, mind numb. The call warning the Elks of the raid had come from Savannah's office.

She closed her eyes and leaned her forehead against the cool side of the refrigerator.

Franco had been right. Savannah had chosen to protect her People over all others. Over her best friend.

And wasn't that exactly what Nicky was doing now? To save Savannah, she'd plead with the tribe to use sovereignty. Her grip tightened on the receiver. If that didn't work, she'd negotiate with Dax, do whatever he wanted.

The handset was gently tugged away. Her eyes snapped open. Franco. Ryan stood at his shoulder.

"You could get in a lot of trouble for this." Franco's tone was grave.

Her eyes burned. "I had to know."

"Had to know what?" Ryan asked. Soot streaked his skin and dulled the brightness of his hair.

"Who called to warn the Elks," Nicky said.

Ryan stiffened, his gaze suddenly fierce. "Who?"

When neither she nor Franco answered, he grabbed the handset and punched in the code. Savannah's message filtered out, tinny and faint. Ryan slammed the phone down. "I don't believe this. She would never—" He stopped and stared at Nicky. "Why didn't you tell me?"

Heat flared, and her eyes dried. "What she's done might be bigger than the tribe. A conspiracy with Chen Cano and the Crybabies. She's protecting them when they pass through Fire-Sky land."

"She'd never—I *know* Savannah. *You* know Savannah." He stabbed a finger at her. "You should have talked to her, *warned* her. You call yourself her friend. You betrayed her."

"I've betrayed her? *I just risked my career for her.* It's you—" Nicky choked.

"How many times has she rejected me, Nicky? This time for that dyeetya, Howard Kie. I begged her, only to be pushed away because I'm not good enough. Not *Fire-Sky* enough for her."

"She's under pressure from her father, Ryan. He's dying. You can wait."

Ryan's jaw clamped. The kitchen fell silent except for a whistle of wind through the back door.

"This is getting us nowhere," Franco said quietly. "We need to talk to Savannah, ask her directly before—"

Nicky's cell phone rang. She tugged it out of her pocket. "It's her." She pressed accept and brought the phone to her ear. "Savannah?"

"No! RJ. This is RJ. The house—I was at kiva—she gave me her phone. The house—" His voice broke, agitated. "Front door. The lock's busted. I can't find them. Noreen! Savannah!"

Nicky suppressed a spike of panicked adrenaline. "Mr. Analla, slow down." She heard barking through the line. Franco and Ryan crowded closer.

"Oh, oh! I found them! Nicky, I found them. Oh, God!"

Nicky's stomach plummeted.

"Someone tied them up, taped their mouths. Let me—"

Precious seconds passed. Clatter sounded through the phone.

"Nicky. It's Savannah." Her voice shook. "J WhiteHawk broke in ... in the door and ... and tied us up, locked Diya in the bathroom. No, Dad! Don't. Shut the door! *Dammit.* Diya got out. I'll have to—" Sound was muffled for a few seconds. "Nicky, WhiteHawk took Dyu'ami. Dyu'ami's his *son.*"

"I know. Are you and your mom all right?"

"Just shaken up. You knew?"

"How long ago did this happen?"

"One hour and forty-two minutes ago. I looked at the clock. No! *Dad.* He collapsed—I've got to—"

"Call nine-one-one. Get EMTs over now," Nicky ordered.

Ryan snatched the phone from her hand. "Savannah, baby. Please tell me you're all right." There was a pause. "No, baby. I'm not close enough." Ryan straightened, face slack. "She hung up."

Nicky grabbed the phone and called in an APB on WhiteHawk to Fire-Sky Dispatch. Cochin answered and took the details.

"We have to go." Nicky pivoted to the door leading to the living room and swung it hard. It banged against the wall. "WhiteHawk has almost a two-hour head start—"

Gemini stood alone in the dusky light of the room, his lined face shadowed. "I know where they are."

Nicky made to brush past him.

Gemini grabbed her arm. "Muuk'aitra. The warehouse. He will need to destroy things, and rescue artifacts only Dyu'ami can touch."

She stopped. "*Tsa'atsi y'aauni.* The spirit stones."

Gemini nodded. "The stones are too valuable to be left. He will use the boy to retrieve them. After that...."

Her throat tightened. "Dyu'ami knows too much."

"Haa'a."

"WhiteHawk won't harm his own son, Nicky," Franco said. "Besides, the boy can't speak."

Nicky whirled on him. "Yes, he can. The moccasin print at the ciénega, the one at the shrine. Don't you understand? They were deliberate. The drug cache was in the tree he climbed when we were here. The fetish in Gianetta's box. He wanted someone to find it, to link it to Seneca's murder. My owl." Nicky dug in her pocket, thrust the little stone at him. "He left it for me because WhiteHawk was training him to make spirit fetishes. Dyu'ami's been talking to us this whole time. We just didn't know how to listen."

She pushed her fist, owl inside, to her forehead. "It's over an hour to the warehouse through Dyaitse Pass, longer by the freeway."

"There's another way. Come." Gemini led them out the back door.

The storm gusts had strengthened, and a metallic tinge of rain burned Nicky's nostrils. The old man strode toward the corral. He whistled, and the little horse she'd found at the ciénega trotted up to him, tossing its head and snorting. Gemini grabbed the braided rope halter and laid a calming hand on the animal's neck.

"Over the mountain is a path." He raised his voice against the sound of the wind. Thunder crackled, closer now. "It will save time."

"On horseback?" Nicky yelled to be heard.

"Haa'a." Gemini unlooped the braided rope from a ring under the halter. "You must go."

Both Ryan and Franco protested, but Gemini cut them off.

"Dza. The boy trusts her. And she has been chosen."

"This horse is too small for either of you." Nicky scrambled over the fence.

"Haa'a. Cow pony," Gemini said.

The horse's nostrils blew large as he sampled Nicky's scent, liquid eyes assessing. "You remember me, boy. Neck rein?" she asked Gemini.

"You ride, too?" Franco's voice winged high.

"Let him go when you get there. He will find his way back." Gemini stepped away.

Nicky stripped off her heavy Kevlar vest, secured her Glock and two magazines. She looped the rope over the horse's head, grabbed two handfuls of mane, and swung onto its bare back. Muscles bunched as the animal sidestepped and tried to duck out from under her. Her thighs tensed, but she swayed with him, reading his movements, countering his tricks. Legs squeezed tight, she tugged his nose down to his chest. He stopped, front legs braced. She met Franco's gaze.

"I'll be fine, I promise." Nicky reached out her hand. He grasped it tightly, searched her eyes, worry marring his. "Open the gate."

CHAPTER FIFTY-SEVEN

Nicky reined in her pony. He tossed his head and blew, and she ran a soothing hand down his sweaty neck. Breathing almost as hard as the horse, she checked her phone. She'd pushed the horse, but he was strong, and it had paid off in time saved.

Down the mountain, the pines opened to the narrow valley. At the bottom, the blunted glow of skylights was visible through the tops of the trees. Suddenly, the boil of clouds above the valley shimmered with brilliant strobing white. She tightened the reins and counted under her breath until thunder cracked. The chestnut pony jerked but didn't try to bolt. Three seconds. Nicky ground her teeth. The storm was heading straight for her. Of all nights for the drought to break.

She squeezed her legs and urged the horse forward, the clicks of dislodged rocks loud against the background of wind sawing through pine boughs. Each step vibrated through her body as he picked his way along the path. Nicky counted the minutes, praying she wasn't too late.

They dropped below the warehouse rooftop and onto a smoother section of the road. Nicky kicked the horse's sides and bent lower on his neck, wrapping one hand in his mane. He lifted his head, ears perked, and picked up speed. She pulled him to a stop not two hundred feet from the chain-link fence.

Murmuring praise, Nicky kept her eyes on the glowing lights of the boneyard at the back of the warehouse complex. She threw her leg over the pony, slid to the ground. Her legs felt like wet noodles, and the insides of her thighs screamed. The little horse snorted. With soothing noises, she removed the bridle and hung it on a tree branch.

Blinding white lit the forest, and thunder boomed. Nicky fell to one knee, head covered with her arms. Like that would help if she were struck. She straightened and stared up the trail, listening to snapped branches and thudding hooves until the sound died away. Throwing up a quick prayer the horse would find his way back to the Elk ranch, she hurried down toward the fence. Each step she took jarred, but the stiffness was abating. There'd be cell service here. She unclipped her phone from the holder on her belt.

Two missed calls from Franco. She hit redial. He picked up immediately.

"The pass is blocked. Wind knocked over a tree. Hell. Trees. We could backtrack to I-25, but that'll take longer." She heard muffled voices and the buzz of a chainsaw. "ETA an hour at least. They there?"

"I can see lights but don't have confirmation. I need to get closer. If you get here before I call again, no lights, no sirens."

She veered off the path and wove through a thicker stand of pines. Underfoot was slippery with needles, and she found herself grabbing rough bark to keep steady. The trees ended some thirty feet from the chain-link fence. A buffer zone in case of forest fire, but it hadn't been kept up. Waist-high weeds and scattered saplings, brown and dried by lack of rain, swathed the ground. Her gaze rose to trace the spirals of concertina wire along the top of the fence. She pressed her lips tight. Not good.

On the other side, carcasses of wrecked cars and trucks lay scattered in the boneyard. The huge garage door was closed, but the window in the door to one side glowed with thin yellow light. Nicky listened for sound from inside, but if there was any, it was obscured by the rising wind and dead branches crunching to the ground behind her. She hugged closer to a trunk, careful to keep her face out of direct light. A four-wheeler sat in a shadowed niche next to the warehouse. *Bingo.*

Nicky crouched, ready to run to the fence, when the door opened and WhiteHawk, arms burdened with plastic storage containers, stepped through. A rifle was strapped diagonally across his back, wooden stock in easy reach above his shoulder. He called back inside.

"*Ba'nah'ah.* You stay here. No. No! Stay. I'll"—the wind snatched his words away—"back. You stay. Good, good."

Her heart rate accelerated. The only person she'd ever heard spoken to that way was Dyu'ami.

WhiteHawk kicked the door closed with his foot and strode to the four-wheeler, his lanky figure casting a long shadow. The dull silver of a six-shooter strapped at his left hip caught her eye, and her hand slipped to the butt of her Glock. She estimated another fifty minutes for backup to arrive, barring no more roadblocks. That was a long, long time if WhiteHawk was almost packed. She might have to stop him and rescue Dyu'ami all by herself. A thrill of excitement coursed up her spine.

WhiteHawk slid the boxes on the back of the four-wheeler and lashed them down. He climbed on and drove down the long gravel parking lot toward the gate and into darkness, the lawn-mower rumble of the engine fading, headlights a diminishing bubble in front of him. Nicky edged out from behind her tree. As he passed the strip mall near the entrance of the warehouses, a spotlight switched on over the last shop—his shop. He skidded to a stop and took the boxes inside. The light popped off within seconds.

Nicky bolted toward the fence. Hunched, she scuttled along the chain-link, periodically yanking at it, praying for a cut section. On the fourth try, the metal bowed toward her. Thank God for the apathy of Fire-Sky maintenance crews. She slipped through, the cut ends scraping across her clothes. The four-wheeler engine started up, and she dove behind a rusting stack of front bumper guards. She dropped her face and eyes when the headlamp swept her hiding place, but peered up again when WhiteHawk parked in his niche. He climbed off, took two steps and, with unnerving speed, slid the rifle from the scabbard, shouldered it—

And pointed it over her head into the darkened forest. Nicky didn't blink or breathe.

Lightning strobed, illuminating the hard planes of his face for brief instances. Rushing air whistled through the pines, and the thuds of falling branches punctuated its sound like uneven beats of a drum.

Incrementally, WhiteHawk relaxed. His rifle dropped, but he stayed still for a long time. Finally, he pivoted, walked to the door ... and hesitated. He cocked his head one more time as a crackling boom echoed down the mountain, then keyed in the code and disappeared inside.

Nicky released her breath but didn't rise until she was sure WhiteHawk wouldn't throw open the door and confront her. She'd been in situations where a niggling sense of danger had tickled her neck. No reason to think WhiteHawk hadn't felt her presence in the same primordial way.

The stack of brush guards didn't give her the cover she needed. She scanned the area and decided a listing SUV, top crushed in a rollover, would provide a better vantage point and protection. Glock in hand, her gaze never leaving the door of the warehouse, she ran to it and tucked in behind the crumpled hood.

Within minutes, WhiteHawk emerged again, more storage bins in hand, and drove back to his shop.

From her position, she could see down the long parking lot to the gate as well as keep tabs on the warehouse until backup arrived.

Or ... A sense of recklessness permeated her body. *Or* she could grab Dyu'ami and head into the forest.

Nicky's mind raced. Based on the timing of his first trip, she'd have about ten minutes. Coiled, she'd readied herself to run when the wail of a siren pierced the wind. Nicky swiveled, heart plummeting. An SUV crashed through the gates, headlights bouncing wildly, red and blue strobes lighting up the darkness. *No, no, no.* Backup wasn't supposed to come in hot. The truck accelerated up the gravel lot, heading straight toward Nicky.

She raised her arm to shield against the lights and raced toward the warehouse door. Burnt white circles peppered her vision.

A rifle shot cracked, and Nicky flung herself to the ground. The truck swerved, its tires spinning on loose gravel, headlights illuminating the warehouse wall. It jumped the curb and slammed to a halt in a weed-and-grass-choked flower bed. The driver's side door opened, and Chief Cochin leaped out, weapon in hand. She ran to the end of her SUV and returned fire.

Nicky scrambled for cover behind the back half of a car split in two like an egg. She screamed at Luz, "Move your truck! *Move the truck! Move—*"

A shock wave of heat ripped through the air as flames burst from the undercarriage of Cochin's vehicle.

CHAPTER FIFTY-EIGHT

BOILING clouds of smoke lit with tiny orange sparks swept up the side of the warehouse. Cochin staggered into the parking lot, away from cover. WhiteHawk's rifle barked again. The chief spun and fell.

Nicky laid down fire as she sprinted into the open. Cochin reached out her arm, and Nicky latched on to her wrist. She continued firing as she hauled Luz behind the crushed car.

Cochin let go and pushed herself into a sitting position, cradling a forearm drenched in blood. "Literally shot the gun out of my hand." Her voice carried a strained note of humor. Shadows wavered across her face and body, their motion dictated by the growing fire.

Nicky surveilled the dark avenue. Nothing. "How bad?" she asked.

"My wrist, through and through." Blood welled between Cochin's fingers. "WhiteHawk?"

"Yes." Nicky holstered her weapon, praying he wasn't creeping up on them. "I need your duty belt. What's our ten eighty-two?"

Luz raised her arms. Nicky unbuckled and slid the belt from her waist. She quickly stripped off the holster and pouches.

"No backup," Luz said. "I came alone. From the freeway."

Nicky bit off a groan and tightened the belt at the chief's elbow.

"How did you get here?" Luz asked. "The child?"

"Inside the warehouse. No time for a recap, Chief. Where's your gun?"

"By the car. I didn't see where it fell."

"Do you have a backup?"

Luz's gaze met her eyes. "No." She'd thrown that gun into the fire after she'd shot Mangas.

"Take mine." Nicky replaced the depleted magazine, racked the Glock, and handed it to Luz along with the second magazine.

Suddenly, the shadows marring Luz's face disappeared, and her eyes reflected a wall of flames. Nicky twisted, and her muscles tightened in horror. A conflagration of orange and red capped the warehouse roof as banks of leaves and pine needles, collected over years, caught fire.

"I have to get Dyu'ami." Nicky shoved to her feet and bolted to the warehouse.

"It's too dangerous," Luz yelled. "Stop!"

A map of the warehouse's interior crystalized in Nicky's head. Stored cars parked haphazardly, heaps of office furniture, machining equipment, car parts, boxes of old paper files, and stacks of tires. All fuel for the growing fire.

The air compressed and brightened around her as the chief's SUV exploded. She punched in the code and slipped inside. Bending low, she took cover behind the nearest car. The skylights above cast an eerie yellow glow, and thick, writhing tendrils of smoke crept across the ceiling. Seams smoldered between the wavy corrugated metal of the warehouse wall.

At the far end of the huge open area sat the single-story office. White fluorescent light leaked between window blinds. The door was closed. Dyu'ami had to be in there.

But where was WhiteHawk?

Nicky scuttled left. At each vehicle, she crouched, assessed her path, then headed to her next position. But with each step, the fire's light grew above her. Her body throbbed with adrenaline. She closed her eyes, fighting thoughts of self-preservation, mortality, and exhilaration. Dyu'ami's face swam in the darkness of her mind. He must be so scared.

She opened her eyes, and her gaze lit on her next position: a car shrouded in a tarp. Her heart leaped. Her mom's Mazda. Nicky tamped down an almost hysterical laugh. The complete loss of the car would plumb the depths of her mother's forgiveness.

Nicky hurried to the rear of the car to survey the area in front of her. The office was closer now but still seemed a ridiculous distance. Crouched, she pushed at the uncomfortable knot of keys digging into her thigh, picked her next target—

Keys. The large red button that raised the garage door was easy to find in the yellow glow streaming through the skylights. She looked up at the ceiling light. Electricity still on. She and Dyu'ami could drive out of here. But she'd feed the fire if she opened the garage door now. It would have to wait till the last minute. Nicky grabbed the canvas and yanked it off. A single press to the key fob. Headlights flashed, locks disengaged. Time to get Dyu'ami.

Nicky dashed across the remaining distance and flung open the office door. The stench of putrefaction slammed into her.

"Dyu'ami." She hurried around the room, peering under desks and tables lining the walls. He wasn't there. "Dyu'ami!"

Her gaze slid over the items on the table and desk surfaces. Dirt-encrusted fetishes of all shapes, colors, and sizes were jumbled with arrowheads and tiny pots.

Offerings. They had to be from the desecrated shrines.

But that wasn't the worst of it. Gray entrails lay half submerged in plastic pans along one wall. Nicky crept forward, her hand pressed over her nose, eyes watering. The pouched bag of a stomach, tied at one end by a leather thong, bulged in each tray. Handwritten labels were stuck on the pans: BEAR, ELK, BOBCAT, COUGAR, BADGER, EAGLE. Realization struck her. Entrails from poached animals, paid for by J WhiteHawk. A paring knife rested on a cloth. She seized it and, with a quick swipe, slashed open the nearest stomach. A gout of milky liquid surged through the cut. She thrust the knife inside, heard a tiny click, and scraped out a hard object.

A bear fetish, its features still blunted, immature to its final construct.

She sliced a second stomach and found a badger fetish, this one with only a mineral sheen overlaying a wooden form. WhiteHawk was using his son to create fetishes worth tens of thousands of dollars. Manipulating the little boy for monetary gain and cultural standing. Making him into the next tribal fetish carver, eliminating heirs by murder. She had to find Dyu'ami.

Nicky darted out the door. A skylight above her exploded and rained shards of plastic and flaming jetsam down in front of her. The sky through the ceiling was a hellish red.

She backpedaled, a scream rising in her chest. *"Dyu'ami!"*

A hubcap seemed to fling itself off the top of a ring of tires. Hair on her arms and head prickled painfully as the cap clanged on the cement and rolled toward her, only to spiral to a stop a few feet away. This had happened before, when she'd dropped off her mother's car with Jinni Sundry.

Nicky squinted at the jumble of car parts behind the tires. A pale round face appeared in the open window of a detached car door.

"Dyu'ami!"

The door leading to the boneyard banged open, and the pop of gunshots punctuated the roar of the fire. WhiteHawk stumbled through the threshold, right arm limp at his side, shoulder and chest dark with blood. He pointed a gun outside the opening and shot. The scabbard on his back was empty.

WhiteHawk slammed the door behind him and rotated. His gaze collided with Nicky's, and silver flashed as he raised his arm. She dove, and the bullet shattered an office window behind her. Her hand automatically slapped her holster. *Empty.* Scrabbling to her knees, she angled at a dead run toward a large heap of car parts—and Dyu'ami. There was a gap behind it. She'd seen it when she'd been there with Jinni Sundry.

A place to hide, but no way out.

CHAPTER FIFTY-NINE

Dyu'ami huddled in the gap, arms wrapped tightly around his knees, rocking back and forth. Nicky slid in beside him and covered him with her body. WhiteHawk took another shot. The sound ricocheted off metal.

"Matthews! I want my son!"

Nicky lifted her head and peered between the tangle of car parts. Through the smoke, WhiteHawk staggered across the cement, gun aimed in her direction. He disappeared inside the office. Nicky freed herself from Dyu'ami. She ran her hands over him, checking for injury. Other than a rip in his jeans and a fresh scrape, he appeared unhurt. Her hand cupped his face.

"Are you all right?"

He rocked in response, eyes moving back and forth. Nicky snugged his head into her shoulder.

"We have to get out of here," she said. Light from the fire blossomed, and smoke continued to roil from the roof. A second skylight exploded. Dyu'ami buried his face deeper into her chest.

"We'll go to my car—you know which one, don't you, sweetheart? You left me a gift there, traded me for apples." Nicky straightened and slipped a hand inside her pocket to extract the keys and the owl fetish. "I lost my owl, and you found it for me." Her fingers trembled as she extended them.

Tentatively, Dyu'ami lifted his head. One hand disengaged from his knee, and he touched the owl with his finger. Nicky thought he smiled, and her heart lightened. They could do this.

"Stay close." She pushed the owl back into her pocket, then tugged Dyu'ami to his feet. He stooped to grab a backpack from underneath a bumper and slung it over his shoulders.

Stacks of car parts gave them cover. His hand tucked in hers, they darted and hid until they were opposite the office door. A muffled *whumph* sounded above the noise of the flames. She knew that sound —exploding gas tank. Nicky peered around the pile of tires. Fire engulfed cars parked on the far side of the warehouse and jumped from one vehicle to the next. The acrid stench of burnt rubber permeated the air.

Nicky towed Dyu'ami behind a blue compact. She scanned the warehouse before she swiveled to study the office. Door closed, lights on. She tightened her grip on Dyu'ami's hand, and they ran.

The door swung open. WhiteHawk staggered against the jamb. "Dyu'ami!" He raised his gun. "*No!* Don't take him from me!"

Nicky ducked and huddled with Dyu'ami alongside of her mother's car. WhiteHawk stumbled into the open. Dark blood saturated the whole of his left side, down to his hip and thigh.

She opened the passenger door and scrambled across the console, knee banging painfully on the handbrake. Dyu'ami crawled in after her.

Her hand shook as she tried to push the key into the ignition and failed over and over. Dyu'ami laid his fingers on her arm. She slotted the key in and turned the engine over.

She glanced back toward the office, and her eyes widened. WhiteHawk stood not ten feet from the car, pistol pointed directly at her. Nicky stared, frozen in horror as his eyes rolled in his head until they were completely white.

Marked for death.

Shadows enveloped the car. A thick column of gray spiraled down from the rafters. It morphed into a huge owl, smoky wings enveloping a screaming WhiteHawk. He fell, his arm covering his head.

Nicky punched the gas, and the car leaped forward. Cranking the wheel hard right, she hit the bumper of a silver sedan and pushed it away. She swerved and wheeled between the graveyard of vehicles, some already aflame. The garage door was a hundred feet away. Tires squealed, and she torqued the wheel. Eighty feet. She snaked between tightly packed cars. Fifty feet away. The fluorescent light above flickered. *Please stay on, please stay on.* Thirty. A burning truck blocked the switch for the overhead door.

"Stay inside, Dyu'ami, until I come back," she said and flung open her door. Her exposed skin smarted, and her eyes burned against the painfully intense heat. She ran to the red button, pressed it. The garage door rumbled up. *Thank God.* She whirled to get Dyu'ami.

A horrible metallic groan sounded above. Nicky screamed as part of the ceiling blossomed a brilliant orange and fell in slow motion, taking the light, air-conditioning, and ductwork down on top of her car. The garage door slammed to the cement with an irrevocable boom.

"*Dyu'ami!*" Without thought, she leaped over twisted metal and flung herself to the passenger's side. The roof was crushed, the door twisted, glass shattered. She wrenched open the back door, searched the interior—

Gone.

Frantically, she swept the warehouse.

WhiteHawk and Dyu'ami, arms laced around each other, hobbled toward the office, stumbling over panels of gray insulation. Her gaze slid to the outside door—she could escape. No one would blame her. No one.

Another skylight imploded. Dyu'ami and WhiteHawk toppled to

the cement, WhiteHawk covering his son with his body. Nicky made her decision. She ran, dodging fiery debris. WhiteHawk had pushed to his feet when she reached them, Dyu'ami latched to one arm, supporting him.

"We can still get out," she said. WhiteHawk swung sunken eyes in an ashen face toward her. His lips moved, but she couldn't hear his voice. Nicky leaned in close.

"I'm spent. Done."

Her gaze flew to his chest. The gunshot wound pulsed blood.

"Take Dyu'ami. Please. Save my son." Feebly, he attempted to unwind Dyu'ami's arm from around his waist, but the boy tightened his hold. He thrust his chin toward the office.

Suddenly, the stench of smoke was overwhelmed by the odor of death. Nicky lifted her head. The gray man stood in the darkened doorway, the club in his hand aglow with a blood-red flame. Blank white eyes caught her stare. He faded into the darkness of the room.

"You see him," she whispered.

Dyu'ami tugged at his listing father.

"No. Let him go," she pleaded. "We don't have time—"

A tremendous groan sounded behind them, and the wall and ceiling folded inward. Escape completely cut off.

Hope leached away.

They had no choice. No other place to hide. Nicky looped her arm around WhiteHawk's waist, and the three of them lurched into the office. Nicky slammed the door behind them, but it wouldn't matter.

Ryan's worst nightmare had become her own.

CHAPTER SIXTY

THROUGH THE BROKEN WINDOW, light from the fire illuminated the office in a ghastly, dancing glow. WhiteHawk lay on the floor near the back cabinets, Dyu'ami crouched by his side, his arms tight around his knees, rocking and staring into space. Blood stained his clothes and smeared the knuckles of one hand.

The middle table held a pile of rags. Nicky grabbed a handful and knelt next to WhiteHawk, pressing the wadded cloth to his chest.

"No use," said WhiteHawk.

Nicky lifted the already-soaked pad and peeled away the remnants of his shirt. She grimaced at the ragged hole sluggishly pulsating blood. "Why didn't you run?"

"I couldn't leave my son."

She made a derisive sound as she pressed fresh rags against his wound. WhiteHawk grabbed her wrist with surprising strength. His eyes were back to normal, fierce, but fading.

"I love Dyu'ami."

Nicky shook his hold away. "Gemini said you didn't claim him because the publicity might be bad."

With a grunt of pain, WhiteHawk swept his hand over Dyu'ami's head. The boy stilled.

"Not the real reason. When I confronted his mother, she threatened me." His smile was forced. "Things I'd done in the past, after I left Montana, before I had my few minutes of fame. Things I did to survive, confessed to her when we were together." He blinked and pulled in a breath. "But it cut both ways. If it ever came out she'd thrown away her autistic child, her reputation would be ruined. People don't like it when mothers aren't maternal. We were at a standoff, and I wanted to protect Dyu'ami."

"*Protect* him? You infected him, used him to make spirit stones, to get rich."

"What do you think would happen to Dyu'ami, the way he is, when Gemini passes? When Clint and Roy are gone? Those cousins of his ... would neglect him or turn him out. I had no choice." He paused to take a breath, coughed weakly. "Had to focus Gemini's attention on my son. If Dyu'ami became fetish carver, the tribe would be forced to care for him."

"Geronimo was a good man. He would've taken Dyu'ami in."

"Except he killed himself." WhiteHawk's head lolled back. "We'd become close. That night, he called me, crying. Couldn't talk him down. I heard the shot, went to him."

"You didn't report it."

"Didn't want the publicity. I built the descanso for him." He squeezed her wrist, his brown eyes intense. "*The descanso*," he repeated. "For Dyu'ami."

Nicky frowned. "You contained Geronimo's spirit fetish?"

He gave a feeble laugh. "No. I took it. You know how much *tsa'atsi y'aauni* carrying a soul is worth?" Prickles shivered down Nicky's arms. "Just like I took from those shrines and sold the artifacts. Down payment on my son's future. He gets ... almost no distribution because of his ancestry. Because his mother's white."

"But I found Geronimo's fetish at the descanso."

"Dyu'ami." Gray lips twisted. "Wondered what happened"—he gasped—"to it. He took ... Seneca's, too. Dropped it in ... Gianetta's box. Traded for candy."

At each pause, he labored for breath. Nicky applied more pressure to the wound.

"Gianetta told me," she said. "But it wasn't until I questioned Gemini and Clint that I understood why you murdered Seneca."

His face hardened. "Bastard fed my boy drugs. Pleasure ... to hold him under till he drowned. Fit my purpose. After Cochise's suicide ... Gemini whined about how none of Clint's boys were worthy ... like it was a royal succession. That's when I realized ... what I needed to do. Seneca ... then Mangas. If their deaths looked like suicides or accidents ... no one would suspect. Gemini'd choose Dyu'ami, especially if he ... had *tsa'atsi y'aauni* inside him."

Nicky changed the blood-soaked rags for new ones. "The *tsa'atsi y'aauni* organism caused your nephews' destructive behaviors."

Worry puckered on WhiteHawk's brow. "Gemini isn't sick."

"His older brother was infected and burned himself to death. Didn't you ask about the family history? Or didn't you care?"

"I *love* my son." His eyes pleaded with her.

As much as she wanted him to suffer for what he'd done, Nicky relented. "Gemini says for some who are colonized, there is little effect."

"Thank the Creator," WhiteHawk whispered.

A shattering crash on the office roof jerked her head to windows glowing crimson. Smoke seeped under the door and through the broken glass. They had very little time, before—

Ryan's voice played in her head: *Would you have the strength to do what needed to be done? Not only for yourself, but for a child?*

"Seneca's rifle and gun," Nicky said.

"Too valuable ... to leave." WhiteHawk stared at his son, his complexion gray, his expression soft.

"We never would've linked anyone to Seneca's death if you'd left them." Sudden tears gathered in her eyes. She blinked, and they streaked down her cheeks. "Where's your gun?"

"Dropped. Another in ... Dyu'ami's pack." WhiteHawk labored a breath. "Don't know where ... he got it."

Nicky bowed her head on a sob. Releasing pressure on the chest pad, she gave Dyu'ami's braid a gentle tug.

"Hey, buddy." She cleared her throat. "I need your backpack."

He pulled it off his shoulders. It fell with a muffled thunk to the tiled floor. Nicky unzipped it and peered inside. Jumbled with a change of clothes and a few toys was Chief Cochin's backup M&P Shield. Dyu'ami's final lunge at Mangas.

Her hand grasped the butt, drew it out. Crying silently, she ejected the magazine and counted bullets. More than enough.

She glanced down at WhiteHawk. He lay on the floor, staring blankly into the distance. He'd slipped away, wouldn't have to face ... She envied him in that beat of time.

"Dyu'ami?"

He scooted around his father and into her arms. He met her gaze, but it was still like he stared through her.

"I'm sorry." Nicky clutched the grip so tight, her arm vibrated. She'd been confident when she'd told Ryan she could do this. Reality was different. *So hard.* She pressed the gun under his chin. His beautiful hazel eyes fluttered closed, lashes feathered against his cheek. Nicky tucked her chin to her chest, convulsed with pain. She had to do this, had to—

Small fingers curled over her hand. Nicky blinked away tears ... and gasped.

Dyu'ami's eyes focused straight on hers. An angelic smile graced his lips. One little hand wrapped around the gun and tugged it away. The other hand slid to her pocket. He tapped at the lump there.

"You want my owl?" She fished it out and handed it to him. If that's what he needed before she....

Dyu'ami stood, the fetish cupped in his palm, and stepped away.

He lifted it high, then placed the owl on the floor before he scurried back to drop into her arms. She hugged him, tightened her grip on the gun. He raised a sooty hand and tugged her earlobe.

He wanted her to listen. But to what? Through the crackle of flames, Nicky heard.... Brows knit, she cocked her head. Heard....

A scratch against the wall behind her. Another. A whine followed, then a high, yipping bark. Prickles raced down her spine.

Dyu'ami threw his head back and grinned. He let Nicky go and scrambled to a cabinet. Nicky stood slowly, arms slack at her sides, gun dangling. Dyu'ami grabbed the handle on the cabinet door and swung it back. She stumbled toward him, ducked her head, and gaped. Through the back of the cabinet, a narrow section of the wall had been cut away. How had she missed it?

A dog bark sounded again from the open warehouse behind the office.

"Diya?" She dropped to her knees and peered through. Smoke hazed the air, but the fire hadn't spread behind the office yet. If the dog had gotten inside unharmed, there must be another way out. Excitement jolted.

She pushed Dyu'ami toward the opening, but he resisted and darted to grab the owl fetish before he crawled on his knees to his father. With tender fingers, he passed his hand over WhiteHawk's hair and gently tugged his braid. Then he scrambled to Nicky and squirmed through the hole. On her belly, Nicky wiggled out. She stood, and Dyu'ami grabbed her free hand. Another bark and a flash of red darting around the corner of the office. *Diya.*

Dyu'ami pulled, and they hurried after the dog, turned the corner —where an inferno of smoke and flames confronted them. She slid to a stop, but Dyu'ami tugged and thrust out his chin.

"No, Dyu'ami. We need to go back—"

From behind the flames, a low shadow hovered, and Diya barked again. The boy yanked away and leaped into a wavering gap in the fire. Nicky dashed after him. The opening narrowed as she hurtled through the searing blaze. Dyu'ami grabbed her hand and ran to a pile of car parts, dropped, and crawled into a tunnel under the debris.

She slid after him to an open pocket by the outside wall. The ceiling groaned and metal screamed as another section of the roof fell. Dyu'ami pounded against the wall, and Nicky tore her attention back to him. A hatch, cut square and low to the ground, was latched closed with a combination lock. He slapped at her hand. The hand that held Cochin's gun.

"Behind me," she said. Dyu'ami scurried to her back. She angled the muzzle of the gun toward the latch.

The blast blew a hole in the wall, but the latch remained partially attached. Nicky swiveled on her butt, braced her arms behind her, and kicked with all her might. The door bent. She kicked again. From outside, gloved hands grasped the metal edge and tore the panel away. Nicky shoved Dyu'ami through the opening. He disappeared. More hands grasped and dragged her outside into a pouring rain. Bulky shapes looped arms around her and sprinted from the warehouse. Metal screeched, and an unholy red lit the darkness. Nicky craned her neck over her shoulder and watched as the whole warehouse imploded, spewing flames and sparks high into the cloud-shrouded sky. Out of breath, she was pushed against the chain-link fence as the firefighters ran back toward the fire. In the trees, a wisp of red darted between trunks, heading up the mountain. Diya. But ... why was she leaving? Why hadn't she stayed with them? With Dyu'ami?

Nicky started when Dyu'ami took her hand. Pressed between their palms was a hard lump. She knew what it was, could feel its heart. Its *w'in'uska*. The owl fetish. They both watched as the flash of fur vanished into the darkness.

A heavy hand landed on her shoulder and spun her around. *Franco*. She let the boy go, fetish tucked in one of her hands, Cochin's gun in the other.

Franco wrapped Dyu'ami in a silver blanket. He straightened

and stared at her, his eyes bloodshot and swollen, lashes and hair beaded with rain.

"I thought you were dead," he said.

"And I just ran through fire." She smiled up at him. "So you'd better be worth it."

Nicky threw an arm around his neck and pulled his lips to hers.

CHAPTER SIXTY-ONE

"Nicky!"

Nicky shut the refrigerator in the fire station great room, juice boxes clutched in her hand as Ryan enveloped her in a hug that threatened to squeeze the breath from her lungs. But she didn't care. She held on just as tightly.

Ryan pushed her away, hands still on her arms, his gaze roving her face. "I got you dirty again." He slid fingers down to her hands. "Apple juice?"

She grinned. "Breakfast for Dyu'ami. He's at the police station with Franco, playing video games."

"Did you hear from Savannah?"

"She called me from her mom's house earlier this morning. Her dad's fine. EMT checked him out, and he didn't even need to go to the hospital. Franco and I'll drop Dyu'ami off with them in a little while."

More men and women shuffled in the door, as soot-streaked as Ryan.

"I guess the fire's out?" she asked.

"Yeah. We were sent back to clean up and get a couple hour's

rest. Thank the Creator for the rain. If it had spread to the trees...."
Ryan shook his head, his smile melting. He sighed. "We found
WhiteHawk. Did you shoot him?"

"No. Cochin. My gun, though," Nicky said. "Before he died,
WhiteHawk confessed to raiding the shrines and creating and selling
sacred fetishes. And murdering Seneca Elk."

"I saw the evidence. That room didn't sustain much damage. A
miracle, I think." Ryan's hazel eyes pierced her. "Lots of miracles
between yesterday and today."

Even though none of the other firefighters were nearby, Nicky
leaned in. "His eyes. WhiteHawk's eyes went white, right before I
saw the gray man in the warehouse."

"Then WhiteHawk was beyond help."

"But Dyu'ami. The same thing happened—"

"The white eyes represent a mark of death, but maybe it's only a
warning. When circumstances or situations change, the mark is
erased."

Nicky stood quietly, the juice boxes cold in her hand, and
digested his words. The gangbanger at the sting operation; his eyes
had rolled white, but his murder could've been prevented if it hadn't
been for Dax's arrogance and the police's belief the man was safe
against Chen Cano's retaliation. With Mangas, maybe she could've
talked him down, but Cochin took that choice from him with a bullet.
And Dyu'ami....

"You said I'd been chosen. Could it have been to save Dyu'ami?"
She lowered her voice. "Gemini Elk said I was the third warrior."

Ryan's eyes widened. "Did Gemini say who the other warriors
were?"

"Cochise and Mangas, but their offerings weren't accepted.
That's why they died."

He nodded slowly. "They must have approached the fire for
selfish reasons. Not to save the tribe. Only themselves. And the
fourth warrior?"

"WhiteHawk?"

"I doubt it. He was desecrating the shrines, creating sacred objects to sell. The gods don't like that."

Nicky bit her lip, her mind adding and shuffling Ryan's reasoning. "I had nothing to offer."

"You ran into that warehouse not knowing if you'd come back out. You offered yourself to save another, the most precious gift of all."

Like Gemini when he'd run into the fire to save his brother. Had she lived because she'd been willing to give her life for another?

"But I did what I was trained to do. What I *had* to do." Nicky drew in a deep breath. "Still, it feels like I have a second chance. With my friends, my house. Franco." She smiled and shook her head. "I'm not explaining this well."

"Yes, you are. You're giving yourself permission to let go of your past and move forward. It's a lesson we should all learn. I told you your visions are a gift." Ryan hugged her again, his arms tightening almost painfully before he let her go. "You should get back. I'm sure Franco's wondering where you are."

He stepped away, but she stopped him.

"Ryan? Is everything all right?"

He paused a long moment, then smiled faintly. "Everything is fine."

NICKY STARED out of the SUV at the rain-swept landscape. Rivulets of water snaked across the sand on their way to arroyos that fed the Rio Grande. Scrubby trees and bushes, stained dark by moisture, raced by, a blur, the sky shrouded in thick blue-gray clouds.

Her fingers played with the damp hair of the boy, whose head snuggled in her lap. His face was quiet, lashes draped in a sweeping curl across his cheeks. Seated in back, they were both dressed in cozy gray sweats with the Fire-Sky logo printed over their hearts. Dyu'ami swam in his, cloth rolled up around his ankles, sleeves pushed high up his arms. His hands were curled and relaxed, tucked under his chin.

"Hey," Franco said over his shoulder. "He asleep?"

"About two seconds into the drive."

"You okay?"

Nicky exhaled. "Yeah. Just want to get him settled at the Anallas' before we talk." She met his gaze in the rearview mirror.

"About what?"

"Evidence that Savannah called the Elks before the raid. About the gun I gave you at the warehouse." She licked her lips. "Us."

His smile was slow, sexy, and her body flooded with warmth. "Let's hold off on that last topic until later tonight at my place."

She smiled back. "Or mine."

His eyebrows shot up, and his lips widened to a wicked grin.

Nicky brushed a long strand of Dyu'ami's hair behind his ear. A stalling tactic. She was having trouble gathering her thoughts.

"Almost there." Franco pointed the truck down a dirt road, slowing to avoid mud puddles. "How do you feel about the tribal council absolving the Elks of narcotics distribution?"

"It won't go over well, not after Chief promised—" She broke off grimly. No way Luz could be elected to tribal council now.

"Anyway, all of the Elks have been released and are back at their compound, preparing for more funerals. They're going to grave-guard for WhiteHawk, too."

"He was the youngest son of the youngest son." Nicky stared out the window, fingers again stroking Dyu'ami's hair.

Franco pulled into the Anallas' paved driveway. Their home was a dark brown ranch-style with a patchy lawn out front, surrounded by three huge cottonwoods. On one side, a horno oven sat next to a melting adobe structure—the first Analla homestead on this property.

"Social worker's here," Franco said. A mud-splattered Prius stood parked behind RJ's truck.

"Dyu'ami?" Nicky rubbed his shoulder. "Buddy? Wake up."

The front screen door opened. RJ and his wife Noreen, the social worker, and Savannah filed out. Behind them stood Diya.

At the sound of her bark, Dyu'ami's eyes blinked open and he sat up, searching. He quickly climbed out of the truck after Nicky and ran to a wiggling Diya. He dropped to his knees and held out a hand, like he couldn't believe she was really there. But Diya was impatient. She pushed him backward and licked his face and hands until he threw his arms around her neck. The dog tucked her head over his shoulder and sighed, her eyes closing. They both stilled and held each other.

Savannah ran to Nicky and hugged her.

"Diya is *here*," Nicky said. "How...?"

Savannah wiped away tears. "After I realized Dad was okay, I followed her tracks. She was already a couple miles down the road, heading toward the mountains. If I hadn't brought her back, I think she would have gone Lassie on us to find her boy."

But at the warehouse, Nicky had seen ... Her brows knit. No. She hadn't really seen Diya. Only flashes of a red coat. But she'd heard a dog's bark.

Hadn't she?

RJ, leaning heavily on the porch railing, beamed and beckoned them to the house and out of the rain. "There he is! Dyu'ami Elk, the next official fetish carver on the pueblo. As I was telling ... ah, well, if *I'd* been here when J WhiteHawk came and took Dyu'ami, it never would have happened."

"Way to throw Mom and me under the bus," Savannah said.

RJ frowned at her. Noreen, an older, softer version of her daughter, brushed by her husband to give Nicky a quick hug.

Franco slid a warm hand up Nicky's back to cup her neck, a caressing gesture that caused Savannah's eyebrows to arch beneath her bangs. She smirked and leaned in to whisper, "Whole story."

Nicky grinned and mouthed, *Later.*

As soon as the screen door was open, Dyu'ami and Diya disappeared down the long hall. Nicky tucked into Franco's side as the social worker shuffled through more paperwork, everyone signing and initialing.

"Now, don't you worry," RJ assured them all. "He'll be fine here with me, uh, with us. We already have some of his clothes from the first time. I heard old Gemini Elk—"

"Agent Martinez?" the social worker interrupted. "Can you move your truck? I need to leave."

Franco nodded and stepped to the door, Savannah and RJ following. Noreen headed to the kitchen.

Nicky was alone. She slipped her hand in her pocket and walked down the hall. Dyu'ami sat on the bed, Diya beside him.

"Dyu'ami? I have to go soon. You'll be fine here until your grandfather is ready to take you home."

Dyu'ami tipped his head, his eyes again distant.

Nicky slowly opened her fingers. The little stone owl sat upright on her palm. "This *tsa'atsi y'aauni*. It has your *w'in'uska*. Your heart. It was your offering." She placed it on the nightstand next to the bed. "Diya's spirit came and helped us, didn't she? Maybe she's the fourth warrior." Nicky ran a hand over Dyu'ami's hair and tugged his braid. "Or is it you?"

Dyu'ami's beautiful hazel eyes flashed to hold hers for a brief moment, turquoise shards sparkling. He stroked his dog and stared into space.

Through her tears, Nicky absorbed his peaceful smile.

CHAPTER SIXTY-TWO

NICKY TUCKED the covers over Dyu'ami's shoulders. He was asleep within moments, Diya snoring faintly at his feet. Her own exhaustion was catching up to her, and she laid her head on folded arms at the edge of the bed, closed her eyes.

"Nicky! Nicky, please come!" Noreen's voice contained a high note of hysteria. Nicky pushed to her feet and ran out of the bedroom.

Noreen met her at the front door. "They're arresting Savannah. They say she called and warned the Elks, that she's responsible for Mangas Elk's death." She clutched at Nicky's arm. "And—and something about that horrible gang from Albuquerque. Your friend is here, from the state police. They just came"—she waved a frantic hand—"while you were in the back with Dyu'ami. They just came. Please. You have to stop him."

Nicky slammed outside and skidded to a stop. Savannah, hands and legs splayed against a state police unit, was being patted down. A second officer explained her rights. Two more vehicles—one FBI, the other a large black SUV—blocked the driveway. Franco, his back to the scene, held on to RJ, who was yelling at the police. Dax Stone and

James Vallery stood to one side. Noreen darted past Nicky and went to her husband.

Nicky ran into the rain. "What the hell's going on?"

"You should have told me about her involvement in the Chen Cano case," Dax said.

Nicky's breath left her lungs like she'd been punched. Face stiff, she said, "It's an ongoing investigation. No conclusions—"

"Bullshit. You submitted a search warrant for her personal and office phone." Dax stepped in close, too close, but Nicky stood her ground. "Do you know what they show? Calls from her cell and office lines to burner phones in Albuquerque, one of which was linked to a suspected Crybaby gang member. They go back for over a year." He paused, then lowered his voice. "If you'd told me your suspicions, I could've helped. Instead, I had to find out from another source, and it was taken out of my hands."

He started to step away, but she grabbed his arm.

"What do you mean, another source? I thought I was your only internal contact for the Cano investigation."

Dax leaned in again. Fine lines crisscrossed underneath tired red eyes. "Of course you did."

Nicky dropped his arm.

"I alerted Chief Stone and the FBI after I spoke to Chief Cochin at the hospital," Vallery said.

Nicky looked back and forth between the two men. "You brought both the director and chief into this investigation and didn't tell me?"

"You brought in Martinez and didn't tell me," Dax countered, his dark blue eyes cold as ice. "His name's on the warrant."

"You're jealous?"

"Please, Sergeant," Vallery interrupted. "This is hard enough without bringing in your personal relationship with Chief Stone."

Nicky stabbed a finger at Dax. "There is no personal relationship."

Vallery's gaze sharpened. "Then Chief Stone didn't cover the balloon payment due on your home?"

"*What?*"

"We got an anonymous tip about your financial troubles during your five-year audit this summer. The tipster said you were desperate for money." Vallery narrowed his gaze. "A few days ago, your mortgage was paid off. Twenty-five thousand dollars. Anything connected to you became suspect. You work on Savannah's computer. You have her passwords, could have used her cell phone. I had to ask myself, was your home more important to you than your friend? Than your job? Chief Cochin believed you were Cano's contact, was adamant you be arrested. She even told me you'd asked for the deconfliction logins so you could cast suspicion on someone else."

Nicky blanched. Luz Cochin had decided to neutralize her. Accuse her of collaborating with Chen Cano. Take her out before she got a chance to submit her completed report about Mangas's shooting.

"When James and I met this morning to coordinate Savannah's arrest," Dax said, "he laid out the evidence against you. That's when I told him you were part of my investigation and I had complete trust in you." His voice was loud, reassuring. "I confessed we'd restarted our relationship, that I'd paid off your debt. My driver, Kevin Archibeque, corroborated. He waits in the truck for me when I ... visit your house." He stared into her eyes. "Nicky, I'm sorry you had to hear about my gift this way. I had a special dinner planned to tell you. Tonight."

The patter of rain filled the silence, but the sound seemed distant to Nicky. Everything swirled in her head. Dax had paid off her loan?

Dax raised his gaze, looked over her shoulder. "Agent Martinez."

Nicky's stomach slid to her feet. She spun around. *Franco.* His expression was stony. He wouldn't look at her.

"I'd appreciate your discretion," Dax said. "Publicity about Nicky's and my renewed ... relationship could harm her career even more than it has in the past. And, of course, there's my wife to consider."

With a curt nod, Franco turned away. Nicky made to follow, but Dax grabbed her arm.

"You fuck this up by throwing yourself at his feet, you can kiss your career goodbye. We need to talk. I'll contact you." He let her go and strode to his SUV.

Nicky squared her shoulders. She'd clear everything up with Franco later. Right now, Savannah took precedence.

RJ and Noreen clasped each other's hands at the open window of the SUV.

Savannah sat cuffed in the back, worry furrowing her brow.

"I didn't do this. I didn't warn the Elks or call Chen Cano's gang."

"I know," Nicky said.

"Don't let Dad do too much, please. His heart...."

The driver started the truck. As the window slid up, Nicky said, "We'll follow and have you out before dark!" She stepped back to stand next to RJ and Noreen as the cars filed down the road. "Let's get you changed into dry clothes before we leave, Mr. Analla."

RJ nodded, and they hurried back inside the house, Noreen trailing behind. "Don't worry," he said. "We'll hire the best lawyer for her." He caught Nicky's gaze, his expression anxious. "You told her not to say anything? Not to answer any questions? There's no telling what they might do to make her confess, who she might implicate."

"RJ! Savannah didn't do this," Noreen said. "She wouldn't betray the pueblo in such a horrible way."

"Horrible way?" RJ shook his head. "She protected her People against sickness outsiders have always brought onto our land."

"Stop. Please, don't fight. Mrs. Analla, you're okay to stay with Dyu'ami? Franco and I will—" Nicky stopped and looked around the room. She shoved open the screen door and stepped outside. Franco's unit was gone.

"I thought you knew." Noreen placed a hand on her back. "He left."

CHAPTER SIXTY-THREE

NICKY STOPPED her unit in her driveway and slammed out of the truck, striding to the patio. The front door to her home was cracked open wide enough to leave a golden wedge of light on the rain-slick cement, and the scent of coffee drifted out through curtained kitchen windows. She'd asked for Dax after they'd bailed out Savannah. Now she knew why he'd been nowhere to be found.

Heat flared up her neck. He'd done enough damage to her and Franco's relationship that morning at the Anallas', and she'd had it with his interference in her life.

She shoved the door and blasted into the narrow foyer. "*Dammit, Dax! Get out of my house and out of my li—*"

The cold muzzle of a gun pressed into the soft underside of her jaw. She froze in her tracks, anger flipping to heart-jolting surprise and a sharp pang of fear.

"Muévese." The man's voice was raspy and muffled, and his breath stank of cigarettes and very good coffee. He'd been behind the door, waiting. She tipped her head to the side, slanting her eyes in a vain attempt to see his face. He pushed the gun deeper, and she swallowed.

"Okay." Nicky spread her fingers, brought her hands higher, elbows bent. She forced out another "Okay," heard the wobble in her voice, the spiral of panic. She hauled in a slower breath, centered herself. Took in details.

Shorter than her, mouth shoulder-high. Tucked to the right side of her body, too close. Adrenaline and his cheap cologne seared her senses. His left hand slid up to cup the back of her neck, skin callused, rough. He stepped away slightly, and the gun dropped.

"Okay," Nicky repeated and planted her foot.

She torqued her torso to the right, grabbed the gun, and twisted it viciously. His trigger finger broke with a sickening snap. He yelped as she jerked the weapon away. Nicky swiveled at the waist and torqued again, right elbow high. His nose exploded in a crunch of blood. She slammed the butt of the pistol into his temple, and he dropped like a stone, one finger bent at a sickening angle. She pointed the snub-nosed .25 at the man's head. Nicky didn't recognize him.

Booted feet pounded on the tile floor behind her. She spun again, stepped into her Weaver stance. Three men in dark clothes, bandanas over their noses and mouths, pointed guns down the hall. The double clutch of a shotgun pump was all the greeting they gave.

Nicky stared into the large black bores of a sawed-off. Her eyes teared, and the coppery taste of fear coated her throat. Muscles drained and joints melted painfully at the sound of her own death. She could drop one or two, maybe, but in the narrow hallway, there was no way to avoid the blast of a shotgun. It would split her in half. She'd be dead by the time she hit the floor ... the walls ... the ceiling....

Which begged an important point.

Why aren't I dead already?

Nicky met the cold gaze of the man with the shotgun, mind racing. In the last couple of weeks—and in alphabetical order—she'd almost drowned, been infected by an organism that could kill her, kicked a poacher's ass, saved two boys, survived multiple devastating fires, and had not one but about a dozen different people point guns at her. Okay, the last one wasn't in alphabetical order, but it seemed the most relevant.

No one spoke; no instructions were given. A tendril of recklessness grew and blossomed in her chest. The effect of colonization? Maybe, but she welcomed it. She straightened, firmed her body, then forced it to relax infinitesimally.

Might as well give it a shot. After all, what the hell did she have to lose?

Nicky cocked a half smile. "Put your guns down, fellas," she ordered. "You're under arrest."

CHAPTER SIXTY-FOUR

As NICKY'S command faded away, laughter, smooth and musical, filled the silence.

Feminine laughter.

The delicate *tap-tap* of footsteps announced the presence of the woman who walked toward the phalanx of armed men. A figure-hugging dark blue dress wrapped her body, the sheen in the overhead light marking its composition as raw silk. The five-inch heels of her sleek pumps were twig thin, but she walked with the confident sway of a woman who lived in shoes that high. Straight brown hair shot with red highlights rippled over her shoulders. Her mouth was a slash of matte red lipstick, and midnight-blue eye shadow cooled her brown eyes.

Nicky sucked in a gasp. "I know you."

"Of course. Please, Officer Matthews. Give your weapon"—she gestured with a graceful sweep of her hand—"to Javier. We did not come here to kill you, but...." She shrugged, a smile twitching on full lips. "It would be a pity." A melodious Spanish accent flavored her English.

The man on the floor behind Nicky groaned, and the woman lifted a delicate brow.

"Ella me rompió la nariz." His voice was thick, clotted, whiny. "Mi dedo."

"Estúpido. Men. Always underestimating the strength of women." The woman rapped out instructions in Spanish, her tone hard. One of the armed men stepped forward—carefully. His hand covered the gun in Nicky's grasp. She tensed.

"Please," the woman said. "Do not. Daniel's shotgun will not discriminate between you and Javier, and it's very difficult to get blood out of tile grout."

"Clear—not blue—laundry detergent mixed with a sugar scrub." Nicky released the gun and raised her hands as Javier patted her down. Why did these guys always smell like the bottom of an ashtray?

The woman's expression arrested. "Really?"

"Laundry detergents are packed with enzymes—proteases, lipases. They chew right through blood." Nicky grinned into the woman's eyes and tilted her head toward the men. "I imagine with these bozos, stains are inevitable."

The woman's lips stretched into a wide smile before she tipped her head back and laughed. This time the sound was real.

"I like you, Sergeant Monique Nicky Matthews. We might yet become friends, but you are the police, and I—" She stopped, the smile lingering on her mouth but dropping from her eyes.

"You are Luna Guerra, mother of Han Guerra, the little boy I saved from the trailer fire at Green Meadow Springs. An alias, of course."

Luna dipped her chin in acknowledgment.

"How is Han? That's really his name?"

"Yes." The woman's face softened. "He is well and safe. Luckily, he is too young for the fire's memory to haunt him, though it has littered my sleep with nightmares."

"Burning alive the men who started the fire didn't help?"

"Not as much as I would have liked. Murder leaves a mark on one's soul, no matter how deserved." She smiled. "Come. Sit. We have many things to talk about."

The man with the shotgun—Daniel—swung it like a waving hand, motioning for Nicky to move. The other men fanned out, their guns still aimed at her. She walked out of the foyer and into her open den and kitchen. Three cups of coffee sat steaming on the table.

"Javier was disappointed you had no cream. He says all Americans have cream. He will cuff your hands behind your back, for precaution only, you understand."

Javier sidestepped around her and snapped on cuffs. Nicky tugged. She couldn't slip her hands out, but they weren't too tight.

As he grasped her elbow and led her to the sofa, she said, "Well done. Ex-cop?"

He didn't respond but lowered her to the couch. She caught his eyes and smothered a gasp. He faded back, hands clasped and elbow resting above the butt of his holstered gun.

"Not so *ex*," the woman said as she sat. "They are easy to buy, you know? And the corporation I run—"

"Corporation? *Que* fancy!" Nicky said. "I hope you follow the tax codes. Part of my salary is paid with federal grants, and I definitely want them to get their cut of your ... profits."

"Many legitimate businesses reside under my label. How else would we launder all the money that comes in?" Luna made a coy moue. "Although one of my most profitable international market sites is shut down now. Compromised." Her lacquered nail playfully tapped Nicky's knee. "Your doing, I think."

Nicky's mind worked as she tried to assemble the pieces of this conversation into a clear picture. She smiled modestly.

"I'm just a little ol' police officer on a little ol' Indian reservation in the little ol' state of New Mexico. Doing my part, keeping my nose clean, fighting crime to the best of my ability within the law."

Luna laughed. "And that is why I will always win. This is not the old American West. You must abide by rules, your behavior controlled by pieces of paper written by politicians who don't know—or care—what danger hides in plain sight. You are outgunned and outnumbered by an army who would die for me."

A shiver traveled through Nicky's spine at the unadulterated truth. Except....

"No. Your army is a force you purchase. Men and women who can't leave because it means their death. My colleagues work for a higher cause."

"What? Good over evil? Right over wrong? For the American way?" Luna chuckled, and the men rolled their eyes and shook their heads. "How quaint."

"We put our lives on the line for crap pay, yet we wake up every morning and get to it. That should scare the hell out of you because you have to ask yourself, why? What makes my job worth dying for?" Nicky held Luna's eyes. "Tell me. Would any of these goons have run into that burning trailer to save your little boy? Because every last one of my fellow officers would've."

The silence stretched, broken only by the shifting of booted feet on the floor.

Finally, Luna dipped her head.

"Tienes razón," she said. "But we have become too serious. Instead, let's talk about your police officer's salary. It's not enough to save your home."

Nicky stilled. "How do you know about that?" Her voice tightened with anger.

"The money you so scorn also buys information." Luna folded her hands in her lap. "And pays off mortgages."

Nicky blinked. Realization struck, and her mouth dropped open. "My God. *You* did it. You, not—" Not Dax. She narrowed her eyes. "I still don't know who you are."

"I am a woman who owes you a life debt."

Nicky opened her mouth, but Luna held up a hand.

"I didn't realize you were undergoing your personnel audit and the timing would seem suspicious. It was never my intent to harm you after what you did for me—after you saved my son. The money has been withdrawn from your account. A bank error." She withdrew a crisp white envelope from the leather purse at her feet and laid it across Nicky's lap. It was from her bank, postmarked two days earlier. "Evidence of the mistake."

"Thank you."

"You thank me, yet you will lose your home." Luna stood and smoothed out nonexistent wrinkles in her dress. "Since I could not repay my debt by saving your home, I want to give you the person who has helped the Crybaby gang over the last year. Perhaps it will be of use to you, perhaps not."

The snitch. Nicky's heart pounded. "I have a question about that."

"Police. Always with questions."

"The informant allowed the transport van to get busted at the CampFire Casino. Why?"

"The informant explained what happened, and we wrote off the loss, although one of the escorts obviously talked before his position was ... terminated."

"Okay. What about the Elks?"

"The men who sold product without permission? Four sons dead in such a short period. Maybe that's enough punishment." She cocked an eyebrow. "Maybe not."

Luna nodded to Daniel, who laid a flash drive on the lamp table.

"I don't need to tell you it would be suicidal to follow. Or that you put your life and the lives of your friends in jeopardy if you reveal my identity, que no? For now, let's keep it between us."

As if one, the four men surrounded the woman in a protective square. The man from the hall held a bloodied handkerchief to his nose. He shot Nicky a hate-filled glare as Luna swayed to the front door.

"Wait!" Nicky called. She scooted to the edge of the sofa. The letter on her lap fell with a tick of sound to the floor. "You never told me your name."

"You haven't guessed?"

Nicky shook her head.

"Liar." Her brown eyes glinted. "Me llamo Chen Cano. *I* am Chen Cano."

SINCE HER EXTRA handcuff key was tucked in a top desk drawer in her office, it took Nicky all of a minute to unlock them. She stared at the cups of coffee. No one had seemed too worried about prints or DNA. Still, she bagged them.

They'd left her cell phone on the lamp table, and she contemplated calling the police but discarded the idea. Luna—Chen—hadn't lied. They would kill her if she followed, murder her friends if she talked. Her hands were effectively tied. For now.

The envelope lay on the floor beside the sofa. Nicky picked it up and dropped it on the table. She grabbed her laptop, poured herself a cup of coffee, and stirred in three spoonfuls of sugar—she made a mental note to make a new doctor's appointment. Then she listened to the voices on the flash drive until they faded into silence.

Her cup of coffee grew cold as she ordered her thoughts.

When the morning sun brightened the room, she switched off the lights around the house and picked up her phone.

Time to rock and roll.

CHAPTER SIXTY-FIVE

"THANK YOU FOR COMING IN, Mr. Analla." Nicky closed the glass door of the administrative foyer at the police station. It was cooler after the rains, and the air had a feeling of fall. "I'm sorry it's under such terrible circumstances, but attribution of the fetishes found at the warehouse is vital."

Savannah's father paused to catch his breath, and Nicky placed a hand on his elbow. Straight hair swept across a pallid forehead, but pink tinged his cheeks, and his eyes were bright.

"Young lady, I only accepted your invitation because that man WhiteHawk stole our heritage for money. That's what we get for letting outsiders on our land. But I cannot say enough how this nonsense with Savannah has upset me." He slanted her a glance. "Have you found more evidence against her?"

Nicky gestured for him to follow her along the corridor that surrounded the glassed terrarium courtyard. He used the wall as support, his steps slow and vaguely unsteady.

"Contacting the Elks from her office phone before the raid was bad enough," Nicky said. "But state police and the FBI have known for some time the Crybabies had a collaborator on the pueblo. Calls from her cell and office phone lines to gang-member burner phones closed that loop."

RJ gave her a sharp look.

"Still, we don't really know who made those calls. It could have been anyone at the department. The only evidence against Savannah is sort of nonevidence. She was out of town with you when we planned our most recent bust. Your last series of tests at UNM Hospital? Theory is she didn't have time to alert Cano's gang to our CampFire Casino sting." Nicky matched his steps, her hand behind his back.

"You're using her absence against her?" He let out a derisive snort.

"If she conspired with Chen Cano, she can expect prison time."

RJ stopped and grasped her arm. "I'm sure she meant well. That it would help her People in some way."

"How? Warning the Elks put our whole operation in danger. A man died."

His fingers dug into her sleeve. "They are the last fetish-carving clan. You wouldn't understand, but their importance can't be minimized. They must be protected."

Nicky stared into RJ's eyes and nodded slowly. "That would explain motive." She took RJ's arm and continued down the hall. "But helping Chen Cano's gang? That's a whole different level of evil."

She reached to open the door to Captain's office, but RJ stayed her.

"Savannah didn't take any money."

"As far as we can tell, she took nothing for her help, except"— Nicky paused—"except Cano's drugs have practically disappeared from the reservation. Maybe that was the bargain struck. The Crybabies would keep their drugs off the rez in exchange for information on our operations."

"Yes! Don't you see? Savannah was *protecting* her People. She should get a medal." He ran a shaky hand over his head. "Her brother died because of this drug cancer. The deal with Chen Cano built a barrier against evil. Savannah's wrong turned into a right for us."

"A devil's bargain, sir. It allowed the gang to get their drugs to cities across the country, and their human trafficking operation thrived." Nicky opened the door and ushered him inside. "You know everyone, don't you?"

RJ hobbled in to shake Captain's hand then pivoted to greet Director Vallery.

"I'm glad you could come, Mr. Analla," Vallery said, his tone grave. "This is very important, and we value you as our resident expert."

RJ stood taller. "I would do anything for Fire-Sky."

"Certainly." Vallery nodded. "We're waiting for a couple more people to join us—" The office door swung open. "Ah! Chief Stone. And Savannah."

Dax ushered Savannah into the room. Nicky stepped forward and hugged her tightly. She searched Savannah's face. Tired eyes stared back at her from behind wire spectacles.

"Savannah?" RJ said.

"Dad?" Savannah's gaze shifted to her father, then back to Nicky. "What's going on?"

RJ hurried over to Savannah and engulfed her in a hug.

"Nicky outlined some of the evidence, sweetheart." He held her by the shoulders and peered into her eyes. "It's not good."

"But I didn't make that call. You were with me in my office. We stayed all night. I only left once, to get you coffee when you asked—" Savannah blinked at her father. Slowly, she pressed a hand to her mouth.

"No, no, daughter. I went to the men's room first. You were alone in your office for a few minutes before I came back."

"Are you sure, Mr. Analla?" Nicky asked quietly. "Your daughter's future rests on your recollection."

"Yes, I—" He swung toward Nicky. "Yes."

Nicky nodded to Captain Richards. He tapped his computer. Voices sounded from a speaker on his desk.

"*No one questions my presence at the station.*"

"*And you will assure us safe passage?*"

"*No, I can only tell you when police operations are scheduled. The rest, you have to take care of. But my information comes with a price. I want none of your drugs sold on our land. If they are, I'll disappear, and you'll have to take your chances.*"

"*But this access. How long will it last?*"

"*As long as you stick to the bargain and no one talks.*"

Captain Richards tapped the computer again, and the voices stopped.

"I'm afraid someone talked, Mr. Analla," Nicky said. "That call was recorded a few weeks after the crash on I-25 last year."

"No." RJ's face grayed.

"Your conversations with Chen Cano's gang—dates, times, places—were recorded."

"No. It was Savannah. She's young. A-a few years in prison won't hurt her." RJ grasped Vallery's arm. "It will kill me."

"Robert Johnson Analla." Dax stepped forward, handcuffs dangling from his fingers. "I'm placing you under arrest for conspiracy and obstruction of justice. You have the right to remain silent—"

"Savannah. Tell them." RJ extended his hand to her. "It was you. Savannah!"

Savannah turned her back to her father and stared out the window. Nicky followed her gaze. Dark clouds streaked across the blue sky, and the gray green and browns of the desert glowed with a richness that only came from the rain.

"Don't worry, N'aishdiya," Savannah said. "We'll get you the best lawyer we can buy."

NICKY HELD open the door as two state police officers escorted a still-protesting RJ out of Captain's office. She'd take Savannah home and then return as part of negotiations with Dax for the flash drive evidence. He'd already pressed for its provenance, but she'd been adamant that unmasking her source was nonnegotiable.

"A moment, Sergeant?" Vallery beckoned Nicky to one corner of the room.

"I won't be long." She exchanged a glance with Savannah, who nodded and left.

Vallery wouldn't meet her eyes. "I had a conversation with Chief Cochin after your phone call this morning. She'd like to apologize for her belief that you were Chen Cano's informant. She also admitted to shooting Mangas Elk and that she gave the gun to you immediately for safekeeping. That, of course, explains how you had her backup weapon in the warehouse."

She frowned. "But, sir, that's not—"

Vallery held up a hand. "Luz Cochin would not only become the first woman but also the first law enforcement officer on the Fire-Sky Tribal Council and an ally we can't afford to lose. Her bravery under fire at the warehouse has already gone a long way to mitigate what occurred during the Elk raid." He tugged at his shirt cuffs. "While I would never condone filing a false report, I'm sure we can come to a compromise on this issue. A way to present your narrative in a, er, positive manner. For the chief. It would be the right thing to do, Sergeant."

Nicky stared at Vallery, her mind adjusting, reevaluating, before she nodded slowly. "Yes, sir."

"Good." He cleared his throat. "Very good. We'd be in your debt."

"In that same spirit, sir. Chief Stone?"

Dax stepped to her side.

"I found this in my mail last night." She extracted the letter from the bank and handed it to Vallery. "The payment to my account was the bank's mistake."

Vallery pulled glasses from his pocket and scanned the letter. "You lied about paying off Sergeant Matthews's debt, Chief?"

"Yes, sir, to protect me," Nicky said. "The wrong thing for the right reason. Seems there's a lot of that going around." She held Vallery's gaze until it slid away.

Dax laid a warm hand on her arm, a faint smile on his sculpted lips. "If you need the money, my offer still stands, Sergeant Matthews."

"Thank you." Nicky was surprised that she really meant it. "I'll handle it myself."

CHAPTER SIXTY-SIX

Nicky climbed into her unit and stared through the water-beaded windshield. Scalding Peak was wreathed in clouds, and gray pillars of rain seemed to hold up the sky.

Savannah clicked her seatbelt closed. "Can I use your cell to call my mom?" She hesitated. "Nicky? Why wasn't Franco here to back you up?"

Nicky grabbed her cell and read the second message she'd sent that morning.

Please come to Captain's office at one o'clock. I'll explain every-thing. Please.

Franco's answer had been succinct and absolute.

Nicky quickly deleted the texts and handed the phone to Savannah.

"He said I didn't need him."

CHAPTER SIXTY-SEVEN

THE SUN HAD JUST DROPPED below the clouds when Nicky parked her unit next to Howard's battered Suburban in front of Savannah's home. She stretched her back and rolled her shoulders, taking in the start of a garish pink sunset, letting the chill air wash over her skin. A brief flash of a fire-sky lit the clouds as the sun approached the horizon. With one last deep breath, she strode through the front door and headed for the kitchen. Negotiations with Dax and the federal attorneys had gone well, and she had good news for Savannah.

Howard sat on the sofa in Savannah's den, watching TV, an open bag of Flamin' Hot Fritos nestled by his hip.

"Why is he always here?" Nicky said. She settled in more comfortably on a barstool, and Savannah handed her a cup of coffee. She took a sip, grimaced, and stirred in two heaping teaspoons of sugar. Her doctor's appointment was scheduled for tomorrow —finally.

"He's not that bad. And he's appreciative of everything I do. Unlike my father." Savannah, a large lavender towel wrapped around her head, peered in the oven's window. The rich scent of cinnamon permeated the air.

Nicky swirled her cup, staring intently at the oily black surface. "I'm sorry about your dad, Savannah. And I'm sorry it had to be a surprise."

Savannah stared at her, light from the ceiling glinting coldly off her glasses.

Nicky stilled her hand. "It wasn't a surprise."

"Oh, it was." Savannah rubbed briskly at the towel. "But everything adds up. I'd heard from some of the night-shift cops that he'd drop in to see if I was working late on days I wasn't. Everyone knew him. Treated him like an uncle or grandfather."

"How did he get into the deconfliction database?"

"He found the password on my phone. I gave him and Mom all of my personal passwords in case something happened to me—car accident, rattlesnake bite, kidnapped by an evil scientist. It never occurred to me he'd do something like this." Savannah hesitated. "Why didn't you tell me I was a suspect?"

"I didn't have a way to clear you. And I didn't want my personal feelings to get in the way." They had, though. Nicky added another spoonful of sugar to her coffee. "I know why your dad did it."

"I figured that one out." Savannah clasped her hands together. "I really do care about what happens to my People, but not at the expense of others. That kind of messed-up tribalism does no one any good."

"He felt like this was an opportunity to save the tribe from something that had killed his son."

"No. He decided to be a hero. That was more important to him than me."

"Savannah."

She waved a hand. "He's never seen what I do for Fire-Sky, only that I haven't married and increased the population of our People by popping out babies." Savannah tipped her head toward the den. "Hence, Howard."

Nicky dropped her voice. "If I remember correctly, you agreed to that coupling—"

"Ew, don't use that word."

"—because you could control him, like you couldn't control your dad." Nicky paused. "Or Ryan."

Savannah sighed and tugged the towel off her head. She carefully draped it over the seat of a barstool. "You're not gonna let that drop, are you?"

"No. But we can circle back later," Nicky said. "Since the tribe has all the evidence, state police and the Feds had to cut a deal. With tribal sovereignty, your dad won't do jail time."

"My mom won't have him home, at least for a little while. Not until she forgives him." Savannah peeked at Nicky. "So ... Dax didn't pay off your mortgage."

"No. But he could have. I thought he did."

"So did I."

"So did Franco." Nicky couldn't keep the bitter note out of her voice. She took another sip of coffee, fingers tight around the cup. "He should have trusted me."

"Oh, jeez, Nicky. Can't you see how Franco might feel? You wouldn't invite him to your house, you wouldn't let him—or any of us —help you. But you let Dax in, a guy from your past you have no reason to trust."

Nicky cradled her cup, letting the heat seep into her cold hands. "I know."

"Apologize," Savannah said.

Nicky picked up her phone and waggled it. "He ghosted me."

"He'll hear the gossip soon enough, find out Dax lied."

The ticking of the timer was loud in the silence that fell between them.

"Why aren't you more upset about your dad?" Nicky asked.

"You don't think I am?" Savannah rolled her neck and stared at the ceiling. "I'm so angry and hurt, I'm afraid to let it out. But I also feel free for the first time in a long while." Her eyes narrowed. "In fact...."

Savannah marched into the den. She picked up the remote and

turned the television off. Howard scrutinized her, mild interest on his face.

"Howard. I'm breaking up with you."

He frowned and slowly stood. They were about the same height, but Howard was rail thin. Nicky wondered how, considering all the junk food he ate.

"Does that mean I don't have to keep wearing these clothes?" He was dressed in red skinny jeans and a plaid flannel shirt, with heavy Doc Martins on his feet and a checkered scarf around his neck.

"You don't like them?" Savannah asked, obviously taken aback.

"They bind my junk. I did it for you, but you're too controlling. I'm an eagle who needs to fly free."

"But—"

Howard pressed a finger against her lips. "No more talk. Just know there can be no us."

Nicky choked on a swallow of coffee.

"I'm sorry to break your heart, but I must go." He dropped his finger and gave her a sad smile. "Can I take those Hot Pockets in the freezer with me?"

Nicky pressed the back of her hand to her mouth and shook with silent laughter.

"Yes, Howard." Savannah's voice trembled.

The timer chimed.

"And a couple of those muffins?"

Savannah's face softened. "Yes, Howard." She leaned in and kissed him on the cheek. "Nicky, can you take those out? Howard, don't touch them until they're cool or you'll burn yourself." She hurried through the archway toward the back bedrooms.

Howard wandered into the kitchen, his fingertips against the spot Savannah had kissed. Nicky slid the pan of muffins onto a cooling rack.

"See how she is? Bossing us around. It wouldn't have worked between us." He opened the freezer door and extracted an enormous box of pepperoni Hot Pockets. "I'll have more free time now. If you

want, I can spend it with Dyu'ami. I like him. He makes me feel ...
necessary."

"I think he'd like that, too," Nicky said.

"He'll stay on Fire-Sky?"

"Yes. After an evaluation, he'll move back in with Gemini."

"Dyu'ami will be the next fetish carver. He will always have a
home on our land."

WhiteHawk had accomplished what he'd set out to do, Nicky
thought, but the cost....

Howard opened the refrigerator and plucked out the condiments
in the door, dropping them into a bag.

"And you, Sergeant Matthews?" He paused and stared at her.
"No blackness follows you now."

"I'm kinda hoping I'm cured of ever seeing visions. Why are you
shaking your head?"

"Because this hasn't closed your mind to spirits. It's made you
more powerful to them." He held up his finger and thumb about two
inches apart. "This much more. If you'd told me about your owl
fetish, I wouldn't have forecast your death and scared you the way I
did."

"Really?" Nicky raised an eyebrow. "That's convenient, now that
you know everything."

Howard smiled sweetly and opened Savannah's pantry. "Graham
crackers." He grabbed the box and put it in the bag. "What will you
do about your house and the mortgage?"

"Ha. You weren't watching TV. You were eavesdropping."

"People don't much take me into account," he said.

"My house? I don't know. Hope for a miracle, I guess." She gazed
out the kitchen window, not really seeing the view. "I always felt if I
didn't fight for it, I was letting my grandmother down. I realize now,
the house is just a house and the furniture just furniture. People
count. Friendships count. I count."

"I have money saved up. I could give you some."

"Thank you, but no."

"And Agent Franco Martinez?"

Nicky raised her brows. "None of your business, my friend."

"You consider me your friend?"

"Of course."

Howard's face split into a huge grin. "Then, as my friend, will you go with Savannah when she visits that Chishe today?"

"Ryan? You think she'll go see him?"

"She baked cinnamon muffins." He dropped a can of Vienna sausages in the bag. "And she is out from under my spell and her father's control, so now she can love him openly. I want her to be happy." He touched his cheek again where Savannah had kissed him. "Why else do you think I broke up with her?"

Nicky's heart ached at Howard's expression. "I'll go, if only to see the look on Ryan's face."

"Good. It's nice they'll get a happily ever after. Can you reach that can of coffee?"

CHAPTER SIXTY-EIGHT

SAVANNAH STOOD in front of Ryan's door, clutching the plate of cinnamon muffins. Nicky smirked, arms crossed and shoulder against a post, as she cataloged Savannah's nervousness—shifting feet, quick breaths, puckered brow. But at her core, she was deeply happy for her two best friends.

Best friends. Dax had been her lover, her rival, even her enemy. Never her friend. Franco, though. He could have been her friend.

Could have.

Savannah squared her shoulders and rang the doorbell.

"Give me a break, Savannah." Nicky gestured to the screen door. "Turn the handle and go inside like you've done a million times before."

"Why are you here again?" Only the slightest hint of strain colored Savannah's voice.

"Moral support. Oh, and because it's about time."

Savannah glanced at Nicky, and her face relaxed.

"I know. I hope he can forgive me for the hell I've put him—us—through. I wouldn't blame him if he doesn't. I probably have a lot of work to do."

Ryan's silhouette materialized in the darkened entrance hall. He stared out through the wrought-iron scrollwork that covered the screen door, barefoot and shirtless, mussed golden-brown hair haloing his head. Sleepy eyes widened.

"Savannah?"

"I'm so sorry, Ryan. Did I—we—wake you up?"

He stepped closer and peered behind Savannah. "Nicky?"

She waved.

"Can I come in?" Savannah hugged the plate. "I'd like to talk. Please." Her voice dropped low. "I have so much to say—to tell you—"

"Ryan? Sweetie? Who's at the door?" A second shape advanced down the hall, curvy legs and feet bare. Long, almost black hair tumbled around her shoulders, and a soft, clinging T-shirt draped over her torso and outlined the swell of her abdomen.

Nicky levered off the post. She stood like she'd been struck and stared at Jinni Sundry as the woman curled her arm around Ryan's bare waist. Jinni's head dropped to the curve of his shoulder, and she grasped his hand to place it over her pregnant belly.

"Sergeant Matthews? Savannah. You woke us, I'm afraid. After Ryan put out all those fires, he came straight home and fell into bed. And I can't seem to get enough sleep right now." Jinni snuggled deeper into Ryan's chest.

A shaft of lingering sunlight glinted off a passing car. Somehow, it caught the stone embedded in the ring on Jinni's left hand. Nicky's gaze dropped to it and darted back up to Ryan's expressionless face.

Jinni slipped her arm from behind Ryan and touched the fiery opal set like a brilliant flame in the purest of silver. She tipped her face up and smiled at Ryan. "It seems fast, but I think we're one of those lucky couples who just know."

"You're engaged." Savannah's voice was strong.

Nicky caught Ryan's gaze, and for an instant, his eyes burned with pain before he blinked it away.

"Ryan said he's always wanted to be a father. After we're

married, he's going to adopt my baby." Jinni twined her fingers in his and pressed their hands back onto her stomach. "*Our* baby."

The silence seemed to stretch forever.

"Congratulations." Savannah thrust out the plate. "I brought you muffins."

CHAPTER SIXTY-NINE

Nɪᴄᴋʏ ꜱᴇᴛ the brake on her unit and steadied her breathing. The sun had yet to rise, but the mountains to the east were edged by a pale grayish-pink sky. She scanned the parking lot, gaze coming to rest on Franco's personal vehicle—a late-model double-cab pickup, silver, lifted over thick knobby tires, long running boards on each side. His conservation unit, a battered white truck, sat two slots to its left. She'd position herself in between. He couldn't miss her.

They had to talk. Had to deal with this stupid misunderstanding over Dax Stone and her home and her debt. Had to salvage the trust they'd built up over the past months working together professionally, which she needed so badly in her personal life. The trust she'd damaged but—she hoped—hadn't destroyed. Savannah had been right about Dax but didn't understand that he was familiar, someone she could handle because of their past. Franco was still an unknown in so many ways. A risk. Nicky closed her eyes and swallowed on a dry throat.

After a quick check of the time on her cell phone, she opened the door and slid out onto the pavement before reaching in for two cardboard cups of coffee tucked in the console. Steam curled from the small openings in the lids. Breath short, a knot of tension expanding in her stomach, she closed the door and walked to the end of the painted white line dividing the empty parking spaces. Conservation personnel met early on Mondays—she'd checked and rechecked their schedule. Briefings were short, and then the officers would set out to their assigned patrol regions, usually before the dawn, sometimes not.

But it didn't matter. She'd wait for him.

The pink sky became tinged with gold. Streamers of light shot over the Ortiz Mountains and painted the clouds. Nicky stood motionless, facing the double doors leading into the building that housed Conservation. A minute passed, then two. The doors cracked open. Her fingers tightened around the cups.

Franco stepped out. He was dressed in hiking boots, khaki camo pants, and a long-sleeved khaki shirt, his head turned to throw a laughing comment to someone behind him. Her heart seemed to stop before it thumped to life. He pivoted and saw her. She was sure of it because he paused for an instant. Nicky squared her shoulders. Franco strode toward her, staring straight at her. He dug into his pocket and pulled out keys. She shifted, relief so profound she smiled. It would be okay.

"Franco, I—" She took a step. Her voice jammed in her throat.

He wasn't looking at her. He was looking through her. Like she didn't exist. Face a mask, he veered to his silver truck. It chirped as the locks disengaged. He swung open the driver's side back-seat door and retrieved a backpack and a rifle case before he closed the door and walked to his unit, passing so close that the rising steam from the coffee cups swirled in his wake.

He used a key to open the passenger's side door—it was an old truck—deposited his backpack on the floorboard, and stowed the rifle behind the seat.

Nicky tipped her head back and choked down a laugh. The sky blurred above her. The truck door slammed. *It will be okay.* She blinked and straightened and watched as he walked around the front of his truck, keys dangling from his fingers. He unlocked the driver's side door.

"Franco," she called, vaguely proud her voice was so steady. "For what it's worth, I'm sorry."

He slid inside the cab, closed the door, and started the truck. Nicky sauntered toward the large trash can by the front doors of the building. She dropped both cups of coffee through the dark round opening, spun on her heel, and headed back across the parking lot to the police station. Might as well get some paperwork done before her shift started.

CHAPTER SEVENTY

THE DESERT around Nicky was green. Plants whose life depended on scant rain took every advantage of the moisture to sprout and flower in a flash of time. She tipped her own face skyward, savoring the waning sunlight, enjoying the solitude.

Waiting.

The Jeep appeared as a red speck on the horizon. It bumped and splashed through playas filled with thin sheets of water. Nicky leaned her back against the side of her unit, the first day in two weeks she'd been in the field. The antibiotics she'd been taking to get rid of the colonization had chewed her up, but she'd insisted on working. Needed the money. Mandatory desk duty sucked, but it had allowed her to do a little digging on unanswered questions in the J White-Hawk case file.

She rested her hand on the butt of her gun. Time to tie up some loose ends.

With a squeal of wet brakes, the Jeep halted on the opposite side of Geronimo Elk's lonely descanso. The engine idled at first, as if the single occupant was deciding whether to stay.

Finally, the engine cut off, a door latch clicked, and a foot encased in a high leather boot stepped directly into a puddle. A faint curse.

"I still don't understand why we couldn't have met at Starbucks. Or is this a better place to dispose of my body?" Ruth Jäger slid her sunglasses over the top of her sleek blond head, blue eyes narrowing. Makeup couldn't conceal the dark smudges beneath.

With a low chuckle, Nicky pushed off her truck and strolled closer to the descanso. "A few years ago—when I had no use for you— a thought like that might've crossed my mind."

"You have a use for me now? I'm surprised." Ruth circled nearer.

"Please, don't take it as a compliment. I have completely no respect for you as a person." Nicky dropped to a squat and studied the seam around the second tier of the memorial.

"Not over your infantile petulance yet? It's been almost six years. The Randals hired my firm to do a job. It wasn't personal."

"It felt personal." Especially since the results continued to affect her life. Nicky stood. She braced her hands on the top of the metal cross and gave a push. It rocked.

"If this little meeting is about influencing the Gianetta Green or Hopinkay cases, you're too late. I've already submitted plea deals. Gianetta has agreed to pay a substantially reduced fine, and the Hopinkays and George Chester will lose their hunting privileges for a year but won't forfeit their weapons or vehicle."

"And the threats of police brutality against me?"

"Bluffs. Leverage." Ruth sniffed. "You know the game."

Nicky hummed a response. "It still surprised me."

"What part?"

"The speed at which you submitted your deals after J White-Hawk's death."

Ruth's face drained of color, and Nicky felt a curl of satisfaction at the woman's distress.

"But I'm getting ahead of myself." Nicky propped her hands on her hips. "The real reason I called you out here was to help me with this." She gestured to the memorial. "If both of us push—"

"What are you talking about?"

"The builder rigged the top to open. There's a hinge under the metal flange in the back."

"The base is pure cement! This is ridiculous. I'm leaving." Ruth pivoted and marched back toward her Jeep.

"And a hidden compartment underneath. That's why I think J kept emphasizing the descanso right before he died."

Ruth halted, body stiff.

"I wonder what he squirreled away inside. Documents? Photos? Evidence of a past life?" Nicky asked.

Ruth's steps dragged as she returned. She pressed her palms against the horizontal arm of the cross.

"On three...." Nicky counted, and they both pushed, bodies strained, backs arched. The tier creaked up an inch, caught, then swung open. She staggered, catching Ruth's arm before both of them fell.

Nicky peered inside the exposed hollow. "Well, what do you know. An internal shrine, just like the ones WhiteHawk looted in the mountains."

"I don't know anything about that," Ruth said quickly, her gaze riveted on the plastic-wrapped box inside.

"Sure you do. But we'll circle back to that later." Nicky knelt and grabbed the thick, clear plastic package covering a metal box. She heaved it out of the hole. "That's heavy! You know, maybe I should take this back to the station and open it there. I mean, who knows what a thief and murderer like WhiteHawk could have tucked away inside?"

"Stop this stupid charade." Streaks of red stood out against the gray skin of Ruth's face. "How much do you want?"

Nicky almost took pity on her. Then an image of vacant hazel eyes shot with turquoise swirled in her mind. Sympathy passed quickly.

"How much is it worth? Let's do a quick inventory." Nicky extracted a multitool from her pocket, sliced away the plastic, and stuck the blade under the lock. A twist and the hasp broke. She flipped the lid open. "Wow." Nicky held up a thick packet of cash. "Did you know a one-inch stack of hundred-dollar bills is over twenty-three thousand dollars? Plus a sack of"—she opened a velvet bag and tipped the contents onto the cement—"gold and silver coins." Nicky picked up a large manila envelope. "I wonder what's in here?" She undid the clasp and riffled through. "Flash drives. Photos. And a copy of a ... Kansas birth certificate." She tugged it out. "'Mother: Karen Ruth Hunter.' That was a nice touch, translating your last name to German."

Ruth looked away.

"'Father: unknown.' Tsk, tsk, Counselor. Lying on an official document. 'Child's name: John Wayne Hunter.'"

"J told you," Ruth said.

"It would have died with us if we hadn't gotten out of that warehouse fire. It was a miracle that Dyu'ami and I did. That's his name now. Dyu'ami." Nicky allowed her contempt to show. "Have you seen your son since you abandoned him? Or don't you care?"

"Don't judge me. *I tried.*" Ruth tipped her chin up. "Even when he was a baby, I couldn't connect with him, couldn't handle him. He wouldn't listen or mind. He threw tantrums, wouldn't stop crying. My career was taking off, and I was a good lawyer." She stared at Nicky, eyes angry with tears. "I thought—"

"Thought you could get a payout from WhiteHawk," Nicky said flatly.

"No. I loved J. I thought my pregnancy would bind us together." Ruth rubbed a shaking hand over her brow. "He laughed, denied the baby was his. Another man I'd been involved with helped. Gave me money so my aunt could care for the boy. When she died, I didn't know what to do. I was Ruth Jäger, up-and-coming lawyer, not some groupie from southern California anymore. When I got the job offer in Santa Fe, I decided to—"

"Abandon your son?"

"I'm not heartless. I met with Gemini Elk and explained. He took to Johnny immediately. And Johnny was calm around him, manageable. Gemini didn't even want money, just that I cut all ties. I agreed. The boy's with a grandfather who loves him."

A knot grew in Nicky's chest. She didn't want to think about a mother *not* loving her child.

So Gemini had known who Dyu'ami's mother was. That conniving old— Nicky pinned Ruth with her gaze. "How did White-Hawk come back in the picture?"

"Publicity of the Randals' civil suit against you. He'd had a change of heart. Not about me. About his son." Ruth laughed bitterly. "After he moved to New Mexico, he contacted me for a few legal questions, that's all. Then, he calls. Tells me if I don't help him with Gianetta and then the Hopinkays, he'll go public. Tell everyone I callously offloaded my Native American child because of his disability. Do you know what would've happened to my career?" She turned her head, jaw tight. "So I helped him. Kept him apprised of your investigation."

The silence that followed her admission was only broken by the chitter of birds and the distant low of a cow.

"J blamed himself for the autism. Thought he caused it with his drug use, drinking," Ruth said quietly. "If that's why it happened, it could just as easily have been me. I'll pay you for those papers, to keep this quiet." A desperate, bitter note crept into her voice. "That's why you called me, isn't it? For money?"

"Yes." Nicky hooked her thumbs into her belt and shifted to widen her stance. "I've had an odd epiphany these last few weeks about the line between right and wrong, about who you can trust. Who's got your back." She fought against the tightness in her throat.

"You're only figuring that out now?" Ruth gave her a pitying glance.

"Fool me twice," Nicky quipped. Savannah had abruptly left to visit family in Arizona. Ryan was busy with work and focused on Jinni and her pregnancy. And Franco, the way he'd looked through her when she'd tried to apologize, had yet to acknowledge her after two weeks.... She shrugged.

Whatever.

"We've gotten off topic," Nicky said. "Since I now have enough information to, er, blackmail you, I've decided to use it. If you don't give me what I want, I'll ruin you."

Ruth's lips twisted. "A cop on the take. Why am I not surprised?"

"You will set up and administer a trust for Dyu'ami with all this money."

"You don't want any of that for yourself?"

"No."

Ruth's brows lowered. "But ... I could use this to ruin you, too. The money was illegally obtained, gained from the sale of stolen artifacts and illicit animal harvests."

"I know this sounds cliché, but WhiteHawk did the wrong thing for the right reason. For Dyu'ami. I've decided not to question it." Nicky swallowed, her stomach churning. "I also need to speak to you about a patent and a settlement."

"You want to hire me as your *lawyer?*" Ruth's voice rose in astonishment.

Nicky held the woman's gaze for a moment, then dipped her head in acknowledgment. "It seems that I am—was—the host of an organism that could potentially make the tribe a lot of money. I want a cut and need someone to negotiate." She released a long breath. "It's a complicated story."

Ruth tapped her lips with a finger. "I'm expensive."

"And I'm broke and about to lose my home."

Clouds hid the sun again, and the breeze took on a faint chill as it washed over Nicky's skin. Drops of rain hit the cement base of the memorial, leaving dark, ragged circles.

"Well—Nicky. Shall we close everything up here and I take you to dinner? We can discuss the trust fund for ... Dyu'ami, and you can tell me your complicated story." Ruth stepped closer and tipped her head to one side. She held out her hand, her turquoise gaze surprisingly candid. "Deal?"

Nicky's fingers tightened on her duty belt like it was a lifeline, touching the cold metal of her shield. Her thumbs slid along the leather, and the fleshy pad of her palm rested on the butt of her sidearm. She pressed into it until it bit her flesh, left an impression.

Then she let it go and grasped Ruth's outstretched hand.

"Deal."

<<<<>>>>

ALSO BY CAROL POTENZA

Hearts of the Missing: A Mystery

The Third Warrior: A Nicky Matthews Mystery

Coming 2022

Spirit Daughters: A Nicky Matthews Mystery

Unmasked: A De-Extinct Zoo Mystery

Coming 2023

Sting of Lies

IF YOU ENJOYED THIS BOOK...

Authors live for honest reviews. They help other readers find their books in a world where millions of books are published each year. So if you enjoyed this story or any other of my books and have just five minutes, leave a quick review at Amazon, Barnes and Noble, Kobo, Google, or my website...

Short or long, your words can make all the difference.

Thank you.

ACKNOWLEDGMENTS

I want to thank my family, my friends, especially CH, EK, and SA, my writing group, my editor, and the people who have asked me over and over when the next book is coming out. You gave me courage to publish this story, and, boy, did I need it.

ABOUT THE AUTHOR

Carol Potenza was a biochemistry professor by day and is a mystery author by night. She loves the combination of her two careers because it gives her the ability not only to teach her students about the biochemical effects of poison, but also to use said poisons very creatively in her murder mysteries (along with other diabolical methods). She lives in the beautiful state of New Mexico with her husband, Leos, and grumpy chihuahua, Hermes.

For more books and updates

www.carolpotenza.com

CPSIA information can be obtained
at www.ICGtesting.com
Printed in the USA
JSHW032231040822
28921JS00002B/11